DARK ECSTASY

"Sir, while I understand and appreciate your need to win me, you need not pretend that I appeal to you—"

"But you do." His mouth was whispering words with that voice that brushed my nerves with a bristling excitement. "Shall I demonstrate?"

No.

"Has a man ever kissed you, Alicia?" His lips asked against my cheek.

No.

His eyes outlined my silent lips. "You have much to learn, my sweet. And I will find it incumbent upon me to teach you."

His arm drew my body closer. His mouth, that wide slash which could appear so menacing, loomed closer, softer, more tantalizing.

My eyes fell closed.

In one crush, he pressed his mouth, his chest, his lean, long legs against mine. And my arms went round him. And my lips met his warm, seeking ones.

And I loved it.

I loved it when he gave some hoarse sound and slanted his mouth fiercely across mine, seizing, exploring. I loved it when his tongue touched mine and I lost my breath, my heartbeat, my . . .

JO-ANN POWER

THE LAST DUCHESS OF WOLFF'S LAIR

ZEBRA BOOKS
KENSINGTON PUBLISHING CORP.

to
Stephen, Jason, and Ann,
who are my three joys

Chapter One

Tragedy, they say, strikes in threes. Today we buried my father, the third of my losses in twice as many months. The first was my grandmother, the second my betrothed.

How could I possibly survive a fourth tragedy?

Yet it was what I was being asked—no, commanded!—to do. And by none other than that kind and tender heart who had sired me, steered me, and now ordered me to walk the earth shackled.

I sat forward in my chair and asked my father's solicitor the question that had burned in my brain this last half hour. "How could I possibly consider marriage?"

"Miss Pennington." He squinted at me over his beak nose. "I am merely the conveyor of the message. It was your father's wish that you marry. And that you marry this man within—" he checked the document that bound me to a stranger, "—yes, within sixty days."

I could sit still for this no longer. I bolted and went to stand at the window. The window, swathed in swirls

7

of fringed wine velvet, let in little light, less air. I pulled back the swag and saw simply stark December sunlight. I blinked, then inhaled deeply but felt no air of freedom, no relief.

How could my father have done this—with never a word to me?

I spun and faced my family. Five of my six brothers watched me in various states of shock or wariness or fear.

I scanned them individually. Mark, the second oldest and a minister, anointed me with pity. John and Paul, both gentle souls who made their daily bread as tenant farmers, stared wide-eyed with surprise. Luke, who worked at the village inn and served people with a smile day in and out, could offer me only confusion. Thomas—rational, blunt Thomas—tensed his square jaw and avoided my eyes. When he spoke, however, he came right to the point.

"Alicia, it sounds wonderful."

"Enlighten me, Thomas. The purpose of this provision of Father's will escapes me."

Leaving his seat before the solicitor's desk, Thomas came to stand before me. Not quite as tall as the rest of my strapping brothers, Thomas looked straight into my eyes.

"The purpose is to provide a good future for you. I correct that—a *superb* future for you. The logic reads as easily. You are the only daughter. And as the only daughter, and one without a dowry or any means to make your way in the world—"

"Oh, but I do have a means, Thomas. You know that the church school—"

"My dear Alicia, *I* know that the church school is

supported by parishioners' donations, some of which come in the form of pennies, not pounds. Its financial success is always marginal, dependent as it is on factory workers' donations and a few merchants' tithes. You have done a wonderful job teaching these poor children to read and write. But, my dear, you cannot make a living from it! No self-respecting woman could."

I glanced at my hands, knotted in white-knuckled frustration at my waist. "I need to try. It is my life, Thomas. Just as Father's life was ministering to his flock."

"Don't think for one minute that this work can support you. I know the financial condition of Father's parish, and I know what went into that school! I tell you, Alicia, you could not hold a roof over your head with what comes in. Let alone pay for the daily supplies!"

"I could live there!" I was clutching at any solution. "I could make a trundle bed there. Live by the fireside."

Someone groaned.

I glanced about and found it was Luke who shook his head and rose to pace the room.

"You can't, Allie." He paused long enough to stare at me with sorrowful green eyes. "You'd die in there during the winter—and winter is upon us, my dear." He swept his hand to the window, beyond which three inches of new-fallen snow covered everything in sight. "How could you survive this?"

"Luke, I'm resourceful. I—I would watch my pennies very carefully. Cut wood to save on coal—"

Suddenly it was Mark who was out of his chair. Mark who was coming toward me, taking my hands in his and holding them firmly while he spoke as if to one of his flock.

"Allie, sweetheart, let us pause now and consider this. We have heard Father's will. He stated very clearly what he wanted for you. And even in the first document, which Mr. Bettelsby indicated was written three years ago, Father wanted you to wed within two months of his death. He even discussed it at length with your Edward Perry before the young man went off with his regiment to the Punjab."

"Oh, yes, I know, Mark. I know. Edward and I had a talk after he asked Father for my hand. Father agreed to such a long engagement only on Edward's promise that he marry me as soon after Father's death as humanly possible. Little did we know then that Edward would be quartered in that horrible place for so long . . . or that he would be wounded and . . ."

I searched Mark's eyes for his understanding, his compassion. I wrung my hands.

"Oh, Mark, even though Father amended that provision after we knew Edward was dead," I swallowed back fresh tears of grief for my betrothed, "how can I marry a man I do not know? Marry him within two months? And—and live with him so far, so very far from all of you? How can I find any comfort, any happiness?"

I sank into a chair, my hands to my chest, my heart knowing all the answers my head refused to accept. I willed myself to stop shaking and looked up into the face of my brother Mark as he went to his knees before me.

"Sweet Allie, if I could save you from this, you know I would. But I can't." He turned slightly and swept

10

out a hand to indicate our brothers. "You know that none of us is in a position to help you, even temporarily, let alone for months or years. We are poor men, darling.

"All six of us Pennington boys make our meager living in the world as best we can. Two farmers from Crewe, both married, barely able to subsist off the land they rent to till. One innkeep's assistant in Chester, young and burly and able, but without the means to buy into the business except by the sweat of his brow. One foreman in a factory in Manchester, living in a hovel while he tries to better himself by doing the owner's bookkeeping. A Methodist minister and his wife and three children in a poverty-stricken area of Liverpool. None of us has any more ability than the others to support or even assist a young spinster, educated and charming though she is."

I pushed aside Mark's overly kind compliments with waving fingers, but he persisted with more irrefutable logic.

"Even our most prestigious brother, Matthew, were he back from China to witness this, would say the same as what I will now: you have no choice but to do as Father commanded. Father had no savings. You know he gave everything away. Even the house you both lived in belonged to the congregation. The newest minister must move in the first of next month. You have no choice, Alicia.

"Marry the man. You needn't do it today or tomorrow. In fact, you have two months! Two months is a long time to become acquainted, sweetheart. Do you know, I have seen couples—particularly in London—who break down my door wanting me to marry

11

them when they have known each other for scarcely a day or two? Of course, I always counsel against such rash decisions. True love develops over time—"

"Yes, Mark. And with knowledge of the other person." I spread my hands wide. "But I have no knowledge of this man to whom Father commits me. How am I to grow to love a husband whom I have never seen, much less appreciated?"

Mr. Bettelsby, the solicitor, who had sat by stoically these last few minutes, cleared his throat with deliberate drama.

We all turned.

"According to your father, Miss Pennington, you *have* met your future husband. In fact, the gentleman was so impressed with your demeanor that it was he himself who sued for your hand. It was definitely not your father who petitioned him."

I almost harumphed. "That is utterly astounding, Mr. Bettelsby, since I have absolutely no remembrance of any such encounter with the gentleman in question."

The birdlike fellow nestled back in his chair and shook his head. "It seems your father initially had quite a time discussing the matter with the man. When first approached by him, your father told him you were already engaged. Your fiancé, Edward Perry, was then still alive, and the Reverend Pennington had promised you to the man upon his return from the Orient."

I was confused, amazed, astonished that such discussions had occurred and I had had no idea of when or how or why.

"Mr. Bettelsby, my father never mentioned any such discussions to me. Why would he to you, sir?"

"Because, Miss Pennington, the Reverend knew his heart worsened drastically. He had been told by the local doctor he was not long for this world. He feared for your future and, knowing how often Her Majesty's Armies require the ultimate sacrifice from their recruits, your father thought it best to have a contingency plan for your future, should any disaster befall your Mr. Perry. The good Reverend wanted me to know immediately of the offer for your hand lest he fall ill before he could sign this newest codicil. However, as to the occasion of your meeting with your new intended husband, I have no knowledge of what occurred, only where and when."

When I lifted my brow and tilted my head in question, Bettelsby smacked his lips and raised his nose, giving over the information as if it were a choice morsel.

"You were on your way to your grandmother's house near Manchester last spring."

I frowned. "As Grandma lay dying?"

Bettelsby shrugged. "Precisely."

Precisely? My mind spun back to that dreadful period last March when the rains began and brought with them this deadly period of mourning that never seemed to end.

I had gone to nurse my grandmother, who had written me of her growing infirmities. Fast approaching her eightieth birthday, she had written me she would not live to celebrate it. She had such a bad case of gout she could no longer walk at all. Her consumption racked her minute by minute, shaking her useless limbs to exhaustion. When I arrived in the grand old house I adored, I ran from her front hall, where her loving maid Mattie greeted me with giant tears in her eyes.

"She's worse, Miss Alicia, and she worried so she would not see you before . . . before the end."

I smiled at Mattie as I handed over my traveling coat, my reticule, my umbrella and hat "I came as soon as I could. Father is so bad I had to get Mark's wife to come stay with him. Show me up quickly, Mattie."

She led the way down the long, mirrored hall, and as she went, I patted my wayward hair into its chignon and straightened my skirts. One did not appear before the *grand dame* of my mother's family looking disheveled. We climbed the delicate circular alabaster stairway in silence. The pristine walls glowed bronze with a thousand gas flames, and I let the joy of seeing my mentor carry me along with speed.

When Mattie reached the master bedroom, she turned and skewered me with her eyes.

"Don't be surprised by her condition."

I promised with a solemn nod.

Mattie flung open the door and I entered the suite as Mattie left us alone.

Grandma lay back amid a mound of ivory lace and eyelet pillows. Her face, once so lively, once so lovely even in advanced age, had lost its heart-shaped delicacy to the ravages of time. And now disease had robbed her of her vibrant pink complexion.

But her senses were still good. At the sound of my footsteps, her forest green eyes found mine. In serene joy, she slowly smiled. Then she strained to sit up and spread her arms in welcome.

"Darling Alicia!" She hugged me to her sunken

14

bosom and planted a wet kiss on both my cheeks. "Let me see you, let me see you!" She pulled my face close to hers to examine it, then shoved me away and pushed her glasses up her straight nose. "These infernal things grow useless."

She adjusted the rimless spectacles and peered at me with her usual subjectivity. "Hmmm. How long has it been since you've been here, Alicia? A year? Two?"

I smiled at her teasing. "Ten months, my dearest."

She grinned and wagged an index finger at me. "Longer, it seems. Let me see you!"

I took a step away and held out my arms at my sides the way she always wanted me to whenever I first arrived for a visit.

"I came last summer on the train, if you remember. We sat outside, and I read you Byron while the roses bloomed. I know you remember. Say you do, and then tell me I can cease this posing. I'm tired, Grandma. The train was very crowded."

"Hmmm, yes, but you're such a sturdy lass, you survive anything. No, no, you can't deprive me of my look, and my eyes are so much worse these days. Turn to the left. Turn, I say. Yes, yes. Still firm and substantial looking. Still have fire in that glossy hair. And good teeth—judging by the way you are gritting them at me. Turn," she rasped, "turn back and to the right. Yes, that's it. Still too damn tall to be the current rage, my sweetheart. But who needs the popular, when the practical can be so much more rewarding, hmmm? Yes, yes, you'll do. Those breasts and those legs should make a man happy to come home to you!"

I blushed. "Grandma, you wrote to me and asked me to come because you wanted good company! Now

15

you mustn't be so bold. Am I to think you had me come all this way to badger me and make me surly?"

I was joking with her, and as she threw me a grin, she suddenly began to cough with such incredible virulence that I ran to her side and eased her back against the pillows.

"Darling Grandma." I took her free hand in mine and stroked it. "You must rest. I will help you. I am here now. And Mattie and I will see to it you feel better in no time."

But she could not cease coughing and her face reddened. I rose to run for Mattie. I opened my mouth to call her, and then spun. But I reeled backward, my mouth open and working, my breath stolen by the specter at the window!

Big, long, and lean . . . a giant male creature hovered there.

A man?

Yes. Yes, surely.

Definitely a man. Wrapped in a black cape head to foot, he dominated the very air with a sinister grace. A dark angel. The most handsome devil I'd ever laid eyes on.

Blue-black hair with one silver streak waving across his noble brow. Silver eyes that glistened in the gaslight. Eyes that traveled every inch of me and in their passing, roiled every nerve to pulsing life.

"Sir? I—I had no idea there was anyone here. I must run to—"

He took one step toward me and I stood my ground, my eyes devouring his severe oval face, his perfect round brows, his inquisitive eyes, his straight nose, his slash of a mouth, his massive jaw.

"Here." He thrust something into my right hand.

When I would not move, he pressed his strong hand over my shaking one. "Give it to her, Alicia."

I looked down. Water. A glass of water. I spun back toward Grandma. She reached for the glass I held in my hand. I went to my knees and gave it willingly.

She sipped it greedily, and when she was done, she sagged in my arms and sighed.

"Thank you, sweet. I—I must rest. Introduce yourselves, please. I would do the honors, but I—I—can't." She turned to look at her visitor. "Forgive me, please. I know I promised you, but I . . ."

And with that, my grandmother sank back into her featherbed and clamped her eyes shut in pain. I wiped her brow with a cloth from the bedstand and for minutes arranged her pillows and her covers. Then, sure she was asleep, I gathered my courage to face her visitor, her friend.

All my life I had done what she had wanted of me.

"Learn the pianoforte, Alicia."

"Learn French, Alicia."

"Learn how to behave like a lady, in spite of that fact that you haven't the usual means to rise beyond being a parson's daughter. You'll never be sorry."

And so today, she had ordered me to introduce myself. And though the memorable image of the man seared my brain with his beauty, and the very idea of speaking to such a creature made my tongue grow thick in my mouth, I intended to do as Grandma bade me. Then, for the rest of my days, I could comfort myself that I had met one man—one rare specimen of God's creation—who stole my breath with his wild virility.

And so I turned, my eyes going to the window. But

17

he was not there. I stood and searched the corners of the suite. He was nowhere to be found. He was gone. Gone!

And I could not explain to myself why I felt forlorn. Cheated.

For the next three weeks I remained at my grandmother's side, nursing her, tending to her household, until we buried her one bright spring day in the vicarage churchyard. Three days later, I packed up the house, sent Mattie off to her sister's with her pension in hand, and returned home to nurse Father.

Occasionally since then, I had shards of memory of the man in Grandma's house. But they were simply that, sharp fragments of memory cutting into my days and nights with the remnants of my initial surprise and fascination with his dynamism.

I dismissed my recollections as girlish dreams. Certainly, I told myself, nothing had ever come of the meeting. Whoever he was, whatever his relationship with Grandma, I never knew. Certainly he could not have been too close a friend because he did not appear again, not even at her burial. Yet amid my grief that sorrowful day, I must admit, if only to myself, that I watched for him.

But I never saw him again. Nor had I met any other man while there last spring.

Now I tore myself from the memory. Reason surfaced. Yet my mind denied the logic. Was the man to whom I now found myself betrothed that same man who'd been in my grandmother's bedroom that night?

I frowned at Mr. Bettelsby.

"Is this gentleman tall, very tall? And very, very dark?"

18

Mr. Bettelsby smiled through thin lips. "So, you do remember him."

"No. He was never introduced to me, really. That is all I know of him. His looks." His infernal good looks.

"Precisely. Some call him the Rake of London."

Mark gasped at Bettelsby's bluntness. "Good heavens, sir. This is my sister's intended you speak of. Surely the man—"

Thomas raised a hand. "Now, Mark, don't ridicule Mr. Bettelsby. He speaks only what he knows to be the truth. And I will tell you, Mr. Bettelsby does speak what many believe to be the truth."

I gaped at Thomas, who once more avoided my eyes.

Bettelsby went on like a proud crow. "Well, the man does have a bit of a reputation."

Thomas snorted. "A *bit?*"

I licked my lips. "Thomas?"

Thomas walked toward the fireplace and took a match from the marble mantel and a thin cigar from his inside coat pocket. "I have heard about his reputation with women. And as our father taught us, I know gossip can be vicious. And perhaps untrue." He lit the cigar and drew deeply on it. "So I will tell you what I know to be true. His reputation as a businessman is sterling.

"As the foreman at the cotton factory in Manchester, I live a simple life. I run the shop, keep it staffed, and keep the accounts. I turn them over each month to the solicitors for the owner. But the owner is none other than your intended, Alicia. He owns four other such factories in Lancashire, all of which he tries to run with one eye toward profit and one toward his

19

workers. One goes hand-in-glove with the other, if you ask me. That is why, among other things, your intended is a very wealthy man."

"Precisely," interjected Bettelsby again. "Maximilian George Dumont Wolff." Bettelsby smiled even more ceremoniously. "Some say the fourth richest man in the kingdom. A businessman of great repute. Yet he is also sixth Duke of Worminster. A very, *very* wealthy man, and a very noble man. Very, very noble indeed."

Thomas took a deep puff on his cigar and for the first time in minutes, he let his eyes meet mine. "Among other things."

I sought a chair and sat down with a thud. Noble. And wealthy. The former I could accept. So many noblemen lived with the appellation and not the wealth to bear it out. But this man enjoyed both. I had never dreamed of living either noble or wealthy, and the very idea that I might be called to live in such manner snatched my composure from me. I swallowed and looked at Thomas.

"Tell me what you imply, Tom."

The others were up out of their chairs, milling about and mumbling.

John shook his head and stared at Thomas. "Yes, explain yourself."

"Should we let her go to this man?" asked Paul.

Thomas shrugged and drew on his cigar once more.

Mark went to stand before Thomas. The two of them, so alike, so red-haired, so intelligent, so intense, stared at each other.

Mark whispered. "Tell us, Thomas. We need to know. She is our only sister. She's only nineteen. We cannot send her off to a man if he is not worthy of her. She is too kind to throw away on someone who will not value her, honor her, keep her—''

Thomas glanced at Mark and turned away to dash his cigar into the fireplace. "He is a Wolff." He declared it like an epitaph. "Surely you know what that means?"

Mark nodded. "A distant relative of ours. Must be some sort of cousin, I'd guess."

"A cousin, yes. Through Grandma's family."

I shifted, growing testy hearing things we all knew so well. "So he is a cousin, Thomas. And he is obviously the Duke of Worminster, so that makes him a direct descendant of Grandma's brother, the fourth duke. But why would he want me, of all people, to become his wife? I haven't a title, a genteel background, a dowry. Nothing! Why would he want me?"

Thomas braced his hands on the mantelpiece and hung his head. "The curse on the Wolffs."

I'd barely heard him, much less understood his implication. "What? What did you say?"

I rose from my chair. My brothers advanced toward him with me. Each of them muttered his confusion.

Mark took up the lead. "Turn around, Thomas. Tell us what this curse is."

As if in pain, Thomas dropped his hands and pivoted. He surveyed each man's face and then settled his eyes in mine.

"The curse on the Wolffs. Placed on the family by a jealous mistress of Charles the Second. A woman reputed to be so eager to share the monarch's bed, she cursed his current mistress, Morgana Wolff, and her newborn son."

Mark tsked. "I will not listen to this. I do not believe the forces of evil can prevail so easily that a woman can curse—"

Thomas scowled at Mark. "Curses abound, Mark. How can you not believe in curses when children starve in the streets and people die of overwork in the factories?"

Mark put up a hand. "Yes, Thomas, but that is not so much the work of the devil as it is the neglect and ignorance of humankind for its own."

"Brother of mine, whatever the cause, the evils persist. The same is true of the family of the Wolffs."

I put one hand up. "Please, do not argue. Tell me about this so-called curse."

Thomas checked my eyes and flexed his jaw. "The woman declared that any male Wolff would sire scores of daughters and few sons. Each Wolff daughter of the family would bear her husband scores of sons. The women in the family would be prolific, but the men would go in want for healthy male offspring."

I was unaffected. "Thomas, there have been a total of six dukes of Worminster, and to my knowledge, all five of the descendants came directly from the original."

He nodded. "Yes, a direct line of five male heirs."

"Well, then," I persisted, "if the curse is to be believed, each duke of Worminster has been able to hand down the title and estates without too many problems."

"There is more, Alicia."

I tilted my head in question.

He obliged me by going on. "If you look to the family records, each duke has outlived his duchess."

Mark paced back and forth, agitation in every muscle of his body. "This is no curse, Thomas. This is reality. We know many woman have a difficult time in childbirth. Alicia, the Duke of Worminster merely wants a wife—"

"No, Mark," Thomas interjected. "He wants a wife from the Wolff family because he needs her qualities. He seeks to mate the best of the litter to the worst of it. Our Alicia, as the only daughter of our mother, should bear her husband—whoever he is—many sons."

I nodded. "Just as Mother was the only daughter among ten children. Just as Grandma—as the youngest daughter of the third duke of Worminster—had four sisters and only one brother. It all follows the rule of the curse. So naturally, this sixth duke thinks that I might be able to produce many sons."

"Yes, my dear. This duke seeks to end the curse."

Mr. Bettelsby cleared his throat once more and we turned to him. He still sat behind his desk, preening like a tiny peacock. "And you should be so grateful, my dear Miss Pennington. After all, the duke could have had anyone in the realm. Anyone at all. And he chose you. You are so fortunate, so very fortunate."

Thomas snorted. "Really, Mr. Bettelsby! I think Alicia should judge his worth for herself."

In my mind's eyes, I could see the Duke of Worminster as I'd seen him that dark night. I saw not just his stark handsomeness, but his endearing concern and ready help for my grandmother. I saw his humanity. And in that moment, I recognized the dichotomy between his appearance and his essence. I was intrigued. Enchanted.

Wondering what other characteristics I might add to

23

that picture, I smiled at Thomas. "Thank you, Thomas. Having taken all your logic to heart, I think I will go to meet the man."

Bettelsby fluttered in his chair. "Oh, I am so happy to hear you say it, Miss Pennington. The duke is so very influential. So well known. This will certainly be the news of the day throughout Lancashire. Throughout the realm!"

"I did not say I would marry him, Mr. Bettelsby. Only that I would see him." I would offer myself one more glimpse of him before I . . .

Bettelsby laughed, a thin chuckle. "But they say that to see him is to love him. All the women do. Certainly there's proof for that!"

Thomas scowled at the solicitor. "Sir, Alicia doesn't listen to gossip."

I frowned at Thomas, but addressed Bettelsby. "What do you mean by 'proof,' sir?"

I supposed he was about to reveal the existence of scores of illegitimate children born by many mistresses. I was suddenly—and inexplicably—sad and angry. No, I was furious! Furious that the one man who had so attracted me could find so many other women attractive. Suddenly, I needed either salt or solace for my wound. And I needed it now.

"Tell me, Mr. Bettelsby."

The little solicitor now inched a forefinger inside his starched white collar and stretched his neck high above it. His flickering eyes checked those of my brothers', especially Thomas's. When he spoke, his voice sounded weak. His words wobbled.

"Popular word says—" he licked his lips and cleared

his throat, "that the Duke of Worminster can captivate a woman merely by looking at her."

Oh, how I wanted to laugh it off, dismiss it for the silly rumor it was. But I knew the truth of his words and I was not amused. I let him rush onward.

"Popular word says that this is part of the Wolffs' masculine power and part of their family curse." Bettelsby's beady little eyes settled in mine. "Popular word says that this duke is more handsome, more devastating than any of his ancestors. Because, despite this duke's great way with women and despite the family curse, no other duke has needed more than one wife." He paused and swallowed repeatedly, his pointed little Adam's apple working furiously.

My mind reeled. "One wife?"

"Well, Miss Pennington, naturally, I thought you not only knew His Grace but also knew his personal history. You are related, after all, and I—well, I—"

"Mr. Bettelsby, explain your riddle."

"Ahem. Well, yes, yes. My dear Miss Pennington, His Grace is unusual in many ways. Not only is he a direct descendant of Morgana Wolff and Charles the Second. Not only is he rich as Midas from his textile manufactures. But he is quite unique among the Wolffs. He has taken two other women in holy matrimony. And two of them he loved. Two of them he lost. Abruptly. Sadly. Rumor says he cannot keep a wife. Rumor says he . . . is too . . . how shall I put this? Too potent a personality. That his women die of living with so virile a man."

My heart pounded at the thrilling idea that one could die of living with so virile a man. Surely, I knew I could live loving such a man.

But loving or living with this man was not my calling in life. My call was to help the helpless.

I gathered my courage and stood.

"I thank you all for your kindness, your concerns, and your information. I will go to see this gentleman. He expects me, and I will not be rude. It is the least I can do to repay him the honor he has given me by going to him and declining his generous offer in person. I will tell him of my chosen path and help him to understand I was not meant for him. He will accept my reasons and begin to look elsewhere for his third duchess."

Chapter Two

I stuffed my hands inside my ancient rabbit fur muff and sank against the umber leather squabs. I sighed at the soothing caress of its sumptuousness. Warm and secluded from the world here inside the Worminster coach, I could admit I could grow used to such luxury. But not far behind was another silent admission: for yet one more time today, I told myself I was terrified of meeting the man to whom I'd been given.

Terror? Yes, tenfold. I lolled my head against the smooth moroccan upholstery and closed my eyes. I had rehearsed my speech so often I felt like a marionette, a wooden figure whose recitation projected from some other lifeless being.

"I cannot marry you," I'd say to this man, this cousin, this duke. "I am not the type of woman you require, no matter this family curse." I'd then give him full well to understand that I did not put credence in such things. And even if I did, I still would not be the woman for such a man.

The bald truth was he was too much man for me. Too noble. Too worldly. Too much married.

I stared out the window of the family coach he'd sent to fetch me. Then, as ever truthful to myself, I admitted the final piece of negative evidence, gleaned from my memories of that night in my grandmother's house: this man was too handsome. Much too handsome for the likes of me.

The scenery wended its way into my mind. Miles northeast of the land where my grandmother's house stood, this territory was new to me and sparked my curiosity. I knew Lancashire to be vast, flat plains. Yet this part of the shire consisted of rounded mountains and valleys in never-ending volley. The dense snows of last week had dwindled in the winter sun to spots of white upon the brown, grassless fields. Geese, surprisingly still fat, pecked at the earth. Tiny birds, brave little fellows to stay so long in such a clime, swooped up and down from the stunted trees bent permanently by the gales that stormed in even this far from the sea. Now an hour or more from the train station, a long wall of lush woods appeared. Pines and evergreens announced the increasing elevation to colder climates.

Above the treetops, something drew my eye, something tall, reaching for the heavens. Something pointed, focused toward some goal. I sat far forward and peered at the needle in the sky. This was no needle, I soon realized, but a spire. Then not just one spire but another appeared. This one was shorter, more bulbous. And then another appeared with its mate, both shorter and squatter than the first one. As the coachman led us closer, the spires of the house disappeared amid the foliage of a serpentine driveway, so secluded, so overgrown even in winter's pall that I marveled anyone found their way in or out of the compound.

28

"That's why I've been sent for you, Miss Pennington," the coachman had declared, when he'd met me hours before at the train in Manchester. "His Grace knows how difficult the terrain can be if one is not accustomed to it. Besides, he wanted no hired cab for you, Miss Pennington."

He smiled. I acquiesced. Then, I pointed toward my one piece of luggage and picked up my voluminous skirts to follow him toward a huge black carriage with four matching ebony horses. Standing before the titanic conveyance with the silver ducal seal upon the door, I speculated on the Duke of Worminster's real worth. Never had I seen such a carriage, not in real life, not depicted in any fiction, not even in my mind's eye.

Now before my eyes loomed an even greater fantasy. The house—no, the mansion—that appeared before me confirmed my conclusion of last week when the full intent of my father's will was revealed to me. This duke, this cousin, this man was not for me. No . . . he was too rich for my blood.

Along a curving drive, the coachman slowed as he took us toward the entrance. Two massive stone forecourt gates, each like a beastly four-eyed sentinel, forbade entry, save to those who had been invited. Through the center passage, I saw the square portecochère and two large doors. The ivory brick house, unadorned by shrubbery, sprang from the ground like a Minoan palace, a multistoried, many-windowed monolith.

I inhaled deeply. Here I would begin.

The coach drew to a stop. The footman who had ridden postchase opened the door for me and cast his eyes downward. I murmured my thanks and looked from his bowed head up into the eyes of the man who could be none other than the head butler.

Tall, pallid, and proud, he had the pinched look of one who remains too long indoors.

"Good afternoon, Miss Pennington. I am Bigelow." He averted his bulging brown eyes to the ground.

Knowing he had nothing of interest to admire in my modest traveling costume, I understood his reserve and his need to look elsewhere. My long pelisse was two years old and cut from a bolt of cloth given my mother by a grateful member of our congregation who was a cottage dyer. The sapphire blue tweed did little for my complexion, but I had not the money to invest in a new outfit. Besides, even though I would have wished to come before the Duke of Worminster in grand style, I would soon leave him. What need had I to impress a man whom I would never see again?

"His Grace the duke awaits you," Bigelow announced. "Follow me, please."

He pivoted and led me up the wide steps across the porch through the massive front doors, held open by two footmen.

If the forecourt struck one dumb with its perverse power, the entry hall soothed the startled mind and delighted the eye. I halted at the splendor before me.

Alabaster, black, and gold twined together in the tiny inlaid tiles upon the floor. Marbled white walls veined in gold drew the eye in a wide sweep from gilded window frames where cherubs danced about the mullioned windows up to the hanging candle fixtures. Higher still, my eyes ran up three stories, each floor surrounded by a filigree railing round each walkway. Straight overhead, I stared at a ceiling of tromp l'oeil blue sky with clouds and birds and yet more angels. I could not get my fill of its beauty.

"Miss Pennington, I say, may I please have your coat and umbrella?"

I tore my eyes from the scenery to look at a perturbed Bigelow.

"Oh, yes, absolutely. Forgive me." I turned over my muff, my sturdy umbrella, and finally the heavy tweed coat.

"Your hat, Miss Pennington." He sounded bored, a churlish teacher of a backward student.

My hand went to the ribbon under my chin. "I wish to keep it, thank you. I will not remain long."

His bulbous eyes grew large as autumn onions. "His Grace will be offended if you leave your hat on in his presence. I would not advise it, Miss."

I inhaled and pulled on the bonnet's ribbons. Very well . . . I would retain all the proprieties. I did not wish to offend the duke, God knew! No, indeed. I meant only to explain my case and leave. If removing my bonnet meant I'd have an easier time of winning him to my point of view, so be it. I took the navy straw from atop my head and patted back any escaping tendrils into my chignon.

Bigelow took the hat as if bearing the Queen's crown. Turning, he disappeared with all my goods through a large gilt door—the cloakroom, obviously. When he stood before me once more, he nodded and we turned down one of the three corridors.

Going left off the entry, we traversed a corridor lined with gray-striped wallpaper and a Turkey runner of plums and grays and black. Then, once again we turned, this time right, down a similarly decorated, similarly dark passageway. To my left and right we passed doors, doors, doors. The very number of rooms, the overwhelming size of the main floor, astonished me. It surely could contain my parents' small rectory in Crewe five times over without a dent to its magnificent walls.

We turned left again, and this corridor was just as wide, just as dark, but longer, longer! Where did this house end?

Bigelow stopped before one oak-carved door, his hand upon the huge brass knob.

"My lord the duke's den, Miss Pennington." His eyes ran down my figure and then peered into mine, as if to ask if I were prepared.

I inhaled deeply and nodded.

His bulging eyes went to the floor in acknowledgment of our silent communication. With one flick of his wrist, the door swung open. His hand swept out. "Miss Pennington, if you please."

He had been given orders, I supposed, to have me enter by myself. Unusual and irritating. Was I not worth announcing? My pride was pricked at the slight.

But with head held high, I walked forward. The door closed behind me on the resounding click of a thick latch. Inside, the den was just as one would expect. Like its owner, it was huge and dark.

A library whose works ran round the walls in ornate bookshelves, the room stood three stories tall. Round each floor, catwalks gave the reader access to the wonders of its literature. I viewed the small room to one side, an office commanded by one massive Georgian desk, the expanse of which equaled the foredeck of a small craft. I stood rooted in the center of the wondrous room and noted the thickness of the Chinese carpet beneath my feet, the numerous settees and chairs, the tables full of open tomes. The nooks and crannies. The smell of oil and wood and leather. The quiet joy of it. The welcomeness of it.

Someone liked to spend hours here. I smiled.

A low-throated growl had me catching my breath.

I spun!

Another growl met my ears!

I searched for my menace. My mouth opened and I stood nailed to my spot as two colossal dogs loped across the carpet.

"Do not move!" came a thunderous order from above me.

My eyes riveted on the creatures who now circled me. So tall I was positive I could have touched them with my fingertips, both were big black dogs. Both sniffed at my skirts as they eyed me.

Footsteps descended a staircase somewhere behind me. As I knew help drew near and as it dawned on me these dogs meant only to become acquainted with me, I relaxed. I stretched out my hands, and gingerly, each one touched his nose against my fingers.

"That's right," came the voice, to soothe me again.

Rough and resonant, I remembered that bass voice from months before and surprised myself that I recalled its timbre. After all, in my memories, it was the specter's appearance which had most roused my nerves. So naturally, in my turmoil of the last months, I had completely forgotten how his voice had soothed me.

"Let them know you," said my companion. "They are fierce, of course—hunters and protectors by their

33

very nature. Yet for me they are quite tame. Rolf and Hans, I call them. I have told them of you and ordered them to behave.''

By now, the two took to licking my fingertips, their red tongues warm and wet. I dared to scratch them under the chin. When they brushed against me, a chuckle came from the man behind me. And then I turned.

Oh, lord. I had always prided myself on my memory. It was how I made such a good practice of teaching in the church school. Without books, one had to use one's memory of literature and history and science. But my memory had not served me well here. No. Not only had I forgotten the symphonic potency of his voice, I had quite forgotten the quaking power of his person.

My bones dissolved at the scorching silver fires of his gaze. Those eyes, eyes that sought and assayed, consumed my reason. I stood, speechless.

He stepped forward and gently took one nerveless hand from my side and brought it to his mouth.

''Alicia,'' he murmured, as his lips met my skin.

Never had a man kissed my hand. So courtly a gesture was for the upper classes. So divine a gesture was for women who knew how to respond to such homage. His brand upon my body stunned me into further flustered silence. What did one say after a man offered such romantic attention?

I watched him as he lifted his dark head and drew himself up to his full height. Even taller than I remembered, he smiled down into my eyes from quite a few inches' advantage. Few men were taller than I, so that this feeling of being dominated comforted and intimidated me all at the same time. But he was speaking, and I forced my mind to his subject.

"You had a pleasant journey, I trust. My carriage met you at the train and the coachman recognized you without difficulty?"

"He was very kind, Your Grace."

"So should he be." His eyes left mine to study my attire. "You have had a long trip. Shall I ring for tea, or can I pour you some sherry, perhaps?"

"No, Your Grace. Hot chocolate is my favorite when I do partake. But I wish nothing, thank you."

"Well, then, come sit down." He turned, his hand still possessing mine, and took one step toward a settee.

When I did not follow, he halted and looked back at me with a cock of his head.

"I do not wish to sit, Your Grace. I—I really do not intend to stay." There, I'd said it. "I—"

His eyes snapped wide until the whites shown all about the circumference.

"What?" A whisper. "What did you say?"

Frozen in fear, I would not fall back. Yet his rasp had my ears ringing.

"My lord, I will not stay overly long. I wish to discuss the matter—no, the impossibility—of this marriage. Then, I would ask one more courtesy from you by requesting that you have your coachman drive me to the nearest inn."

Looming closer, he uncurled his fingers from my hand and let the offending appendage fall back to my body. He glared at me. His words came forth as carefully measured punctuations to his anger. "What—exactly—are—you—talking about, Miss Pennington?"

It registered in my mind that I liked it a thousand

35

times better when he called me Alicia. I dismissed the revelation and stared into the black pupils of his eyes. They became my only point of reality at the moment. "Sir, I—I must discuss this matter with you calmly. Rationally."

"The agreement was concluded calmly and rationally with your father, miss. There is nothing to discuss."

"Oh, but there is. You see, I—"

He waited.

I groped.

"I have thought much on this marriage this past week, and I know I am not the best choice of a wife for you."

"I think *I* am the best judge of that, Miss Pennington. I do nothing lightly. Especially not marrying. What gives you to think I step so easily into a contract which has the ability to create so much chaos in a person's life?"

"I intend no insult to you, Your Grace. Please believe me. But I—well, I am my father's child, sir, in many ways. He taught me much of life here and beyond. My mother taught me other truths as valuable. And so you see, by the example of their marriage and the examples of their religious teachings, sir, I—I believe no true marriage exists without a true marriage of minds. This—this union between you and me would be no such marriage. And therefore—in all good conscience, sir—I must declare that I cannot marry you."

He glanced at his fingernails. Pursed his lips. Ran his eyes around the room above my head. "You are very idealistic. That's what comes of being raised a minister's daughter. I should have known," he looked into my eyes, "but I assumed you would be more docile than idealistic. More fool I!" He smacked his lips. His eyes ran down my figure, and in cool judgment, he lingered over me as if I were a yard of cotton for sale. "You are quite an amazing woman, Alicia."

He made me feel foolish and young. My ears rang now from fury.

"Your Grace, I am not interested in your view of me."

His eyebrows rose as much in surprise over my boldness as in question over my true meaning.

"I am here, sir, out of the courtesy you did me, asking for my hand as you did—"

Now his brows rose to touch the waving streak of silver in his hair. And he opened his mouth in mirth.

I rushed on, eager to have this out, over, and done with before my courage flagged.

"I am here to tell you in person why I cannot marry you. I felt I owed you that much."

He squinted at me with those silver eyes. "Do go on, Alicia, I am eager to hear this."

I glanced about me. Given permission now to plead my own case, I felt like a schoolgirl petitioning the board for some sweet treat. I knew my petition was worth more than that, but still I hated his—what was it?—his tolerance.

I stared at him.

He waved one hand at me and then folded his arms. One foot thrust out before the other, he tilted his head to one side. His superiority taunted my courage.

"I cannot marry you, sir, because not only do we not know each other, we do not care for each other. We have nothing in common, no peg upon which we might hang a union of like minds. We are too different. You, from wealth and privilege so far beyond my experience and—yes, beyond even my fantasy. And me, from a cottage in Crewe, sir. With six brothers, all working men with not a title nor a penny among them.''

He mulled that a moment and dropped his hands. ''Is that all?''

All? ''It is everything, sir.''

His eyes delved into mine with joy! Then, with a look that crinkled the corners of his eyes, he smiled at me. ''No, Alicia. That is *not* everything, my dear.''

He walked away from me toward a long Jacobean cabinet. Upon it stood decanters of every size and shape, crystal goblets and glasses of every cut. Taking one decanter, he poured two glasses of amber liquid. Then, one in each hand, he came toward me and pressed one into my hand.

''Go on, drink it. I know you probably have never had spirits, but you'll need it before we're done here. Drink it, I say.''

I stared into the glass. The vapors rose to my nostrils. I glanced to my side and placed the glass on a small deal table.

The duke snorted in laughter.

''I see you don't take to orders well, either. My, my. What will I do with such a stubborn, disobedient wife?''

I was trying so diligently to be polite while defending my own cause. But I had never survived any needling very well. And his words loosened my tongue. ''Sir, you need not *do* with me at all.''

"But I will. And you, my lovely lady, will *do* with me."

I shook my head. "There is no reason."

"There is every reason, every reason in the world." He took a sip of his drink and savored it a moment. "It seems you need a list. Very well. I shall recite."

"Please, sir, there is no need—"

He pounced on my statement. "There is *every* need. I have listened to you. Now, my dear, you shall listen to *me*.

"From time immemorial, the male and female of the species have united in body long before the mind even understood."

I groaned. Such discussions were *never* had. Not between two people who barely knew each other, not even between mother and daughter, let alone between men and women!

"Yes, my dear, I know. One does not speak of such things. But today we will." He took another sip and then put it aside. "Today we will speak of many things others never dare dream of. It will be the beginning of something vital between us—a meeting of the minds, as you call it. You see, I desire such accord as well. And since you require it, we two will create it here and now. And we will name it honesty."

I opened my mouth in surprise.

From across the darkening room where the shadows of evening began to fill the corners, I felt more than saw the magnetism of his smile.

"Yes, my dear, as you see, it is easy to begin a relationship. Far more difficult is the task of building one founded on equal devotion and equal honor. If both exist from its inception, the relationship can become priceless. I know of such relationships. And it is what I wish for us, my dear. Above all else, it is what we shall have.''

I would have objected, but he put up one hand. ''No, Alicia. Let me speak. Honesty—brutal as it might be—will be our watchword. And I tell you in all honesty, you are mine. I have not bought you. I have not won you. Nor have I sued for your hand by winning your heart first. And for such an independent miss as you, I imagine that rankles. But there is nothing for it. It will be this way.''

I stepped forward, eager to rebut.

He would not permit it and put out a wagging fore-finger.

'Ah, ah, ah. There is more. You say you will not stay, but where will you go? Yes, after you leave the local inn in Wolfsson, where will you go? To one of your brothers? You yourself said your brothers—whom I know would welcome you into their homes in a min-ute—cannot afford to keep you. A woman, a young woman, without prospect or inheritance. What would happen to you? I'll tell you: you'd go from brother to brother, from week to week. Without a penny to offer them in recompense, what happens to your self-respect, Alicia? Your pride? What happens to any prospects you might have for a suitor? They decline as well. No, no.'' He flourished a hand. ''I am your first, your last, your very best hope of a decent future.''

What could I reply? I don't want this future you offer me? I don't need this future you depict?

Economically, I needed it. Socially, I could learn—oh, yes, I could learn to enjoy it. I could even relish its benefits and revel in my ability to use my place and money to spread earth's joys about the lands of the duchy of Worminster. But what of the other aspects of such a marriage? I could not give myself, body and soul, to a man I did not know, even if I was attracted to him for purely physical reasons.

Still, I did not want the other life he painted, either— the dreadful one of me resented by and resenting my benefactors. The one of me growing older and grayer without hope of home or husband or children.

I considered the floor. "Your Grace, I recognize the logic of your suit. For a woman of my station and circumstances, it is not only a superb honor, but it makes tremendous good sense. If I were to accept, I would possess all those elements of a domesticated life. Every woman's desire, so to speak, fulfilled. Yet there is much that warns me from such a match because those elements are only trinkets, tokens taken in trade for the whole substance I desire." I forced my eyes to his.

He did not flinch. Surely he must divine my meaning.

I stood in the void and forced myself to reveal everything. "That is why, sir, I have made arrangements for me to teach at a girl's school in the town of Lancaster. I will teach English. And in return, I will be housed and fed and receive a small monthly fee for my services."

"Is that the full measure of your self-worth, Alicia? A post at a girls' school in a small town?"

"No, Your Grace." I bit my lip and began to knead my hands. He wanted honesty; I would give it. "I have thought of more. Often. Too often. It is one of my—" I remembered my father's word for this trait of mine, "—my vanities. But his death and my fiancé's have

41

taught me much, sir. Humility is far better a trait than fanciful daydreaming. With time, I shall acquire more of it."

His eyes fell closed. The sweep of his ebony lashes cast shadows across the planes of his face, making him more classic statue than mere mortal. Finally his eyes opened, and when he spoke, his words were full of regret. "You are much like any other woman."

I bristled.

He came toward me and gave a crooked smile. "And yet, not like most I've known in that you see substance and desire that. But fortunate as you are to be bright, you are not yet wise."

That was an insult that made me swallow back sharp words and bite my lip.

He came within inches of me.

"I admire your courage, my dear. It will stand you in good stead here in Wolffs' Lair. We have need of a woman such as you. *I* have need of a woman such as you. And that is why you will marry me."

"I see no compelling reason there."

"I will give you one." He searched my eyes. "What say you to a bargain?"

"My church's teachings do not permit me to gamble."

"But this is no gamble. The prize is certain, won by good deeds. Surely your religious teachings allow a person the gains of his or her labor. And your winnings shall be won by your labor, my dear. Quite literally, I daresay."

I blushed violently.

"My God, you were sheltered, weren't you? I shall have to change my ways so as not to offend you. For I would not have you offended, Alicia. I would have something far different." He reached out a hand, and with the backs of his fingers he traced the line of my jaw from chin to ear.

A butterfly's wings could not have been gentler. No man had ever touched me with such reverence. I reveled in it so that when he took his fingers away, I swayed forward.

His eyes gleamed brightly at my willful response.

In a haze, one part of my mind asked if this was the way he would always touch me; another part asked if this was how he had caressed his two wives, how he'd seduced his other women.

Maddened by my waywardness, I stepped back and turned. I found a window, and outside it, the winter remnants of a topiary garden. I found animals sculpted out of faded greenery. Finally, I found some sanity, some words to cloak my jealousy—and my need.

"Your bargain. I would hear your bargain, Your Grace."

"You will consent to become my wife and with the birth of our first son, let us say at his first birthday, I give you the means to leave me, to support yourself independently of me."

I spun and stared at him. "You would divorce me?"

"No. Never such a distasteful thing as that, Alicia."

I sagged and closed my eyes.

"I would allow you to take the boy and retire, shall we say, to your own abode."

"Why?" Why would a man marry to obtain an heir, then allow the child out of his sight?

"Why, indeed. I wish to see you happy."

"You do not know me well enough to have a care for my happiness."

"My," he was chuckling, "you think me shallow. Tsk, tsk, my dear. That is no way to ingratiate yourself with any man, let alone your intended."

I would have objected, but he stopped me with a shake of his head.

"I want a son. I would have him by you. *Why* would I have him by you? Well, there are many extraordinary reasons, my dear. First on my list is that you are reputed to be so good with children. In the church school, you are well liked. Yes, I have inquired not only of your father, but of others. They all agree that you mix discipline with love. Second, I wish my children reared by a lady who *likes* them, by God. I have had my fill of air-filled governesses—"

"Governesses?" What need had he for governesses?

He gave a rueful glance at me. "Ah, I can see your brothers did not tell you everything about me, did they? Both kind and irrational of them, wasn't it? Yes, I have children."

Children! I smiled, pleased beyond reason. I frowned, confused by complications I had not anticipated. Children sweetened the pot.

"Yes, it surprises but interests you, doesn't it? I knew it would. I have two daughters, Alicia—both in need of a firm but friendly hand. I see you as providing that, my dear. Bringing a sense of stability and order to a house too long without a good woman. Which brings me to my third reason for selecting you. You are, above all else, a woman I can prize. You are a Wolff."

"Really, sir. If you refer to the so-called family curse, I must inform you I put no stock in such silliness."

"Neither do I. But the fact remains that you are a Wolff. And as such, you are subject to the family, shall we say, tendencies. And the evidence for them abounds. You are the only daughter among a family of seven offspring, correct?"

"Yes."

"Your brothers, those that are married and have children, have few sons, do they?"

"True." Matthew had two girls. Mark, the same. John and Paul, one each. Luke and Thomas, since they were not yet married, had no children. "Of the six, only Mark has a son."

"Yes. Which follows the trend, curse or not."

"That does not prove in any way that I can bear you a son any more than any other woman."

"No, that alone is not evidence enough, is it? So we should look at other members of the family. Your mother was an only daughter, too, wasn't she?"

"Yes. She had nine brothers."

"And you know these brothers well, do you not?" When I nodded, he continued. "Seven of them have daughters. Fourteen daughters among them. One has one son. One has no offspring at all, having declared himself a Catholic and taken his vows at age eighteen. Therefore, your mother's family shows the same tendencies as your own."

"True. And my mother's mother, my grandma, did come from a large brood, and—"

"She was a Wolff."

I looked into his soft gray eyes and knew I could not win here. He would have me speak the facts. "Yes.

45

She was the youngest daughter of the third duke of Worminster.''

"The fifth daughter of the third duke, my great grandfather. And the youngest sister of the fourth duke, my grandfather.''

"Wolff or not, sons are born to this family.''

"Eventually, yes.''

"*Always* eventually, it appears. Why use me to create the inevitable? Surely, Your Grace, you could have any lady in the land for the asking.''

He snorted. "I could, eh? Your brothers have left much untold, I fear.''

Angry, I let emotion overwhelm politeness. "They have told me you have a certain reputation with women.''

"Oh?'' One long brow rose to the silver wave that dipped along his forehead.

"They say you have—'' I knew I colored at the subject, "—mistresses.''

He froze, his eyes locked to mine. "What else do they say?''

"That is all.''

"*All?*'' He narrowed his eyes at me. "Don't ever lie to me, Alicia. What else do they say?''

"I do not know. My father and mother taught us to scorn gossip as idle talk. I do not know rumors because I do not ask.''

"But someone spoke about my having mistresses and you heard. It is enough to make you question my character.''

"Yes.''

"The disastrous thing about rumors is that once they start, it is the very devil to prove them false. So then, would it help for me to say that in anticipation of this marriage, Alicia, I have given up my mistresses? All of them.''

Them? ''How kind of you.''

I turned back toward the garden. Enflamed, I tried to control my breathing.

Yet when he came near, when he stood just behind me, so close I felt his human vitality seep through my taffeta bodice, I could not control my rampaging heart. His voice, now richly melodic, imparted words straight to that beating, bleating organ.

''I *am* kind, Alicia. And I *am* honorable. When I take vows, I keep them. I would not have chosen you if I felt you would not do the same. For richer, for poorer. In sickness and in health. 'Til death us do part.''

''Except in our case, it would be 'til I produce a son.''

He paused for interminable moments. ''I hope longer. But if that is all the time given us, yes.''

I gazed at barren trees, the symbol of life dormant, withered, dead. What would my life become if I did not marry this man? As barren, as dead as the scenery, loving other women's children to the end of my days. Yet what would my life become if I did marry him? Any better? I had to probe.

''And what kind of life would I have, Your Grace? With a son, the heir, in my charge, and society to shun me for my rather peculiar status? Married but not, I would be a subject for gossip.''

''But you would be rich, and capable as you are of winning people to your goodness, you would make a happy life for yourself. And for our boy.''

"How do I know that you will honor this agreement?"

"I will put it in writing. My solicitor will make it binding. I will even add something to sweeten the reward."

"Money is not a prize for me, sir. Only a means."

"I will sign over to you your grandmother's house."

My heart sang! I pivoted, and to my surprise and delight, I had spun right into his arms. "You would give me her house? But why?"

He smiled slowly as his warm fingers stroked my forearms. "Because she told me you loved the old place. Because it is still my property to give away as I choose, even though she lived in it for over five decades. Because it was once called the Wolff Dower House, yet no Wolff duchess has ever lived long enough to take up residence. And finally and foremost, because your grandmother thought you would consider the bargain if you were given proper motivation."

"You mean to tell me my grandmother *approved* of this—this marriage between us?"

"Not merely approved, my dear—suggested it herself."

I fell back against the cool window glass. The contrast of cool pane at my back and warm man to my bosom made my body tremble. "My God. I never thought that *she,* she of all people, would have—"

"She had your best interests at heart."

"How could she?" I searched his eyes for answers he might not possess. "How could she when she knew I was betrothed to Edward Perry?"

The duke pursed his lips. "Yes, well—I know not my Aunt Constance's thinking on it, other than to say, she sent for me to propose it. And I thought it had merit, particularly after I saw you."

I nodded. "Last spring, when I went to visit her and you were there in her room."

"I knew then from the looks of you you were the right woman for me."

I almost harumphed. "Please. Now you are being kind."

"No, I am honest."

I shook my head.

He shook me. "I need you to believe me, Alicia. You above all others." Then, his two hands came up to cup my face and hold it so my every feature was available for his scrutiny. "You are so honest yourself. So upright. So fair. In thought and deed and beauty."

"Please. I know what I am, sir. Too tall. Too strongly colored. Too strongly tempered."

He threw back his head to laugh and then when I did not laugh with him, he suddenly stilled. His fingertips caressed my cheeks.

"Look at me, Alicia. Yes, by God. By normal standards, you are too tall a woman for most. But for me, you are—shall we say?—fitting. By normal standards, you are too red-haired, too green-eyed to pass for delicate. But for me, you are—shall we say?—enticing. By normal standards of propriety, it is true that no duke, no earl, no baron, no man in his right mind, would want a woman with such an independent bent to her thinking. But I have never been accused of being in my right mind. Quite the opposite. And so for me, you are exactly what I need."

I stood my ground. "You must understand, sir, that

while I understand and appreciate your need to win me, you need not pretend that I appeal to you—"

"But you do." His thumbs were stroking my cheekbones. His torso was moving closer to mine. His mouth was whispering words with that voice that brushed my nerves with a bristling excitement. "Shall I demonstrate?"

No.

"Has a man ever kissed you, Alicia?" His lips asked against my cheek.

No.

"Not your Edward?" He breathed against my earlobe.

No.

"Not any boy from your congregation?" He lifted my chin. His eyes outlined my silent lips. "Wonderful. Then you have much to learn, my sweet. And I will find it incumbent upon me to teach you."

His one arm drew my body closer while his other hand went to my nape. His mouth, that wide slash which could appear so menacing, loomed closer, softer, more tantalizing.

My eyes fell closed.

In one crush, he pressed his mouth, his chest, his lean, long legs against mine. And my arms went round him. And my lips met his warm, seeking ones.

And I loved it.

I loved it when he kissed me once, testing, leading. I loved it when he gave some hoarse sound and slanted his mouth fiercely across mine, seizing, exploring. I loved it when his tongue invaded and I lost my breath, my heartbeat, my . . .

He jerked away and the world returned with unwelcome sanity. I felt cold air rush around me when the only part of him on me was his hands to my shoulders. I felt bereft and somehow incomplete. I sought his eyes.

He gazed at me with surprise and something I would call tender admiration.

"I will give a few more lessons, and in quick succession, I think." He combed a lock of straggling hair back into my once-tight coiffure. "For now, tell me you accept the bargain."

Reason ranted at me to be bold, just one last time. "What if—what if I never give you a son?"

"I doubt that. But if it does not happen, we could do as many couples do and spend the rest of our days together. After all, that would not be long for you, my dear. I am more than twice your age and most certainly will not live into your prime."

"You—you would not divorce me for failure to—?"

"To get an heir? No, Alicia. I have had two wives and have two daughters. I marry you, my dear, because you are my last, best hope of producing an heir and because—well, frankly, I find you damnably refreshing. I intend you to be my last duchess."

I frowned.

"I could put that in writing as well, if you like. Yes, I see I will have to. You need to learn to trust me, don't you, my dear? Well, I shall see to that. What can I do now—immediately, to show you I am trustworthy?"

I swallowed hard and considered the frenetic foulard of his cravat.

"I see you have a thought on that. Out with it. If we are to be man and wife, we will speak of many things in private the world would not allow in public."

He grasped my chin between thumb and forefinger. "Tell me."

I adored his eyes, so sweetly searching mine, so tolerant of my fears. Yet, I could only whisper. "I wonder, sir—"

"Max."

"Max. I wonder if you might give me time to—to become accustomed to the idea of marriage?"

"I would like us to marry before Christmas. I want my girls to have a happy holiday this year. That gives you twenty days at most before the ceremony. Choose any day that suits you."

"Thank you, sir—Max. But I—" I bit my lip, "—I had another issue in mind when I spoke of—well, I—I wonder if you might give me time to become acquainted with you, to learn your habits and your preferences, to understand you a bit before—before we—"

"Ah, yes. I see. Before we consummate our vows. That is what you're talking about, isn't it?"

I blushed and gave one curt nod.

"If you accommodate me by marrying me before the Yuletide, I will promise you I will not pressure you to consummate any vows until you are ready."

I exhaled. "Thank you, Max. I am grateful."

"However," he placed a forefinger against my mouth, "because of the very nature of our bargain, that reprieve cannot endure indefinitely. Therefore, you have three months, Alicia. Three months from the date of our wedding to come to me. After that, I will choose the right moment with no prior notice. What do you say?"

I shivered with the thrill of success. Three months

was more than enough time to bring myself to perform my wifely duty. Many women had had less with offer of less reward. With less of an appealing husband, too.

"A fair bargain, Max. I accept."

Chapter Three

Now when Max reclaimed my hand, I let him keep it. Literally and figuratively, I had committed my hand into his keeping. He smiled, almost triumphantly, and with that told me he recognized the willingness in my gesture.

"Come," he squeezed the appendage that gave him such power over me. "I would introduce you to my family."

I nodded. Anxious to meet his daughters, eager to make a good impression on those two who would become my charges, I rued at once my choice of traveling outfit. Serviceable, it might have been, for travel, if not for discouragement of one determined duke. But impressive it most definitely was not. And I wondered if they were old enough to judge me by my attire. Suddenly I was afraid.

Good God, what had I just done? Committed myself to a man—a duke, no less!—whom I did not know and did not even understand. How could I have been so obsessed? So possessed?

I could not pause. I could not think. I could only

follow. And pretend. Pretend I was not quaking more violently with my every step toward some unknown vista.

Max led me toward the hall, and as I walked beside him, retracing my steps of mere minutes before, I clenched my teeth. Now, when the tile and marble and plush carpet passed my view, I realized with wide-eyed awe that what I had just agreed to do made me the future mistress of this . . . this . . . labyrinth!

At this great salvo to my faked composure, I balked.

Max turned slowly, tilting his head in query and pausing momentarily before a sylvan painting hung upon the papered wall. His dark grace seemed a very part of the wooded scenery. So searching, so astute were those silver eyes of his that I felt mesmerized and dissected all at the same time.

"The house was begun by the first Duke of Worminster. But the service wings were added by my father. He hired an architect whom George the Fourth favored. The decor is rather heavy Georgian as well. Can't say as I favor it all. But I can see from your expression, you debate its style."

"It's not so much the style, Max. I know so little about style. But the size *is* rather daunting. And I haven't seen but the library so far!"

He gave a little laugh. "Nothing you won't get used to, Alicia. Perhaps this room will suit you better."

He thrust open one alabaster portal and my eyes saw the purple and black of the hall give way to a riot of yellows, reds, and greens. This glorious scheme was more to my liking. I must have shown him that by my expression, because when I turned from the Indian calicos of the divan and armchairs, he was once more grinning at me.

"I am happy to see you won't be changing everything about the mansion. There is much I like. Particularly the brilliance of this room. And," he stepped to the far corner, where he grasped the handle of another door, "this recent addition."

He threw open the door and a fragrant gush of air met me where I stood. Moreover, the sound of running water soothed the ragged ends of my emotions. What was this?

"My conservatory," Max informed me, as I walked past him into the verdant forest that beckoned unmercifully.

I barely noticed the cool tile beneath my thinly shod feet or the white trail it wove through the dense brush. I smelled only a floral perfume and saw only green.

Green so rich it warmed my nose and ears and toes. Green so lush the fronds of one plant reached out to embrace the stalks of another. Green so black that even the radiance of afternoon winter sun did not dim its lure. I tried to part one plant from another. To my joy, only more of this man-made jungle filled my eye. I stopped and glanced up at Max.

"I have never seen such rare wonders."

"Nor I," he whispered, as he delved into my eyes, sounding vaguely like my father when he preached on something holy. He shook himself to awareness. "I ordered this glass-and-iron dome constructed solely because I enjoy nature, raw and pure."

I wandered between two giant ferns, brushed one pink geranium blossom from my cheek, and reverently touched one deep-blue tree violet. "You are a botanist, then?"

He nodded. "And you, I see, are one as well."

"Well, no. I simply appreciate nature, too. In its purity."

"In its raw power?"

Now I examined his set features. His noble forehead. His broad shoulders. His long-fingered hands with a dusting of black hair across the knuckles. If ever I had seen raw power, it was here before me, personified in this one figure whom many called the Cotton King of the North. The most powerful and the richest man within hundreds of miles.

He employed hundreds of men, women, and children in his many mills across the Lancastrian plains. These workers left the hovels they called homes each morning before dawn and labored until hours past dusk. They toiled in cramped, cold, dark factories, stopping only long enough to eat a cut of bread with perhaps a slab of cheese. These workers were often sick, always weary, and forever in debt. They wandered from one day to the next, in search of a living. What they found was a living death.

I knew because I had seen such people in Crewe and Chester and Lancaster. I had seen them when I'd gone with my father on his circuit rides, when he would try to buoy these people with talk of how hard work brought just rewards. I had heard these laborers reply that the cotton manufacturers were ruthless men to work them so hard for so little recompense. They had so little joy, and less hope. And though I had heard no one speak against the Duke of Worminster specifically, I knew he was one of those men. And I, daughter of my socially responsible father and mother, now knew I would tutor my husband in his social responsibilities.

I drew myself up, girding myself with righteousness, and faced him. "That is where you and I will disagree, Max."

He stood bemused. Surrounded by the savage growth, he looked somehow totally in his element. Yet he remained the gentleman and waited for me to continue.

"I think there is much to improve in raw nature. Particularly man's nature. Reason is the force of men. More of it must prevail. Lest the tendency to wildness shall sap our efforts at progress."

"So, humanity comes to the rescue of the wild and primitive world. I must say, my dear, I do not share your value of the wisdom of humankind. Far too many ignore their instincts in favor of reason and find themselves the poorer."

"Yes. And others can justify almost anything if they do it calmly, sanely."

He chuckled, throwing his head back and finally folding his arms. "Well, I do hope you are not going to concentrate solely on the sanity in *your* nature."

I bristled. "I am what I am, sir. The daughter of a Methodist minister who shepherded the working classes. You must not assume I am uneducated or—"

"I assume nothing of the kind, Alicia. In fact, I never *assume* anything. Not in business, and certainly not in my personal life. Not anymore. No, I find out the truth. And I make a particular point to find out about women." He stepped nearer and ran a finger down my cheek. "Women who interest me. And you interest me. You intrigue me, have intrigued me since that night in your grandmother's room. You are such a mix of this and that. You favor betterment of living conditions for the average mill worker. You even insist on teaching them how to read. Furthermore, you have a rather extraordinary understanding of Latin, and you consider yourself an expert on the War of the Roses."

"And the Cromwellian interregnum."

"Ahhh. Really?" His silver eyes grew merry. "I must tell my investigator he is lacking in thoroughness."

"Investigator? You had me—?"

"Oh, but of course. I told you, I find out as much as I can about people. You do not think a man of my means would take to wife a woman about whom he knows little or nothing?" He seemed to sneer at his own words. "Bah! What folly. What folly . . ." His mind drifted then. Far, very far from me. And as the distance increased, his features marbelized.

And the hair along my arms rose up and I became afraid. Afraid of the creature before me, whose silver eyes took on the glaze of fury. Afraid of this menace with winged brows and clenched iron jaw. I quaked. Yet I wanted the other Max to return. Wanted him so desperately, I instinctively placed my hand on his wrist.

My touch seemed to drain the wildness from his countenance. His eyes slowly softened to dove gray. His brows lowered. His jaw relaxed. And he spoke to me with rasping sweetness.

"I chose you, my dear, for your background and your breeding. I desire all that is educated and rather bluestocking about you. But I also desire all that is instinctive in you, else I would not prize you as such a good mate. Perhaps that sounds obtuse to you now, but I warrant you will soon see it proved."

He raised my hand from his wrist and brought it to his mouth. Turning it over, he placed a warm and lingering kiss into my palm. The softness of his mouth brought memories of moments before, when his lips had pressed mine in delicious abandon. I shivered.

He noticed and gave a little smile. "Do not be afraid to show me what is instinctual about you, my dear. After all, we *are* family. The same family, even before we mate. We understand each other at an elemental level. Recognize it, Alicia. Let us begin to enjoy it."

He reached for me and following his lead, I went instinctively, blindly, wholeheartedly. His arms enveloped me, his eyes ravished me, his lips swooped to brand me and I gave every—

"There you are, Max!"

I gasped. Max growled in protest. I staggered backward.

Max braced me with an arm at my waist and spun to face our intruder.

"Caroline! My God!" Max raked his hair and recovered his breath, if not his composure. "You nearly frightened us to death!"

"Max, do forgive me. I never meant to frighten you." The petite, henna-haired woman apologized to him, but turned curious Wedgwood-blue eyes on me. "I meant only to remind you that we awaited you, as you requested. We did hear voices, and I thought I would come to see if indeed it was you. And, of course, it is. Max, you are forgetting your manners. Introduce us, won't you?"

"Yes, Caroline." He stood aside so that I now got

60

a full view of her. "Caroline, I would like to present Miss Alicia Pennington, formerly of Crewe. Alicia, this is my Aunt, Lady Samuel Wolff. She is the widow of my father's brother."

Recovering myself to the point of remembering my manners, I extended my hand. The lady took it as she cocked a brow at me.

"Pennington, Pennington . . . are you related to the Penningtons who are descended from Constance Wolff?"

"Yes, Lady Samuel. Constance Wolff was my grandmother. My mother's mother." We shook hands perfunctorily.

"Really! How interesting." She gathered her red wool shawl about her arms. "You must be the granddaughter she prized so highly. The few times we saw each other, I remember her speaking of you so reverently." She turned porcelain eyes on Max. "Do come introduce your guest to the rest of us, won't you, Max?"

"Precisely my intention, Madam." He swept out an arm to part the foliage for her. "After you, Caroline." He let her lead the way and then turned to offer me his arm. "Alicia."

I twined my hand through his arm and hung on to him. He had not told me about this aunt. Indeed, I had never heard of her from my grandmother, and I wondered where the lady lived. I was now adrift in more unknowns and very distraught. Distraught, above all, that this lady—his aunt, no less!—had found us in a most undignified pose. My cheeks blazed with shame.

Lady Samuel sailed through the meandering pathways of the conservatory with practiced ease. She must have visited often, I thought, as she led us toward a clearing where one young man and one young woman sat, both with expectant looks upon their faces. At our approach, the man stood, while his female companion folded her hands in her lap.

The man was no match for Max. Not in height or handsomeness or sheer grace. He was perhaps six inches shorter, a shade blander, a trifle less assured. If his lack of assurance was due to the necessity for the ivory-handled cane he held, I had no clue. Yet through it all, I could see at once the familial resemblance.

Not so his female companion. Bedecked in a rose-and-white lace confection of a gown, she mirrored Lady Samuel, decades younger. She was slender, with natural red highlights in her plain brown hair. She had the same opaque eyes, the same retroussé nose, the same pride of place. Indeed, she sat like a reigning presence, awaiting a subordinate's introduction. *My* introduction. I armed myself, sensing an enemy.

Max resonant voice brought me to myself. "Alicia, I would have you meet my most immediate family. My cousins—and yours also—Lady Adair Wolff, Caroline's only daughter, and Lord Gilbert Wolff, Caroline's son."

I nodded and smiled at Adair, who reciprocated my politeness. Gilbert took my hand and paid his homage with a continental kiss of my fingers. Beside me, Max stiffened.

I sought to smooth the passage and smiled more broadly at both. "I am delighted to meet you. I have not met many from the Wolff side of my family."

Lady Caroline sniffed. "I should say not."

Max trained mean eyes on his aunt.

She spread her mouth in a sorry semblance of a smile and looked at me. "Your grandmother may have lived in the Dower House, but while her father and her brother were alive, she most certainly was not welcomed into the other houses of the Wolffs."

"Caroline," Max warned, "those are old troubles. We have no need to speak of them here. Aunt Constance is dead. Let her troubles be buried also."

Caroline assessed me a moment with those milky blue eyes of hers. "You do not know, do you, my dear? No, no, I see not. But I say, if we are to forget things, first we must know them. A shame no one told you. I shall, lest you think us all priggish. The reason was a dictum by my father-in-law, who was also your great uncle. We did not associate because of your grandfather, Constance's husband. He was, so the story goes, not of our class. A solicitor's son who saw your grandmother Constance and persuaded her to run off—actually elope—with him. Oh, he was soldier. An officer, to be sure. But one who had purchased his commission and then marched off to fight in whatever war was available, leaving your grandmother to live off the dregs. Then circumstances often forced her to come to her father, the third duke, to subsidize her meager allowance so that she might feed her brood."

At this soliloquy, the others had frozen like ice sculptures. Even Max stared at the woman who had ignored propriety as well as his wishes.

"The duke, her father, took great pity on her, even though she had married far beneath her station, and he gave her the right to live in the Dower House until her death. Her brother, however, chose to cut her off in every other way. No money, he said. A pity. Money becomes a judge of so many people." She sighed. "The Wolffs chose not to associate with her."

"That's not true for all of us, Caroline." Max had recovered enough to speak. "Aunt Constance received many of us. You simply did not *choose* to be associated with her. Do not put the onus on others for your own choices, madam."

Uncowed, she looked into Max's eyes. "Quite right, Max, my dear."

Lord Gilbert cleared his throat. "I say, Miss Pennington, are you here for a visit?" He smiled, more at ease now. "The holidays, perhaps?"

I turned to Max, bewildered. Didn't they have any idea why I was here?

Max lowered his lashes, then glanced up at a curious Gilbert. "Yes, Gilbert, you might say Alicia is here for an extended stay. In fact, she is here permanently."

Lady Caroline went rigid as the dead. Lady Adair sent one hand to her fichu-covered throat. Only Lord Gilbert seemed accepting of his cousin's explanation.

"Permanently?" Gilbert turned his eyes and his charm on me. But before I had time to be truly startled at his interest, Max spoke the words that had all three gasping.

"Married?" whispered Gilbert.

"*Married!*" cried his mother.

"No," mouthed Adair. "No, Max." She rose from her wicker chair, her rosy silk skirts billowing about her as she faced down her cousin. "How *can* you?"

Then she turned, not so much toward me as against me. As tall as I, she met me squarely face-to-face. Her blue eyes—those extraordinary eyes she could have used to charm anyone—examined every feature, every line, every asset and liability I bore. Suddenly her mouth opened, attempted words, failed, and snapped shut. She pivoted to face Max. Her lower lip trembled. Her shoulders convulsed. And then she swirled, grabbed up handfuls of her gown to avoid touching mine, and sailed past me, as if I were a pillar of poison.

"Shocking." Lady Caroline struggled for the wicker chair her daughter had vacated so abruptly. "Shocking."

Lord Gilbert watched his mother and sister with nothing but tolerance. But when he turned to Max, he stuck out his hand. "Wonderful news, Max. I *am* thrilled to hear it."

Hesitating a moment, Max finally took Gilbert's hand with aplomb. "Thank you, Gilbert. I accept your congratulations."

"You must excuse Adair, of course. I expect her to come around shortly. She doesn't take to change well, you know. Her 'nerves,' as the doctors say." Gilbert turned to me. "Adair will recover, do not fear—not only her composure, but her manners. As we all will." He indicated his mother and then cocked a brow at me, striking a haughty pose that reminded me once more he was a Wolff as much as Max.

Gilbert's mother, meanwhile, had placed a handkerchief over her mouth. She was gasping repeatedly now, and her face became splotches of white and purple. Gilbert went to her side to stroke her back and murmur encouraging words.

"There, there now, Mother. Relax and your spasm will end. That's right. That's a good girl."

She stopped almost immediately, wiping her mouth

and then her watering eyes. Then she gazed at me with what I felt must be rare warmth.

"Forgive me, my dear Alicia. I—I simply was so shocked."

She checked Max's expression and something there made her eyes widen. Suddenly, she was fully recovered and standing and then—amazement above all others!—she was kissing my cheek.

"Dear girl," she murmured into my ear, "how happy I am for you. For you both." She drew away and clasped my hands in hers. "How delightful to have a new mistress of Wolffs' Lair. How bad of Max not to warn us, not to drop even the tiniest hint." She sniffled and smiled serenely, fully in control of herself once more. "You must be in an absolute thrall about the engagement. Come sit down here and tell us all, my dear. Gilbert. Max." She sat, indicating we should all join her, and that I should take the chair opposite her. But when Max did not sit but came to stand behind me, her lips narrowed in distaste.

Undaunted, she proceeded. "I did tell Bigelow to serve tea in here, Max. I do hope you don't mind. Gilbert, do toddle over and pull the bell, will you, like a dear? Thank you."

She settled her eyes on me as her son struggled to cross to the glass wall and the bell pull. Meanwhile, Max's palm cupped my shoulder.

"Well, Max," Caroline laid her hands into the mounds of her prune satin gown, "do tell us how this engagement came to pass. You have known each other for years, I suppose, and just recently came to the realization of your mutual affections?"

Serene in her discourse, she was smiling, scrutinizing, searching.

I would have replied, but Max squeezed my shoulder ever so delicately. "Alicia and I have met, yes, Madam."

She lifted fine feathered brows. "And you are so young, my dear girl. What are you? Seventeen? Eighteen?"

"Nineteen."

"Yes, quite. And your father has just passed on, has he not?"

I nodded. "Yes. And my mother has been gone almost four years now."

"So . . . you are an orphan."

"I do have six brothers, Lady Samuel."

"Please, we are family, call me Caroline. *Six* brothers! How interesting." She glanced up at Max. "Follows the curse, doesn't it, Max?"

Whatever his reaction, hers was lost as Bigelow made a clattering entrance along the tiled path with a tea cart, teetering and tottering with china, sweets, and jams. Whatever Caroline's impertinence to have usurped Max's role as host by ordering the tea served here, none of them acted oddly when she said to Bigelow, "Lay it here before me, Bigelow. I shall pour, unless you wish to, Alicia?"

"No, Caroline, please, you do it." I smiled, feigning graciousness, but really fearing her eyes would find more to criticize about my upbringing than I cared her to understand.

"Very well." She bent to her task, arranging cups on saucers, passing the plates about, and removing the cozy from the flowered Minton pot. As she worked at passing the scones and the butters, she kept her eyes on her tasks but her mind on my marriage.

"Well, I think it a lovely idea that you invited your betrothed here for the holidays, Max. It will certainly give you an opportunity to announce your engagement. Perhaps the duchy's Christmas reception and ball would be a lovely time. Was that your thought, Max?" She prepared to pour the first cup of tea and smiled at me. "What do you take in your tea, dear?"

"Two sugars, thank you, Caroline."

She poured, added the sugar, and placed a teaspoon on my saucer and passed it across to me. "You like sweet things. Candy? Hot chocolate?"

As I received the cup, I told her she was correct. "My greatest foible is a craving for sweets."

Caroline's eyes slid up to Max. "We shall have to see she is satisfied, won't we, Max?" She smiled no smile. "Satisfy me with a few details of this wedding, Max."

"Caroline, we will not be announcing our engagement at the Christmas party. My thought was that instead, we would be announcing our marriage."

Her eyes widened and then slid to my waistline.

Max's hand tightened on my shoulder.

I could have flinched at the pressure of his wrath or his aunt's, both were so potent, so menacing. But it was Max who recovered some shred of civility first.

"I have proposed, and Alicia has accepted. I see no reason to wait. Neither does she. We will be married before Christmas Day, Caroline. That is less than three weeks, I know, but I wish it this way. I would hope you and Adair and Gilbert will find it in your hearts to wish us both well."

"Of course we will, Max." She glanced at her son and back to Max. "Adair always recovers herself. It's just . . . well, my dear Max, less notice than six or seven months is so extraordinary that . . . well, the gossip, my dear. The gossip will kill us all this time. What *will* people think?"

"Whatever they wish, Madam."

"But my dear boy, they . . . you . . . we cannot expect that people will forget . . . They will talk of this to their graves! We shall never live it down! Max, surely you know what I mean!"

"Yes, Madam, I do. In my darkest hours, I suspect people will *never* forget. *Never* relent. But I have given up living by others' rules, in case you hadn't noticed. I live by my own rules, and the rest of the world be damned!"

I closed my eyes. The puzzling pugnaciousness of the moment made my stomach churn. I put my cup and saucer down upon the second tier of the cart. I put my hand to my head.

"She's ill," murmured Gilbert.

"She most certainly is," declared his mother.

Max crouched beside me. "Dear, what's the matter?"

Caroline harumphed. "Good God, Max, in her condition—"

Ohhhh, I groaned in shame. Caroline insisted on thinking that I was—was—

Max put a hand to my forehead and examined my face, but he growled at his aunt. "Just *what* condition is *that,* Madam?"

"Don't be indelicate, Max!"

I raised my eyes to a worried Max and turned to

69

this impossible woman and her impertinent thoughts. I was determined to find the physical courage to correct her false impressions.

"Caroline, Max and I have met only once. That night was last spring, a few weeks before my grandmother's death, and . . ."—good heavens, how could I utter the words that revealed how little I knew this man?—"our meeting was for a bare five minutes, if that. So, you see, Caroline, I am not with child. Max and I do not marry to give a child a name or home. And so we do not marry out of passion, let alone love."

"Then, I am at a loss, Max. What can be the rush? What is the attraction?"

"I speak only for myself, madam," Max offered, somber as the grave. "While Alicia has assured you that she and I do not marry out of necessity to an unborn child, I will assure you that I marry out of dire necessity to my already born children. I want them loved and cared for by a good woman."

Caroline's eyes narrowed, but she waited for the rest of his disclosure.

"And I want this to happen now, soon, *tomorrow,* if Alicia will have me. But I want more than that. Alicia may not marry me for love—perhaps not a romantic love—but that is acceptable to me. No, instead, I wish a quiet, consoling love, gentle in its tone, unassuming in its grasp. This gentle woman," he turned toward me now and settled his gazed into mine, "this parson's daughter will bring me that. And I would have that above all for myself and my children."

His words, his regard for me, made my heart stop with sweet longing.

Caroline was sputtering. "And so the possibility exists that you will have yet *more* children, Max. Male children. Heirs."

Max turned on her once more. His face was kinder, even if his words were not. "Yes, Caroline. That is true. You—and Gilbert and even Adair—will have to accept that possibility. In the meantime, and for as long as you wish it, I still give you my protection and the hospitality of my home."

Oh, my, my. They lived *here?*

I fell back in my chair.

That was why Caroline had ordered Bigelow to bring the tea. Why she'd poured. Why she was so officious in Max's house. She and her children actually lived here!

Gilbert smacked his lips. "I tell you, Max, I have nothing but good wishes for you and your bride. I never thought to inherit the dukedom from you. Never." He smiled sweetly at me. "And now, with this stunning lady as your wife, I know I won't. She is a Wolff, healthy and strong, and therefore, she will soon bear you a son, and hopefully more than one. I wish you well, Max. God knows, you deserve some happiness. And now, if you'll forgive me," he stood and thrust the cane before him, "my leg pains me. I must retire before supper."

He bowed slightly at me. "Good to have you with us, Alicia. We needed someone without guile, didn't we, Max?"

With that rhetorical question, he hobbled off toward the morning room.

I watched him go while Caroline apologized for her son and Max waved her words away with a quick move of his hand.

71

Summarily, she, too, left us.

In deference, Max rose to his feet. He watched her go, then broke the silence when he suggested I finish my tea. "It will refresh you. This has been a grueling interview. You are tired and need to rest from your trip. I will introduce you to Mary and Elizabeth after you have had a nap."

Was he pratting on? Protecting me? I looked at him now in light of new evidence. This man whom I was about to marry was an enigma if ever I'd met one. Powerful, rich, titled. Tolerant, yet still benevolent to his less fortunate relatives. Caring of his two daughters. Truly a treasure. Yet some inner sense told me he could be dangerous, too. Dangerous if trifled with, if crossed.

Who, then, would have the courage—no, the audacity—to confront him with guile?

I could not ask him. But I was determined to discover who that might have been.

Chapter Four

To discover that person and the reasons for such undercurrents among the family, I needed to know more about them—and quickly.

"Mary and Elizabeth," I began, when Max declared he would show me to my room. "I would like to meet them, Max. Please . . . I'm really not tired, and I'm much more interested in meeting your daughters than in resting."

He smiled, more at ease since we were again alone and our discussions centered on something other than family tensions. "My dear, I would be happy to introduce you. I'd be delighted, in fact. The sooner the three of you meet, the sooner . . . well, the sooner many things will be put to rights."

I tilted my head at him in question and he stood aside to lead me out of the conservatory.

"This way, Alicia." He was not going to elaborate on what needed to be put to rights with his girls. "I'll take you back through the morning room and out into the hall toward the main stairs where you entered.

Don't worry, you'll soon learn the pattern of the house.''

I smiled as I stepped toward him and silently wondered if I'd learn the pattern of its inhabitants as easily. "Please, Max," I urged, as I hooked my arm through his without hesitation, "tell me about Mary and Elizabeth.''

"They are five years of age. Lovely little moppets, I think. Bright and inquisitive.'' We began to climb the wide wine-carpeted stairs.

"Five is a wonderful age. So full of joy.''

"Yes.'' He frowned.

As we took the turn in the stairs, I took the opportunity to look at him fully.

"Are they not good children?'' I ventured.

"Good. Very good. Too good.'' He blinked and tried to smile at me.

"And you have no governess currently?''

"None. I have tried two, both harpies. I personally dismissed the last one. She gave decent references, but after five months of her, my girls are . . . well, you shall see.''

We came to the first landing and he took my elbow to lead me down one wing of the hall. The upstairs reflected the mood of privacy, and I was pleased to see that the colors reflected that as well. Here, the blues and muted greens gave a much-needed sense of tranquility in this house of somber turmoil.

Even now, trouble haunted Max's eyes. And he was quiet. Beside him, I walked down the hall and wondered what he would have added if he'd felt as free to tell me his family's troubles as he'd been to lavish praises over me. While I certainly did not expect him to reveal his every past misdemeanor, I was shocked now at my own proclivity—indeed, my desire—to reveal to him every one of mine.

Had he won my trust so easily? I acknowledged to my inner self that the easy way he'd spoken to me in his den had made it simple subsequently for me to side with him against the indelicacies of his relatives. If my loyalty was so quickly given to this man I barely knew, how long would I wait to deliver to him the essence of his desire—my body?

Shocked to the bone, I felt myself blushing, burning, yearning to be closer to him, yet knowing propriety meant I should move far, far away. I distanced my torso from his and considered the carpet.

He did not notice, so consumed was he by his own thoughts. Instead, he led me left, passed an open door, to what appeared to be none other than the second story of the library. Then he stopped and knocked at a closed door on the opposite side of the hallway. In a second, the door opened and a petite pale reed of a woman bowed slightly in deference.

"Your Grace, do come in. We are just finishing our tea." Her brown eyes met mine in curiosity.

"Thank you, Williams. Alicia, this is Miss Williams, who serves as nurse to Lady Mary and Lady Elizabeth. Williams, this is Miss Alicia Pennington."

I smiled and nodded at the woman, who at forty years or so looked as haggard as a mill worker. From overwork with her charges, perhaps?

"How do you do, Miss Williams. Have you been nurse to the children long?"

Williams checked Max's eyes to see if she might respond to this strange lady now standing in her schoolroom. When she saw his permission given, she dropped me a curtsy.

"Yes, Miss. Ever since they were born, Miss." She glanced at Max. "Will you see them, Your Grace?"

"Yes, Williams, we will. Come, Alicia."

He took my arm once more and led me through the small foyer into the schoolroom. There, sitting with hands folded, eyes fastened on the doorway, were two tiny girls, both with heart-shaped expectant faces, both with wide gray eyes filled with fear.

"Hello, my dears," Max greeted them cheerfully.

Both immediately stood, then cast their eyes to the floor and dropped their father and me a curtsy. They were identical. Identical twins! Dressed in identical plum dimity with plain pinafores on top, they appeared to be reflections of each other. With Max's black hair and his large gray eyes, they were gorgeous children, destined to become gorgeous women.

I beamed at them. They eyed me suspiciously, then greeted their father.

"Good afternoon, Papa."

"Hello, sir."

"Come over here and give me a hug." Max bent and spread out his arms.

They came. Oh, yes, they came. And they hugged him, each in turn. Yet neither hug was an expression of joy or affection. And I felt my heart drop. No, each hug was as cold and indifferent a touch as an icy wind upon a shore. They stepped back, hands at their sides, and stared straight ahead—at no one and nothing.

"I have come," said Max, as he straightened and took on a more officious tone, "to introduce you to a very fine lady. Her name is Miss Alicia Pennington.

76

Alicia, this is Mary and Elizabeth. Mary is our oldest—by five minutes. She is often first in many things."

The little girl in question cast her gray eyes to the floor in modesty, and as she did, I noticed she had a mole to the left of her mouth, the only mark distinguishing one girl from the other.

"Mary is first to learn her alphabet. First to finish her porridge. First in many things. Elizabeth is no laggard, however. She often bests her sister by her dedication to quality. While Mary is quick, Elizabeth is thorough. A most unique way to tell the difference between them, wouldn't you say?"

"Absolutely," I said. "And we shall find more. Mary, what do you like to do best when you are not doing things quickly?"

She glanced up at me and pondered the question. Her thoughts spun in her head, yet she remained composed, true to her form as the leader. "Watch Cook."

I chuckled. "And what do you like best about watching Cook? The good smells?"

"No, Ma'am. The little bites she gives me."

"Any special 'bites'?"

"Cookies. Marzipan and toffee. Lots of other things."

I looked at Elizabeth, who was licking her lips. "And do you like to do that, too, Elizabeth?"

She looked at the floor and scuffed her feet. "Yes, Ma'am," she muttered.

Was she simply following her sister's lead or being shy? I knelt before her so that her line of vision and mine were even. I smiled as I addressed her. "Is there some other sport you prefer?"

77

"I like stories. I like it when Williams tells us stories."

Mary made a sound of displeasure and Elizabeth compressed her lips.

"And do you also like to read them?"

"We have only three books, ma'am. Papa has hundreds in his library. But I can't read them."

"Well, then, we shall see to it that we get a few you can read, Elizabeth." I looked up at Max, who had a look of incredulity on his face. "That will be acceptable, won't it, Max?"

"Definitely. Whatever you three want you shall have."

Thus assured of his support, I rose. "Tomorrow morning at ten, all three of us will take our morning tea together. And we'll make a list of your favorite goodies, Mary, while you, Elizabeth, impart your favorite stories. Then, to be fair, I shall tell you my favorite foods and stories."

While it was clear from their startled expressions that the two girls had no idea how to take this delightful development, Williams reared back in utter dismay. But true to her station, she clamped her mouth shut. Who was she to object?

Max cleared his throat. "Williams, do have the girls ready at ten."

"Yes, sir. Am I to understand, sir, that Miss Pennington is to be the girls' new governess?"

"No, Williams. You are to understand—as are Mary and Elizabeth—that Miss Pennington is to become the next Duchess of Worminster."

Both girls took the news with silence.

But boiling water could not have done more to make

Williams expression go from composed to outraged. Her head fell back as her mouth sagged open.

"But . . . but, sir, I thought . . . that is, I presumed—"

Max cocked an angry brow at her. "Yes, Williams, what did you presume?"

To reveal her complete thoughts would have been so far beyond her station that she could have been sacked on the spot for it. She knew it. I saw it reflected in her worried eyes.

She pressed her hands together before her. "I am sorry, sir. I was mistaken. My thoughts are unimportant."

Max harumphed. "Precisely so, Williams. And I'll not have presumptuous staff in my house. Do it again and you will be gone. Alicia, let us leave Miss Williams to digest that." He extended his arm toward the door.

I could do naught but what he wished, and so I turned for the hall. Struggling to keep up with him, I noted that with his every step, his fury swelled. I barely noticed that we had once more traversed the hall when he suddenly halted and thrust open a door.

"Here is your room, Alicia, until our marriage, that is. I do hope you like it. I'll have Mrs. Timms, my housekeeper, up here in a moment." He strode into the room, which was adorned in brilliant malachite damask drapes and upholstered chairs and throws. Viciously, he yanked at the bellpull. When he turned toward me, he breathed so fiercely, his nostrils flared wide. He avoided my eyes as he sought to control his temper.

"As you can see, Alicia, I have numerous problems with some of the staff and with some of my relations.

All is not well here, but then, all has not been well here for years."

"Yes, Max, I see that. If it is any consolation, I believe that one can do so little to change the behavior of one's relatives. They often think they can abuse one of their own and go unscathed. But if your servants are discourteous, Max, why not dismiss them? I may be an advocate of better working and living conditions for the poor of this world, but I do not condone discourtesy from anyone at any time."

"Thank you, my dear." He tried desperately to smile. He failed. "I welcome your assistance in changing conditions here. In fact, your avid crusade for a better life for all made me think you most suitable for me in my time of need." He faltered for more words of explanation but once more thought better of it.

"Forgive me now, Alicia, I must leave you. I have work to accomplish before dinner. Do introduce yourself to Mrs. Timms. She has been with us since my father was a young man and she'll not be impertinent. And I know she'll like you." He truly smiled now. "Make yourself comfortable. Order a bath. Have Mrs. Timms get a maid to order your clothes for you. And have her show you about the house. I will see you before supper. We gather at eight o'clock."

He stepped toward the hallway with haste and closed my door behind him.

Alone, I inhaled and closed my eyes. So much had happened in so short a time that I grew weary trying to recall all the innuendos and half-statements offered up for my examination in the last hour. I shook my head and opened my eyes.

Never had I had a room so large, so luxurious—and

all to myself. Oh, I had visited my grandmother, and she had given me her anteroom as my resting place. But never had I called the space mine. This room, so green and gold, sent shivers of joy up my spine. It looked like a forest. My forest. And I smiled.

But a knock at the door meant I could not enjoy it in solitude just yet.

"Come in."

The bespectacled woman who opened the door was as round and rosy a creature as even Mister Dickens could have created. Dressed in plain French gray calamenco cotton, she had a flaming pink complexion and stark white tresses that gave her the robustness her undecorous attire merely complemented. She threw me a toothy grin, gathered up her voluminous crinolined skirts, closed the door behind her, and hastened before me. Immediately she fell into a curtsy.

"Good afternoon, Miss Pennington. I am Mrs. Timms, the housekeeper, and delighted to meet you." She rose and, beneath her rimless glasses, her robin's-egg-blue eyes danced over my features. "His Grace the duke informed me last week of his intentions toward you, and I am pleased to meet you. I can see that His Grace has chosen wisely."

"Why, thank you, Mrs. Timms, I am honored at your assessment of me. I hope I shall live up to your expectations."

"Aye, Ma'am, I think you will. You are a minister's daughter."

Amazed that she hadn't pointed out my value as a Wolff first and foremost, I stared at her. "And why would a minister's daughter be vital to this household, Mrs. Timms?" I smiled gaily at her to indicate I might

81

be steadfast but I was also tolerant of others' theological beliefs.

But in the bat of an eyelash, she had gone from sweet to sorrowful. "Oh, Miss, forgive me." She cast her eyes to the floor. "It's not for me to say. It—it really isn't." She was groping for words, but when she found them, her head came up and a smile once more graced her jovial features. "Every house needs a godfearing mistress in it, Miss Pennington. Every house. And we here at Wolffs' Lair have not had a mistress who . . . that . . . well, shall I say, we are eager for a good woman."

Why had she fumbled for words and, when she found them, said exactly the same thing Max had said earlier? *A good woman* . . .

"Thank you, Mrs. Timms. I am eager to assist the duke in his duties and in ordering his household, but I shall rely on you and your years of knowledge to help steer me in the right direction."

Oh, she liked that. She almost clapped her hands in joy. "Yes, Miss Pennington, you can count on me. I have been at Wolffs' Lair since I was a young girl. The previous housekeeper purchased my services at the Manchester Servants' Fair one bright morning in June in 1815. I was twelve. And eager to please."

"Good heavens, twelve! Had you no parents?"

"No, Miss Pennington. I was orphaned when my Mum and Da were caught in a mill fire. My brother died there, too. After their deaths, I made myself an oath I would never work in a cotton mill. And I haven't. I went to that fair that morning after I buried my kin and Mrs. Penrose saw me and picked me out of that crowd, she did. Said I looked like I had a strong back

82

and a stronger mind. I proved her right, too. I worked hard and I studied hard under her, and when she died ten years later, I took over the running of the house. That was just after His Grace, the present duke, married his first wife and—well, the Duchess Cynthia was never a hale or hearty lass. She needed all the help she could get. And me? Why, I was thrilled to give it her."

Cynthia. Curiosity ate at me. "Was she sickly, then, the duke's first duchess?"

"Oh, yes, Ma'am. Always down with a cough or sore throat. We clothed her in the finest merino wools, the best cashmeres. One year, I remember how His Grace brought her a huge white fox throw for her lap. But not much seemed to keep her safe. She was frail; always had been. She could never sit a horse for the hunt after September, and certainly never go outside for a sleighride in winter. She had to stay inside, always before a roaring fire. When I think of all the coal the footmen would haul. My God, it seemed sometimes to be half the bin! She was a sweet-faced angel, with a disposition to match. The duke loved her, without a doubt. Without a doubt. But his love could not save her, not from the ravages of winter."

"Is that how she passed on?"

The look on her face would have frozen hell itself. And I, more the fool, tried to find some avenue by which I might clarify my intent.

"Was Cynthia unable to withstand the winters perhaps?"

Mrs. Timms bored into my eyes with some unspoken question, and at her search, I did not flinch, but oh, did I wonder what I had said to put her off so.

83

Presently she recovered some dignity, some circumspection, and gave me a jerky smile.

"Oh, no, Ma'am. No, sorry to say. If you'd have asked me, though, I always would have said she'd go of consumption or such. But no . . . she went to her maker after delivering to her husband, the duke, a fine, strapping baby boy."

A boy! Max had once had a son! No wonder he wished for another. How long had the boy lived? How had he died? I stared at Mrs. Timms. "What happened to them?"

"Oh, it was tragic, Ma'am. Tragic." Her voice thickened with unshed tears, and she cleared her throat to no avail. "Poor little tyke. Poor, poor Cynthia. I always say that if the two of them had lived, we would have a wonderful life here today."

I examined Mrs. Timms closely. Perhaps in her I could find some answers to my questions of the family's tensions. "What do you mean, Mrs. Timms? Why is all not well here?"

Hastily, she plunged her hand into one of her deep skirt pockets, sending the house keys therein jangling. She extracted a large white handkerchief, dabbed at her eyes, and then blew her nose. With much attempt at dignity, she straightened her face and pursed her lips. "Forgive me, Miss Pennington. I overstep my bounds. I have told you more than I should. I would have you to understand that I do not gossip, do not carry tales."

"Oh, that is quite clear, Mrs. Timms. If it were so, I am sure the household staff would have known of the duke's intentions toward me." Mrs. Timms blinked keen eyes at me and I continued my explanation. "I was introduced to Williams the nurse a few minutes ago, and and she did not know of the duke's betrothal.''

Timms looked pleased and relieved. "I told no one, Ma'am.''

"I know that, Mrs. Timms. And I applaud your ethics. Gossip knows few boundaries.''

"Oh, I know that, Ma'am! I certainly do. I never indulged in it, ma'am. In this house, gossip is never welcome.''

Gossip, again. A plague to Max and to his family. I would avoid its lure at all costs. Yet I needed some basis on which to build an understanding of the troubles here.

"Mrs. Timms, I know we shall work well together. We shall proceed in mutual trust. But now, before we part,'' I persisted in my query, "please tell me in all honesty why the house is not a happy one.''

In answer, she wrung her handkerchief. "I will do much for you, Ma'am. The duke's wish always has and always will be my command. But in this matter I will remain silent. After all, what I would say to you in explanation would be the very thing I say I detest— gossip. For I know few facts.''

Mrs. Timms pulled herself up into what I knew was her most imperious demeanor, the one she would use with her subordinates. It not only fended me off, but warned me off a subject that might hurt us both.

"Miss Pennington, I suggest that you ask His Grace to discuss that issue with you. It is a family matter, and I am merely staff.'' She backed away from me and the indelicacy of the subject. She could not wait to leave me. "Good afternoon, Miss Pennington. I shall send you Dorcas, who will be your maid. Good afternoon."

She turned on her heel and left me alone. Alone to accustom my self to the room and my situation. Alone to run my fingertips across the glossy cherry highboy and the matching dressing table that faced it. Alone to sit upon the bench before the three-tiered mirror, examine my own features, and assess my suitability to assume the title of duchess. Could I preside, command, order a family and a household of such size—and such troubles?

Oh, I was a Wolff, all right. I exhibited the high forehead, the straight nose, the inquisitive eyes. I displayed my own individuality in the fiery red hair and a temperament to match. I possessed the curiosity, the intelligence that my mother had heralded and my father had regaled. I looked into my eyes and into my heart and asked myself if I were equal to such a task as living in a house with secrets and curses and one moody, sensitive, killingly handsome husband.

The answer that rose to my mind was cut off by another knock at the door.

I gave permission to enter and watched through the mirror as the door behind me opened and closed. This time, the woman who stood there was tall, imposing, and stiffly at attention.

"Good evening, Miss Pennington. Mrs. Timms sent me to you. I am Dorcas, your maid."

I rose and faced the woman. Dressed in less expensive gray cotton than the housekeeper's, Dorcas nonetheless reflected every inch a ladies' maid. She was as tall as I, with a handsome but homely square face, plain brown eyes, very thin lips and, beneath a prim white cap, thinner pale brown hair.

She met my gaze squarely.

"How do you do, Dorcas?" I inclined my head civilly, yet some inner sense warned me from smiling at her. "I am pleased to meet you. Mrs. Timms tells me you are quite competent."

"Yes, Miss Pennington. I am. I was ladies' maid to His Grace's last duchess and served as hairdresser to His Grace's first duchess, the Lady Cynthia."

"Ah, so you are adept at many things."

"I like to think so, Miss Pennington."

"I shall rely on your advice then, Dorcas. I am not used to the demands required of me here"—did she suppress a smile at that remark? "—and I do want to make a good impression."

"Yes, Miss Pennington. I shall apply all my skills."

The flatness of her tone, the lifeless acceptance in her eyes piqued my curiosity and my anger. I spun from her and assumed my prior position on the dressing table's bench. I plucked out my hairpins and combs. I fanned my fingers through my wayward tresses. Curls rioted across my shoulders, catching the gas lamps' glow in a thousand brilliant lights.

"What would you do with this, Dorcas? Would you say I should keep it in its coif?"

She stepped closer and her passive face appeared just above mine in the mirror. Her eyes met mine briefly and then descended slowly to my crown. I watched her, feeling the bore of her gaze down into my skull, as if she would view all of my personality by reading the convolutions of my brain. I willed myself not to flinch.

She lifted her hands, and as she did, I noted how

extraordinarily long and thin her fingers were, with unblemished skin, smooth knuckles, and nails shaped like a hawk's pointed talons. I clamped my jaw to seal the shudder in my mouth.

"You have lovely hair, Miss Pennington." Her fingers gathered fistfuls of curls. "Thick and naturally waving." Her hands splayed into my scalp and I felt her body's warmth against my skin as she lifted and fanned the hair out to its full length of twenty inches or more. "It is hair any woman would be proud of." Her forefinger with its perfect nail ran down my crown and created a new part. "This is more fashionable, however." Her eyes met mine.

I tried not to squirm in my seat.

"I can do much for you, Miss Pennington, because you have great assets. Your high forehead reveals a noble brow. I recommend for daytime we coil your hair softly about your face instead of keeping your current severe remove and simple comb. No more nets, either. Your hair is too glossy to be hidden and too long to require such confines. Your profile displays a clean relief, and so for afternoon and evening, we can give you ringlets all about or two long finger curls behind both ears. As Duchess of Worminster, you own hair ornaments of gold and silver, pearls and precious stones. Emeralds, I think will serve you well, miss. And of course, I know how to use them to best advantage. Rely on me. I will make you more beautiful."

Whether she would make me more beautiful than I was or more than I deserved to be, she did not elaborate. I would not pursue it. Indeed, I was rabid now to escape her hands.

"Thank you, Dorcas. I appreciate your thoughts.

Now, if you will please prepare me a bath, I will change for dinner."

She stood there, perplexed.

"Well, what is it?"

"Forgive me, Miss Pennington, but Bigelow informed me you have only one valise for luggage." Her eyes flashed to my attire. "Have you brought clothes for dinner, Miss?"

I inhaled. God, she had me. I couldn't tell her that I came so unencumbered because I had not expected to stay.

"I was so flustered about coming I forgot my luggage." Ohhh, now I was lying through my teeth!

"Forgot it?" She was incredulous. "Do you mean you lost it in your travels?"

Inwardly, I groaned. I could not tell her that because I had told Bigelow I'd packed only that one piece.

"No, absolutely not. I'm not quite sure how it happened, but it did." I was snapping at her, hating myself more than her efficiency. "I shall wear what I have, that's all."

"I can assist you, Miss Pennington. If I may, I can offer you perhaps the perfect attire."

I cocked my head at her.

She folded her long white hands before her and serenely gazed at me. "His Grace's last duchess was about your size. As slender, but not so tall."

I waved a hand and turned away. "I refuse to wear her clothing. I would feel—"

"I assure you, Miss Pennington, that what I have in mind the last duchess never wore. In fact, there are quite a few outfits in various stages of assembly that she never lived to wear. She was not as tall as you, nor of the same coloring, but she was of almost the same proportions.''

"I would not feel correct, Dorcas, wearing a deceased woman's attire.''

"But these she never wore, Miss Pennington. Let me at least fetch one. One appropriate for dinner. If you do not like it still, you can, of course, revert to the traveling costume.'' Her chin came up and her eyes challenged mine.

She was my match.

I bristled. "Very well, bring it to me. There is no harm in looking.''

She spun and within minutes returned, a glistening copper-gold silk dinner dress draped across her arms.

I gingerly touched the delicate stuff.

"Oh, my. I've never seen anything so lovely.''

"Yes. The duchess liked the very best. The black lace trim was a special favorite of hers. While she was dark, very dark, the color will suit you as well.''

I grinned at her. But she, sober as before, merely nodded and said, "I will order the footmen to fill your bath, and meanwhile, I will finish the buttonwork. Afterward, if you can stand for me while I mark the hemline, I can have another maid bring down the other unfinished articles of clothing from the sewing room. There are nightgowns and a new satin-lined robe, a tea gown, and a day dress. All of them half-finished.''

"Oh, I couldn't accept all that.''

"But why not? No one wears them now, Miss Pennington. No one ever will, if you don't. It would be such a waste.''

"Yes, yes, of course.''

I turned away and accepted the opportunity to ap-

90

pear before Max's family in some finery. Even if it had once been owned by his last duchess.

"Has anyone ever seen any of these items, Dorcas?"

"No, Miss Pennington. Never. The last duchess was very strict about no one viewing her wardrobe selections before she wore them. She was very determined in that way. Only I was permitted. I helped her select them, you see."

I nodded and shifted the copper silk between a thumb and forefinger. Yes, I saw. I saw myself arraigned in more splendorous style than I'd ever dreamed.

But it was nothing—nothing!—to the reality I saw an hour later. This time I stood before a full-length cheval glass near the window and twisted this way and that to view the beauty of the gown. High-necked, with long fitted sleeves that ruched at the wrists, the copper silk glinted in counterpoint to the opaque intricacies of the tiers of ebony lace that cascaded down the bodice from bosom to floor. I admired the way the bodice fit me perfectly, even though Dorcas had had to let out the gussets to accommodate my larger proportions. At the waist, however, Dorcas had had to tuck in the princesse waistline.

Dorcas frowned, even with a dressmaker's pin in her mouth. "Too loose still?" she asked, as she removed the pin and took up her needle and thread from the pincushion on the table. "I feared that. My last lady had grown a bit heavier than usual when she ordered this. She was awaiting the birth of the twins and had begun to fill out in the waist. But even *enceinte* as she was, she did not do justice to the full bodice as you do, Miss."

Pleased beyond good sense, I hid my joy in a search

for the gown's matching black lace handkerchief. I asked Dorcas for it and she produced it at once.

"You look wonderful, Miss, if I say so myself. And I am so sure the coiffure does you justice."

This time I did not hide my smile, but showed Dorcas my appreciation with a brilliant look. I pressed my palms to the two long swinging finger curls at the side of my face. "I'm very pleased, Dorcas. I doubt the others will know me."

Her lips extended across her face into a closed-mouth smile. The look rather reminded me of a grimacing fish . . . if fish grimaced at all.

I let her open the bedroom door for me and I made for the stairs. Dorcas had given me directions to the withdrawing room as she had coiled my hair with huge hot irons. I had virtually memorized the layout of this mansion in the time it had taken to tame an unruly mass of curls into the controlled serenity I now possessed.

Assured, thrilled, I sailed down the main staircase, traversed the morning room entrance, and arrived before the alabaster portals to the withdrawing room. I inhaled the powerful air of exuberance and opened the doors myself.

Seated in a small semicircle before a blazing fire were the four members of the family—Gilbert, his sister Adair, their mother, Caroline, and of course, Max. They each turned: Gilbert smiled; Adair flushed; Caroline assessed; and Max strode forward and then halted, mouth open in horror.

The others gasped in unison.

Max glared at me, his eyes white at the rims with icy fury.

God, what had I done?

I put a hand to my throat, but Max grasped my wrist and spun me from the room. In lightening strides, he had me down the hall, throwing open a door to some room whose function I could not for the life of me remember from Dorcas' lessons.

"What—what are you doing?" I cried at Max.

He faced me like a mad dog while his wild eyes consumed the gown. "What am *I* doing? What *am I* doing?! No, no, what are *you* doing? Where did you get this?" He touched the lace at my bosom. "How could you wear it?"

"But it is new! She'd never worn it. Dorcas told me so."

His light eyes narrowed on me. "What? What babble is this? The gown is *hers. Hers!* How did you come by it? And why, in God's name, wear it in front of me?"

I swallowed back the bile of my fear. "Dorcas, I tell you. She said it was an unfinished gown of your last wife's. That your last duchess had never worn it because it was not finished before she passed on. How could I know, Max? I merely wanted to appear before you in a suitable dinner dress and I had none. Dorcas came to my rescue."

"I'll see Dorcas on the street! Impertinent witch! Dorcas would know this gown was taboo."

"How? How would Dorcas know it is taboo?"

"The lace! Dear God, the black lace was *her* trademark. Her calling card! Her every garment foamed with the stuff. I don't care if I never see another scrap of it 'til the day I die. I forbid you to wear black lace, do you hear me? I forbid you now and always ever to wear it! Take that dress off, and for God's sake, burn it! I will buy you anything you wish, Alicia," he clutched my upper arms in an iron vise, "anything on God's green earth. But never, as long as I live, ever wear anything with black lace! Do you hear me? Do you?"

"Yes, Max," I said, as I backed toward the door, and with what courage I retained, ran for my room.

Chapter Five

I stood before the three-tiered mirror this morning once more attired in my only gown, my now-much-used, much-hated traveling dress. I was not pleased, but I was comfortable. And safe—at least from Max's wrath.

Not so Dorcas, who now knelt before me; adjusting the hem of my skirt over my petticoats, and who cast her eyes anywhere but into mine. She, who had been so noble at our introduction, was now a servant. And that because she had felt the sting of my anger as well as her master's last night.

Max had summoned her to him immediately after our confrontation. What he had said to her I could only imagine. I knew only that when Dorcas appeared before me afterward to help me remove the offensive gown, she told me that he had warned her henceforth to be more prudent. While she delivered the summary in circumspection, her words and her nervousness gave me the clear impression that he'd delivered the ultimatum in a red rage.

I listened to her with an iciness that concealed my

boiling fury. I did not trust myself to speak above a muted tone. My words were clipped, perfunctory instructions coupled with one adamant admonition to be very careful, lest her next advice prove as disastrous as this one.

"But I swear to you, Miss Pennington, I did not know about the lace. I had no idea the gown could summon the Duke's vehemence that way."

If I could have peered into her soul to discern the truth of that statement, I would have done it then with the piercing look I gave her. She shuddered, but did not shrink from me.

"Dorcas, I expect you to conduct yourself with integrity and discretion. I would assume that is why you have been assigned to me, and I would assume that is what you provided your last mistress, the last duchess."

"And His Grace's first duchess."

"Yes, we cannot forget what a long history you have of serving the mistresses of the House of Wolff. Well, then. You must be very proud of your place among the staff. I expect you to conduct yourself in such a manner that you will continue to keep it."

"Yes, Ma'am."

She hung her head, then curtsied. "If you no longer need me, Ma'am, I will leave you."

"There is one more thing I require of you, Dorcas."

"Yes, Ma'am, anything."

"Gather all the duchess's clothing you described to me. Then, pack it and take it to the nearest workhouse for distribution to the poor."

"Oh, Ma'am! All that silk and velv—"

"Dorcas," I barely whispered, "do as I say. Tomorrow morning before ten o'clock."

"But—"

I had merely to raise my brows and she understood her peril.

"Yes, Ma'am. Of course, Ma'am. By ten, as you say, Ma'am."

Now it was nearing eight o'clock, and she had already done my bidding. In fact, just after she awakened me this morning, she informed me that she had already completed part of the task: she had packed everything, ready for distribution to the workhouse in the village of Wolffson. I nodded and asked for my bath to be drawn. She quickly complied. I bathed. She arranged my hair in an early morning coif of simple ringlets at the ears, one large coil down my back, and my own modest lace cap atop my crown. I thanked her. She had then helped me don the traveling dress.

Now, I wondered if I could face the family with as much self-possession as I faced this one servant. The thought did much to unravel the carefully wrought serenity I'd knit all night, awake in my room. I'd alternately paced the floor, peering out into the black forest beyond my window, or I'd lain wide-eyed staring at the wall, deducing poor conclusions from half facts and false conjectures. I'd pondered motivations from innuendos and inferences. And through it all, I had concluded nothing substantive. Nothing except that I must be strong.

I balled my hands into fists.

Dorcas shied away from me.

I stood transfixed. Did she think I meant to strike her?

"Dorcas, you need not fear my hand. I assure you, I do not lash out at people to make them comply."

"Thank you, ma'am." She took a furtive glance at me. "I really did not think that you . . . I mean I—"

"Yours was a natural reaction of someone who expects such behavior. Tell me, have there been many here at Wolffs' Lair who beat you?"

"Not many." She either would not or could not elaborate.

But I would not be moved from my goal.

She cast her eyes to the floor. "The last duchess was very particular about her person and her habits."

"Particular to the point of punishing people."

She bit her lip.

"Dorcas, such acts are the work of cowards, those who cannot persuade others to their cause with any but violent means of enforcement. Look at me, Dorcas. I am not one of those people." She nodded once more. "Thank you for your help this morning. I will go down to breakfast now." I stepped away from her and headed toward the hall.

Dorcas's instructions about the house last night served me well again this morning. I saw three upstairs maids bustling to their duties and two footmen hauling coals and water, but I had no need to ask them directions to the dining room. Nor had they any need to speak to me except to curtsy or nod as they passed and called me *Ma'am*.

No one else seemed up and about, and I wondered if the family had dined early and I'd missed them all. If I had, relief would have been my first emotion. But courage—and a certain impatience to have the worst over—made me wish them all present. I compared myself to Daniel about to enter the lion's den.

When I opened the double doors, my comparison became reality. One sweep of the turquoise room told me that, save for Max, the family were all present.

Caroline, seated to the left of the master's chair, turned to me with a poorly suppressed smile of superiority and begrudging welcome. Next to Caroline, her daughter, Adair, tilted her head to one side while she assessed my attire and let her lashes fall before eyes that might reveal too much. Gilbert grinned at me and rose from his chair.

"Good morning, Alicia!" He captured his cane from its resting place against a table leg and took two steps toward me. "I am delighted to see you. Come sit with us. We are at our tea and coffee, as you see."

I offered a "good morning" to them all as Gilbert took my elbow with his free hand. I smiled at his graciousness and allowed him to lead me to a chair to the right of Max's empty one. When Gilbert finished assisting me with my chair, I placed my napkin in my lap and gazed across the glossy mahogany table to Caroline and smiled.

"I trust you slept well, Alicia," she offered blandly.

"Very well," I lied, much too easily for my conscience.

"That guest bedroom you occupy is next door to mine," she continued, as if the fact were of great importance. "It is one of the loveliest in the house."

I nodded as a footman appeared with two pots and offered me either coffee or tea. Although I always preferred hot chocolate, I chose the tea and tried to smile at her.

"Yes, Caroline, the green-and-gold room is stunning."

"But I much prefer the other side of the house, which faces east. My bedroom never receives the warmth of day, except in June. You will be so fortunate to have that warmth after you marry."

"Oh, how so, Caroline?" What *was* she headed for?

"Well, I have never been inside the ducal suite, you see, but I do understand that the appointments are superb, particularly the fireplaces. Those, plus the eastward exposure, must mean that the rooms are quite comfortable."

"Now, now, Mother," Gilbert was resuming his seat as he chastised her politely, "we don't want to give Alicia the impression that we are not grateful for our own appointments."

She inhaled so that she drew taller in her chair. "Gilbert, really. I am not implying any such thing. I was merely trying to convey to Alicia how very fortunate she is—" she trained envious eyes on me, "—to come from such a poor station to such a grand one."

I would not be baited. "Caroline, I am well aware of how fortunate I am. I shall endeavor to deserve it."

Gilbert's eyes twinkled. "Well, well! I daresay that's a novelty for this house." He sipped from his cup, then crossed his arms. "I think I shall enjoy watching you deserve your riches, Alicia. I, for one, can learn a thing or two."

Caroline skewered her son with a flash of those pale eyes. "Don't be a simpleton, Gil."

He stared back at her. "Simpleton. Hardly a good way to begin the morning, is it, Mother? Now that we have someone with us from outside our little circle, don't you think it about time you abandoned your little tantrums? Even you, dear *mater,* might benefit from it." He nodded in my direction. "Forgive me, my dear, I must leave you to your foes. I cannot abide my mother this early in the morning. Her virulence upsets my equilibrium."

And with that, he turned as gracefully as a man with his disability could and, with his cane before him, made his way to the doors. When he had closed them behind him, I felt his loss. Inexplicably, the brilliant room grew grayer.

His mother grew more circumspect. She sniffed. "I see I should apologize to you, Alicia. My son is very right to point out my transgressions toward you. I would not be so rude to most."

"Then why *are* you rude to me, madam?"

Her eyes clouded with tears and she searched in her pocket for a handkerchief. When she found one, she blew her nose. "I am very proud of the Wolff family name. Perhaps more proud than someone who has only married into it should be. But I am a guardian of its power nonetheless." She gazed at me now with a little pity and much resignation. "I always thought that if Max married again, he would choose someone with a title, a dowry, a family name equal to his. I am simply so amazed that he chose a young—a *very* young woman with none of those characteristics."

"And exactly why did you believe he would marry someone like that?" When she seemed unable to answer, I clarified my point. "Who gave you those expectations, Caroline?" If I knew, then I might be able to confront others' objections to the match.

She smiled, a cat over a bird. "Why, Max, naturally."

"Obviously he changed his mind."

"Did he? Or did someone change it for him?"

"I don't know who that might have been. Not me, certainly. I never even spoke to him before yesterday."

"It was your grandmother. How else would he have been persuaded to marry you? Constance told him tales of you that whetted his appetite, and, as he declared yesterday in the conservatory, he wanted a wife soon. You fit the mold."

She made me sound like a horse—worse, a brood mare!—for hire! My ears rang in rage. "So, you dislike me for myself, for what I represent, or because my grandmother interceded for me?"

Caroline paled.

She did not expect anyone could be as bold as she? Ha. Being a minster's daughter might mean one was trained to turn the other cheek, but it did not mean one had to tolerate abuse, verbal or otherwise.

"I find myself apologizing to you yet again, Alicia. You are astute and I am brash. But I will meet your frankness with my own. Yes, I am disappointed with Max's choice. I think he could have done much better for himself. A handsome man, devilishly handsome, so some say. A man of maturing years. Next month, he will be forty. Not old, by any standards, but beyond the bloom of life to take another wife. A *third* wife, no less. And such a young one, less than half his age. It is jarring . . . jarring. And quite inexplicable to think that he has never conversed, never dined, never danced with you. Never discussed nonsense over teacups. I find myself incredulous. So much so that even this morning, I am dazed at his precipitate action. I am even more startled at your agreement. I thought young ladies of your breeding came with an abundance of good sense.''

How could I explain my motives? Could I in all honesty declare I had accepted this proposal primarily because of the good sense it made? Could I discuss my parents' poverty, my brothers' pecuniary status, or my need for a way to support myself? Pride might have allowed it if, in fact, those reasons predominated my thinking.

But I sat here now, confronted by this woman and her objections, and admitted to myself that the only reason I had accepted this proposal was that I was enthralled by the man. His looks. His voice. His body. And while my mind rebelled at the temporal nature of those inducements, my heart and my body thrilled—yes, even throbbed!—at the future that awaited me. A future of marital union, bodily union. The idea that I might welcome such . . . carnality, yes! *carnality*—did not offend me. Or make me blush. Or make me prevaricate. No. Rather, the admission made me strong, stronger than I ever thought to be over such a confession of my . . . humanity.

Yes, instinct—that very knowledge Max had requested I summon to this relationship—instinct leaned over my shoulder and bent to whisper in my ear that I was right. In Max, I had found someone I could care for, as my mother had cared for my father and he for her, as my brothers cared for their wives. The very idea was exhilarating, liberating, justifying. There was no balder way to say it: I was attracted to this man.

As I had never been attracted to any other. Not even to my poor departed fiancé, Edward Perry.

I met Caroline's eyes. "I cannot speak for Max, Caroline, only myself. I will tell you that in many ways, I am as surprised at these developments as you. Yet I agree to them because, whether you might believe it or not, I care for Max. And I intend to marry him and make him happy."

"Yes," she sighed. "I see you do. And I wish you the best of it, but I must tell you, I think you have your work cut out for you. No one can make Max happy. His first wife did not succeed. His second one didn't, either. And who are you to try? I am astounded certainly that *he* would try a third time. After all he has . . . shall we say, experience? . . . with women, and to take yet one more wife is probably the most brazen act of . . . I hardly know a word for it. *Faith,* I suppose. Yes, the most brazen act of faith. God knows, I wish him well. You, too, I daresay. And now, having thoroughly degraded myself, I think I shall take myself off to my morning correspondence." She rose like the weary of the world and with a trembling hand, patted her mouth and set down her napkin beside her plate. She gave Adair and me a vacant smile. "I will see you at luncheon, of course. Good morning to you both."

With baleful eyes, I watched her go. Alone with the third and last of my "lions," I summoned strength for this last attack. I took a sip of my tepid tea and turned my eyes upon Adair.

She sat, fiddling with her teaspoon and contemplating its baroque engravings.

Into the arena stepped an under-butler who tried to tempt me with creamed salmon and potatoes or a poached egg. I chose an egg, whose center looked as cold as my reason. I waited as he served it on my plate and disappeared back into the recesses of the kitchen.

All the while, I took in Adair's pursed mouth and her raised brows and felt the lioness in myself emerge to prowl the room. I could not bear the seat and left it for the blazes of the white marble fireplace. Putting my back to it, I faced her.

"You have lived here a long time, haven't you, Adair?"

Clearly, she had not expected the circumventional approach.

She blinked. And offered me the facts. "Yes, almost three years. Ever since Papa died."

"Your cousin, Max, is most hospitable."

She nodded and put down the fork she had found so engrossing.

"Why does he continue to tolerate such bad manners in your mother?"

Her eyes flashed wickedly. "He is too polite."

"And she is too brash."

Adair hung her head. "Yes," she murmured. "You are so right. But she cannot change. He knows it. As we all do. Even *she* understands herself."

"Help *me* to understand."

"Why should you bother?"

"Why should I not?" I rolled forward on the balls of my feet and with expectation, I arched both brows at her. The look that had gotten so much from Dorcas quelled Adair as easily. As I tempered the thrill of such power, I listened to her explanation.

"My mother is well intentioned, I assure you. She simply has lived so long with so much convention and

105

so little means that I think she has quite forgotten her true station.''

''Knowing nothing of the former, I quite agree about the latter.''

Adair sniffed in flustered indignation. ''She comes from a very good family. She was the heiress of a silversmith in Warwickshire. Bred to marry upward, she was given an education and a dowry to attract a prosperous merchant. But one day, she met my father as he came to Grandfather's shop. She thought he came to buy new goods, so prosperous did he appear. In fact, he came to pawn a few of his family's possessions so that he might settle his gambling debts.

''But she could not know that. She was young and lovely; he was young and impetuous. She did not know he was nobility, a second son whose amusements ran to cards and dice. He did not care she was propertied merchant class. But my grandfather, the old silversmith, cared, and so when he found them in a compromising position one afternoon, he demanded they marry.''

She rose from her chair and headed for the bay window. Head held high, hands folded before her, she appeared to be a nun at her beads as she faced the light of day.

''I am not quite sure what happened when my father brought her home to his father. The old duke, the fourth Duke of Worminster, was very old and disappointed with his life and with his children. All of them had spurned him for his previous profligate life. Evidently, he'd enjoyed many a mistress and sired many a son out of wedlock. His son, the heir, my father's older brother, had followed his father's example, and

106

since he was still in search of a suitable heiress to become the next duchess, he, too, decried my father's choice of my mother.

"Evidently, what had been a loving union for the newlyweds to that point became a living hell. Since it was not clear whether my mother was with child yet, the fourth duke called in a midwife to examine my mother. Above the loud objections of my mother, the midwife declared my mother as yet barren—and then it became even more difficult for the old man to understand why my father had chosen my mother.

"To make matters worse, the old duke demanded that my father request more of a dowry from my mother's family. Outraged, she threatened to leave my father if he asked. But forced into it by his own father, my father did go to his father-in-law and ask for more money. When the silversmith declared he would have to pay in increments, my father returned to the old duke, money in hand. He thought he was done with the bargaining. But he was wrong.

"The old duke, at that point, mortgaged up to his eyeballs in a merchant marine company out of Bombay, needed money more than he needed another mouth to feed. He told my father to use the first increment to pay the company's bad debts, lest the family be ruined with the stain of bankruptcy. But the increment was not enough to stop the creditors. My father, the only one of the family who had any liquid cash, paid the total bill. The old duke allowed his second son to pay the family debt with my mother's dowry, and all the while he held out the expectation that at the end of the ordeal, my mother would be welcomed into the fold of the family as worthy of them."

Adair turned to face me now, and I saw what it cost her to tell this story to a stranger. Pride. Pride would be her price as it had been her mother's so long ago.

"But that was not to be. The old duke had his ways and his ideas. He was raised—indeed, imbued with the idea—that as the fourth Duke of Worminster, he had some God-given right to decide who was and who was not worthy of the smallest respect within his family. He began the degradation of my mother. Slowly, insipidly, he destroyed her. He seated my mother at the end of the table."

Adair gave a little laugh. "Below the salt—far below the salt. He declined to call her by name, but called her 'the smithy's girl.' He scrutinized her attire as if she were too uncultured or too lowly to know the proper way to appear in his drawing room. She objected. The old duke ignored her pleas. My father could do little to rectify the situation and soon quit trying. The marriage deteriorated more.

"My father took another woman to his bed. The mistress bore him three girls, no less. The old duke laughed—the family curse again, he said. But when, months later, quite by surprise, my mother bore Gilbert into this world, the old duke laughed no more. The old man died, proclaiming that Gilbert could not possibly be the true son of my father. And my mother has neither forgiven nor forgotten. The men in this family can be so heartless."

Her blue eyes fastened onto mine. "They can kill a woman a thousand different ways. If they do not do it with words, they find other means."

The skin on my scalp tingled. I clasped my hands to keep them from shaking.

"A truly tragic tale, Adair. I do wonder how people like that go to meet their maker, don't you?"

"The devil was the old duke's maker, Alicia. So, too, his son, the fifth duke."

"There was no reprieve for your mother under the fifth duke's hegemony?"

She snorted. "None. None whatsoever. Like father, like son. Worse, in this case: he threw my father and mother out of this house."

"But why?"

"Improper behavior, he charged."

"By whom?"

"Whom do you think?"

She squeezed her hands together.

I could only wait for her to continue.

"My mother spoke only once to me of this, but I remember her words very clearly. She said, 'He demanded we leave, implying that I had approached him in some affectionate manner unbefitting a sister-in-law.' It was the other way, though. My uncle had approached my mother and when she refused him, he banished both my mother and my father."

Adair was swallowing hard by now. "So you see, we have yet another indication of how cruel the Wolff men can be to the women of the family." She came to stand before me and searched my eyes. "Are you not afraid?"

Reason abounded. "Afraid of whom? Max? I have no evidence to suggest I should fear Max."

"How convenient."

We stared each other down. But it was she who broke first.

She raised her chin and smiled no smile. "You've

109

heard no rumors, then. Too bad for you. Too good for Max. I suggest, for your own safety, you ask Max for his rendition of the recent family history.''

''I have no reason to ask any such thing.''

''You will.''

''You are as rude and as bold as your mother.''

''Such breaches of etiquette may be unforgivable, but then, you must admit I have piqued your curiosity, if not your fear.''

''I do not fear Max.''

''That is your innocence speaking. Use your intellect. You seem to have so much of it.'' She would have left me then, but I stopped her with my words.

''If you fear Max, why, then, are all of you still here?''

She sneered. ''We have discovered that poverty is a worse nightmare than living with the devil.''

''If that is true, then I feel very sorry for the three of you.''

She hooted. ''Ha! Not as sorry as we feel for you, my dearest Alicia. Not half as sorry as we feel for you.''

Mary and Elizabeth sat on either side of me at a little children's table in their nursery schoolroom and peered at me with questions in their eyes.

''I don't think Papa would like us to do that,'' said Mary.

''No, no,'' agreed Elizabeth with a shake of her dark curls.

''You ride ponies. True?''

They nodded in unison.

''And you play ball.''

110

"Yes, but in the summertime, when the sun is shining," offered Mary.

Elizabeth leaned close to my right shoulder and with those marvelous liquid gray eyes like her father's said, "He wouldn't get mad. Not really." She leaned around me to look at her twin. "Let's."

I glanced up at Williams as she poured more tea into my tiny doll's-size cup. "Williams, do get the girls' coats, hats, and mufflers, will you?"

"Well, Ma'am—" her eyes darted from Mary's to mine, "it's so cold, ma'am."

"Yes, Williams. Haven't Mary and Elizabeth any warm wraps?"

"Yes, Ma'am—"

"Well, then," I raised the toy teacup to my lips and ignored her stalling, "there's no reason to delay, is there?" I looked squarely into Williams' dull eyes. "Get the girls their coats and mufflers, will you please? There is no time like the present to begin new ventures." I took up my own pelisse and straw hat and donned them quickly.

Mary was frowning now, while Elizabeth was up and dancing backward toward the hall. "Come, come, do, Mary. I want to go. I do."

Mary was not so easily persuaded. She hung back and shook her head so that her long curls bobbed around her delicate face. "Papa will be mad."

"How do you know?" I asked.

"I know." She looked at her shoes.

"She's afraid," said Elizabeth to me.

"Am not."

"Well, girls," I interjected, "let me tell you this. If

111

your father finds any fault with our little walk, I shall see to it that he finds fault with me, not you."

"See, Mary?" Elizabeth accepted her coat from Williams and began to shrug into the dark red wool. "Don't be scared."

Williams now stood before the recalcitrant little girl to whom she held out her coat. Mary slowly stood, as if she were fourscore of age instead of five. She let her nurse help her on with the coat, a duplicate of her sister's, wine-red and oversized, even though it had been cut down to fit a child's frame. Bulky, unwieldy for the natural graces and exuberances of youth. And Mary donned the apparel like a rag doll. Limp and lifeless, she tried to toggle the frog closures and wasn't succeeding.

When Williams bent to assist, I saw how Mary simply stood, allowing her nurse to do the very thing of which she herself was quite capable. Coddling, I knew, never benefited a child.

I stepped forward and extended my hand. "Come along, Mary. We'll have a good walk and you'll feel better about the whole thing in no time."

Mary grasped my hand, but Williams tried to hold her there by virtue of the unsecured coat. I did not need to look at the woman to convey the message I intended.

"Thank you, Williams, she'll be fine. Come, Mary."

I smiled—oh, yes, I smiled imperiously—and Williams let her hands fall to her sides. "She catches chills very easily, Ma'am."

"Thank you, Williams. That's good to know." I headed for the door, each girl by the hand.

"Ma'am," Williams' voice caught me before I passed the portal, "if someone asks, when may I say you'll return?"

"Soon, Williams. Soon."

I heard the latch click in the door and tried to imagine what the woman behind it was saying to herself. Whatever it was, its content might be clearer after I spent a morning with her charges.

Elizabeth leaned close to my side and giggled. "She hates us to go anywhere without her."

I didn't have to look down to know that Mary shot her sister a look of fire.

"That's natural," I offered, as I headed us all toward the principal staircase. "She has loved you and cared for you just like a mother."

"She's very nice," said Mary, carrying the banner of her nurse high as we marched away from the woman's bastion. "She helps us do everything."

"Not go for walks in the woods," chirped Elizabeth.

"Well, *I* never wanted to," Mary pouted.

We took the landing with measured strides, yet I could feel Mary's reluctance in her every step.

"And *I* don't want to work all day," Elizabeth argued.

"What kind of work does Williams have for you?" I asked.

"Reading and scriptures. Lots of scriptures. The same stories over and over."

Mary shivered. "I don't like them."

"See? See? Better to go for a walk than read those stories all day long."

We traversed the front hall when Bigelow appeared as if summoned.

"Miss Pennington," he bowed slightly. "You are going out? Do you require a carriage? I had no idea that you were interested in—"

"No, Bigelow, thank you. We do not require a thing, else I would have rung for you. We are going for a walk. To acquaint ourselves with each other."

"I see, ma'am. May I say where, ma'am, in case His Grace should inquire, ma'am?"

"Yes, Bigelow. You may say we are going to investigate the grounds. Into that lovely woods I have seen from my bedroom window."

"I see, ma'am." He stepped aside, clearly unsure of his responsibility here.

I suppressed a laugh. Had anyone ever before confounded the imperturbable Bigelow?

He hastened around us to open the front doors. As he flung them wide, I turned up the collar on my pelisse and bent to the wind that swirled about us.I

"Oooo," moaned Mary. "I don't want to go."

"Secure your coat, Mary," I ordered. "You'll be warmer."

She was not happy with me. But then, happiness would come later—I hoped. I lead them down the mansion's front steps, beyond the square porte cochere and into the massive courtyard. Across the pale cobbles, I walked with my eyes on those two stone foregates which had so mocked me yesterday when I arrived here. Yesterday, I had likened them to beasts. Today, I could say no differently. Not quite gargoyles, not quite God's creatures, they no longer intimidated me, only fascinated me.

Elizabeth had read my mind. "I think witches live

there," she confessed, as her eyes fastened on one, then the other.

"Tall ones, with warts on their noses," Mary added.

I considered the structures and could see how one might conjure a demon from the play of shadows when the sun slid through the gaping apertures.

"Do you think witches live there, Miss Pennington?"

"No."

"I have seen them," Mary affirmed.

I frowned at her. "Really? When?"

Mary gripped my hand more tightly. "Always. Even now."

"Where? Show me."

"There," her head came up as her hand went out to point to the very openings where I had imagined the beast's eyes to have been. "She lives in there and comes out at night to dance and fly."

"You haven't *seen* her, though," Elizabeth declared, with a mix of disdain and hope.

"Williams says she's seen her," Mary shot back to her twin.

Elizabeth chewed her lower lip on that.

Fury churned in my chest. "And what has Williams seen, Mary?"

"A witch."

We were stopped now before the foregate where Mary's apparition was said to dwell. I saw only menacing shadows.

Mary saw through her mind's eye. "She's got warts on her nose and long black hair. She's tall. Williams says you're tall, like her, Miss Pennington."

I felt mortally wounded, felled in a battle to which

I'd not yet received a call. No matter . . . one can engage at any point to save one's honor and one's loved ones.

"And do we have other semblances, Mary, this witch and I?"

"She can change to look like anyone she wants, Williams says. During the day, she's pretty, but at night, she's ugly. The devil and his wives are very cunning."

Elizabeth was tugging at my hand. "I want to leave. Let's go to the woods. Let's, Miss Pennington."

The wind whipped up dead leaves to swirl about us. But the chill I felt had much to do with the revelations of this tiny girl. Williams and I had much to discuss. Furthermore, I wondered if Max knew what disservice his seemingly loyal nursemaid did him with his children. I added that to my list of queries and smiled at my charges.

"I want to see this lovely woods. I have lived in a city most of my life and I am charmed by the woods."

Mary trudged beside me, happy to be quit of the foregates and its mythical inhabitant. Still, Mary's next comment brought me up short. "I hate the woods."

"But why?"

"Trolls live there."

"Trolls?" Good God in heaven.

"Williams says they live there to guard the woods from too many men."

Williams. Williams. With how many frightening tales could one nursemaid imbue a small child and continue to serve in her post?

"What trolls live in this woods?" We took a well-worn path toward the pine-dotted forest where skeletal trees shone in gray-green relief. "I certainly see none."

"Well, of course you can't see them," affirmed Elizabeth matter-of-factly. "But the story of the Billy Goat's gruff says there is a troll who lives under a bridge and the bridge where he lives is not far from here. Do you want to see it, Miss Pennington?"

I paused, overcome with amazement. How many ghastly tales of horror had this woman particularized to scare these defenseless little girls?

Max would surely hear of this quickly. Meanwhile, I had to show these guileless children that one adult existed who possessed no motive save to enjoy them.

"Yes. Yes, indeed, I would love to see this bridge. Trolls have never been a favorite of mine, so I doubt I shall see him. You have to believe in them to see them, you know."

"Really?" cooed Elizabeth. "Williams never told us that."

"She says evil exists everywhere."

"Well, I can agree with Williams on that, but not on the power of the trolls to hurt you. If you can't see them, say the Teutonic legends, they can't lay a hand on you."

Elizabeth stopped in her tracks. "How wonderful! That means they can't take us and put their own children in our place. We won't be taken! See, Mary?" she was recovering her natural positivism. "I told you Williams couldn't see all those witches and trolls and things."

I brushed Elizabeth's dark curls back under her cap and cupped her chin to smile into her eyes. "You are so right, my dearest. No one is going to take you away from your home."

Mary was frowning when I turned and knelt to her.

117

"Mary, darling, you mustn't fear these things. If you are good and kind and honest, no evil being can seize you and take you away." I brushed her curls behind her ears and smiled into her worried eyes. "And I know you must be a very good girl. I can feel it."

Elizabeth came to stand close by us both. "Williams says your father was a minister."

I furrowed my brow. "Yes, Elizabeth. What has that to do with this?"

She smiled so broadly I could have sworn the sun was shining with a summer's intensity. "Williams said that you would see our true selves."

"Yes."

"But you think we're good girls. You just said. You did."

"Yes, I did. I see two charming, bright girls, whom I will enjoy teaching and—if you let me—if you want me—I will enjoy loving you, too."

"Will you tell Williams, that, Miss Pennington? Will you?"

"Of course, why wouldn't I?"

"Because she says we were born to evil and she makes us pray on the stone floors of the chapel and eat gruel and—"

"Wait!" I could barely contain my shock. My head reeled. The newest gust of wind did nothing to stabilize my disequilibrium. I took each girl by the wrist and said, "Look at me. You mean to say your nurse has told you you are evildoers?"

They hung their heads and licked their lips. Then they told me tales of horror.

Mary told me of a time she had taken an extra sweet tart from the morning breakfast tray and had to go

118

without food for two days to do penance for it. And Elizabeth told me about one day last summer when she'd slipped off into the coach house to ask the coachman about her father's last trip to 'Manc'ester' and for her mysterious disappearance, she had gotten five lashes with the groomsman's whip.

I sat back on my heels astonished. Sometimes, the worst evil comes from those who seek to instill goodness with the threat of deprivation and suffering, instead of love.

"My dears, your father has welcomed me here to be your teacher as well as your new mother. From this day forward, I promise you you shall not bear the threats and punishments unless I myself mete them out. I also promise you that beatings and starvation are not my methods. There is too much of that in the world already. No, from now on, Williams will come to me for approval for everything. Do you hear me?" I tugged at each girl's hand for a response.

Reluctantly, slowly, their gray eyes met mine.

"She'll be mad we told you," offered Elizabeth.

"She'll yell. *Oooo*, she'll beat us with the switch for fair!" cried Mary.

"No, no, my darlings," I hugged them both close to my heart. "She will not hurt you ever again."

Chapter Six

"Bigelow, where is His Grace?" I handed over my pelisse and hat into his outstretched arms.

"In his den, ma'am."

"Make sure the girls get hot chocolate, will you?" I turned for the hallway.

"But, ma'am! His Grace cannot be disturbed."

"Oh, yes, he can."

Mary ran to seize me about the legs. "Oh, ma'am, don't leave us. Williams will be mad you gave us chocolate."

I threaded my fingers through her hair and smiled at her. "No, my dear, if she is mad, it will be with me. Go with Bigelow to the kitchen."

"Miss Pennington! The Ladies Mary and Elizabeth are not allowed into the kitchen without Williams. It is her strict instruction."

"And it is my sole instruction that they are to have hot chocolate. Shall I tell your master that you have problems with my orders, Bigelow?"

He shrank into his skin. Even his bulging eyes receded. "No, Ma'am."

"Then take the ladies to the kitchen and have Cook dispense something delicious to go with that hot chocolate." I squeezed each girl's shoulder. "Something with raisins, or—"

"Dates," offered Mary.

"Dates," I affirmed for Bigelow. "Go now, I will speak with your father."

They held hands as they followed a reserved but compliant Bigelow.

I traversed the plum gray hall and skewed up my courage. I had not spoken with Max since last night. I had no idea what his mood might be. But I certainly knew what mine was. Anger filled my breast. I knocked against the library door with rapidity. Without waiting for an answer, I opened it.

I saw no one except Max's two dogs, who when they saw me quickly loped to my side and licked my fingertips. Trailing them behind me, I walked in farther to examine each nook and alcove. Finally, what I saw as I stood in the door to his den drove all determination from my mind and replaced it with something I had never felt before. But oh, could I readily name it. Jealousy. Hot, bitter and thick.

Max sat behind his massive desk, pointing to something on very large sheets of paper. Bending over him was the loveliest creature I had ever laid eyes on.

She was small boned, with long, tapered hands that rested, one on Max's desktop and one on his shoulder. She had rosy skin and plump apple cheeks, which she had delicately rouged so that when she laughed, as she did now, she appeared radiant. She was striking with her golden brown hair parted in the center and waved back over her cheeks and ears. And to highlight her great attributes, she was sumptuously dressed, elegant in a lilac taffeta day dress that buttoned down the bodice and displayed her extraordinary proportions to my sorrowful eyes. In my heart I knew those proportions of hers were real; no bust enhancers filled her bodice.

Then, when she looked up at me, I understood why any man might find her intriguing. She had the most amazing eyes—cat's eyes. Liquid purple, and alive with long-lashed, leisured curiosity.

My eyes flitted to Max, who was scowling at me.

"Pardon me, Max. I did not know you were involved."

I wanted to run, but my pride had me overlooking the familiarity between them and saving the situation for myself, if not for him. On either side of me, the two dogs sat on their haunches, waiting for my next move.

"I needed to speak with you," I managed to get out. "Privately. Immediately."

He stood to round the desk and approach me. One step behind, his guest glided forward.

He took my hand. "Do come in, my dear. While this was to be a secret meeting, I see no reason not to introduce you, since you have discovered us."

His words seared my heart. He would flaunt his relationship with a woman in his very home the day after he'd proposed to me? I could not, I would not believe—

"My dear Alicia, I wish you to meet a very good friend of mine."

The woman came abreast of Max and smiled up into my face. She was petite, feline, exquisite—everything

122

I was not. She smiled broadly, displaying a coy dimple in her left cheek. Then, she extended her hand.

"Alicia, this is Madame Lianne Duvalier. She lives in Manchester and works there."

Works there? I scanned his eyes and hers.

Max leaned into me, clearly offended I had not taken the woman's proferred hand to shake.

"Lianne is a modiste, Alicia, the finest in the north. I sent word to her this morning that I needed her immediately and she packed and returned in my carriage."

Relief rushed through me like a gust of brisk December air. A modiste . . . I grasped her hand and smiled. "How do you do, madame?"

"Lianne," she corrected, in a downy-smooth voice. "I could do naught but obey such an intriguing summons." She flashed a dimpled smile at Max. "How could I resist being the very first to meet Max's new bride and to create a trousseau worthy of his name and her beauty?"

Her compliment was lost on me. The only thought I had was that she was a modiste and so close a friend that she'd addressed him as Max. I also realized that her French name had nothing to do with her decidedly British accent. It made little sense.

Meanwhile, she assessed me more boldly.

"I see why you are enchanted, Max. She is lovely. No—even better, refreshing."

"Please, I—" I barely knew what to say.

Lianne tsked. "You are unused to such attention. Let me assure you, I will be as unobtrusive as possible."

Max snorted. "You? My dear Lianne, you have

never been unobtrusive in your life. I brought you here to do my betrothed justice with your needle. She is in need of many things quickly. Be as obtrusive as you must to get the job done.''

Lianne let her eyes roll playfully.

Max was grinning. ''Lianne is here at my request and will stay for a week or two.''

She cast amused eyes at him. ''Am I?''

''I shall make it well worth your stay, and you know it, Lianne.''

''I shall expect it, Max. I cannot leave my business without some suitable recompense. My two assistants are not quite as adept as I would wish.'' She examined me now, head to toe. ''But I welcome this opportunity, Max. I would love everyone to know I had dressed her. Your next duchess is an absolutely stunning creature. With the right colors and the right cloth, my God, she will entice any man.''

Max suddenly scowled again.

She caught the look and something she read there made her hasten to correct herself. ''Oh, surely, Max, you know what I mean. Her height is dramatic, her complexion is clear as fresh cream. And her coloring! All that rosewood hair and those forest-green eyes! Very alluring, my lord duke, very alluring. We shall bring them all to everyone's attention with the right silks and velvets.''

Whatever she was saying did not lessen Max's growing bad humor. In fact, he bit his lip in agitation before he turned from us and regained his chair. With a wave of his hand, he said, ''Very well, Lianne. Take these sketches away. They look wonderful to me, but Alicia must approve everything, of course.''

"Of course." She glanced from me to him and back again. She was at loose ends. She had lost her self-assurance.

And I did not know why.

She walked to his desk and scooped up the sketches. All the while she was talking to cover the change in atmosphere. "I shall find Bigelow," she murmured, "and see if Mrs. Timms has remembered to ensconce me in my favorite bedroom on the second floor. I do love the southern exposure. I shall unpack and set up my forms and such patterns as I have in my anteroom. Perhaps, Alicia, we can meet later to discuss your preferences in material and style."

"Yes, thank you. I must speak with Max first."

She smiled curtly, a worried glance toward Max hastening her retreat. "Until later," she said, trying to sound assured, and closed the door.

I walked forward. I still had my reasons for being here. And foul mood or not, Max would listen to me.

He had directed his attention to a ledger, so I simply stood and waited until he could do naught but look up at me.

"Well? What is it?"

"I must speak with you about Mary and Elizabeth."

In his eyes, I could see conflicting emotions battle for predominance. "Please—speak, then."

"They—they are not treated well."

"Is that so?" He leaned back in his chair and assessed me coolly.

"Yes." I had not seen this side of Max. This frigid, impersonal side. "They are being frightened, unreasonably so I think, by stories that Nurse Williams is telling them."

"Stories? What kinds of stories?"

"About witches and trolls."

He narrowed his eyes in concentration. "My dear Alicia, every nursemaid tells every child such tales to make them obedient."

"Not as many, and not so forcefully." I splayed my hands upon his burnished desktop. "What she does is cruel, Max, cruel. There are many ways to have a child obey. The most important is to live as an example, to instruct with deeds. The second is to instruct with words. The last is to punish when someone strays from the path of goodness. There is no place for tales of evil, no need to make them so specific that a child is frightened out of her wits. Williams tells them of witches who live in the forecourt gates and of trolls who will capture them and replace them with their own children."

"I understand Williams is a godfearing woman who wishes only to instruct my girls in their right paths."

"I am a godfearing woman as well, Max, and I tell you that your daughters are being frightened unduly."

"It is laughable, my dear, that any Wolff, male or female, can be frightened."

"Is it? Why?" I was roiling in fury now. "Have you some notion you are immune from fear?"

"No." He was running a hand through his hair, pushing back his chair and shaking his head. "No, we are not immune. But we are not cowards."

"Courage derives from strength of mind and heart. Strength is not being cultivated in Mary and Elizabeth, only weakness. Weakness developed from fear. And I see no reason why she would do it, except perhaps to make them malleable children. I tell you, Max, if that

126

woman continues her tales unabated, Mary and Elizabeth will become milksops, simpering little children for all their lives. Even now they are afraid to go outside against her will. Afraid to have hot chocolate without her approval. Afraid to walk into the woods or climb a tree. Or skate on the pond."

"You think Williams is responsible for this?"

"Yes, the girls told me so."

He went to his window and gazed out over his lawn. For long moments, he ran one hand over his chin.

"They told you this because they trusted you?"

"I'd like to think so."

He flashed a troubled smile at me, then furrowed his brow once more as he reconsidered the lawn. "You were very right to come to me immediately. Whatever else anyone may say, I love my daughters, Alicia, and don't ever doubt me on that. Naturally, I shall summon the woman and have her to understand that she reports to you from this day forward."

Success came so swiftly, I'd have stammered if I'd opened my mouth then. But he rounded the massive desk to stand before me.

"My dear, I apologize for my bad temper and sullenness. I have had an idea for some time now that something was amiss with the girls, but had no inkling Williams' actions were the cause." A sweet smile tugged at the corners of his tempting mouth. "You are a jewel, do you know it? Priceless. I am most fortunate. I am only now beginning to appreciate you in all your facets."

"Please, I am not accustomed to such flattery."

He tipped my chin up and suddenly his lips were

skimming mine. Satin soft, they brushed along my jaw to my ear. "Then, I shall help you become accustomed by flattering you shamelessly. I shall begin by telling you that I now know you are the most suitable person to teach bravery to the girls."

Lost in the dark magic his lips wrought on my skin, my eyes fluttered closed. "How do you know?"

"Umm. I love your skin, just there where your pulse beats. How do I know? Because you stand up to me even when you assume I have brought one of my mistresses into my home to parade before you."

I shot backward, but he held me firm and grinned.

"You stand up to Caroline when she insults you over breakfast, and then, you handle Adair with as deft a hand."

"I wouldn't call it that."

He chuckled. "Oh, but I would. I heard it from their lips, no less." He placed his hand against my cheek and the warmth of his palm comforted me. He drew me more firmly against his torso and I went, just as blindly, just as willingly, as I had yesterday. Wrapped in his arms, my head tucked beneath his chin, I felt peaceful for the first time since I'd left his embrace yesterday.

He kissed my temple, and when he spoke, his hot breath fanned my hair. "You are doing everything I would wish for in a wife . . . . and more. I shall attempt to be as worthy a husband."

I gazed up at him.

His tone had gone quite grave.

"I am sure you will be a wonderful husband."

"I shall certainly try to be, my dear. I shall certainly try."

128

I stood on my toes to offer my lips to him, but he only brushed his fingers across my mouth and pecked me on the cheek. "I fear I cannot taste you too often before our wedding. The taste would require a complete feast." He laughed and kissed my brow. "Go, darling. Go see what Lianne can create for you."

Disappointed that I would not sample his kisses with any leisure, I hugged him, bade him goodbye, and headed for the hall. The two mastiffs rose as one, noses to my skirts. I had my hand on the doorknob, ready to tell them to remain, when Max quickly assured me that they could accompany me if I wished.

I chuckled. "I have always wanted a dog, sir. But two?"

"Anything I have is yours, darling. Take what will make you happy."

"Thank you, Max. For everything." I smiled and would have departed.

"Alicia, one thing more." I turned to see his face ravaged with trepidation. "I want you to know that I have never been intimate with Lianne. Never. Although the banter between us may give you the impression that we have been lovers, I repeat, we have not been. Her husband and I were friends. Very good friends for over twelve years. Guy chose a woman whose wit and charm I happened to appreciate as much as he. They adored each other, and when he died, she turned to me for comfort and help. And I gave it willingly. So, whatever you do, whatever you hear, please believe that Lianne is only my friend. For many years now, my only friend." I saw him pause as he controlled what appeared to be a trembling mouth. "I hope now I might acquire another in you."

Gratified that he would share that with me, I smiled sweetly at him and did a mock curtsy. "Aye, my lord duke. You have already gained another in me."

His features relaxed. "Good. Now see what you can do about something more complimentary to wear than that terrible outfit."

"Why, sir, I am outraged."

"Not as outraged as you'll be if I see you in that garment again and am forced to tear it off you! Now, go! *Go!*"

It wasn't difficult to find Lianne's room. From the landing on the first story, I could hear chatter and laughter tumbling down the stairwell.

With my two shadows following close behind, I approached her room and, once inside it, I understood her fascination with it. Even at this late morning hour, sunbeams cascaded over the pinks and mauves that pervaded the patterned chintzes and the cabbage rose wallpaper. I stood at the portal and watched Lianne give orders to a gaggle of three upstairs maids.

Meanwhile, stooping over into the cavern of one standing trunk, Lianne busily exhumed a handful of laces and eyelets and ribbons from a lower drawer. She was instructing one of the maids to empty the other trunk into the anteroom's chests.

"Forgive me, Lianne," I called to her above the chittering of the three delighted maids, "I thought I would come to help you."

She turned those wise cat's eyes on me and waved me in. "Wonderful. Come in, come in, Alicia. I am glad you are here. It will certainly help to have your impressions as we unearth some of these fripperies. Not everyone should wear every fashion or frivolity. Bad for the digestion, don't you think?"

"I honestly wouldn't know, Lianne." I walked over to run my hand along one folded swatch of watered peach satin atop the chin-high truck. My two canine friends sank down to fold themselves up just inside the threshold. "I have never had the opportunity to pick and chose among fashions or frivolities."

"Why not?"

"Max has not told you my background, I guess. Yes, well, I see he hasn't. I am a minister's daughter. The youngest of seven, the only daughter. We are Methodists, and while my father has had sizable parishes, none has ever been terribly rich. Nor has he. Therefore, I dress as I can."

"Hmm." She had folded her arms to consider me with arched brows. "Time to learn, then."

"I am not sure I have the ability."

She threw back her head and roared with laughter. One hand to her throat, she almost crowed. "Please understand one thing, Alicia: ability to choose may be a function of taste, but the ability to choose wisely comes from practice and education. You now have at your disposal the means for both. Max has told me to spare no amount of money or time with your trousseau."

She selected a Louis XVI chair with the dignity of Marie Antoinette assuming her throne and sent the servants off. When they had disappeared behind the closed anteroom door, she indicated I should sit in the matching chair.

"Describe to me what you like in materials and accessories."

"I have no idea."

"Of course you do . . . every woman does. The fact that you have not an opportunity to exercise your desires is an omission I am here to help fill." She patted my hand "Now, tell me. Silk? Taffeta? Dimity?"

"Well, not lace," I blurted.

She hooted! "You learned that quickly enough, I hear."

My cheeks blushed that Max had told her.

She leaned close to me. "You mustn't be ashamed. It was not your fault. Dorcas should have known better. But since she didn't, I'm glad to hear Max gave her an upbraiding." She sat back in her chair and examined me studiously. "You are nothing like her, I am delighted to say—nothing like her at all. So if you wish to wear lace, perhaps in time, when Max has forgotten her, you could try a lit—"

"No, I could not. I don't like it for myself, really. I wore that gown last night only because I wanted to dress for dinner and I had only this." I plucked at the wool I hated and sighed. "He loved her terribly, didn't he?"

Her thin eyebrows shot to her hairline. "His last duchess? Love? Not precisely the word for Max's feelings for her. No. No. She was something quite different to him. She was . . . his passion, his addiction."

My heart crashed to the floor.

"She was nothing like you, at all. She was . . . what shall I say? Incomparable? Yes, that suits her. Incomparable."

I blinked back a flashing bright pain behind my eyelids. But, fool that I was, I asked for more. "And his first duchess?"

"The complete opposite in every way. From complexion to temperament, two women could not have been more dissimilar. Yet they were cousins."

"Cousins. Extraordinary. I never knew. But then few speak of them by name. They are his 'first duchess' and his 'last duchess.' They are mythical creatures. Why?"

Her objectivity evaporated like water in a desert sun.

"Max could not bear it. For years after his first duchess's death, he could not bear to hear a reference to Cynthia. To say her name was to place him on a rack and watch him write in abject torment. Then, when the last one died—my God, even I tremble to speak her name—when Maribel died . . ." she panted with the effort the name had cost her, "yes, when Maribel died, he was like a man drawn and quartered. There was nothing left of him. Hollow, a shell of his former self." She fought the urge to cry, and her throat and mouth worked at repression. "Only in the last few months have I seen him recover some of his old vivacity, his buoyance. I attribute that to his Great Aunt Constance and her suggestion that the two of you marry. Now that I see you, I feel much more assured that he will return to himself. You are so right for him." She smiled once more and squeezed my hand.

"Thank you." I wish I knew why she said that, but to ask was to almost plead for some compliment of person that my breeding decried. "I want to make him happy."

"I am sure you do. He needs to be happy. He has

suffered so. I fear what would happen if he lost his third wife."

"Rest assured, I am very healthy."

She chuckled delightfully, clapping her hands. "My dearest Alicia, it was the very first of your assets I noticed. I daresay it is the very one Max saw value in."

My expression fell. Was I perceived by all to be nothing more than a conduit for a male heir? Had I deluded myself these past hours that this—this *contract* was more than a legal arrangement? In the past twenty-four hours, I had come to think I was respected as an equal by my fiancé, and yet here I was considered only a vessel—yes, a vessel!—to be filled.

I rose in rebellion.

"Alicia, forgive me. What did I say?" Lianne had followed me to the window and now placed comforting hands on my arm. "Please, tell me."

"You are quite right, Lianne. It is the first of my assets, as you call them, that Max prized, and probably the only asset I can bring him. I am very healthy. It's almost vulgar to be so healthy, some would say. Yet I admit I have never been sick a day in my life, even though I have nursed many a poor soul. None of their diseases has ever felled me, even for a day."

"Surely then, Alicia, you can understand why Max would find that helpful in embarking upon a new marriage. He has lost his first two wives. He wishes to be married for many years to you. And knowing the horror of raising children without a mother, because he himself had no mother to nurture him, Max wishes his girls to have benefit of a good woman."

"Your explanation makes perfect sense." What it did not do was make my heart grow lighter. I placed my hand atop hers. "Thank you, you have been most kind to sit and tell me these things. I wish it were as easy to talk with the other family members as it is you, Lianne."

"Ahh, yes. I did wonder if you'd had the dubious honor of meeting Max's relatives. Not terribly hospitable toward you, I imagine. Especially Adair."

I crinkled my brow in amused distress. "Adair? Why, I thought Caroline had the tongue of an adder."

"Mmm. Like mother, like daughter, wouldn't you say?"

"Only Gilbert has any manners."

"Is that right? He must be on his best behavior for some reason. Not in his cups these days?"

"You mean he's given to imbibing?"

"My dear, he's given to *wallowing!* It's his downfall, among other, more venial perversions."

"He seems harmless."

"Do us all a favor, Alicia. Don't say that to anyone. Max may explode in rage, Caroline in a mother's mad fit, an the gentleman himself in a hot pink rash."

"You're serious."

"Never more so." She led me from the window and tucked her arm in mine. "Come, let us leave these problems for some fun. I have brought with me two gowns I intended to place in my front shop window. Now, I never did sew up the gussets with any but basting thread, nor did I finish the hems. However," she thrust open the door to her anteroom and ushered me inside, "I think the colors may do you justice. I had the girls dress the mannequins with the gowns. Yes, yes, here they are. What do you think? Are they worthy of the next Duchess of Worminster?"

* * *

"Worthy" was not the word I'd have chosen to describe Max's opinion of the gown I chose to wear to dinner that evening. No, not "worthy."

"Ecstatic." "Elated." "Approving," perhaps.

"Scintillating." He moved toward me and kissed my hand. "Simply scintillating." His gray eyes met mine in silvery rays of appreciation. "You have chosen well." His gaze traveled to Lianne. "Both of you."

"Max, you know it is so easy to dress a woman who has such raving attributes," Lianne said as she fluffed out the silk poufs of my overskirt and stood back a moment to survey her handiwork. "The forest green matches the depths of Alicia's eyes, the pale pink ribbons her complexion. Credit Dorcas with the charming coiffure and then credit me with some foresight for the portrait you see before you. I was simply bright enough to ask your man what your new duchess looked like and fortunate enough to have something so complementary in the shop."

"You have not disappointed me," he twined one of my hands across his arm and took Lianne's hand with his other. He led us forward to the others. "Come in, and, Lianne, let me reacquaint you with my Aunt Caroline and my cousins Gilbert and Adair."

None of them was as interested in me tonight as they were in Lianne. As relief danced through me, I detected how Caroline resented this intrusion of yet another person into what had heretofore been solely her domain. While I had become accustomed to Caroline's formidable nature, I also now had the opportunity to watch Lianne deal with the woman. And she did a masterful job.

She sailed forward and performed her duties of

136

obliging guest with an air of grace so impartial, so warm, that had we not had the revealing discussion of the afternoon, I would never have known she had such poor opinions of Caroline and her brood. Indeed, Lianne took a seat on the rose damask settee opposite me and then smiled and laughed, posed and demurred to the point that I might have even said she was truly interested in Caroline's gossipy blather and Gilbert's carnival views of politics.

As for Adair, no one could have feigned interest in her conversation because she offered none. Oh, true, her demeanor was that of a normal English lady. Quiet, elegant, and restrained, she did not move from the golden silk slipper chair she had chosen as her perch. She sipped her sherry with the air of a woman in a critical state of intestinal pain. I could only note her distress and feel sorrow. My thoughts were filled with the main topics of conversation, the coming holidays, the duchy's annual Christmas reception and ball, and Max's and my wedding.

"When will it be?" Lianne turned eager eyes from me to Max.

From across the room in front of the gilt fireplace, Max pursed his lips and raised his glass to me. "Tell us, my dear . . . when shall it be?"

Lianne laughed lightly. "You mean to say you have not set a date? Oh, Max! I am amazed at you! You let Alicia go so long without naming the moment?" She leaned across to me and placed her gloved hand on mine. "My dearest, do you realize how fortunate you are? How unique? To be able to say that the grand Duke of Worminster has let his future bride choose the date! Max, you are slipping, old man."

"I could not risk her distress, Lianne."

Caroline looked almost benign. "Well, then, do not keep us in suspense. Tell us, when shall it be? We must all prepare, you realize." Her frosty blue eyes settled in mine.

Her attitude nettled me.

I gave Max an engaging grin.

"What is the date of the duchy's Christmas reception?"

"A week Saturday."

"And the event includes everyone from the duchy?"

Max nodded once. "Everyone from the miller in the village and his three small sons to the tenant farmers of Addelmarle in the north, to my managers of my cotton factories in Manchester and beyond."

Adair roused to the subject. "Which means, of course, that your brother Thomas will be invited."

Gilbert was frowning. "And all the assorted Wolff family relatives."

Lianne gazed at me with expectation.

"Wonderful," I concluded, and smiled at Max. "What do you say, then, Max, that we celebrate our wedding with those who are most important to you?"

Had we been alone, I am most sure Max would have done more in response than he allowed himself. He caught my gaze with those mesmerizing orbs of his and probed for my innermost soul. "My dear Alicia, whatever you want that is within my power to give you I will. Name the day."

My heart caught. My mouth watered and I fought desperately to keep up an appearance of social propriety. I wanted to say "today, now." But I knew I could not and mourned my loss. I swallowed back raw desire,

138

turned my most ravishing face up to his, and declared, "Friday. The day before the reception. Does that please you, my lord?"

"Outrageously," he murmured, it seemed for my ears alone, as the others broke into various exclamations of agreement or surprise.

Suddenly Gilbert was on his feet. "I think," he said as he raised his glass, "we should have a toast to the new bride. What do you say, eh?" He surveyed the group.

Max, who now dragged his smoky eyes from mine to his cousin, found voice. "Absolutely, Gilbert. I had Bigelow bring up a suitable champagne from the wine cellars this morning. It awaits us at table." He strode toward me and took both my hands to help me rise. "Shall we go in?" he asked the others, but with his half-lidded eyes, he caressed my mouth. "Gilbert, could you escort Lianne, please?"

The others drifted from the room. When we were completely alone, Max turned my hands over to place a kiss inside each palm. "Thank you, Alicia. You have made me very happy."

At his joy, I thrilled and wanted to joke with him. "You are easily pleased, I think."

"I think you are so right. But then, I am easily pleased only by you."

I tilted my head. "It is a simple thing to declare a date."

"Perhaps. It is a more complex affair to choose one so beneficial to my person."

"Is that not the duty of a wife, my lord duke? To prove beneficial to one's husband?" I was chiding him.

He went quite serious. "Yes. I think I have quite

139

forgotten that." He took my hand and hooked it through his arm. "Let us dine, and as we do, I shall attempt to remember it."

"Please don't remember too well, my lord. I rather like you beholden to me."

"Do you, now?" He threw back his head to chuckle and squeezed my hand with his warm one. "Well, then, we shall explore other ways to have me eat from your hand, my dear."

That the great and noble Duke of Worminster should show such humility made me shiver with delight—so much so that when we entered the dining room, the others reacted to the looks of us.

Lianne grinned.

Adair appeared even more pained.

Caroline sighed and glanced away.

Only Gilbert met my gaze and winked.

He rose, a champagne flute in one hand, and waited until Max had seated me to his right at the massive table.

"To the new bride," offered Gilbert. "The newest Duchess of Worminster, may God grant her long life."

"And many children," Lianne added.

"And much happiness," Max concluded, and they all drank.

It was the last positive note of the evening. In fact, when the last of the fruit and cheese were cleared away, I could count one argument between Gilbert and his mother about the Queen's handling of her husband Albert, one disagreement between Lianne and Adair— yes, Adair—over the use of Italian laces or Flemish in good handkerchiefs, and one standoff between Gilbert and Adair about the importance of a young woman's education in the use of watercolors. I, of course, had no knowledge and little interest in any of it and found myself so outside the general stream of conversation that I once more asked myself if I could hold my own in a family so torn by internecine strife.

When Lianne rose from her chair beside me and excused herself to retire early, Max nodded and bade her goodnight. Adair abruptly followed Lianne's example. Seeing herself in mixed company, Caroline glanced from me to Max, and with a flick of her hand, had Gilbert escorting her up to her quarters.

I sat, deflated and bewildered.

"Look at me, Alicia."

Max stood beside me, his finger tipping my chin up so that I might see him. "Don't brood on this, darling."

I shook my head and looked down at my hands. He seized them and bade me rise. "Come with me, away from here. Please."

His beseeching tone had me following him out of the splendorous dining room, down the hall, through the morning room, and into the conservatory. When we stood once more beneath bowers of fragrant flowers, he faced me and tried to gather me to him.

My hand to his chest forbade it.

"No, Max. Tell me, please, because I need to understand why. Why . . ." I turned distressed eyes up to his own tortured ones, "tell me why Gilbert seems so erratic and Caroline and Adair so bold, so utterly—"

He inhaled and shoved his hands in his side pockets. "Yes, I know how you feel. Words fail me as well. They are simply uncontrollable." He raised his arms and let them fall to his sides. Despair lined his countenance as he turned from me toward the verdant blossoms of roses and wild red orchids.

"As God is my witness, Alicia, I have tried with them. I brought them here years ago when they were penniless—worse than that, when they were in debt. I feel I have been as generous as one can be in my circumstances, paying their debts, housing them, clothing them, even supplying an allowance. Yet it makes no difference. They are as headstrong as ever they were. When we are together, the aggravation does none of us any good. Frankly, I avoid them when I can. Amid the storm, I try to make a home for Mary and Elizabeth. I have not succeeded very well." He drove a hand through his rich black hair and turned to me. "I need you, Alicia. If I suspected it when I first saw you months ago, I recognized it two days ago. Now I understand it. I see it in all its possibilities."

"I am complimented beyond expec—"

He placed one long forefinger over my lips. "Hush. Don't be demure, my darling. Leave that to the simpletons who have so little to offer a man."

"You think me sophisticated now?" I tried to bring him from his despair with a little lightheartedness. "Not long ago, you told me I was intelligent but not wise." I stepped closer to him and his body's warmth permeated the gossamer silk of my gown to tempt me nearer. "Am I to understand you have changed your view of me?"

He ran his hands up bare arms and neck to cup my face. "Yes, my vision was impaired. But no more. You are as wondrous, as different as a rose from this orchid."

He eyes went to the profusion of delicate pink rose

142

petals. "A rose is a splendid creation, meant by God to satisfy the beholder. The fragrance, the composition form a tight bud of complexity and unity. The flower appears to be none other than what it is. Even its defense is apparent, its thorns displayed for all the world to see for exactly what they are—sharp weapons used for any war. But this—" he indicated a huge vermilion orchid, "this is quite different."

Never having seen a specimen like this, I examined it with curiosity. Not understanding his direction, I asked the only question that came to mind. "Do you know the name of this?"

"This, and all the others. Personally selected for a certain rare quality. This one is quite unique. It appears to be an orchid, but is a succulent from the jungles of Ceylon."

I dared to touch a fingertip to the thick petal. Substantial, sturdy beyond visible discernment, the succulent released a potent aroma to the immediate air. Sweet, almost sickening in its intensity, the flower became at once less lovely. My nostrils flared. I backed away.

Max snorted in disgust. I was distressed that I had insulted his sensibilities, and I glanced up. To my surprise, he was smiling reassuringly at me. "Some flowers, like some people, tantalize from afar. But once exposed to the full flavor of their individuality, we are often repelled."

"I have met such people."

He himself placed a finger upon the fleshy lips of the vermilion beauty. "Such people are destructive, like this rare flower whose perfume draws its prey to its sticky blossom. Then, once the prey alights, the plant

143

sends out more perfume to drug the poor victim. He becomes faint and loses his footing. He falls down right into the long cup which, filled with acid, quickly becomes his coffin. The acid eats the body of the poor victim as he struggles in vain to escape. But of course, he is hopelessly trapped. And he dies. Slowly and painfully. Justifiably so, too, I might add. After all, he had the poor judgment to be attracted to her perfume. It is somewhat like being attracted to certain women, you see."

He turned to face me. But he saw someone—one of his wives or mistresses, or even Caroline and her children. But certainly he did not see me. He only ranted on.

"The attraction can be potent. So potent you forget every other being, every other rational act, every other thing you ever held dear, and you throw every ounce of integrity away just to possess her, just to bathe in that perfume. So you fly to her and then," his eyes fell closed and my heart sank in a pit of boiling jealousy, "and then you receive your reward. You die."

What had begun as a description of Caroline and Adair, perhaps even Gilbert, had ended as an analogy to a love affair gone wrong. But whose love affair? Max's, surely. Dared I ask who else?

I had to know.

I pressed myself against his chest. Closing my eyes to the truth I would now beg from him, I listened to the violent pounding of his heart as his arms came around me.

"Have you died?" I choked out.

"Twice before."

No mistresses then, but two wives were those he

144

mourned. His grief for the two women he'd promised to cherish till death assuaged my jealousy. I now told myself that if I had come this far in his affections in such a short space of time, I had justifiable hope that I could ameliorate the disasters of his past and bring some lasting joy into his life.

"May I help you live again?"

His lips in my hair muffled what I thought was a sob. "God, darling, yes!"

He kissed my crown, my forehead, my cheek, and at along last his lips met mine. Luscious, wet, and wild, his mouth seized the essence of my being and plundered for more. I could not care. I wanted him. I wanted to heal him, help him, have him.

He sensed it. I willed it to be so. I could tell when he felt my surrender. I knew when he accepted my will into his keeping.

He was a man enraptured. Enraptured as his arms clutched me closer. Emboldened as his ravenous kisses were met with mine. Empowered as he bent me backward over his arm and pushed aside the silk of my gown to place his hot lips against my breast, upon my nipple to suckle there to both his satisfaction and mine.

I'd have swooned from the voracious pleasure but he caught me, held me, crooned to me of ripe hunger for us to become one.

"I want you, Alicia," his voice was gruff in my ear. His hands were roughly covering my breast with my gown. "I want you, my darling." He was smiling into my passion-dazed eyes as he kissed my nose. "But we will wait. I want a wife in my bed. A wife and a virgin, before God and man and even me. I will not take you here, a newly betrothed woman. No, not here because

145

I want you in a very large bed. My bed. Sans clothes. Sans thought. Sans reason. Sans every inhibition you've ever been taught.'' He steadied me on my feet and cocked a brow at me. "Besides, if I remember correctly, our bargain states that you will come to me.''

I blushed furiously and considered the floor.

"My dearest,'' he tipped my face up and his eyes caressed my features, "I hope I may safely assume that you will not tarry too long in your decision to come to my bed.''

Embarrassed beyond words, I turned from him and was not a step away when his voice once more arrested me. "Rest assured that when that moment comes, Alicia, I will welcome you with even more delight and, if it is at all possible, more passion than we have shared here tonight.''

"Yes,'' I owed him nothing less than truth, "I know that, my lord.''

"I live for it, my darling.''

And so did I.

Chapter Seven

"The strap is too tight now, Ma'am," Elizabeth winced even though I'd stopped wrapping the skating blades' leather braces across her ankles.

"I'm so sorry, my dear." I frowned at the two mastiffs who had their noses stuck in front of Elizabeth's foot, obstructing my view. "If these two gentlemen would kindly move a bit—" I took Rolf's collar and pulled him away, while I nodded to Hans to back off, "we'll be able to loosen those straps. There, how does that feel? Remember, we don't want them too loose, or you'll lose your balance and fall."

"Falling's not so bad," Mary called to her sister, as she glided toward us across the ice. "Come on, Elizabeth. Today I'm better at it. You will be, too."

I finished fixing the straps atop Elizabeth's left shoe and patted her leg. "There, now. Give that a whirl."

She smiled at me, more assured now. Wobbly even after three afternoon skating lessons, Elizabeth remained true to the character Max had painted of her: she was the second child, and the more cautious one.

"Hold my hand, will you please, Ma'am?" she asked

me as she tried to balance herself on the blades strapped to her leather overshoes.

I smiled and took her mittened hand. "Of course, my dear. Come. We'll take a turn about the pond together."

On tiptoe, we stepped from the log where she'd sat to the edge of the pond. It was not a large body of water and not far from the stream where the horrid troll was said to live beneath a ramshackle bridge. I had had to use all my persuasive powers to get the girls to cross that bridge. But they'd slowly learned to trust me and now crossed it with less trepidation. The lure of skating lessons engendered the daily development of courage. I used the lure as often as I could—particularly after the temperature plunged a week ago and brought with it a magnificent snowfall that molded the ground with a white blanket and iced the trees with a glittering display of refracted lights.

I placed my two feet on the pond and led Elizabeth out. She clutched my hand for dear life. "Don't fret, Elizabeth. I won't leave you."

She swallowed and licked her lips. Then, very carefully, she left the solid snow-covered ground and stood upon the ice. Behind her, the two huge dogs sat on their haunches to supervise. I smiled.

"Let's start, shall we? Remember how well you did yesterday? Well, you'll do even better today."

And she did. She glided slowly, and, after a minute or two, so serenely that even Mary slowed to watch. Elizabeth had no eyes for her audience of four. Instead, she turned her sights inward and, as was her wont with her reading and her numbers, she excelled. With every step, she become more confident, more graceful. If she was not so adventurous, so daring as Mary, she compensated, as Max had said, with the quality of her efforts.

Mary skated to my side and grabbed my hand. "I want to skate like that."

"You do very well, Mary."

"Not as good as Eliza."

I bit my lower lip. The biggest—the only—problem between these twin sisters seemed to be this one. And now, after almost two weeks with them, I still confessed, if only to myself, that I had failed to find a solution. Jealousy, especially of one's own siblings, was not an easy thing to adjudicate—worse yet, to dispel.

"You and I shall take a turn ourselves. Now, let us focus on the stroke of your foot upon the ice. Think how it must feel to fly." We were in tandem now, our right feet and then our left feet striking the ice in measured glides. "That's right. Pretend you are an eagle, sailing gently on an updraft—and put your right foot down gently. Good, good. Now, the next updraft. Yes, yes. That's right. Again."

Her stride became smoother, her confidence stronger. I could feel it in the way her body slid across the ice and the way her fingers relaxed in mine. We went round the pond that way once, twice. Then, as her fingers finally unclasped mine, I knew she needed to leave me and try this alone. I skated with her a few yards and then slowed. Making my way to the edge of the pond, I stopped next to a large pine and crossed my arms. The sight of the two of them gracefully taming their fears gave me a glowing satisfaction.

"You have done wonders with them," a husky voice

whispered in my ear, as two strong arms wrapped around me.

I closed my eyes and leaned backward. Max.

He kissed my temple and would have turned me into his embrace.

I laughed up at him and put a palm to his coat. "Don't. The girls—"

"Will have to get used to the sight of me kissing you sooner or later."

I glanced about. "But there may be others!"

"Others? You mean Rolf and Hans? I see no others, my sweet." He kissed me briefly and relaxed against a tree, taking me with him.

"You say I will choose the time and place for our—communion, yet you pursue me endlessly."

He grinned, that sensuously sculpted mouth of his forming a tempting feast. In his black beaver hat and black overcoat, his rugged complexion shone to a tan perfection, while his ebony hair and white streak tantalized me even more. For the thousandth time, I resisted the urge to touch it, crush it in my fist. More, I wanted to trace the line of that white streak that fell boyishly across his brow. God, he was handsome, and so soon to be mine that I shivered.

He clutched me closer. "Are you cold?"

I shook my head and the two of us smiled together.

"Well, I wouldn't blame you if you were. This coat," he indicated the now-much-discussed traveling pelisse, "is totally unsuitable. Which is why I came to get you. The three of you have been out here for over two hours. Williams is fretting like a plucked chicken over them out here, and I can't have my bride come down with a chill on her wedding night, now can I?"

150

"I told you, I am never ill."

"But allow me a husband's right to look after you."

"I welcome it."

"And I am gratified beyond reason."

"I know."

His smoldering gray eyes considered my mouth. But to my sorrow, he must have remembered my admonition to propriety, and he sighed and set me from him. "It's time to come in. We'll send the girls off for hot chocolate, and then I want you to come with me to my den. I have something I want you to see."

With much grumbling, Mary and Elizabeth left the ice.

"We'll come tomorrow," I promised.

They plunked themselves onto the log we used as a stool when donning or removing their ice blades. Rolf and Hans lumbered over to us, Rolf to lean over Max's shoulder, and Hans to scowl at my handiwork.

Max paused as he unlaced Mary's straps. "Alicia, tomorrow is our wedding. What with the guests arriving and the reception afterward, I doubt we'll have time to skate."

I glanced from him to the disappointed twins. "We'll come early, then. Before luncheon."

Max frowned.

The two girls caught their father's look and began to plead with him.

"Oh, please, Papa." Elizabeth looked crushed.

"We'll make you proud of us," Mary pleaded.

He chucked her under the chin. "My pet, you always make me proud of you."

She looked so startled, Max and I caught our breath. Max recovered first. "Why are you surprised,

Mary?'' He probed her eyes. "Do you not know how I love you?''

"Yes, sir.'' She avoided his gaze and squirmed.

Elizabeth was no better.

I looked at Max and shrugged in bewilderment.

He reached for Mary's hands. "I do love you,'' he grasped Elizabeth's hand, too, "both of you. You are my delight. Why would you think I don't care for you? Have I been unkind?''

They shook their heads.

"Inattentive?''

They snuck a glance at each other.

"What, then?'' he urged on a whisper.

Mary pondered a moment. "We're not good for you, sir.''

"What?'' No whisper could have been more tormented. "What are you saying, Mary?''

Tears dribbled down her cheeks. Her twin fought the same reaction.

"We are girls. And girls aren't anything. Boys are better.''

My heart twisted. Society teaches from the cradle attitudes that cut as sharp as knives, severing us from our true selves and our fullest potential before we know it.

"I do not feel that way, Mary.''

Her eyes came up to challenge his.

And with the force of her look, Max fell back.

"Mary, Elizabeth, my dears! Why do you feel this way?''

"If girls were as good as boys, you wouldn't want a son.'' Her blurt made her swallow convulsively. "Ooo,

152

I didn't want to say that—'' She tugged to be free of her father.

He would not let her go.

Meanwhile, Elizabeth reached for her twin to hug her.

Max tried to embrace them and they veered back. He was left holding the air.

"My dears, I love you. It saddens me beyond words to know that you think I value you less because you are girls."

"Why do you want a boy? Williams says you want a boy. You didn't want us. And you're going to marry Miss Alicia tomorrow because you need a boy."

Overwhelmed, he sank back on his heels and lifted his brows. "For a lot of reasons. For a lot of reasons that have nothing to do with you. For a lot of reasons you are not old enough to understand yet."

He checked my eyes, and at my nod, he plunged on.

"The most important reason is that I don't want anything to happen to you both if anything should ever happen to me."

Now I considered him with a frown upon my face.

"You see, I keep in my study a piece of paper which is very old and priceless. It is the piece of paper that was written long ago by a king of England. His name was Charles the Second, and on this piece of paper, he wrote that the Duchy of Worminster was to be inherited by males only. It doesn't sound fair, I know. But there isn't anything I can do to change it. What I can do, and what I have done, is prepare a will for myself so that if and when anything ever happens to me such that . . . I can't be with you any longer, you will have a long, happy life, free from worry about money.

153

And . . ." he gave me a wan smile, "now that I am marrying Miss Alicia tomorrow, you will have someone to watch over you. Someone who loves you."

Elizabeth perked up. "You mean you'd let Miss Alicia be our mother? Even if you're not here?"

"Yes," he grinned.

"Forever and ever?"

"Yes, I want you happy."

The two girls examined each other's eyes.

Mary faced her father now with ease. "So you are not marrying her only to get a boy baby and take us to an orphanage. You are not like that old troll who wants to trade us for another."

If I could have fallen through the earth, I would gladly have gone. Max fared far better. Perhaps years of dealing with the dubious felicities of businessmen and government officials had done that to him. I could not have summoned the aplomb if my life depended on it.

"My dears, I want you with me always."

Mary brightened. "I like that," she murmured.

"Me, too," chimed Elizabeth.

"There, now," he tweaked each girl's nose. "No more of this talk of boys better than girls and trolls and orphanages." He stood. "Come home, now. There is much we must do for the wedding tomorrow. And you must help Miss Alicia."

"Oh, yes," I joined him in his urging. "I need your help, especially to lay out my clothes for the morning."

He clucked his tongue for the dogs to follow as he held out his hands for us all to join together. We walked to the other side of the copse where he had stopped his magnificent red sleigh. I had seen it only once, a few days before, in the coach house, and then in dappled sunlight. Now, in brilliant afternoon, the sumptuous conveyance beckoned to my sense of comfort.

"Oh, Papa, you brought the sleigh!" Mary scrambled forward with her sister close behind. She climbed in and sank blissfully into the plum leather upholstery, her sister emulating her actions a moment behind.

"I thought it appropriate for my three ladies to have a warm ride home after such a strenuous afternoon in the cold." He took a woolen carriage blanket and pressed it around the girls' legs. Then he turned, his face lightened from the cares of the preceding conversation, and assisted me in beside them. When he joined us, we all pressed tightly together and the proximity made the girls laugh while I became once more conscious of Max's magnetism.

As he seized the two massive reins, neither of us gave notice of our closeness—or chose not to—and I breathed more easily. Want him I did. Tempted by him I was. But as his actions and words had indicated in the past ten days or so, he would kiss me and caress me, tease me and teach me, but only so much. Only so far.

For he, above all else, wanted a virgin bride in his bed. He had said it once, then many times again. The expectation was not unusual. Neither was his adamance. And so it was easy to ignore this raging need between us. Easy to be flattered by his courtship of my person. Easy to enjoy his solicitous arm or his outstretched hand. Easy to revel in his lingering looks at table or in the drawing room, with others about. Easy because he went only so far to tempt and satisfy. And then he would step away, leaving me more eager for his next look, his next touch, his next foray against the bastion that was my nineteen years of chastity.

I knew what he did and I knew why. I was his betrothed and found no harm in it. Indeed, in my most objective moments, I admitted that he was probably very wise to do as he did. Without his seduction—for I knew enough to call it by name—how would our marriage develop? How would it mature? And how soon?

I had agreed to three months within which the union would be consummated. Three months! Was I mad? At this breakneck pace of Max's seduction, I could never withhold my wifely favors for three entire months!

He turned quickly to look at me. He had pulled the sleigh to the front door of the mansion and the girls had alighted. "I like to see you laugh."

I hugged his arm. "It's easy when I'm with you. You make me happy."

"Ahh, the feeling is mutual, then." He looped the reins into the side rail and climbed down. Then, he turned and offered me his hand. "Come with me and we'll see if I can make you any happier."

"Much more and I shall be delirious."

He chuckled and led me away toward the door, the two dogs at our heels. "I tell you, I want you fully happy every minute we're together. Then, no one or nothing can take you from me."

I tingled with ribald excitement. My voice dropped to a spare level. "Max, no one will ever do that. Besides, you don't want to spoil me. Too much chivalry and I shall die of utter abundance."

His eyes took one quick assessment of me. "No, you

won't, darling. I know you. You'll return the favor a thousand times."

He patted my hand and led me through the front door and down the hall. Past Mary and Elizabeth, who requested hot chocolate from a perplexed Bigelow. Past Mrs. Timms, who requested a word with us about the reception menu. Past Dorcas, who wondered if I'd like hot chocolate to warm me. And into his study, where he told the two mastiffs to wait for me outside and closed the door against the rest of the world. Then, with dexterous fingers, he stripped me of my hat and pelisse and himself of his hat and coat.

"Come here now and stand before the fire. Close your eyes."

I extended my arms and splayed my fingers to warm them at the blaze while I listened to his footsteps drift away and in five strides return. Then, with a whoosh of air, something heavy descended to my shoulders and enveloped me in downy warmth. I nestled into its delights.

"What is this you have draped me in, my lord?"

He arranged upon my head a hood, as heavy as divinely warm. "Feel."

He took my hands in his and spread my fingers, then crossed my arms and plunged them into the thickest, lushest fur.

"May I open my eyes?"

"Just a moment . . ." He took my left hand then, and on the third finger, he slid a ring. "Now. Now you may open your eyes."

With my fingers still plunged into the glories of the fur, I opened my eyes to view his. He was grinning, expectant as a little boy eager to see another's joy. I looked down and neither of us was disappointed.

"Oh, Max!" I breathed, clutching handfuls of long-haired silver fox. I snuggled into the cape more deeply, nuzzled my cheek against it, and then, remembering the ring, held up my left hand. There, in newest white gold, sat two large emeralds, and at either side, two diamonds of the same size.

"You betrothal ring. I was furious it was not ready for you two weeks ago, but it couldn't be helped. The diamonds I ordered three months ago did not cut correctly. They shattered. I had to select others and hence it was late. I wanted it for you that day you arrived."

He was apologizing? "Max. Oh, Max, you have no need to make amends to me. The coat is luscious, and the ring is stunning. I never thought to own anything like either of them."

He came closer and gripped my arms. "Then it is fitting. Because I never thought to possess anyone like you."

"Please, you make too much of me, Max. And I— I'm not anything like your two previous wives."

"No, my dear, you are not." He took my chin between two fingers to lift my face and peer at me. "But if you mean to imply that you are not worthy of such gifts, I shall be heartily angry with you."

"Oh, Max, I would not anger you for the world." I stroked the rich fur and admired once more the gems on my finger. "But I am no noblewoman, no heiress. I am nothing, have nothing—"

"Stop!" He was shaking me, hurting me with his fingers nipping the flesh of my arms. "Stop it, I say! Do you think me merely a bounder who would seduce you with gifts and honeyed words? A man who uses women? Good God, Alicia! What I said out there to Mary and Elizabeth was true: I do not seek to hurt women, would not tread on their sensibilities simply to have hegemony over them. I am no fake in sheep's clothing. I give you these gifts freely, as a man gives his bride all that he has and she, in turn, does the same."

"But that is precisely my point, my lord. I have nothing to give you in this marriage. Nothing. And you have been so generous with thought and deed. So—beneficent that I am undone, Max. I am astounded that you should care for a too tall, too lanky minister's daughter who can bring you nothing."

"Nothing?" His smile was sarcastic. "Is that what you think you bring me? Nothing?" He threw back his head to shake it. He dropped his hands and walked away from me.

He paced now, a wounded animal in torment.

"No one has told you anything of my previous marriages, have they?" He stopped to narrow his eyes at me. "Or have they?"

I shook my head. "Lianne told me a little. Their names, and that you loved the second one very much."

He groaned, bitterness and agony in ripe mix. He spun from me. "Didn't Lianne tell you how I loved my first wife? How I loved her from the time I was twelve and I saw her in her mother's garden in Liverpool? How I loved her delicate pale blond hair and bright blue eyes? How I loved her silken voice, small and fragile as fine china? How I cared for her in spite of that frailty? How I married her when she was sixteen

159

and I was twenty-two, old enough to want her, yet not wise enough to see what I was doing?''

He walked the floor a possessed man. ''Did Lianne tell you how I loved Cynthia through more than ten years of marriage? Ten years of sicknesses? How she suffered from consumption and brittle bones? How she hated the winters that chilled her through and through? How she refused to go anywhere—not even in the sleigh for a midday ride—for fear she'd catch her death of cold or break an arm or a leg with a misstep? How in spite of her best efforts, she still became ill, and how I rubbed her back with ointments, brought her teas and hot liquors in the middle of freezing winter nights? How, amid it all, I suffered with her when she miscarried time after frightening time? How she so pined for a baby, an heir, that she insisted we share a bed, even though the best doctors told her she would die if she ever brought a fetus to full term? How I wanted to keep her from all harm and she wouldn't let me? How she put temptation in my way, took me to her bed, and there conceived despite my most honorable intentions and then—then how she died after giving birth?'' He pivoted and all hell's fury danced in his eyes. ''Did Lianne tell you that?''

''No. No, she didn't.''

He snorted. ''No. Lianne wouldn't tell it all. She is my friend, and she'd leave the details for me. But I suppose she thought you ought to know something . . . yes, something.''

He stepped before me once more and searched my eyes. ''Do you know what you bring me which I value, Alicia? You bring me a woman blantantly healthy. A breathing, laughing, active, vibrant woman. A woman

160

who braves not only snow and ice, but that cold crew I call my family. You are alive and absolutely pulsing with vitality. And I welcome the opportunity to make you mine, keep you mine. So if, in the bargain, I happen to find you enticing, will you object? Will you turn me away?''

He was angry but he was logical, and he was within my reach. I placed a palm against his cheek. ''No. I will not.''

He put one hand atop mine and his tortured eyes fell closed. ''Darling Alicia,'' he placed a kiss inside my hand, ''trust your good instincts. What you see is no lie.'' His eyes captured mine. ''I find myself more enchanted with you each day. You make me smile, laugh. You do the same for the girls who badly need you. More, much more, I watch you with Caroline and Adair and Gilbert, and you are superb. Polite, certainly kind. Kinder than I could ever be.''

''But, my dearest lord, you are the consummate gentleman with them.''

''It pleases me you think me so noble. But I must tell you, I will go only so far. Past experiences have shown me I spend my efforts on them to no avail. I prefer to find some joy where I can. With you. For as long as I can.''

Errant points of his speech by the pond pierced my brain. I ran my hand through that silver shock of his hair. ''Tell me why you say such a thing. You appear to be as healthy, my lord, as I am.''

''In two months, I shall become forty years old—twice your age, Alicia. I have not long to remain. Ten years, if I am lucky. So you see, health has nothing to do with life expectancy.''

"No? I rather thought it had everything to do with it."

He shook his head and walked to his desk to idly push aside a few papers. Suddenly, he stood at attention. He lifted one of the papers and then quickly pocketed it. He looked at me, but his eyes were glazed.

"If you will excuse me, my dear, I have much correspondence to answer. Much work to do before our wedding."

Sweeping the floor-length fox cape from my shoulders and over a chair, I went to him.

"Look at me, Max. Tell me, darling, are you ill?"

"No."

"Why then do you speak of dying and—"

"Leave it, Alicia."

"What you said to the girls, the way you phrased it, made me afraid. And now you speak of me having to live without you. Why, Max? You're frightening me."

"My love, you are frightened because you have just recently suffered three deaths. You know the tenuousness of life first hand. You perceive things many would not because you have so recently suffered such losses."

I examined every line of his features. "When you and I first talked here in this room two weeks ago, you promised me honesty, Max. I call upon you to deliver it now and for the rest of our days. Telling me part of the truth does not qualify, my lord duke. Doing so makes the act a sin of omission."

For the first time in our days together, I saw his eyes lose their vivacity. I saw instead tears rise there. And since no man ever shed a tear in the presence of another and certainly not in front of a woman, I now feared the very worse for the man I loved. Yes, loved!

"Alicia, leave this discussion where it is. I promise you I will tell you all I can. But not now . . . not now. Marry me, sweetheart. And then I will tell you whatever I can."

"But why not now?"

"Because you would run from me in horror—"

"No!"

"Yes! And I might never have the chance to end the ceaseless bout of evil that lives within these walls."

"My lord, you speak in riddles."

"Riddles? No, I speak of curses, my dearest. Curses. And only you, sweet and lovely as you are, can help me drive them out. Will you stay and be my love?"

"As long as you will have me, Max."

He rounded the desk and brought me close. The movement made the paper in his pocket rustle. He shot me a glance, but covered it with a captivating smile. "Oh, I will have you, 'til the day I die." He bent to kiss me.

"Aaahem! Excuse me, milord—"

We broke apart at the sound of Bigelow's voice.

"Yes, what is it?"

"Your Grace, two of the guests have arrived, sir. They are the group from the afternoon train. They gather in the entrance hall. Miss Pennington's brother, Thomas, and also Baron Southeby."

"Baron Southeby. Wonderful." Max placed a hand at my waist and gave it a consoling squeeze. "Let us go out to meet our houseguests, my dear."

I sighed and turned. This wedding could not come soon enough for me.

Bigelow led us out to the hallway as I turned to Max.

"I'm delighted Thomas could come at short notice.

And even more delighted that you gave him time from his position so that he could leave the factory.''

"Since none of your other brothers could attend the ceremony, I was eager to have him. Besides, I like him. He has performed well at the Number Five Factory and that, in no small measure, because he has a good head on his shoulders for business.''

I hugged his arm. "I hope you might be friends. As much as employer and employee might be.''

"Certainly as much as brothers-in-law might, eh?''

"Mmmm, quite.''

We rounded the corner to the entrance hall and there, awaiting us, stood two men as dissimilar as could be. One, tall and red-haired, intensely studied the painted ceiling, and the other, as tall, but blond and spare, was nattily dressed in cream wool traveling suit with matching leather gloves which he vigorously slapped against his muscular thighs.

As I went to my brother Thomas and embraced him with glee, Max shook hands with the blond man.

"Branford, wonderful to see you,'' Max was greeting his guest. "I hope you will consider staying a few days.''

"It is a long trip up to these woods, old man. I hate to think of getting back on a train to London any time soon. If you and your new bride can stand me for the holidays, I may take you up on that invitation.''

"Good.'' Max turned to me and Thomas. "Let me introduce you to Alicia and to her brother.'' Max put out his hand to Thomas. "Nice to see you again, Thomas. I hope I may call you Thomas without objection.''

Thomas trained accepting eyes on Max and smiled.

164

Clearly, this matter of how Max would receive him had worried him.

And he trembled as they shook hands. "Thank you, Your Grace."

Max turned to his friend and offered introductions to me and to Thomas. "Branford joins us from London, where he has taken up residence these last few years. Branford is my brother-in-law." Max checked my expression. "He is the only brother of Cynthia, my first wife."

That Branford would attend the wedding of his dead sister's husband spoke eloquently of a relationship which appeared untarnished by years of separation or any animosities. That Branford shook hands with Thomas and kissed my hand told me he had accepted his sister's death as some normal course of events. The camaraderie Branford allowed was equaled by Max, whose silver eyes showed no distress that the baron should meet me.

Yet Thomas felt odd. He remained stiff, nervous. I felt it in his jerking movements as he pulled at the jacket of his best serge suit. I leaned into him and tried to tell him without words that he needn't be uncomfortable, but he constantly swallowed and licked his lips as the four of us went down the hall toward the drawing room.

When we had seated ourselves in a small circle before the benefits of a roaring fire, Max offered spirits to both men. While Branford readily accepted, Thomas declined.

Max frowned. "Tea, then? I can easily ring for it. You've had a long journey and it is very cold outside."

"No, Your Grace. Thank you. I don't wish to put you to any trouble, sir."

Max cocked one long brow. "Thomas, you will soon become as much family to me as Branford. You are no trouble. You are my guest."

Thomas, who had spent the last moments with eyes narrowed on Max, seemed relieved, if only a trifle. He smiled, albeit woodenly. "Thank you, sir. I think I'll take that brandy, if you don't mind."

I rounded my eye at Thomas. Drinking spirits was not something we had ever condoned in our family. He took the small sniffer from Max and looked at me with apologetic eyes. "We all change, my dear Allie. Even you."

"Me? No."

"Yes. To look at you is to see a lady. You have a new hairstyle and new gowns. Gold velvet, eh? Mother would be happy for you. Grandma, too. I never thought to see you so—well, I can't quite give it a word."

"Exquisite," Branford supplied, and raised his glass in homage. "I say, Max, she's quite lovely. You do pick them, I'll wager."

I caught my breath. I would not let this conversation deteriorate into one of those silly comments on women's beauty and toilette. Or worse yet, a comparison between me and Max's previous wives.

"Branford, please tell us how you find London. Is there as much snow there as here?"

"My dear Alicia—I may call you Alicia, may I not?—it is dismal in London these last few weeks. No snow, but ice storms. One cannot go out without expecting to skate everywhere! I find it amusing simply to sit in my front window and look out at the comedies of those who have ventured beyond their doorstep." He sipped his brandy with relish. "I tell you, I am glad for the respite. You have always been a good host, Max, old boy. Good food, good wine, the best cigars! No, I am joking, and you know it. I am thrilled to be invited to this little wedding. Honored, in fact."

Max smiled. "Thank you, Branford. Your friendship has always been important to me."

"Well, I certainly would like to see you happy, Max. Curses or not." He was smiling, obviously making fun of the very idea that there could even be such a thing as a curse.

But he saw us all stop and dissembled.

"I say, I am sorry. I really don't mean to sound like a simpleton, but I see I have." He stared at me. "Alicia, I will have you know that I do not put any credence in this silliness of a family curse. My sister met Max when she was quite young, and it seems she insisted from the moment she clamped eyes on the man that she would marry him. She got her wish. Although she was never a raving beauty, she was very pretty and kind and affectionate and generous. And I do believe that in her short, agonizing life, she loved Max more than anyone."

He frowned into his glass and downed a hefty draught. "She died loving him." He looked at me once more. "Max, I do believe, made her a very happy woman. You look to me to be a very level-headed female. So I will now be even bolder than I have been and say here, now, before your betrothed and your brother, that it is my prediction that Max will make you as happy as he made Cynthia."

Grateful for his honesty, I nodded at him. "Thank you, Branford. In the past two weeks, I would say I have come to the same conclusion." I glanced up at Max, who was smiling at me.

"As you can see, Branford, Alicia is an extraordinary woman."

"I wish I could find one as interesting, Max. But few appeal to me. Perhaps you have a sister, Alicia?"

I chuckled. "No, I'm afraid not. I am an only daughter. I do have six brothers."

Thomas grinned into his glass. "And though she was the youngest, she gave us more orders than we cared to have."

I cuffed him on the arm. "Not so!"

"True. True."

Branford centered his attention on Thomas. "Where do you live, sir?"

The question made Thomas once more uneasy, and he glanced at Max before answering. "I work for His Grace. I am foreman at one of his factories in Manchester."

"And very skilled, too," Max affirmed. "I think Thomas and I will be talking soon of a change in his circumstances."

"A head for business, eh, Thomas?" Branford mused. "Good for you, old man. That's something I could never master. Certainly, Max has done well with Cynthia's dowry, doubled it in the first eight years. Right, old man? While I can barely eke out a living from the farms I own. If I had Max's foresight, if I had even turned over my holdings to him to run as he asked me to years ago, I might be rich now. But—"

he raised his glass once more, "I am, as we politely put it, comfortable."

Bigelow appeared at the drawing room door and cleared his throat in his imperious way. "Your Grace, the footmen have settled Mr. Pennington's baggage in his room. The Baron's will take a few more minutes, however, due to the number of preparations we have yet to finish in the men's guest wing. We are prepared, however, to show Mr. Pennington to his room, if he wishes."

Max raised a brow at Thomas.

Thomas rose. "Thank you, but first I wonder if I might have a word with you, Your Grace. I have brought with me the books of the past three months for Number Five, and I'd like to talk with you about the results."

"Very well, let us go into my den. Alicia, Branford, if you'll excuse us? We'll see you at dinner, Branford. Alicia, send Branford up to rest as soon as his room is ready, will you? If he doesn't have his nap after traveling, he is a bear at dinner!"

Branford chuckled. "God forbid I should give you more tensions during the dinner hour than you've already got, eh?"

Max nodded once at Branford and shook his head in familial tolerance. "Good afternoon, Branford. Alicia." And then he and Thomas disappeared.

The man who faced me was less jovial, more circumspect. His merry blue eyes now grew solemn. "Do you love him?"

Such directness was something I should have expected, given the introduction to his relationship with Max. Still, I was struck.

"Yes."

"Thank God." He sighed. "I specifically came to this wedding to see if you did. So few marriages are based on love. Lust, perhaps. Sometimes, lust at best. But that dies. And fortunately, what I have deduced takes its place is tolerance. If one is lucky. How long have you known him?"

I inhaled and kneaded my hands. "Two weeks."

"What?"

"Yes. I know it is not reasonable. But it was a marriage arranged by my father and my grandmother with Max." I then delved into the whole tale of family connections, which then raised the specter of the family curse—which, surprisingly, he avoided.

"Yet you love him."

"Yes. I have come to see him as very kind and wise. A man frustrated . . ."

"Hmm, yes. Frustrated by family tensions you don't understand. I know. I have met the venerable Lady Caroline and her chicks. Why Max tolerates them I will never know. But I conclude he *does* know and won't or can't discuss it. A very dark family, the Wolffs. Interesting that you should be one of them and capable— if one believes in such scourges as curses—of lifting it."

"Like you, I put no credence in it."

He thrust up a hand. "Ho, there! Hear me, Alicia. I put no truck in witch's curses. Food for the foolish, I call it. But I do put faith in facts. And the facts are that the Wolff family has had trouble getting heirs. I daresay the reason that Max is so mad to acquire an heir is simply because Gilbert would inherit if Max died without male issue"

Gilbert would inherit if Max died without male issue. I had never really let that logic permeate my thinking. Gilbert was, of course, the heir presumptive to the Duchy of Worminster. I turned now to Branford with more curiosity than prudence.

"I cannot understand their relationship. But now that you bring this fact to my attention, I wonder . . ."

He snorted. "Wonder nothing, Alicia. These two cousins once cared for each other. Max liked Gilbert's intellect, even had him pegged to take over the shipping end of the family cotton trade. But that was ten years ago, before—" he waved a hand in search of a word, "—before the deluge."

"The deluge?"

Branford checked my eyes. "Poor dear, you've walked into a madhouse, haven't you? And you don't even know it."

He shook his head and tsked.

I waited with halted breath. "Well, I can't illumine you, my dear. Wish I could. Wish I might. Not my job, though. That's up to Max. Only Max knows the truth. Perhaps, yes, probably not all the truth, but enough to make more sense than I would."

He rose and placed his crystal glass upon the carved oak console. He turned and sorrow lined his visage. "Before I go, I must tell you this: I believe Max. I always have. When you hear the story, if you ever brave the wilds of reason to ask it of him, remember that I believed him—and that I have every reason not to."

I clamped my shaking hands together. "Branford, I have no idea what you're talking about."

"Yes, I see that. And I pity you when you learn it."

"Do you imply I should not marry Max until I know this—this secret?"

"Ho, that's far from me to say, my dear. We make our choices in life and we live with the results, don't we? Make your own choices, Alicia. And leave me to my simple existence. I must go up to my room now. It's prepared by now, don't you think? Yes. Yes, well. Until dinner, my dear." He bowed and was gone.

Chapter Eight

I gazed at a large, pale moon drifting across an inky sky. Somewhere in this cavernous house a clock struck two. Today was the day of my marriage to Max, that once dreaded, then once eagerly awaited day. Yet I felt no joy. No anticipation. Only anxiety. And some small shred of fear.

I wrapped my thick quilt robe about my linen nightdress and lolled my head against the wall. For a woman who had only admitted to herself this afternoon that she loved her future husband, I now wondered what so many hinted at that threatened to wound that love in its infancy.

I had no idea. No idea what to think, whom to believe, even where to begin to understand the issues of which few dared speak. I knew only fragments of the past. Fragments called curses and rumors, betrayals and lies.

I knew only that Max had married two women before. That he had loved them both. That both had died. That one, the first, had died in childbirth. And that something which had happened to her was enough to make Branford Southeby warn me of asking questions about it. And certainly, after what Lianne had told me weeks ago about Cynthia and Maribel, that made it difficult enough to broach the subject of their demise without other fuel for the fire. And the upshot was that I was left with half-told tales from everyone, including the indomitable Adair.

I cupped my head in my hands and rubbed my eyes. I felt lightheaded and dizzy, and the hot chocolate Dorcas had brought me had failed to send me to sleep. Torment did that to a person. So I knew that at this pace, I was certain to look absolutely terrible tomorrow, far from the healthy woman Max so valued and Caroline so disparaged.

I walked from the window to the center of my bedroom and paused to admire in the moonlight the dressmaker's figure. Hanging upon it tonight, Lianne had arranged my finished wedding dress. Ivory gossamer silk, the gown was a vision of three-tiered skirts whose hems were edged with quilling of candlelight sarcenet ribbon. Lianne had sent to her shop for the silk and ribbons the night she had arrived. And in the following two weeks, she had slaved over the gown's production with a mother's diligence. She had spared no time or effort or expense to provide me with the very best fabrics, the most fashionable design, the finest handiwork. When I had objected, she'd laughed lightly and shaken her head.

"My dear, it pleases me to do this for you, but also for Max. You see, I owe the man much. When my husband Guy was alive, Max was very generous with his friendship and his time. Guy and Max were old school chums, a brotherhood we English women know little of except to say it is as strong a tie as that of blood brothers. When Guy lost his father, the Comte de Grasse, he lost his estates as well. His father died of a stroke during the Revolution of fortyc-eight when a group stormed his chalet. That revolution destroyed what little was left of the *ancien régime* in France. Afterward, Guy and I left Paris permanently and moved to London and then to the north when Max gave Guy a position in two of his factories. I opened my dressmaking shop and we lived in moderate comfort. Without Max, we would not have been able to do that. So, if I wish to repay old kindnesses with new ones, you will allow me, won't you, my dear? Besides," her eyes twinkled mischievously, "I will find other clients most eager for my skills after they see you. They will credit the gown with the inner beauty you possess and try to equal that." She laughed. "So I will not dissuade them from their imperfect logic. Let me do this for you, won't you?"

So I no longer objected to her dedication. How could I, when I was enchanted with the product? And more delighted with the friendship?

I skimmed my fingertips across the fragile silk bodice and over the delicate fabric lilies-of-the-valley that adorned its center. Suddenly, now, I felt the excitement of becoming Max's wife seep into my soul. Surely, a man as generous, as kind as Max was to so many, was worthy of my meager admiration and devotion.

I stepped to my dressing table and ran my fingers over the square tulle wedding veil and the lilies-of-the-valley which wreathed the crown. My hand shook— and somehow I knew it was not from anticipation. I clasped my hands together to stop the palsy. Determined to see myself in the veil, I lifted it to see myself once more as I would be tomorrow . . . but then I stopped.

Someone was running down the hall, crying. Sobbing.

I flung open my door to find Elizabeth crying and Dorcas right behind her, her fist lifted to knock.

I opened my arms and Elizabeth sank into them, babbling incoherently.

"Dorcas, what in the world is wrong?"

"Oh, ma'am, come, come! The master sent me for you. We need you." She was tugging me down the corridor.

"What—?"

"It's Mary. Mary! She walks the floor. Like the undead! Come with me!"

I bundled Elizabeth more securely to me and scurried as fast as I could toward the nursery wing. When I rounded the door to the twins' bedroom, only two gas lamps lit the interior where Williams stood at the door, anger in her eyes so intense that surely Cerberus at the gates of hell was no match.

She did not greet me, but cast her eyes to the ceiling in a sign of tolerance. "It's only a dream," she bit out. "I don't know why Elizabeth woke her father. I've seen this before."

Before, eh?

I stepped around her.

Gray shadows fell across the spare furnishings. The two dressers. The two trunks. The one almost bare bookcase. The worn braided rug. The two beds of the same small size and linear form. In one corner—the darkest—Max knelt before a tiny mound of wide-eyed, unseeing little girl.

He spoke to her in a whisper, urging her, cajoling her to come with him. But she neither heard him nor cared.

Keeping strong hold of Elizabeth's tiny hand, I knelt by Max's side as he took my other hand and crushed it in misery. My eyes were only for Mary.

"But, sweetheart," Max pleaded with her, "tell me where you are so that I might come to get you."

"In the pit. In the pit," she cried, but no tears fell from her eyes. *"Will* you come for me, Papa?"

"Of course, my dear. Tell me how to find you."

"Down the stairs, Papa."

He swallowed and looked at me. I nodded for him to continue. Whatever her problem, wherever she was, he had entered her fantasy and might yet bring her back to us.

"Don't look—" she suddenly beseeched him. "Don't look!" Her thin voice dwindled to a thread.

"Why?" he whispered. "Why can't I look, my pet?"

"Awful." Her hands flew up to cover her eyes. "Awful. They bleed. They were bad, like me."

"But you're not bad, my dear."

Her little head bobbed in affirmation. "Yes, I am, yes, I am. Oooo, can you get me out, Papa?" Her arms flailed and her legs shot straight out, rigid. "The devil will cook me. You can't get me now . . . here he comes!"

Suddenly, frantically, she pushed at the floor with her feet while her hands thrusted an invisible Satan from her.

Williams, who had come to stand behind us, cleared her throat. "Your Grace, she is having a dream. I tell you, leave her to me."

"Quiet!" he hissed over his shoulder. "Mary, listen to me," he was crooning again. "I am coming down the stairs. Hear me? Hear my footsteps?"

She nodded slowly.

"I want you to tell me how to find you."

"Past the people in Pur'tory."

"Past who?"

"They cry and they tell people not to walk further, Papa. They *do!*"

I leaned forward, my heart pounding. Oh, yes, suddenly I knew where her sleep-drugged mind had taken her. "Past the people in Purgatory?"

"Oooo!" She stomped her feet on the floor and shook her head.

Max gazed at me, appalled.

I shifted to sit beside her. "Those people, darling, can come out. So can you."

I put my hand on her arm, and she did not flinch from me, but frowned in consideration of my words.

"Mary," Max appealed, "here I am." He sat forward on his knees and took her hands. "Come with me."

With the touch of his hands, she dissolved into a gush of tears and threw herself into her father's arms. "Papa. You came. Oh, Papa, you came."

He held her fast as she repeated the litany of her wonder. Max's eyes met mine as he consoled her with soft words and the safe haven of his arms.

Within a minute or two, she was hiccupping and

178

clutching his arms. "Why am I on the floor?" she asked finally, and gazed about her in wonderment.

We all breathed heavily in relief.

Max stood with her in his arms and went to lay her in her bed. But she clutched at his neck and clung to him, her head in his chest. "Noooo!"

"But, my dear, you—"

"Can't stay here. No, Papa, don't make me."

He stroked her hair and cuddled her closer. His eyes sought mine. Triumph, fear, and a plea for help mingled in their limpid gray depths.

I went to brush her hair and help quiet her.

But she was sobbing into his robe, her thin voice a shrill horror. "Papa, I don't care if you are evil. I want to be with you."

My hand paused in midair. My mouth fell open.

Max gaped at me.

Williams stepped forward with outstretched arms. "Sir, I will take her now. She—"

Mary huddled into Max's chest, clearly trying to burrow away from Williams. Max moved aside so that Mary remained out of reach and out of sight of her nurse.

He peered at the woman. "Williams, what is the meaning of this statement from Mary?"

"Your Grace, Mary is highly strung."

He cursed viciously. "If she is, she was educated to become that way."

"No, sir!"

"Oh, yes, Williams. I know my daughters." At that, Elizabeth ran to catch him round the legs. He put one hand to her curls as she hid her face in his robe. "Why does Mary dream of Purgatory, Williams? Why does

179

she dream so forcefully of it she walks in her sleep? I told you the other day that I didn't want you frightening my children.

"Good God, witches and ghouls. Trolls, for pity's sake. And now this. And don't tell me, it is the last governess's fault! I took that explanation months ago, but no longer. What I have seen and heard here shows me the culprit to be you, Miss Williams. And I'll not have another night of it. You are dismissed. Now."

"If it makes you feel holier, throw me out! You'll not win. The Lord God says 'Vengeance is mine.' "

"And mine. Out you go. And I'll do it myself, if I must." He thrust Mary into my arms and put Elizabeth's hand in mine.

And then he stalked her across the expanse of the nursery.

Oh, she gave ground.

But she preened like a peacock and smirked. "I meant to teach them godliness. They're tainted, coming from that woman and you. I was doing the best for them, saving them from the sins of their mother *and* their father!"

"Like hell you were," he snarled. "Get out of my house!" He was hunting her as she eluded him.

"I've never been so happy to leave a house. The house of the Wolff! The ravening Wolffs! With their ravening sin!"

His teeth bared, he lunged for her.

But she was quicker and dodged him. She spun toward the hall, and as she took its length, we could hear her laughing, screaming.

"You're no good! You and that woman! The devil himself, and his witch in wolf's clothing!" She cackled.

180

Max collapsed against the door frame, his face to the molding.

I tried to go to him, but my head spun wildly and my two precious burdens writhed in my arms, pinning me to my spot. Dorcas fell against my back and cried loudly.

At the raised sounds, Max turned to face us. But his long fingers flexed in white anger and his eyes, dark now with violent blood lust, rolled over the walls and appointments.

I stretched out my hand to him not only in supplication, but also in the very need to steady my reeling world. Never had I seen Max so possessed. I wanted him the way I knew him. Strong. Bold. Logical, gentle.

Presently, his visage fell into compassion. He crossed to us to encircle his daughters and me in his arms.

"Williams will really go?" Mary hiccupped, as wide-eyed now as when she had been in the clutches of her nightmare.

"Yes, my darling," Max promised. "She was very wrong to teach you those things."

Elizabeth gazed at her father with wonder. "She said you and our mother were very bad people and that we have to be good to make up for it."

Now Mary rallied. "If she goes, will we be able to become good people without her?"

"You already are good people, my dears."

They didn't believe it and cast sad countenances to the floor.

I could not remain silent any longer. The sight of children in fear of God was a sight I could not tolerate.

"Yes, both of you are very good people," I said.

181

"You did your lessons today, didn't you? And you washed—even under your fingernails and behind your ears? And you were polite to people? And you were courageous. That I know because I saw you both be bold and skate upon the ice again." I hugged them each in turn.

"But Williams says that babies are born bad," Mary offered. "That the devil wants to take them, and that—"

"Williams is wrong about you," I assured them. "Remember that I told you my father was a minister and he always told me that each man and woman must make his or her own way in the world. And so must you both. God would not let small children start with bad marks against them. That wouldn't be fair, would it? And God, as I know him, is very fair, my dears."

For a long moment, they examined my face in a search for truth. I glanced up into Max's eyes and saw unabashed appreciation there. I smiled and kissed each girl's cheek.

"Now, let us put you to bed. You need your rest. We have a wedding here tomorrow."

They clung more tightly to me than ever before.

"Please stay," cried Mary.

"Yes, don't go," demanded Elizabeth.

"My dears," Max was shaking his head, "Miss Alicia needs her rest. She *is* the bride, you know, and—"

They turned huge gray eyes of disappointment on him.

"She can sleep in with me," offered Mary.

"Or on the cot that's tucked under my bed!" cried Elizabeth.

Mary caught my hand and stared at me with tears in her eyes once more. "Please, ma'am."

"Very well. I will stay." I looked up at Max and he tried to smile, but couldn't manage it.

"Good night, then, my dears. Sleep well, all three of you."

"We will," chirped Mary, and I wondered if any of us would manage it.

Manage? I managed little. Elizabeth went off to sleep in a moment, her eyes meeting mine in a smile just before she sank into sweet oblivion. Mary took a bit longer. But with another pat to her hand, she drifted off into a dreamless, deep rest.

My own sleep took much longer. Instead, my mind's eye replayed the scene in the nursery. The indomitable Williams, saving children from the sins of their father. The raging Duke of Worminster, saving his children from a self-righteous nurse and her abuse of their young, delicate minds.

Williams deserved to go in the middle of the night. What she had done to those children was unforgivable. And no justification on earth could truly support such a dastardly effort.

I did not drop a wink until the rays of dawn cast brilliance into the girls' bedroom. Then, I slept until well past ten.

I suppose all three of us would have continued had not Dorcas come to urge us awake. At the sound of her voice, I sat up, blinking and confused. But soon, it all came back to me. The place. The reason. The night's events. The day before me.

183

I had hugged myself in shivering anticipation. Even Dorcas's proffered hot chocolate had done little to warm me or calm me. In fact, my headache ceased, but the floating sensations returned after I downed the liquid. Thankfully, no hand convulsions returned to steal some of the luster from the joy.

Only now, as I gazed about the drawing room crowded with the guests of my wedding and my new husband beside me, did I have the time to consider the import of the occasion.

I was married. Married to a man I loved. Married to a man I knew to be kind, generous, and loving to his friends, his children, and his relatives. Yet his past had been checkered. By two wives who had loved him. By two wives who had died. By his relatives, whom he kept in the finest of styles right here under his own roof. By a nursemaid who taught his children to fear him and ridicule him. The very power of those virtues scoured every vestige of fear from my heart.

I gazed up at my new husband, so tall, so dark, so devastatingly handsome in his wedding attire, and I inhaled in joy that he was finally mine.

Max squeezed my waist. "I am thrilled, wife, to see you smile. I was worried I might never see that glorious look upon your face again."

I cast my eyes lovingly into his. These were his first words to me since he had spoken his vows minutes ago. And it had been painfully clear to me at the beginning of the ceremony that he questioned my health and my resolve to really marry him.

Yes, at my first sight of him standing here in a brilliant black suit with blinding white shirt, I saw him discern my mood in a moment. He was wondering if

I had slept at all, looking at my hands to see if they shook, peering into my eyes to see if they wavered. When he found a bride who looked a little the worse for only a few hours' sleep but who, despite her eerie sensations of floating, was calm and committed to this sacrament, he closed his eyes briefly and then opened them again to slowly smile at me.

As the vicar began the words of the ceremony, Max took my hand in a sturdy grip and then spoke his vows with a solemn resonance that thrilled my vanity and soothed my nerves. He placed a glorious wedding band of thick yellow gold upon my finger and then seized me and kissed me with a brisk fervor that made me gasp. Now, sheer minutes later, he was once more admiring me with that savaging look that never failed to take my breath away.

"It is the excitement." I nodded toward the twenty-odd wedding guests who assembled for the receiving line. "I have received many guests, my lord duke, but never any for my own wedding."

"Tomorrow's crowd will be even more staggering." He took my hand and kissed it lightly. "But you shall endure beautifully."

"You have great confidence in me."

"And why should I not? You survive every trial so well, my dearest. You are a paragon."

"You are too complimentary."

"A husband's right."

I could not suppress a grin. Through every tribulation, Max charmed me. And, like any young woman in love, I adored his courting, his care, his caressing words and deeds. I took them, enjoyed them, and sealed them in a tender corner of my heart where in-

185

nuendos and trepidations could not reach. I cocked a brow at him and twined my arm through his, pressing my breast to his strong body. "A wife's right to enjoy every bit of it. You'll hate it when I become greedy."

He gave me another little hug and cleared his throat. "I could never hate you, my dear. Quite the opposite, I know "

I examined the depths of his silver eyes. He was declaring his love for me? How could that be? A duke in love with a minister's daughter? A woman he barely knew? A woman of little breeding?

Yet the glow in his eyes told me it was possible. My veins filled with fluid desire as quicksilver as his gaze.

"Accept the congratulations of our guests, my darling. And then you and I will excuse ourselves for a wedding supper in my chambers. Or I should say, our chambers."

The joy, the terror of such intimacy made me bold. The first guest came forward, and, unseeing who it really was, I extended my hand and smiled broadly.

I was smiling at Caroline.

As the nearest relative, she, of course, would be the first to offer her best wishes to us. And if I blanched, if I regretted my heartily extended hand, I was astounded to see that she took it with much enthusiasm. Certainly, she took it with much more enthusiasm than I ever expected her capable of.

"Your Grace," she called me, and gave me a deep curtsy of impeccable precision. "Best wishes to you both." She met Max's gaze with forthrightness. "I do hope you will be very happy. Max, you deserve it. And Alicia, I have the distinct impression you will bring it to him."

186

"Why thank you, Caroline," Max was meeting her halfway. "I do appreciate your felicitations."

She turned her accepting eyes to mine. "I have many faults, Alicia, but stupidity is not always among them. I shall contribute to your peaceful life as much as possible. You have only to call on me and I shall comply."

I nodded. "Thank you, Caroline. Max and I are very happy, and we will seek to make everyone in the household that way as well."

"Yes, if last night's episode is any indication, I trust you to weed out the hideous growths in the household."

Max threw her a black look. To refer to the incident at a wedding party was truly bad taste. But then, when had bad taste stopped Caroline?

"I had a feeling something was wrong there. Months ago, I told you, Max, it was not the last governess who was doing the dirty deed of turning your children against you. But you wouldn't listen to me." She saw fury mark Max's brow now, and she skewed herself back up to some more proper plain. "Yes, well, forgive me. I do try for propriety. But I did want to clear my own name because I had interviewed and approved of that last governess, you know."

"Yes, I know," Max bit out. "Now, if you would please avail yourself of the champagne, Caroline, while Alicia and I greet our other guests?" It was no question, but an order.

And for once in her life, she took it. She moved off toward one footman who held a tray of champagne flutes and Max fought for composure.

Beneath his breath, he cursed even as he was smiling at the next in line.

Adair. Adair, who usually looked so defiant, today appeared as accepting as her mother. She smiled and offered her hand, her best wishes, and a curtsy to me. Unlike her mother, though, she said nothing other than the necessary words, and then she, too, sailed toward the same footman her mother had chosen.

Gilbert came next. Leaning upon his cane, he stepped forward and grasped Max's hand with gusto.

"I am very happy for you, Max. Very happy. And you, Alicia, I know you shall bring us all great joy as the next duchess."

"Thank you, Gilbert." I smiled as he leaned over, embraced me with one arm, and kissed my cheek.

Without a backward glance at Max, Gilbert joined his family. Had he looked at Max as I had, he would have seen a man as wildly furious as a parlor's confines permitted.

"Max?"

Through clenched teeth, he enunciated very clearly, "He is not ever to kiss you, do you understand me?"

Stunned, I could not reply instantly.

His eyes captured mine and he shook me by the arm. "Do you?"

"Yes, of course, I—"

"Good." Then, as if he exchanged one mask for another, he smiled at his next guest with an élan that had me utterly perplexed.

"Branford—"

The two men hugged each other.

But when Branford tried to do the same with me, I shrank back. Branford was not dissuaded, and seized me anyway. Stiff as a board, I received his congratulations, and when he moved off, I stood like a statue, afraid of Max's reaction.

He took my hand and gently caressed the palm with his thumb. "Branford is no threat, my dearest."

I stared at Max, and whatever sweet sorrow I saw in his eyes was torn from my vision by the sight of my brother Thomas stepping toward me.

"Alicia?"

I went to his arms in a panic.

He clutched me. "Alicia, what's wrong?" His voice in my ear brought me to sanity.

I shook my head. "Nothing, silly of me, really. I am so glad you could come. It's wonderful to have you, since none of the others could come on such short notice."

He stood back in my arms and glanced from my husband to me. "Yes, sad that Mark couldn't leave his congregation. But Christmas is in four days and he has much to do."

"Yes, yes, I do understand. But I am very pleased you are here. It makes me feel at home."

"Yes, well . . ."

Clearly, Thomas felt ill at ease. His only sister had just married a man who owned the factory he worked in, the Cotton King of the North, one of the richest men in the realm. So far above a minister's family, so different, so rich, and . . .

Suddenly, I glanced about me at the decor, the guests, my gown, my groom, and I felt as out of place as Thomas.

Max watched me and I knew he read my thoughts. He frowned and my heart began to crack like fine glass in a vise. He took my arm.

"Alicia, darling, perhaps you would like to sit down. Forgive us, Thomas, but Alicia had rather a short night's sleep because of a little trauma—"

"Yes, I heard. Mary walks in her sleep."

"I don't wish to sit, Max. I am fine."

"I insist," Max said, and led me a few paces to a fat Queen Anne chair. He leaned over me, and whispered in my ear. "I ask your indulgence, my dear. And I beg your forgiveness for my speaking so bluntly to you. Here," he waved a footman over to us, "take a drink of this. It will calm you."

It was champagne, frothy and cool. I sipped it and closed my eyes. When I opened them once more, Max was hunched before me at eye level. His voice was whisper-soft, but his countenance was just as brooding and forceful.

"We will finish our duties quickly here as bride and groom, my dear. Mary and Elizabeth came to me earlier this afternoon with a lovely surprise for a wedding gift for us, and I would like you to see it before the sun goes down. Then, we will retire." His finger outlined my jaw. He tried to smile and failed. "You need your rest."

I nodded, we stood, and Lianne rushed forward to ascertain if I was recovered. Behind her, the remaining wedding guests lined up, offering congratulations and best wishes. Because they consisted mostly of the household staff, lead by Mrs. Timms and Bigelow, we were done in a matter of minutes.

"Come with me, now, while they're eating and drinking," Max urged, and he gave Bigelow a flash of his eye. Bigelow disappeared, and in seconds, he returned with Max's ebony beaver-trimmed coat and hat and my new silver fox cape.

Max donned his coat and then helped me into the cape, all the while leading me from our chattering guests toward the front door where Hans and Rolf stood guard. Outside, the sleigh awaited us. Then, with a *whoosh*, Max swept me into his arms. He lifted me easily, so easily I felt giddy at the might he displayed.

"Where are we going?" I tried to sound gay as he set me into the plush upholstered seat.

"To see your wedding present from the girls."

Chapter Nine

Max climbed into the sleigh beside me and arranged a blanket around my lap as the two mastiffs took up their posts opposite us.

"What are they doing out here? Why couldn't they put it in the ballroom with the other presents?"

"Hmm," he took up the reins and slapped them once. The horse responded immediately, and off we went through the snowy courtyard over into the woods. "They couldn't put this present on display anywhere but out here."

"Riddles again."

He frowned. He let the horse slow and reached for my hand. "Alicia, about last night, I—I really—"

He shook his head, unable to continue.

I turned to him. The torment on his face made me regret my fear of him. Yes, he was a moody man, but he had suffered so much for so long. Now, I dared to hope that I could make things right for him. Whatever they were.

"Darling Max, I am your wife now. Sworn to uphold you in sickness and in health, in sorrow and in joy, and I wish you would share everything with me."

He grabbed my hand. "I have been unfair to you. Not completely truthful with you, and I said I would be. Letting others eat away at your natural inclination to trust me simply because I would not share with you everything. You must forgive me, though. I had a superlative motive. I wanted you." He mesmerized me with those eyes. "I want you more now. I was afraid if you knew everything there was to know you would run from me in horror."

"That is not possible, my lord."

"No?" He did not believe me and turned away. "Others have."

"I am not others. And I, too, have my motive." I tugged at his sleeve, looked deeply into his eyes and smiled. "You see, I am in love with you."

"Are you, my dearest wife?"

"Totally."

"Papa!"

"Papa! Alicia! Please come over here!"

I could not tear my eyes from his. In those crystaline depths, such sweet torment mixed with such tender joy that I was spellbound.

He placed a gloved forefinger beneath my chin. "I never thought I could care for a woman ever again. But *you,*—my sweet, strong Alicia—you, I adore."

"Papa!"

He outlined my lips with his finger. "Later, I will demonstrate the full meaning of adoration, darling." He threw me a secretive grin and then slowly turned toward the sight of his daughters.

Bundled in warm clothes against the brisk winter

winds, they scampered on the edge of the pond on their ice blades. Without the assistance of me or Williams, they had instead enlisted the aid of a footman, who stood against a tree, one leg propped upon the log we always used as a stool.

"What are the two of them doing, Max?"

"Showing you their progress. They came to me hours ago, begging to do this for you. Let's see how well they've practiced."

He stood and offered me his hand to assist me out of the sleigh.

I climbed down, picking my way across the snow in my new leather shoes and lifting my wedding gown to avoid ruining its hem. The two dogs loped beside me.

But as we came closer, instead of waiting for us, the girls skated toward the middle of the pond.

"How do you like us, Mother?" Elizabeth extended her arms like an angel and sailed smoothly across the ice.

"Papa said we could call you that." Mary grinned as she circled past us.

"It's all right to call you that, isn't it?" Elizabeth asked, as she skated straight for us.

I grinned at her and wished I could hug her. "Yes, of course, it is. I'm thrilled to be your mother."

Max's arms came round me then, and as I leaned back into the comfort he provided, he whispered, "Not as thrilled as I am to have you as my wife."

"Watch us now, Mother!" Mary grinned broadly and began to take long strides with great lunges. She sped away with an ease that astounded me.

"Children learn so quickly," I observed, as I closed

my eyes to feast for one small moment on the giddy sensation of his long, hard body fusing to mine.

"Yes. All the more reason to ascertain exactly what it is they are learning." His hand tightened on my arm. "I could have strangled Williams last night. If she hadn't gone willingly, I think I would have killed her. I am sorry you had to see that."

"I am sorry Mary and Elizabeth had to endure the woman's zealousness. Children have so many hurdles to jump that it's a shame to put more before them."

He cuddled me closer, his breath fanning my cheek. "Now with you, they will have a better life." His body cupped mine as masterfully and securely as a glove.

My arms wrapped over his and I sighed.

He kissed my cheek. "Promise me something, will you, Alicia?"

His severe tone made me turn. "Anything."

"That you will take care of them if anything ever befalls me."

I searched his eyes. "Yes. But nothing will ever befall you, Max."

He stepped back. His eyes took on that haunted look of the night before. He tried to speak, but no words came.

"Darling, are you ill?"

He shook his head.

"Do you not wish to live with me, then?" I was joking, of course.

But he was not laughing.

"Tell me why—?"

He pressed his hand to his coat pocket, and I distinctly heard a paper crinkle there. Another paper? The same as yesterday? No, it could not be. These were his wedding clothes. Unless . . .

I put my hand over his. "Max, tell me what—"

"Papa!"

"Papa! Mama! Look at us!"

Both of us turned toward the pond to find the two girls almost to its center, circling its core.

"Oh, Max!" I walked toward the pond. "They're too far out, Max."

"They're fine, darling."

I didn't believe it, but strode to the edge of the water. With narrowing eyes, I surveyed its surface. Solid blue-white, the ice appeared whole. But I was not convinced.

"I have never taken them out that far to the center. The temperature fluctuates, and the ice could not be as deep as I remember it last week."

The girls were skating so well they glided upon its glistening surface like two overdressed little swans. I had not ever seen them so merry. Not even at the ceremony.

"Girls," I called across the water, "come in."

They shook their dainty heads and giggled.

"Girls!" I stepped onto the pond.

They laughed and continued their figures on the ice.

I spun toward Max. "Make them stop, Max. Please, I—"

The dogs advanced, and I waved them back.

A rumble vibrated the ice beneath me feet. My eyes met Max's. I spun toward the girls.

They had heard it, felt it just as I did. And they had slowed, frowns upon their faces.

"Come in, Mary. Elizabeth, do as I say." I walked smoothly now out to them.

Elizabeth was the first to recover her thought and she gave a few good shoves in my direction.

But Mary stood stark still. Then another rumble resounded in our ears. Her eyes met mine.

"Gently, Mary, gently skate toward me." I took measured steps upon the ice that now trembled with my every move. Behind me, someone's weight cracked the ice. I turned my head. "Go back, Max. You're too heavy. The ice will crack more. You, too, Haskins," I shot a warning look at the footman who had also ventured out in rescue. "Go back to the shore."

"Alicia, I won't leave you to—!"

"Get me a branch of a tree, Max. Scoot it across the surface to me. Yes, yes. That one will do." He had quickly made his way to shore and grabbed up an old tree limb that was as round as my wrist and as long as my legs.

"Slide it to me."

I very gently bent, and when he slid it toward me, his aim sure and true, I seized it and held it aloft. I displayed it to Mary, who now had a look of utter horror frozen upon her little face.

"Whatever you do now, sweetheart, do it slowly and gracefully. The very best skating is required of you now, my pet. Take a step toward me. Yes, that's right. Another. Good. Another."

At each step, I searched the ice around her. In back of her, a long jagged crack snaked its way behind her. To her right, blue water bubbled from beneath the ice's surface. That crack wended its way toward me, and I stepped gingerly to my right to avoid its divisive course.

Separated now by five or more feet of moaning ice and two long right-angled cracks, Mary and I gazed at each other.

"Do not panic, my pet. Come forward, just one more step, and I will extend this limb to you. You will grasp it and never let it go, do you hear me?"

She swallowed more audibly than she spoke. "Yes, ma'am."

An then she tried to take a step, but the ice shattered beneath her foot. She tried another direction and her footing held. Then, she extended her hand to take the end of the limb. In the next moment, she lifted her right foot. But before it ever met the ice, the patch of which she stood trembled and groaned and her face registered shock, despair, anguish—

And she screamed!

I ran forward, but the ice beneath me gave an echoing cry and I too, began to sink.

I put out another foot and felt—somehow—secure. But my ankles met ice-cold water. I panicked and instinct made me lurch in the direction of security. I landed, somehow upright, on a sturdy floe still attached to the shore. I gazed about me in wonder. But my eyes sought Mary, who now still clutched our tree limb.

I flattened myself on the ice and skidded across its slick surface. This way, hand over hand, I could still hold the limb. This way, she saw me coming for her, even as she sank.

"Mary," I was whispering now, "don't let go. Don't fight. Remain still. That's good. I'm coming for you. There, see? Grab my hand. Good. Now come, let me pull you. Don't fight the water. That's right. That's right." And slowly, awkwardly I pulled her from the water. Pulled her from the center toward the shore. Toward her sister and her father and a whimpering footman.

"Get the blanket from the sleigh, Haskins!" Max was yelling as I dragged Mary toward her father's outstretched arms. He caught her close and wrapped her securely against him as Haskins dropped the blanket over the drenched, shivering little figure. From somewhere, the man had found a matching blanket and did the same for me. Max brought me close to him and kissed the top of my head in frantic worry.

"Haskins, help me get them in the sleigh. Here, here, take Mary. It's all right now, my pet. Get into the sleigh with your sister, dear. Alicia," he wrapped me in the lock of his embrace, "give me your cape, darling. We'll get you another."

My heart pounding, I let him do with me as he would. I stared at him, wondering what in the world he was raving about. The only thing that registered was that he was laughing. Laughing, but tears were streaming down his rugged face as he lifted me high into his arms and carried me to the sleigh, the dogs whining at his heels.

My teeth were chattering, out of fear more than cold, and my eyes were only for Mary, who sat wide-eyed and silent, huddled in the plaid wool blanket.

Sitting with Mary on one side and me on the other, Max brought us close and rubbed our arms. Elizabeth clung to her sister. None of us spoke as Haskins the footman took the reins and sped us home through the woods and into the courtyard.

When he ran inside with a stoic Elizabeth in his arms, he emerged in minutes without her but trailed behind him an anguished Bigelow and a hysterical Mrs. Timms.

As Haskins took Mary, Max caught me to his chest and strode inside with me. The wedding guests formed a circle of gasping surprise.

"What happened?"

"Oh my heavens! *She* saved Mary?"

"Good God, look at her gown! She's sopping!"

"My word! No foibles for this Worminster duchess!"

Thomas appeared before me and cupped my face. "Sweetheart, are you all right?"

I nodded.

"She's going to have a bit of a chill, Thomas, if I don't get her up to bed soon." Max elbowed his way past my brother and Branford and the inquisitive servants, all the while shouting orders for hot chocolate and boiling water and dry clothes for the girls and me.

Shocked and still a little speechless, I rested my head against the strength of my husband's shoulder. He smelled of sandalwood and brandy, and instinctively I nestled closer. By the time we'd made the first landing, he was chuckling in relief.

"My darling, I can see you are recovering quickly."

I pressed my lips to his strong jaw. The fact that he was clean-shaven, so unlike his peers, who thought the height of fashion was a full beard, held particular appeal to me. "I'll recover even more quickly with this special attention you give me."

He threw back his head to laugh, then he shouldered open a door. "Your Grace, your chambers." He glanced back over his shoulder and groaned, "And your two faithful bodyguards are close behind, but unfortunately," he kicked the door closed, "unable to join us."

My eyes were all for the chambers. Indeed, my finest fantasies would never have equaled the glory of this room. Pale silver wallpaper, ebony furnishings, and plush black velvet drapes gave the cavernous room an otherwordly eminence. Even the abundance of mirrors and silver fixtures lent the room a brilliance I could never have matched in my dreams.

"Your dressing room is through that doorway," he explained, as he pushed back the crushed black velvet bedhangings to set me down upon the matching counterpane. "Our sitting room is in that direction, and beyond that is my bedroom."

"It's breathtaking."

"Mmmm." He turned me about and began to work at the hooks at the back of my wedding gown. "Not so breathtaking as a great bout with fever will be, if we don't get this wet gown off you."

"Can I assist you, Your Grace?" Dorcas breezed in, carrying a tray with a porcelain pot, one cup, and a saucer.

"No, Dorcas," Max said. "Draw Her Grace a bath, will you? A very hot one. What have you got there?"

"Hot chocolate, milord, Her Grace's favorite."

"Well, bring it here. Alicia, I want you to drink all of it, darling. Then, I want you to steam in a hot tub and rest."

"Mama?"

We three turned to see Mary standing in her nightshift at the door. Her hair was matted to her head, but her eyes were limpid with expectation.

I opened my arms to her. "Mary! Come here, my dear."

She ran like the wind. And then, she buried her face in my throat and squeezed me so hard I thought I'd pop.

"Sweetheart," I stroked her hair back from her forehead, "are you all right?"

She nodded and clutched me harder. "Can I stay with you?"

"Yes, love. You may. Anything to make you happy."

"Mama?"

We turned to the doorway which now held Elizabeth.

I knew what she wanted as well. "Come here, darling." I opened my arms and she ran to me. I looked up at Max. "I think we will all do well to recover together."

But we recovered nothing that night.

Not lost sleep from the terrors of the night before.

Not respite from the horrors of the day.

Not even health.

No. As I lay in my marriage bed that night, I lay between the two girls who were now my daughters. That night, in my grand ducal chambers, without my new husband, I desperately tried to sleep. But fears ran amuck in my brain. And with every sore muscle and bone screaming for release, I could only stare at the ruched canopy of silver above me. Above it all, I tried valiantly to wish away the violent dizziness that rampaged through my brain with the ferocity of a cyclone.

Then, as I lay there mere inches from my girls, I felt them both grow warm. Elizabeth tossed and turned, moaning in her sleep with her malady. Soon Mary began crying and perspiring.

Much like the previous night, she could not see me or hear me. But tonight she had viable physical reasons not to do either. Her eyes were glassy, her cheeks red as cherries. I put my palm to her skin, which had grown as hot and dry as twice-burnt toast.

I stumbled from the broad bed without throwing on my nightrobe. My head reeling, I fell back on the mattress. But I got up and ran through the sitting room and managed to knock on Max's door.

He opened it quickly, his royal blue satin dressing robe tied securely about his waist, his hair combed and neat.

"I couldn't sleep," he told me with a rueful twist to his mouth. "My God," he caught me as I cupped my forehead and began to slide down his body. "Alicia, what's wrong?"

"The girls are ill."

"And so are you, sweetheart." He caught me up and took me to his bed. Very gently, he turned down the counterpane of gold and laid me into cuddly napped sheets. "Darling, what's the matter with you?"

"A wild dizziness. Oh, Max, see to Mary and Elizabeth. They both have fevers. I wanted to ring the bellpull for Dorcas. Get some help, please."

"But you—"

"Don't worry about me, Max. Go."

Chapter Ten

I sat before my dressing table and ran my hands across the décolletage of the creation Lianne had made especially for me for this occasion.

A deep green brilliantine lined with pale blue crepe overskirt and capelet, the ballgown made me feel more like a duchess than anything else had thus far. The wide collar fell off the points of my shoulders with just the right tension to keep the gown modestly on me while exposing the most pale skin to everyone's view. Dorcas, who had dressed my hair in hot iron finger curls, had done a noble job of matching the gown's color by inserting dyed blue bird-of-paradise feathers into the back crown of my hair.

I loved the effect because never in my life had I ever thought to look like such a grand lady. A duchess. The willing mate to His Grace, the Duke of Worminster. The idea appealed to me. But the fact—ah, yes, the *fact*—appealed to me more.

"I would predict you are the loveliest woman at the reception and ball, Duchess."

I swirled to find Max lounging against the door

frame to my bedroom. With his hands stuck into his trouser pockets, he seemed lighthearted and charming. The way I preferred to see him. The way I'd seen him only a few times, the last of which was before the girls' accident yesterday.

I laughed and twirled about. "You do like it?"

"No."

"No?"

He strode past my two sentinels Rolf and Hans and all the while, his silver eyes darted over me like bolts of lightning. "I like *you* in it." He caught me around the waist and let his eyes travel the line of the bodice across my rising breasts.

I grinned in nerve-ripened satisfaction. "Well, then, my lord, I think you didn't pay Lianne enough."

He cocked a brow. "I think I've created a fiend!"

"You'll probably discover I eat too much as well and I'll grow fat . . ."

He was tsking.

". . . and ugly . . ."

He was nodding.

". . . and demanding."

"Of what?"

"Money. Jewels."

"What kind?"

"What kind? How should I know? Diamonds! Rubies!"

"Emeralds?"

"They'll do."

"Will these?"

He pulled from his trouser pocket a strand of sparkling green gems alternating with blue-white ones. Each was a perfectly cut square in a silver link.

I put one finger to a stone. "Oh, Max . . ."

"You like them."

I swallowed as he handed the necklace into my keeping. "I hate them."

He let his head fall back and roared. "But you'll wear them anyway."

"If only to make you feel wonderful." I walked to the mirror with them and sat down. I draped the jewels around my neck and held each end out for him as my eyes caught his in the mirror. "Come secure the clasp."

He grinned and took the two steps to my side. He bent and I watched him. So devilishly handsome in a white stock and berry-red waistcoat topped with black satin evening suit. So endearingly solicitous as he had been all last night, helping Dorcas and me with the girls. So much man. So much my man.

I tingled as his body drew nearer. I vibrated as his warm hands to my nape made me close my eyes. As his soft lips to my shoulder made me tilt my head back against his taut torso. As his gentle fingers turned my face up and made me offer my mouth to him. As he took it.

Lavishly.

Hungrily.

Repeatedly.

"Madam," he was breathing heavily as he tore his mouth from mine, "I regret to say we have guests."

I sank back against him and sighed. "Two hundred?"

"And twenty-eight, to be precise."

I smiled slowly and sought his eyes in the mirror. "A full evening's festivities."

"God help us all." He grabbed my hand and tugged me up.

"Wait! Wait! My fan and gloves." I seized them as we passed the chair where Dorcas had laid them.

"I'm amazed you don't want to take these two buggers with you as well!" He eyed Rolf and Hans who stood and stretched as we passed them.

"They'll stay here tonight," I told him and them at the same time.

Max gave me his arm and we made our way to the stairs. "I looked in on Elizabeth and Mary before I came to your room. Elizabeth had some broth and tea for dinner, and her fever seems gone. But Mary's remains."

"Hopefully, tonight it will break."

"Yes. I want to see you rest properly, too." He squeezed my hand. "How are the dizziness and headache?"

"The only reason I'm dizzy now is because you are near me," I assured him. "But the headaches get worse, it seems, just before bedtime."

"Why would that be?"

I shrugged.

"You've never had problems like this before?"

"I told you, I was very healthy, Max. The floating sensation could be a reaction to all the changes in my life recently. And the headaches may be the same. I hope so. I always thought they were for . . . well, I always thought they were for frivolous women who had nothing else to do with their days except . . ."

"Except?"

"Dote on themselves."

He laughed. "I agree. However, in your case, I fear something else."

"Oh? What might that be?"

Now at the entrance to the Worminster grand ballroom, he paused and looked deeply into my eyes. "Some terrible malady that may take you from me."

I wanted to say "Don't be ridiculous, Max." But I couldn't. I stood before a man who had lost two wives. Each in her youth. And he had loved them. And though he had not yet declared his total affection for me, he had cared for me enough to court me and marry me. Enough now to express concern for my health. I could not repay that with some vacuous dismissal of his fear. Especially when I myself could not dismiss the symptoms.

Instead, I reached up to place a kiss upon his cheek. "My darling husband, nothing will take me from you."

He shuddered and cupped my cheek in his palm. "And no one."

"Now or ever."

"I think it's time we celebrated with a little dancing, don't you?"

"I don't dance well, sir, I warn you."

"Surely a waltz?"

"I'll try. I've waltzed only a few times. I haven't had the practice, and I don't mean to shame you."

"My dear, don't you know I chose you because you could never shame me?"

He was opening one of the double doors to the ballroom, and I was frowning at him. Meanwhile, the question that hung in my mind disappeared as Bigelow

208

came forward to take us to our stations before the massive white marble fireplace.

Here, the family milled about waiting for Max and me to appear. Here, at the far end of the ballroom, whose walls were adorned with sculpted gilt angels and Louis the Fourteenth candle wall sconces and whose radiance was refracted in the thousand tiny crystals of the pendulous baroque chandeliers, the tenants of the Worminster duchy gathered waiting for the master to announce his new wife. Here, old and young alike, rich and poor, elderly hunchback and perfect newborn baby, collected to have their annual chat with the man who held their welfare in his hands.

My husband. And my master. Never had that come home to me as much as it did now. Never had I thought to accept any man as my master. Never had I thought to marry anyone, except perhaps jolly Edward Perry, an army man, a solicitor's son, a man with few expectations and fewer prospects. And yet suddenly, almost inexplicably, here I stood next to Maximilian George Dumont Wolff, the sixth Duke of Worminster. And I was his bride.

I looked down the row of guests waiting to be received and smiled in abject pleasure.

So they came, in no particular order and no set scheme. The miller and his painfully thin wife. The farrier from the village where Max had his horses shod. The butcher, his second wife, and their bawling baby son. The costermonger, who lived in Wolffson and came to the kitchen door each morning with fresh mussels and cod.

"Yes, mum! I comes ever' mornin'. Ask ol' Cook. With fish as fresh as if they was wigglin'!" he bellowed at us with a black-toothed grin. "Aye woun't sell ye anything rotten, I woun't! Not ol' Marty, 'ere. No, sir."

"I'm sure of it," Max grinned, and pressed the usual seigneur's yuletide gift of a gold piece into the coster-monger's palm.

He moved on to be replaced by a plump, kindly looking gray-haired woman who gazed up into my eyes with strident curiosity. Max took one look at her and froze. Yet he introduced her to me with the same kindness as any other.

"My dear, this is Hannah Mead. Also a resident of Wolffson."

"All my forty-two years, Your Grace." She curtsied, never taking her black eyes from mine. "You are pretty, you are. Jus' like the other two." She winked at me and leaned close, so that I knew she had imbibed more of the punch than the average woman. "You look strappin', though. I hope you'll be callin' for me soon, lass."

I didn't have to look at Max to know that whatever her full meaning, he was furious. Diplomatically, he bent down to speak in a rigid undertone. "We'll let you know if we need you, Hannah."

She winked at me again. "I think it'll be soon, eh? Nine months to the day?" She chuckled so that her whole body shook like set custard. "I'm the midwife, lassie. All the girls call for me."

I smiled politely. "If we need your services—"

"Oh, you'll be needin' me, Duchess. I could wager two whole quid on it. Your husband is a ripe one, he is."

"Thank you, Hannah," Max pressed the sovereign

into her hand and indicated with a nod that she should move on.

But whatever alcohol she had consumed in the punch made her bolder. "It's the curse that does the duchesses of Worminster in, ain't it, Your Grace? Not me. I'm good, I am. What happened to the first duchess wasn't my fault, was it, Your Grace?"

He was shaking his head, eyes to the floor. "Hannah—"

"Oh, I know, sir, ye've no wish to remember that night. But I do. Plain as I remember today. And you, my lady, from the looks of ye, you'll not have the problem she had. I bet even Doctor Quentin would say it if he were here tonight to look at you. No, ma'am," her dark eyes twinkled. "You're too healthy and too wise to let another wom—"

"Hannah!" Max bit out. "Why don't you go have another round at the table?"

She jumped at his bark. "Yes, sir. Sorry, sir." With one quick grin from her copious mouth, she curtsied and gamboled toward the long supper table at the far end of the room.

I examined Max as completely as a doctor might. He avoided my eyes. Avoided the topic. Indeed, he raked his silver shock of hair and looked so disturbed that I was positive he considered abandoning me to perform the Yuletide duties of the duchy alone.

Instead, we stood for almost three more hours, receiving our guests and mingling with them. And I enjoyed it, learning names and occupations and hopes and dreams. Learning of the collective past of the Duchy of Worminster. Learning how they revered their dukes, honored them. And how Max seemed to be different from the previous duke, his father. How Max was more generous, the gold Yuletide sovereign being just one gift he gave them. How Max was more devoted a landowner, his knowledge of farming extending to breeding animals and improving the quality of soils. How Max had already had two wives, while the usual Worminster duke took only one. How Max hated this topic and would make some excuse to take me on to another group of people whenever someone spoke of his first or second duchess. And how the guest, male or female, young or old, would examine me with narrowed gazes or fretful mutterings or soulful sighs.

Gratefully, I welcomed the opportunity to open the dancing. But even that went badly. Max held me indifferently, his eyes everywhere but in mine. We made a graceful picture, I'm sure, but not exactly a happy one. As soon as the others took the floor, we left it to mingle a little more.

Hours later, I hailed the end of the festivities. As the last of them drifted from the ballroom, I saw Max make his way once more to my side and offer his arm.

"Thank God, that's finished. You look exhausted."

I arched my back and sighed. "I am. I want to take a look in at the girls, and then I'll have my hot chocolate."

Stoically, he led me up the stairs and around toward the nursery wing. I knew his thoughts centered on the midwife's talk. She had spoiled the evening for us both. I could tell when he had taken me out to begin the waltz and his hands had held me with all perfection but no intimate care. I could tell now by his rigid body, his set mouth, his unseeing eyes. And I acknowledged that somehow, the fragments of the past that had been

212

revealed tonight cut into our relationship more, tearing us from each other and the joy we'd experienced briefly before the reception. Desirous of more joy, I could not broach the very subject that threatened to rip us further apart.

I let him open the door to the girls' bedroom and preceded him inside.

The two girls occupied their respective beds. And though Elizabeth slept, Mary stared wide-eyed at the ceiling, while the upstairs maid who now tended them wiped her brow with a cloth from a water basin.

I hastened to the maid's side. "Nora, how is she?"

"Worse, Mum. She's coughin' and burnin' up, she is."

I felt her forehead. "My God, strip those blankets from her. Get me rubbing alcohol, Nora."

"But mum, yer gown!"

"Get me a robe or an apron. Now."

"Yes, mum." She curtsied and scurried off.

"Shall I get Doctor Quentin, Alicia?" Max was helping me strip the blankets from his daughter. "He is tending a patient in the village, from what a few told me tonight."

"Yes. I'd feel better if a doctor looked at her, although I fear it's pneumonia now, and what he could do, so can I."

Elizabeth struggled to sit up and rubbed her eyes. "What's wrong?"

"Your sister's very sick, darling. Would you like to sleep in my bed?"

"Mary'll be all right, won't she?" Elizabeth looked from me to her father.

"Yes, my love," Max assured her. "She caught cold

213

when she fell into the ice yesterday. We'll make her better. For Christmas.'' He wrapped her into her quilted velvet robe and then gathered her into his arms. ''You can sleep, and Alicia and I will make Mary better.''

''Promise?'' she circled her arms around his neck.

''I promise. Now kiss your mother goodnight and I'll tuck you into her bed.'' Elizabeth pecked me on the cheek and with one searing look into my eyes, Max left me to tend to his other daughter.

But tending her and curing her were two different things. Tend her I did. All night. Through a fever that made her delirious and rosy as any vermilion flower from Max's conservatory. Through alcohol baths that cooled her and shivering bouts that rocked her. Through torment with Max pacing back and forth, anxiously glancing from me to his daughter and fighting the need to speak of the events of the reception. Through hours when the doctor did not appear because his patient in the village was dying. Through hours with Nora running to and fro for clean cloths, dry night clothes, and fresh bed linens. 'Til dawn, when Mary sank back against her pillows, cool to the touch, peaceful and sweetly smiling in her sleep.

I sank into a chair and my head fell back.

Max was beside me in a moment, his fingers combing my straggling hair back from my brow. ''Would you like some breakfast? Your usual hot chocolate?''

I had forgotten about it. Forgotten everything, along with my exhaustion. ''No, thank you. I think I'll just go to bed.''

He stood, and when I did, he scooped me up into

214

his arms. Still avoiding my eyes, he made his way down the corridor. "How's your headache?"

"I don't have one."

"Amazing. You've been up all night and no sign of one?"

I shook my head. "When we came up, I had one, but it disappeared hours before dawn." I hated being held so close and being spoken too so matter-of-factly. "Really, Max, I can walk, you know."

"I know."

"I must be rather heavy."

"Not really."

This pointless blather made me eager to have the whole subject out in the open.

"Max, we must talk."

"Wait—" He passed my bedroom door to our chambers and then opened his own. Shouldering his door closed behind us, he strode across its regal length.

My recollections of the night before had been dimmed by the violent dizziness and headache and by the fear for the girls' health. But now the sight that met my eyes confirmed my impressions of the night before. This was no mean room.

Gold and white, the ducal chamber of the sixth master of Worminster sparkled more vibrantly than my imagination of heaven's hallowed halls. Just as the duchess's chambers shimmered in silver, this was its full complement. A ducal palace meant for the pleasure of the lord.

Max set me down on one chaise lounge of cream brocade trimmed in gold braid. I watched him as he left me to go toward a large cabinet, extract two tiny liqueur glasses, and pour two drams in each. He returned to me, one hand outstretched with his offering.

"Take this, it will help you sleep."

I shook my head, my eyes in his.

"Stubborn woman." He tried to smile and failed. Then he took a draught of his own liqueur.

"Max, what did the midwife mean when she said those things?"

"She tended Cynthia at a few of her lyings-in."

"A few? You mean to say, Cynthia had more than one child?"

"So, someone has told you stories already, have they?"

He whirled away so that I could not see his face. But I knew what was written there. Anger. And was there also fear?

He stood before two French doors whose drapes had never been drawn against last night's bitter winds.

"As my wife, you deserve to know some things from my lips," he declared. Then he took another drink and inhaled deeply. "Cynthia was so delicate that she was often brought to bed with birthing pangs before full term. She would lose the babies, always. I told you that." He swallowed back some painful thought.

"Cynthia brought only one child to term. A boy. He lived only a little while. Only a few hours. If he had lived to this day, so much would be different. So much would be simpler."

"What? What would be simpler, Max?"

He rounded on me, wild with a furor that fired his eyes to Vulcan's rays. "Cynthia would not be dead. I'm sure of it. I never would have been tempted to marry again. You would not be here. You and I never would have met. There would have been no need." He thrust the liqueur glass down with such a jolt I thought it would crack upon the wooden console. "I would have had a son, and there would be no need for you and me to try to create one."

I hated to know more, yet I had to. "Why does the midwife—?"

He stole my thoughts and my words. "Why does the midwife think you'll need her services soon?"

He laughed wickedly.

My skin crawled.

"Didn't you hear Williams the other night? I am the very devil himself." His eyes blazed. "The devil, with all manner of evil at my command."

He came forward and crushed me to his chest, placed his hot mouth on mine, and showed me heaven and hell in one kiss.

I gazed at him through a haze of desire and moaned for more.

He complied and his mouth went for my breast. But as his wet tongue drew a moist path across the swell, he stopped and thrust me from him.

I rocked on my heels.

He strode the room like a madman.

"My God!" he railed. "To think I could have married a woman who didn't know about me! Didn't ask! Who trusts me for what she *sees* and *feels* I am. Your marvelous *instinct!*" He raked his hair and spun like a dervish.

"Ahh, sweet Christ, Alicia. You undo me, sweetheart. I thought I could marry you for simple reasons, dynastic reasons. Offer you the Dower House for the simple favor of a son. Now I find I am hopelessly in love with you and I want you for yourself, not for any son you'd bear me. And I can't bear to have you or your feelings in peril. Can't bear you to know the very thing that would make you run from me."

He loved me?

I stood with my mouth open, my heart pounding. I went to him.

"Max, I am your wife. You may tell me anything, my husband. Anything, and I am still yours."

He twirled to face me, his eyes ravaged with the torment of the damned. "No."

I reared back. "No? You won't tell me?"

"No. I won't chance it." He had me by the arms, his fingers digging into my skin with an animal's ferocity. "You are mine. And you will remain mine. Until our bargain is complete and you bear me a son. Then," he smiled ferally, "then you may ask me anything you want about Cynthia or her successor. Anything, and I will answer. Until then, you are mine. Mine, blindly. Mine, completely. And I forbid you to ask *anyone*, including me—most especially *me*, about my past. Do you hear me? Do you?"

How could I not?

More frightening still, how could I do as he wished?

Chapter Eleven

I did not ask. Not him nor anyone else. Yet the need to know haunted my every move, my every deed. Worst of all, it cast a spell between Max and me that darkened our nascent love for each other.

He avoided more than my eyes now. He avoided conversation and—if I were really looking for worse—I could say he sometimes avoided me altogether. Taking his breakfast earlier than the usual seven, visiting the recuperating girls at hours when I was at my bath or reviewing menus with Mrs. Timms. Retiring early and alone to his room with only a chaste kiss to my cheek. Yes, he left me to my own company.

I was miserable.

In mind and heart and body.

I had no one to confide in, either. Lianne had left the morning after the reception. Her business, she declared, had endured without her this long, but could no longer. And so she departed with a special hope that the girls might recover quickly so that our holiday season might be bright.

"The girls need some joy, Alicia. But Max needs it more," she said, and kissed me goodbye.

But try though I might, I could not give it to him because my dizziness and headaches intensified. They ruined Christmas morning for me, though Max had bought me a cashmere stole of such elegant weaving that I could only hug him and murmur my thanks. Ruined my help of Mrs. Timms with the annual servants' party for New Year's Eve. Destroyed Max's and my most pleasant hour together New Year's Eve, when I had to cut short yet another intimate supper because I could not bear the blinding pounding in my brain.

Disappointed because I thought this supper in our sitting room might be the right occasion for me to make amends to Max, I had to rise from the table, one trembling hand to my forehead.

"Forgive me, Max. I can't go on."

He had caught my arm and swept me close to kiss my temple and stroke my hair. "Darling, I wish I could take these episodes from you. They're getting worse, aren't they?"

"Yes, and now, I am often breathless, too." I clutched at the lapels of his dressing gown and inhaled the power of his manly scent. "I am sorry, Max. I had hoped—"

"I know, my love," he said ruefully. "I had hoped as well. However," he led me into my room and assisted me into my bed, "that will come in time. For now, I want you well. I'll ring for Dorcas."

But Dorcas never came.

Mrs. Timms did instead.

Kneading her hands and showing traces of tears on her cheeks, she told us that Dorcas could not come.

Instead, at that moment, Dorcas lay sprawled in the servants' hall on the floor, a victim of a slippery floor and a little too much New Year's cheer.

"She's screaming something terrible, Your Grace, and I wonder if I might send for Doctor Quentin. It's her leg. From the way it juts out at an odd angle, it's very broken, I fear."

"Do send for Quentin. I'd like him to see Her Grace as well."

I started to object, but then went quiet. Perhaps I did need to see someone. Perhaps I was wrong and there was more amiss with me than a change of residence, family, and routine. Perhaps the terrible pains weren't going to disappear as mysteriously as they'd come.

Mrs. Timms eyed me with increased concern. "Are your troubles back, Your Grace?"

"I'm afraid so, Mrs. Timms. Your compresses have been wonderful, but the relief lasts for only a little while."

Lines appeared on her round face, marring its usual jovial nature. "You must not worry, ma'am. There can be many explanations for your maladies." Her face spread in a consoling grin. "Many delightful explanations."

I smiled at her. Good Mrs. Timms was trying to imply I might be with child. "Yes, thank you, Mrs. Timms. How right you are."

When she left, Max turned to me with a tight grin. "Timms is always the optimist. Would that she were right, darling, and you did have another reason for these infernal problems." He bent to place a kiss on my nose. "But that will come. Tonight, we'll get

221

Quentin in here to set you straight." He squeezed my hand. "Now, close your eyes and go to sleep if you can."

"You'll stay with me?"

"Absolutely."

In minutes, Nora arrived. Nora, the upstairs maid on whom we now relied to help with the children, took one look at me and muttered to herself, then turned on her heel and left. She reappeared with a pot of tea, hot compresses, and the latest news that Dorcas had ceased her screaming and was more comfortable in her own bed, awaiting the arrival of the doctor.

While I tossed and turned upon my bed, Nora went back below stairs to join the others for the end of their festivities. Hours later, as my headache lost its virulence, the village doctor arrived.

Quentin was a tall, thin, gray man. Overworked, overanxious, overzealous for his patients, he squinted at me through red-rimmed eyes.

"How do you do, Your Grace." He did not bow, but came and shook my hand and then Max's. "I shall help you as much as I can. Tell me what ails you, ma'am."

I was as detailed as I could be. He was as thorough as I'd ever heard a doctor be. I was pleased, even if he was not.

He frowned and scratched his trim gray beard. "Your afflictions sound like nervous disorders to me, ma'am. I could prescribe laudanum."

"Doctor, I know laudanum is the usual remedy, but frankly, I've seen more women get worse after taking it. I am not inclined to believe it works. Instead, I'll take fresh air and sunshine."

"Hmm. Well, unfortunately, madam, you'll not see fresh warm air and sunshine for another five months. What will you do in the meantime? Allow yourself to become worse?"

I sighed. He handed me a small blue vial from his black bag and I took it.

"Thank you, Doctor." I smiled in reassurance, but silently reaffirmed my own intention never to unplug the stopper.

I watched him go and sank back against my pillows. Max came to take my hand.

"Go to bed, darling. I am fine."

"You'll take a draught of that?"

I smiled, unable to bring myself to a lie.

He kissed my forehead and retired alone to his suite once again while I grieved for another opportunity denied me.

I did not grieve for long, however. I could not.

Two mornings later, Max received a messenger from Thomas at the Number Five Factory in Manchester. A fire had swept through the building the previous night and the damage was almost complete. Thomas, who knew how to rebuild a schedule or restore confidence, pleaded for Max to come to the city. Within the hour, Max kissed me goodbye and told me to recover quickly.

Amazingly, I did. Oh, yes, that first day, the dizziness was gone and no hand convulsions disrupted my peace. By the next day, the headaches had disappeared. But in their place came a more dreaded malady: vicious stomach cramps. Like nothing I had ever known. So powerful, so debilitating that I doubled over in my bed and softly cried into my pillow.

Nora had no idea what to do to ease my pain. I—for all my experience with illnesses—could suggest nothing.

"It's as if ye had a hex on ye, mum," Nora grumbled, as she wiped my brow.

"I don't believe in the family curse, Nora. Whatever is wrong with me has an explanation."

"Oh, I just said it seems like a hex. But it ain't. These aches and shakes ye've got, they're just like me sister's mistress, who died of poisoning."

I stared at her.

"Yes, she did, mum. Drank too much o' that laudanum, she did."

"But I don't take laudanum." I refused to take it even though I hid the vial under my mattress and poured a little of the bitter-smelling stuff into my washbasin each morning just so its contents might decline.

"I didn't think you were that kind, ma'am. Still, your shakes and dizzy spells are a sign you did drink it, and the stomach pains are a sign you're not drinking it now."

Cold fear crippled my reason. I rose up while she patted the pillows behind me. Then I sank back as I pondered my condition.

The absurd idea set my mind racing. Anything—absolutely *anything*—was possible. I had certainly learned that at my father's knee. But this—this attempt to hurt me, even kill me—was it probable?

I had eaten with the others. I had always eaten with the others. I took food from the same platters and serving trays, morning, noon, and night. Except for one time, just one time during the day when my needs were served separately. When Dorcas brought me my hot chocolate. Dorcas . . .

Dorcas had always seemed so agreeable. So reliable. So caring of my person. Especially since we'd come to congenial terms with each other after that first horrible incident over Maribel's gown. Why would Dorcas wish to hurt me? Unless Dorcas had some motive I knew nothing of . . . some long-held grudge. How could I discover what that reason might be without being obvious and giving Nora or anyone else facts to deduce my cause?

"Does everyone know I have convulsions and dizziness, Nora?"

"Oh, yes, mum. Dorcas told us."

Dorcas again.

"And do they think I take laudanum?"

"Well, mum, most ladies do. But I know you don't."

I smiled at her. "And have you let that be known among your friends below stairs, Nora?"

She blushed.

"Come, come, Nora. I know servants talk among themselves."

"Yes, mum, they do. And—I did tell them that you are a strong lady and have no need of such mixtures as laudanum. 'Let the Duchesses Cynthia and Maribel take it,' I said to them, 'but I know the Duchess Alicia wouldn't touch it.' "

My God, the other two had taken it. For reasons Nora thought normal. But were they normal reasons? And if they were not, who'd acquired the drug, and who had administered it? And why?

I had to know. But more important, I had to be careful.

"You've been a very good nurse. Thank you, Nora."

She curtsied and left me to my thoughts.

Thank you very much, Nora.

That afternoon, the stomach pains subsided and I rallied to dress for dinner. My two canine shadows and I looked in on the girls, who had recovered beautifully. Leaving Rolf and Hans to amuse the girls, I descended the master staircase just as Branford rounded the top landing.

"Ho, Alicia! By Jove, it's grand to see you up and about." He took the last few steps between us to grasp my hand in his and kiss it lightly. "Awful about those maladies, my dear. Glad they're better."

"Hmm. Gone, in fact."

"Really? Well, I say, that's wonderful." He looped my hand through his arm. "I get to escort the loveliest lady in the house to dinner, then. Missed you at table, you know. I have enjoyed the library and the stables, even if Max has not been here to squire me about this time."

"You have visited often here, haven't you, Branford?"

"Yes, and damn good host our Max is, too." We made the foyer now and headed toward the dining room. "Good table, good conversation. Good man, your husband."

"Yes, I thought so."

He harumphed. "Some don't."

We were about to enter the dining room and I put my hand to his. "Branford, tell me something, please. Did your sister—" Gad, this was outlandish! But I had to know.

"Did Cynthia what?"

"Die peacefully?"

He sucked in air. "Who told you she didn't?"

"No one. But I wonder, did she take any medication? Or some other preparation from an apothecary, perhaps? Some restorative?"

He eyed me unmercifully.

I could not stop what I had begun. "Did she perhaps suffer from dizzy spells?"

"Yes. She did."

"And Maribel? Do you know if she did, too?"

"Yes, Maribel was our cousin, and like the other women in our family, she had them, too."

Despite his acceptance of the headaches as a family trait, the affirmation that both drank laudanum petrified my soul.

Branford put one hand to my elbow. "What are you saying? That you wonder if all three of you have the same malady? But you are not a Southeby. You're a Wolff!"

"My reasoning ran more to the issue of how they acquired the laudanum and why they died."

"How does anyone acquire the drug? Through a doctor or a medicinal shop. Most ladies send out their maids, who discreetly fetch a tiny vial of the stuff. But neither Cynthia nor Maribel died of opium addiction. Surely you know that by now?"

"No, no one tells me anything, Branford. And I haven't asked."

227

He tipped up my chin and his eyes roamed over my face in sweet compassion. "Listen to me, Alicia. Cynthia had headaches because she *always* had headaches! She had everything. She was sickly. Maribel did whatever was fashionable, and taking laudanum is becoming distressingly fashionable among women. I have no idea how or why you have your headaches, but one symptom does not a conspiracy make. As for why the two women died, it's not a subject for delicate ears."

"Branford, my ears are not delicate. I am sturdy stock, no hothouse flower."

"I should never have opened the subject with you."

"You are always leaving me with half-told tales and caveats, Branford."

"I leave you with what my heart says I can give you and what society says I should. Ask your husband what facts you miss."

"I can't."

"I know and I fear you risk sanity to ask."

"I fear I have lost sanity already, Branford. Now, what I fear is losing things far dearer, such as my husband and my life. And that I will not do. Tell me why Cynthia and Maribel died, Branford."

He shook his head and flexed his shoulders. Some wild emotion made him tremble. "Both died immediately after childbirth."

I stared at him.

He raised his eyes to the ceiling. "The curse on the Wolffs came home with a vengeance to this sixth Duke of Worminster. Not only has he had great difficulty conceiving an heir, he had seen little success in birthing one. Cynthia died hours after the birth of a sickly little boy. Maribel died after what appeared to be a fairly easy birth of twin girls. The villagers say . . . well, they say it is the curse. Whatever was responsible for their deaths, perhaps only God Himself knows. I avoid the gossip. I suggest you do, too.''

I had my answers; still, none of them made much sense. They created in my heart only more fear.

I straightened the skirt of my pink silk moiré gown. ''Since you have helped me as much as you can, Branford, let us go in to dinner. I am suddenly very hungry.''

But dinner brought me nothing but the usual tension.

Adair was as cool as custard, just as before, while Gilbert wobbled in his chair, quite pickled.

Caroline, ever changeable, greeted me with a warmth I would never have predicted.

''I am so glad you feel better, Alicia. I worried over your condition.''

''Thank you, Caroline,'' I told her, as I took my seat at the head of the table. ''It was a passing thing, as you see.''

''Yes. I'd hate to think Max's third wife would suffer from the very same condition that afflicted his first two.''

To my right, Branford stiffened.

I fought hard to appear serene. ''Cynthia and Maribel had similar problems?''

''Oh, my, yes.''

Gilbert leaned both elbows on the table and grinned at me lopsidedly. ''Cynthia had every malady there ever was. But lovely Maribel had every one that suited her.'' He cast a glance at Branford. ''Forgive me, old man, but you know it's true.''

Branford nodded slowly, fear vivid in his blue eyes.

The three footmen hurried about, serving us our soup. Aware of them, I refrained from becoming too frank and chose another route to my goal.

"Well, I intend to have no more maladies, fashionable or not."

Adair sniffed. "Formidable of you, Alicia."

Gilbert waved a spoon. "Bravo, Alicia! Determination will win the day. Maribel said the same thing, of course. But she was not half as strong or smart as you."

Adair smirked. "Gilbert, Maribel was not smart. She was wily."

Wily? I frowned at her.

But she turned on her brother with a harpy's vengeance. "If you had kept your thoughts to yourself then, she would still be alive today."

"Children!" Caroline thundered, "stop this! Branford and Alicia have no need to hear this silliness."

"Well, Gilbert has no need to get so sodden, either, Mother."

"I'll do as I damn well please. After all, it's Max's liquor, Max's money I'm drinking up. There's a certain satisfaction in that, wouldn't you say, sister dear?"

"Gilbert!"

"Shut up, Mother! Or would you prefer, *Mater* dear, to have your lovely daughter Adair soaking up the money? Yes, yes. That's the nub, isn't it?" He laughed so hard he had to hold his stomach. "Ho, ho, forgive me," tears watered in his eyes, "I must retire. Not interested in food, anyway."

He stood and shuffled his way to the door.

Caroline snorted, then looked to me and Branford.

"I beg your forgiveness. Gilbert's drinking becomes more of a problem each day."

"The best thing for him would to be put away," muttered his sister. "Far away, where he can't get to liquor."

"Abstinence helps sometimes," I said. "A little understanding helps more. My father worked with men who needed to learn temperance. Learning is very hard for some. Sometimes they drink to forget an incident they recall with shame."

Adair and Caroline checked each other's eyes across the dining room table. Silence was their pact.

I was not deterred, but left the subject hoping we might hit upon another that cracked open the secrets of the house.

But the interminable evening offered me nothing.

I retired to my room and donned the ivory silk nightgown and peignoir Lianne had made for me but which I had never worn. Tonight I longed for my husband. I wanted him, not only because I felt much restored in health, but also because I wished to ease the ache, fill that hollow which was my unconsummated vow. I yearned to fill all the hollows in his life with laughter and love and children.

I stood before my French doors and looked out upon a winter night with snow deeply laden on the ground. I yearned for him. And wondered where he slept, and if he thought of me.

The pressures of my long illness and the turmoils of tonight's revelations made me take to my bed early.

Yet in the stillest hours of deep morning, I opened my eyes to see Max over my bed. His hand went to my brow. I caught it to my chest. He smiled sweetly.

"Hello, my love. Go back to sleep. I only meant to see if you were well."

"Quite well. I missed you."

"I missed you, too. Go to sleep."

I would not release his hand. "Stay with me."

He frowned. "Why? Is something amiss?"

"No. I merely want you."

He laughed lightly. "I want you too, my love. Very much. But I told you once, I want you—all of you. Now is not the best time to begin such discoveries. Sleep."

I smiled and closed my eyes.

And when I opened them in the morning, he was there again. Dressed to go out, he pointed to my morning breakfast tray and apologized with a rueful look.

"Sorry, darling. I have an appointment with my solicitor in Wolffson. We must speak of the factory, you know. I didn't want to wake you this early. But I'll be back for luncheon."

I scrambled up on my knees.

His eyes traveled the sheer gown in appreciation.

"Come home and we will have luncheon together . . . here." I grinned suggestively. "By the fire."

"Madam, if you dress like that, I will share any meal you wish." He leaned over to peck me on the cheek. "I regret the appointment deeply, darling. Goodbye. See you at noon, or just past."

But he did not come. Not at noon, or at one, or even at two. And I had long ago dressed for the afternoon, ordered luncheon taken away, and gone to do the reading lesson with the girls.

Even dinner came and he was not about.

I could not eat, but stalked the conservatory, furious at him for not sending word.

Adair sailed in and paused when she saw me so peevish.

"Walking the floor, eh? He told you he went to see his solicitor, I heard. Yes, well, you'll wait quite a while, from what I gather. The 'solicitor' is an old excuse. Maribel suspected what he was up to when he went calling in Wolffson. You should, too."

"I have no idea—"

"That's right, poor little parson's daughter. You have no idea. Well, I'll tell you, the solicitor who lives in Wolffson has a daughter. A very lovely daughter. Nancy is her name. Ask Max about her. Ask him."

I could not move.

"No, you won't ask, so I'll tell you. Max has kept Nancy in a lovely style for many years. Adding to her house. Buying her the latest clothes. New jewels. Just like the new ones he gave you." She trilled a wicked laugh and leaned close, her eyes ablaze.

"He didn't see fit to give you the family heirlooms, did he? No, not for the little minister's girl. He gave you new ones rather than have you tarnish the glory of the Worminster collection. I could see how proud you were of them. Suited your vanity, didn't it, to think he'd buy you precious stones? Not so innocent and moral as you seem, are you, dear girl? I bet you meet his passion in bed, too, don't you? Well, how does it fit your passion that he has Nancy, eh? Has had her for years. She is his light of love, as they say. His whore." She chuckled.

"You get real satisfaction from trying to destroy people, don't you?"

She glared at me. "When that's all that's left to you, yes, you do."

"I feel sorry for you."

"Don't waste your emotion, Duchess. It's you who's got the problem, not me."

I left her where she stood. Then I retired to my room, donned a soft Belgian linen nightgown, and tried to read. Dickens did not amuse. Scott did not appeal. I opened the connecting door to our sitting room and saw my needlework awaiting me on a side table. That did not interest me either.

I went to open Max's bedroom door. The glorious golden room was dull without him. Yet, in an attempt to conjure his presence, I strode among the furnishings to touch a part of him. His matching chairs of cream and gold. His manly, massive writing desk. His gilt-edged diary.

I stared at it. It was locked. Locked against intruders. Locked against seekers of stories unspoken.

"Were you looking for me, my love?"

I jumped at the sound of his resonant voice. He stood in the doorway, his hair windblown, his coat off, his valet a pace behind him.

"Rolland, you may go. I can take care of myself this evening."

He shut the door and stood there a moment, surveying me. "I apologize for being so late. I should have sent word not to wait supper for me, but—"

"I told Bigelow to serve without you."

"I see." He dropped his coat in a nearby chair and walked over to me, all the while undoing his waistcoat and cuffs. "You are angry with me."

"I can't hide much from you, can I?"

234

He stood before me now and raised my chin so that our eyes met. "You are too honest. I read your every thought." He narrowed his eyes. "And I see you harbor some resentment. Pray tell, love, what is it I have done?"

"Not come home."

He raised both palms. "I am here now. Do with me as you will."

I harumphed and would have walked away.

He caught me by the arm.

"No, love. Come back." His fingers tugged, but I resisted. He stepped forward and put his arms around me. "Stubborn woman." He buried his lips in my hair and whispered, "My solicitor sends his greetings."

"Does his daughter also?"

He pulled away and stared at me. "Look at me. Please. What do you know of the solicitor's daughter?"

"What should I know?"

"That her name is Nancy. That I have known her for many years, all my life, in fact. That she is a widow—"

I wrenched to be free of him.

He pinned my arms to my side and clamped me close. "And that for the past four years or so, when I have been without a wife and she without a husband, she has comforted me in many ways when I was lonely and needed a woman's perspective."

"And a woman's body."

"And a woman's body." He sighed. "Furthermore, you should know that I was as generous with her as she with me. And that I saw her today—"

A sob escaped me and I jerked away from him.

He would not let me go. "And that I told her our

relationship would henceforth be based on friendship. She understood and did not cry or accuse me of false pretenses. Nancy is a very logical, intelligent woman.''

"And is she wise, as well?"

He combed his fingers through the length of my hair, over my shoulders, and across my thinly veiled breast. "Yes."

Trapped in his arms, I could only close my eyes.

"She told me to go home to my wife, whom she has heard is classically beautiful and utterly charming."

"The first day we met here in your den, you told me you had given up other women."

"These past few years, the only one I ever had was Nancy."

"But when I said there were many women, you didn't deny it."

"My love, I told you gossip abounds about me. I cannot be held accountable for all its fictions. I wanted you to know that I intended for no one to come between us. I would hope no rumors would, either." He placed his lips against my cheek. "Darling, my greatest sin today is that I did not send you word I would be so late. I promise you I will correct that. But I swear I did not lie to you. I had not seen Nancy in the last few months because I did not want to. Nor did I want rumor to spread that I visited her. I saw her today quite by accident when I was in her father's house. I did not lie to you. I never have."

His voice warmed my cold pride. But I was not totally convinced yet.

"Max, are you proud of me?"

He pulled away and peered at me. "What's this? Have I not shown you how much you mean to me? I buy you gowns and fans and gloves and frills. I give you my house to command, my children, my name, my heart, and—"

"And a new necklace and a new betrothal ring."

"You do not like them? Fine. We'll buy others."

I shook my head. "No, sir, please. Don't."

"What is it, my dear? What would you have me do that I have not?" His words melted their way into my resolve, and I shook with the power of my need to hold him close.

But he did my heart's bidding. He brought me flush against his warm, hard length.

"Take me to bed."

"Sweet wife," he whispered, "my fondest desire has been to make you mine. I want to show you how no other woman has ever meant a thing to me compared to the love I bear you."

"Please," I cried and circled my arms around his neck, "please do."

And at my surrender, he took me. Took me into a bruising embrace. A flaming kiss.

A kiss that scorched all thought. Burned all reason. And torched every inhibition.

I pushed away and worked at his braces and shirt studs, soon stripping him of the white expanse and being rewarded with the feel of thick, curling black hair wending through my fingers.

His big hands went to my breasts, covering them, cupping them, thumbing the nipples through the material in languid delights that made me eager and made me bold.

"Instinct told me," he crushed me close to rasp against my ear, "that you would want me this way.

237

God in heaven, darling," he hooked two fingers into the neckline of my gown and sent it sliding over my curves, "how have we waited this long to have each other?"

Naked, I pressed myself against the furry sculpted planes of his chest. Every nerve screamed for more. My hands went to his trousers, but he stayed them and caught me up to carry me to his bed. With a swift move, he flung the counterpane away and set me down.

His eyes sluiced up over me from the point of my toes to the hair on my head. With deft fingers, he undid his trouser flies and stepped out of his pants and his small clothes and his shoes and hose. Then, as God created him, he came to me.

And I welcomed him with open arms. Stretched upon me, he became the eighth wonder of the world to me. With his iron-hard muscles, lean, long limbs, wet, seeking mouth, he was the one delight I'd ever crave. The one sin I knew I had every right to indulge.

"There is so much I want to teach you," he was murmuring, as his lips traversed my neck and collarbone. "So much I want to give you."

My hands danced along his spine down to his hard buttocks. "Give me you."

"Me you shall always have. Allow me to show how we will have each other."

And then he kissed me, caressed me completely. Beginning with my hair. He threaded it out upon the plump pillows. Then took tendrils of it to tantalize me and himself with leisured drawings along my arms and around my heavy, tingling breasts. He took my fingers and kissed each one, then traced them over his rough, wild torso in patterns that made him close his eyes and moan for more. He used his own fingertips around my nipples and sent shivering rays of ecstasy down my belly to some quaking center of my being.

The exquisite tortures extended to eternities. My skin blazed where he touched and yearned for more when he moved on. I wanted his hands on me everywhere, and I pressed myself to him in agonized longing to tell him so. He understood and gave me only more of the ravishing enticements. I spun out of this mortal place. His body, his words became my only anchor to this earthly realm.

"Sweet," he bathed one areola with a wet tongue and trailed a moist path to my navel, "every inch of you is sweet. And spicy," his mouth traveled lower to claim my secret places. "And hot."

My hips rose up off the mattress as his mouth sampled me, devoured me. Madness tore through my body and I was convulsing, crying, reaching out to him.

And he was there. Looming above me, arms braced on either side of me, his dear face growing flushed as his eyes bore into mine.

"Here, love, is our union." With delicate fingers, he parted me and then in a series of tormenting, torrid liquid thrusts, he tenderly, slowly, serenely placed himself inside me.

"And here," he said as he paused partially inside the portal at my virgin's barrier, "is the only pain I ever mean to give you." He bent to kiss me thoroughly, then slid through and watched me as I enjoyed it and smiled.

"But here," he moved his hips in a smooth, slow rock, "is the essence of our marriage."

My eyes grew wide as his long girth moved higher,

surer inside me. My mouth opened and he claimed it as then he claimed all of me. Then he took me to some heaven I'd barely known existed for mortals. He showed me the pleasure points of my body and his own and we came to a crashing, vibrant surcease that I knew was our private paradise.

I returned to myself moments later and inhaled deeply.

He grabbed for a blanket, but stopped to chuckle.

I opened my eyes. We were at the foot of the bed. And from the looks of it, it was no small wonder he was having trouble covering us. We were not only at the foot of his massive bed, but we had completely destroyed its order. We had used every inch of it.

I blushed furiously and sought to cover my nakedness.

He brought me close. "I would feel your body next to mine for a while longer. I have waited so long to have your long legs wrapped around me, I will be a glutton and feast on my bounty."

I hid my face against his throat. "You say such wonderful things to me."

"To me you are wondrous."

"Why?"

"*Why?*" he moved away to peer down at me. "Because you are so unlike any woman I have ever known."

"I am not unique."

He cupped my face. "To me you are quite rare. Shall I tell you how?"

"Please."

He smiled and hugged me close. "Well, for the first

thing, you always say 'please.' You are the most un-selfish creature I have ever encountered."

"Surely you have met women with manners before."

"Women with manners, yes. Women who sought to get something from me after using them, too. You have no ulterior motives, my sweet, save those that make my body burn for yours and make my heart as light . . . lighter than I ever thought it could be again."

I rose up on one elbow now and peered into his dear eyes. "I know you loved both your previous wives and I—I am honored—no, more than that . . . thrilled is the right word, that you could love me, yet—I am not lovely, and they—"

He cursed roundly. Then he rose from the bed.

"Come here—"

Stark naked, I balked. Yet, trusting him, needing him, wanting his happiness, I went with him to stand before a full length, three-tiered mirror. I refused to look into it and pressed my head back against his chest.

He stood in back of me and his arms went around my waist while he spoke in my ear.

"Listen to me, Alicia. Look into the mirror, darling. Do it! Yes. You think I can't love you because you are less than the other two. That is not so. They were both ladies. Rich, yes. Pretty, certainly. Cultured, supposedly. But what are those qualities to yours? Look at you, darling. Look!"

I forced myself to do his bidding.

His eyes met mine in gratification and he smiled in heavy-lidded sensuality. "Look how sweetly you blush, darling. Down to your lovely breasts. Neither of my duchesses would ever have let me love her totally naked

241

nor would have ever left a bed for me unclothed. It is no small thing to have a wife who does your will even against her training.

"But there are other differences among you, differences that mean the world to me. No, you are not rich, but I have no need of money. No, you are not pretty by conventional standards, but I do not need prettiness as much as the stunning creature you are, outside and in. No, neither lady was as appealing as you are to me, darling. Neither Cynthia nor Maribel had compassion or understanding. Both were vain, self-centered, sometimes heartless. Whereas you," he nestled his warm loins and chest into the comparable curves along my back, "fit me perfectly.

"Look at your coloring, your bone structure. Yes, sweetheart, look at you. You are a Wolff, a mate for me. That russet hair and those green eyes, the look of the forest, darling. God meant you for me." His hands came up to hold my breasts, the globes now aching with his wooing and the nipples puckering at his ribald scrutiny. "You possess a gorgeous body, my lady. Built to inspire great love, and great devotion, and to produce many children."

His hands delved lower to span my hips and then to caress my private places now pulsing with his fondling. I watched his hands in utter fascination as my knees buckled and my inner core melted in the volcano he stirred.

He kissed my ear. "Tell me, sweetheart, how could I not love you? You are a mix of modesty and brazenness. Truth and beauty mixed to one incredible potion for all to see. What is more the mystery, sweet, is why you are in love with me."

I opened my mouth to explain.

But he turned me in his embrace and slanted a fore-finger across my lips. "I would prefer it if you would tell me with your body why that's so."

And so I did. I led him to his bed, watched him lay down in bold invitation, and knelt over him. With my mouth, my hands, my eyes, I enjoyed the way he tasted, the way he smelled, the way he looked. With my heart, I freed myself to enjoy his every bulging muscle, his every sensitive spot, his most secret desire.

He shuddered. He moaned. He grasped the iron bars above his head and asked for more. And everything he wanted I gave and gave freely. This was my husband, my love, my life.

Then, he wrapped his long arms and legs around me and rolled me to the mattress.

"You take my breath away," he murmured against my throat. "You are every lovely thing I've ever prayed for."

That night became a revel of delights and satisfactions. A celebration of one man, made in Adam's mold, and one woman, made in Eve's. This Adam displayed no regrets; this Eve no coyness. This union of flesh on flesh blended to one pure ecstasy, one blessed commingling beyond my mortal skill for definition.

Soon one night became another so that a string of nights turned in on each other and wove together in an intricate pattern which became the fabric of our marriage. The texture of our days and nights transformed my view of my mission here on earth, wherein I loved a man and he loved me. Thus could I say I was suddenly, inexplicably, and utterly fulfilled.

But one morning more than a month later, I arose

from our bed of pleasure and a violent nausea gripped me. I managed to make my own bedroom before I wretched into a chamberpot.

Max, who had already dressed and gone down to breakfast, did not see me. No one did. And I said nothing.

Nothing.

The next morning, I stayed abed as he left early for a two-day trip to Manchester, once more to check on conditions at his Number Five Factory. Again I was ill.

I knew my malady this time.

I was pregnant.

I was overjoyed and terrified. If I told him, he would be thrilled. Now I knew him intimately enough to predict that he would welcome this manifestation of our love as well as the proof of our union. But I also feared the other—the secrets he vowed to reveal. The secrets I had asked to hear and now dreaded would take him from me. The secrets that might kill our marriage in its splendorous youth.

Chapter Twelve

I could not tell him.

He returned from Manchester and our intimacies resumed. Although our sojourns into the realm of sensual love made our nights bliss, by morning I was careful not to let him see me in my sickness and just as careful to put on the brightest attitudes for the rest of the day. In some ways, that was not difficult.

Many in the household left us alone. Branford returned to London. Adair went to visit a cousin from her mother's family, while Caroline took herself off to some friends in Yorkshire. Only Gilbert and I remained in the house during the day while Max was away at one of his factories.

I had no idea how Gilbert occupied his hours, nor did I ever think about it until I listened to the stillness of the great mansion without all the other adults. Oh, we had the general noise that comes with two children and two dogs and a bevy of staff, but not the purposeful activity I was so used to. It made for melancholy days.

Cold February brought with it frostier winds and deeper snows. Yet Bigelow had long ago taught his footmen and his maids how to build a fire high and keep it so through winter's dreadful storms. I walked the mansion during the day, teaching the girls, playing with them, and then retiring to the library, where the Brontës or Keats awaited me. Or when I wished not to think, I would pick up my needlepoint and try to push my agonies away with each thrust of the needle.

Ever, always, the issue plaguing me was when to tell Max. For surely, at some point, I must.

Yet I quaked to tell him. And knew when I did, I risked my future and his, as well as our child's. Still, whatever the secrets of his past, I wanted to know. I deserved—yes, I *needed* to know! And yet I feared it as surely as the fires of hell.

I hoped for some way—some stroke of God's hand—that might change all the conditions. I found myself wishing that Caroline and her two children would inherit someone else's fortune and disappear from our lives like a bad dream. I wished that the servants had a lesser code of honor so that one of them might reveal to me the rumors of the house. I would stare at Max's diary and wish for it to unlock itself, open its pages, and render up its secrets. That way, I would know the problems I faced and remain true to Max's dictum that I not ask. But the book did not open of itself, and I could not bring myself to do so immoral a deed as pry into my husband's private writings.

What did happen were two occurrences that set me to trembling even more. The first took place one day at my desk in my sitting room as I searched for more writing paper and found something else too terrifying for words. It was a crumpled notepaper that had lodged its way into the back portion of a drawer, and from the looks of it, had stayed there for years.

It was dated August 10, 1846, and the hand was feminine yet bold. The signature was Maribel's. The note was addressed to her "darling," and the words were desperate and commanding all at the same time. I read it with growing revulsion.

> *Darling,*
> *I think Max knows about us and so we must not meet again until my confinement is ended. Trust me to know how to handle him. I know what's best for us all. I promise you we shall be together soon.*
>
> > *All my love,*
> > *Your own Maribel*

Evidently, the reason Maribel had rewritten the note was because she'd crossed out a portion. She did not want the recipient to read the last sentence.

I crushed the note and held it to my bosom. Maribel had not remained faithful to Max. Worse, she had conspired against him.

I felt rocked by the knowledge. Yet I wondered who else knew. I promised myself to wait—to wait unto the end of time, if I must, to see who knew.

But then another question hit me: had Max ever truly discovered this about Maribel? Instinct told me he was no man to take adultery with any understanding. Base instinct told me he would certainly kill any man who took his woman. Perhaps he'd kill her, too.

I hid the note in my jewelry box, to which I alone held the key.

My awareness of the note's existence was never far from my hand or my thoughts. And if that wasn't enough to spoil my days, the second terrible event occurred when Dorcas returned to me as my maid. Out of her splinters now, she walked, limping slightly—but she walked. And, so said Mrs. Timms, she was well enough to resume some of her duties.

If I had become an actress when I was with my husband, I now became an even better one with Dorcas. Suddenly, I preferred tea, not hot chocolate. And I always ate in the dining room, never from any tray Dorcas brought me. She accepted my new preferences and did not comment on them.

But no sooner had she been assigned to me again than she fell ill with a winter's cough and fever. Nora once more replaced her. And I breathed more easily.

But a few days later Mrs. Timms and I sat in the drawing room, deciding on the week's menus, and I found more reasons to worry. Max had had to depart suddenly for an extended business trip to London. He was to be gone a week or more, and so I needed to change the volume of foods and number of courses Cook would serve.

As we finished our menu changes, Mrs. Timms gathered up her papers and prepared to leave. "I do hope you are satisfied with Nora's services, Your Grace. Dorcas is really the more senior maid, but what can I do?"

"Nora is wonderful, Mrs. Timms. You needn't fret about her."

"Dorcas has so much more experience, though. Before she worked for the first or second duchess, she originally worked for Lady Adair, you know."

"No, I didn't."

"Yes, they'd played together as children, much against the wishes of the old duke. He thought it was so improper. But Adair and Dorcas got along famously. Fast friends, I think, even today."

"Yes, well, that's good to know, Mrs. Timms."

Now I had another reason to doubt Dorcas's loyalty. This coil between her and Adair made me more afraid of Dorcas than before. Would she support her friend Adair to the point of poisoning a woman whom Adair disliked?

I had to admit to myself that I had absolutely no insight—no instinct—about the true nature of Dorcas's character. Furthermore, I had no substantive motive to assign to Adair for disliking me as she did. Unless, of course, I could believe Gilbert's innuendo of a few weeks ago that Caroline or Adair herself wished her to become mistress of the House of Wolff.

Nora was my only hope. At the risk of diminishing Nora's opinion of me, I decided to encourage her to tell me the family gossip. Unpretentious as she was, Nora gave me nuggets of information that tickled and teased.

One day Nora confided that Bigelow always put a newspaper back in its original order before giving it up to a footman to cart off to the trash heap. Mrs. Timms, she revealed, loved a spot of brandy with her tea before retiring. Haskins, the footman, had a devil of time helping Mr. Gilbert into bed after he'd drunk himself silly each night. And Dorcas, sick as she was, was pining for Lady Adair to return from her trip.

"Oh," I busied myself removing my crinolines, "why is that, do you suppose, Nora?"

"Oh, Mum, them two is right tight. Two peas in a pod, you know. Word has it that Dorcas was the by-blow of Adair's father."

I shut my mouth, trying not to gape.

"Yes, Mum Them two is stepsisters."

Frantic at that news, I went through the motions of my day with little relish. I spent the afternoon with Mary and Elizabeth, doing their lessons and reading them a story. So, by nighttime, I paced the floor of my bedroom.

Still, unable to rest, I tied the sash of my robe around me and made my way to the library. Sequestering myself in a little nook with a romance by Mary Shelley, I curled my feet up into my chair, pulled my robe about me, and read in fascination her tale of a man-made creature forced to commit evil. I lost myself in the woes of Doctor Frankenstein and his wayward invention, the man who was none.

"Can't sleep, huh?"

I jerked up. Gilbert had propped himself between two narrow rows of shelves.

"I wanted to read."

"Pshhh." He reeled away from me, headed for the sideboard where Max kept his liquors. "Came to get another bottle."

I watched him as he opened the cabinet door and rummaged about, finally extracting a large black bottle and facing me. "Join me, Duchess?"

"No, thank you."

"You don't drink intoxicating fluids, do you?"

He had never been nasty to me. I would not give him an opening to be now, either. I returned to my book.

Still, he would not be stayed. He wove his way toward me. Swaying slightly, he grinned down sardonically, then uncorked the bottle and drank without benefit of glass.

"Miss your husband, do you? Hmmm, no wonder. I've been told he is no gentleman in bed. An animal with an animal's appetite."

I shut the book and began to rise.

"Got to get away from me, eh, Duchess? Don't blame you. Wish to hell my mother would leave me alone. And Adair. Women, hell . . . even Maribel wanted to get away from me in the end." He took another swig and glared at me as I tried to go around him. He grabbed my arm.

"Don't want to hear that, do you, Duchess? Don't want to hear the sinful stuff of family life. Against your virgin breeding—op, but you're not a virgin anymore, are you? No, I'd say he's done the deed by now. Had to. Wouldn't want ol' Gil to inherit the throne, would he?"

"Let me go, Gilbert."

"That *is* why he married you, you realize. Because he hates me." He came close, so close I could smell the spirits he'd been consuming. His breath made me reel. His fingers bit into my arm. "He got a good bargain in you, didn't he, though? The gorgeous daughter of the minister. A lush piece for his cravings. The sweet virgin who overlooked his sins and took him to husband anyway."

He threw back his head to laugh mercilessly.

I yanked myself free and strode for the hall.

But he caught me in a swift lunge. Suddenly, his arms wound around me and crushed me close. He plunged his hands into my hair and backed me up against a bookshelf. Grinding his body against mine, he held my head like a vise and then seized my mouth. Brutally tasting every bit of me, he plundered my soul. Ripping at my robe with his hands, his mouth traveled my throat and bosom.

I was wild to be free of him. But a man who is drunk can be appallingly strong. And it did me no good to pound him and push him, no good to try to kick him. He went on and on! And when he had me naked to the waist and his mouth came back to mine, he inexplicably drew away.

His hands clamped my face and he peered into my eyes.

"Oh, Christ," he moaned, "you are crying."

His whole body fell away from me, and sorrow stood in his gray eyes. "You're not Maribel. Not that traitorous bitch."

I tried to cover myself.

He shook his head and out of habit he raised the bottle to take another taste. But he stopped short, glared at the thing, and then flung it across the room.

It shattered into a thousand pieces as the liquid stained the carpet black.

"Oh, God," he bent over and ran his hands through his hair. "I loved her. And I loved him. Like a brother, and yet I did that to him. I can't do the same again. Not with you. You . . . you're not even like her. She . . . she didn't love him. She loved me. Or so I believed. And he found out. And unmans me every day of my life in retribution."

He spun to face me. A drunk's lucidity lined his features.

252

"Don't let him hurt you, though. Don't. Leave here while you can. You deserve to live."

"Gilbert, you are very drunk and don't know what you're saying—"

"The hell I don't. Don't let him do to you what he did to Maribel."

"I don't know what you're talking about—"

"No, that's clear, or no woman in her right mind would have married the man. And you, little parson's daughter, you *are* in your right mind, aren't you?"

"Yes, enough to know I'm going to bed and leaving you to your ravings."

"That's right. Put your head in the sand again. Don't look. Don't listen. But when your time comes, you'll wish you had."

"Never." I was at the threshold.

"Your husband killed her, you see. He killed Maribel because he thought the twins were *mine*. Mine! But then, that's not the worst of it, because he had killed Cynthia to get Maribel. Because Cynthia stood in the way of what he thought was a perfect match with her licentious cousin. Poor, silly, sickly Cynthia. She never knew what was going on between them, right here in her own house. And neither one of them knew what a sexual appetite he had—how he does unnatural things to women. Maribel told me. Your husband, lady, is a fiend."

"You're mad!"

"Am I?" He made his unsteady way toward me. "Ask him, Duchess. Ask him how his other wives died, and then ask him how he's going to do away with you. Because he will, you know. He'll find another woman who'll suit him, his whims, his perverse appetites, and he'll do away with you, just like the other two."

His words held me spellbound.

"God has done more than curse the man, Alicia. He has let the devil take him and make him in his image."

I took to my bed but found no rest, no respite from the terrors Gilbert had revealed. I was up early, wondering what to do, where to go, how to deal with this dilemma. But my day was one long nightmare. By evening, I was still possessed by my thoughts. Soon, my deliberations were cut short by Nora, who knocked on my sitting room door to announce a visitor.

"Who is it, Nora?"

"Well, mum, he says he's an old friend o' yours. Here's his card."

The sight of the name made my knees buckle. "My God! Edward!" My eyes flew to hers.

"He said you'd be right surprised to see 'im, mum. Said I was to get smelling salts before I came to tell you."

"Oh, wonderful, kind Edward! No, Nora, I won't be needing smelling salts."

"He's in the conservatory, mum, where Bigelow put him."

I took the stairs at almost a dead run. At the doors to the conservatory, I saw Bigelow exit.

"Bring us some tea will you, please, Bigelow?"

"I already asked the gentleman, ma'am. He's had a long trip in the cold weather."

"Thank you, Bigelow. You are very kind."

I walked into the warm glass room and found Edward amid the roses. He turned as he saw me approach, his kindly brown eyes twinkling at my approach.

I went into his open arms.

"Alicia." He gathered me close and kissed my hair.

I pulled away to examine him. Never handsome, he had always been rather craggy looking. Now, after his ordeal in the army, he was even thinner than before, with a touch of gray edging his soft brown hair. But his eyes were still lively and warm.

"What a shock, Edward. What a surprise." I pressed my hand to his cheek and he kissed it, then took it between his two as we sat to talk.

"I knew I might frighten you. I certainly frightened my parents. Even though the army had sent a notice to Whitehall, the messenger seemed to have lost his way or his resolve before he got to Crewe. I walked in the door—a man who was the walking dead—and my mother fainted. I thought my father would have a seizure. But they recovered."

He smiled sweetly, his thin lips stretching across his big teeth. He recounted a tale of ambush and capture and subsequent release for ransom by natives who desired concessions and money from the British Crown.

"And so you see before you a man who has collected a regimental honor and a citation from the Queen. Small compensation for the fright of my life and six months in a squalid prison. But I will forget. What all the accolades cannot return to me is you. And that is my biggest loss in all this. I was the one who was shocked when my parents told me you were not waiting for me, but indeed married to another man."

"Oh, Edward. I would never have broken our engagement if I'd known."

"Dearest, I did not come here to fault you for believing I was dead when Whitehall said I was. No. I came to see you because I thought you should know I was alive, but more important, because I wanted to assure myself that you were happy. And well."

"Edward, thank you. I would have never forgiven you if you did return from abroad and not come to display yourself in the flesh. I grieved for you."

"I'm sure you did, dearest. When you agreed to marry me, I knew you cared for me, if only as a friend. I hoped you would grow to love me and so I asked you to become my wife. But circumstances changed all that. Your father died. And so, he sought to make a life for you."

"You know all this?"

"When I returned and learned of your father's death, I went straightaway to see Mr. Bettelsby. He told me everything."

I hung my head.

"Dearest, do not be ashamed."

"Oh, I'm really dreadfully sorry."

"So am I. I loved you. Love you still. I came today to content myself . . . to assure myself that you are happy." He clutched my cold hand. "Tell me, dearest, that you are happy."

Happy?

I stared at him. Friend, confidant, yes, he was those things to me. Could I lie to him and be successful?

"I am very happy, Edward."

"So, then, what they say about the man who is your husband is just vicious rumor."

Ohhh, God. How could I ask?

Edward was incredulous. "Surely your brothers told you!"

I stood to turn my back on him and finger the lush petal of a giant red rose.

"Surely Thomas told you!"

I froze.

He came and turned me to him. He could have been whispering, for all the force behind his words. "Maximilian the Wolff. The animal who marries and then destroys his wives."

Ahhh! The words made me double over in agony.

He caught me and took me to my chair.

"Dear Alicia. Why have you not come to terms with this? Surely, what I say is not news? Or is it? My God, you've been married for months! And his reputation is notorious. I learned the tale years ago. Christ, it's almost forklore in all of Lancashire! How could you not know?"

I was gulping for air. "Know? Know what? I put no stock in rumors, trifling gossip. I made my life listening to the good things. Edward, how can you have me believe that the man I married is a cold-blooded murderer?"

"It is not I who say it, dear. Everyone does. Did. It seems the two ladies in question died mysteriously. I know only the smallest detail. The first died after childbirth, a difficult one. The story goes that he found her, bleeding badly, the midwife drunk, and the newborn babe dead, perhaps suffocated. The story says he let his duchess bleed to death. He got no help for her because he wanted her cousin as his next wife. A cousin who was comely and seductive. A cousin whom he had

257

taken to his bed long before his wife had died. The saying goes he killed the one to have the other. And then, later, he did not want the other wife, either.

"He discovered she was having an affair with a man, someone he knew well. As a result, he went mad. Crazy. When she was brought to bed with twins, he claimed they were not his but the other man's. Her lover's. She, fool that she was, agreed with him. The next day, she was found alone in her bed, dead of eating something spoiled. Many say she died of poison administered by him."

I stared at him in horror. Everything made sense. All the tensions. All the hatreds. All the bitterness in the family. Yet how could a man who seemed so dear, so sweet, so loving, kill two wives?

"I can't believe it of him."

"Then why would he bribe a magistrate not once but twice not to look into their deaths?"

"He wouldn't."

"But he did."

"There is some explanation. There must be."

"Really? Why, then, did the man confess this on his death?"

"Confess? To whom?"

"Your father!"

"Oh, God, no! How do you know that?"

"The man confessed on a city street where he'd been run over by a carriage. Villagers called the nearest parson. It was your father—and about twenty others who heard the magistrate's confession."

"Edward, Edward! If this were so, why would my father then commit me to a marriage with a murderer?"

He shrugged. "I have no answers for you there, dearest. Perhaps that truth is buried with your father."

"Or perhaps—" came a deep voice from the depths of the garden, "you'd better ask your husband."

I spun.

And there he stood. My husband. My love. My nemesis.

"Mister Perry—" Max strode forward, his eyes only flickering to Edward briefly and then back to me, "I'd like you to leave my house. Immediately. I must speak with my wife now, as you may well see. Go."

Edward stood there a moment, wondering what to do.

"Go, Edward. Please. Max and I must talk."

"If you want me, Alicia, I'll be at the Inn in Wolffson."

"Thank you, Edward. I'll remember."

With a glance at Max, he made his way to the door.

"Goodbye, Alicia."

"Edward."

Max had not once taken his eyes off me.

"So you've found out."

I nodded. Rocked by the knowledge last night and its confirmation tonight, I questioned—if only momentarily—my ability to endure this third bout.

Yet I squared my shoulders and met his gaze.

"Why, Max? Why wouldn't you tell me?"

He gaped at me. And then he laughed! He threw back his head and laughed uproariously. "Oh, that's rare, that is. Why wouldn't I tell you?" He covered the space between us. "What do you take me for? An idiot? Why would I tell tales such as that?"

"To be honest with me. As you said you would be."

"No! You did not listen! I told you I would be as honest as I could be. I never promised you more than I knew was humanly possible."

"Then why not tell me what facts you knew?"

"Why? So that you could look on me in horror?" He seized me by the upper arms now. "You! The only good thing that's ever happened to me! Why shouldn't I take the only thing God ever gave me that was bright and honest and totally good and keep it from harm's way? Hmmm? Tell me!" He was shaking me.

"Why?" I was crying. "Why? Because I loved you."

"Do you? Did you? If that were so, would you truly believe these tales now?"

"I don't know what to believe. Gilbert, Edward—"

He stepped back. "Gilbert! What about Gilbert? Is *he* talking behind my back? Again he destroys me, eh? Well, I'll cure him once and for all—"

He was turning, striding toward the door, and I was running after him.

"No! No!" I was grabbing him at his sleeve, his lapel, ripping his jacket at the pocket so that it tore off, and a small bottle rolled across the tiled floor. I looked down.

A bottle. A little vial. Blue. Such as laudanum was kept in. My bottle, from beneath my mattress. The one I'd refused to use. Why, why would he have it?

I stared at him and backed away.

His whole mood changed now. He saw me make deductions, and his eyes took on the sorrowful concern I knew him to have when I'd suffered my headaches.

"Alicia—darling . . ."

I was backing into the roses, and the thorns tore at

my gown and my hair. My hands were covering my mouth.

"And to think I loved you—"

My hands covered my body where our baby grew.

"I adored you, Max, and you were trying to kill me all along!"

"No! Alicia, listen to me!"

"No!"

He reached for me and I ducked to escape him.

"Don't touch me!"

I circled around him and backed toward the door. "I'm leaving. Don't stop me."

"Very well, leave me. There was no other answer for it anyway. I knew if you ever found out, you would hate me."

His features hardened now into the man I'd never seen but had heard others describe. "Go. Take the Dower House. It's yours. You earned it." His eyes dropped to my thickening waistline. "He is not born yet, but I give you that which I promised you. The house, and a future without me. Go. Go quickly. And leave me alone."

Chapter Thirteen

Alone. I had never been so alone. But never had I loved. Never had I lost.

But oh, I did leave him. Running from the conservatory, I left him just as he'd ordered me. I ran to my room and locked myself in. Too terrified to cry, too overwrought to move, I stood in the middle of my silver-lined room and stared at nothing.

There came a knock at the door. I clutched my throat.

"Your Grace, it is Mrs. Timms. Please let me in. We must make arrangements."

I opened the door. With averted eyes that blinked back tears, she murmured how the duke had instructed her to help me leave for the Dower House. In addition to stores of linens and supplies and staples for the pantry, he had given instructions that I was to take Nora, Haskins, and my ever faithful Hans.

The next morning, after another sleepless night, I joined the other two and the huge mastiff to journey the five miles from Wolffs' Lair. I did not see Max before we departed. Locked in his den, he did not emerge before I left that morning. Without a word from him, Nora, Haskins, Hans, and I climbed into the ducal coach and traversed the snow-laden country to open the Dower House, take the ghostly dusters from the furniture, build new fires, stock the pantry, and begin a life alone.

Three days later, a hired carriage pulled up to the front door. Haskins, seeing that it was not the ducal carriage as he expected, opened the portal against violent winter winds. Within minutes, he came to tell me Edward Perry awaited me. Edward inquired as to my health and begged to see me. Unable to see anyone, least of all Edward, I wiped my tears for the thousandth time and told Haskins to tell my caller I was not at home. Nora came later to tell me that Edward had left, but not without an argument with Haskins about my state.

Two weeks later, Thomas was the second to come to the Dower House.

"Max came to Manchester last week. He told me that you and he had parted." Thomas crouched before me as I sat in my grandmother's wine-red drawing room.

I dared not speak about it, lest I open a wound too raw for probing.

Thomas, persistent Thomas, would not let it go. "Dear, I am so sorry. I know you began to care for him."

My eyes drifted to his sad brown ones. "You knew."

"That you cared for him, yes."

"That's not what I meant, and you know it. Tell me why you said nothing, Thomas? Why?"

"Father asked me not to. And Grandmother, too."

"But why?"

"Father came to me to ask what I knew about the Duke of Worminster, my employer. He came to me when Grandma proposed the idea to him, soon after your Edward Perry was presumed dead in that ambush. I told Father I knew the duke to be a prudent businessman—and the man whom some decried as a murderer. But Grandma knew Max very well, and to my surprise, Father knew a little about him. It seems Father took a confession of some sort—"

"From a magistrate."

"Quite. Father took a confession from a man who claimed to have accepted a bribe from Max. The magistrate claimed that Max paid him money not to pursue a line of thinking that indicated Max had killed his last wife. Tortured by this unethical conduct, the magistrate confessed before a horde of people. That incident only added to the gossip about Max."

Thomas rose and went to stand before the giant window that overlooked Grandma's rose garden. Beyond the terrace, I saw the bare spines of the bushes, spare as my hope.

"I, of course, knew the gossip. Had known it for years. Maximilian the Wolff, they call him. So you can imagine that when Father first summoned me and told me about his plan, I was horrified. 'How can you give her over to such a man?' I cried. And do you know what he told me? He said that he had Grandma's assurance that the man was tortured by many mysteries, not the least of which was who had killed his two wives."

I rose and went to face my brother. "You mean she thought someone else killed both of them?"

"Yes. Father and she were convinced, I know not why or how, but they said circumstances continually pointed to Max, but that no one could ever prove otherwise."

"Yet, since Max was the only one who knew what happened on the occasions of their deaths, he had to clear himself."

"But marrying another would not clear his name. And more to the point, why marry me?"

"Precisely for the reason stated: he wanted an heir. You were a Wolff, and family curse or not, you were young, healthy, and in need of a husband. Max had learned much about you from our grandmother and even more from Father. Evidently, the man wanted you for his wife, sight unseen. Yet Grandma insisted that the two of you meet, and so she arranged it. He left for a business trip to the United States soon after, and when he returned, Father had passed on, as well as Grandmother. The will only remained to be carried out."

"Still, neither one told me. They never even intimated it. And neither did you. I feel foolish, having been kept in the dark by everyone who ever meant anything to me. God," I ran a hand across my brow, "all of you must think me stupid."

"On the contrary. Grandma thought you were intellectually and morally strong enough to endure the revelation and help Max clear his name."

"Well, she was wrong."

I was far from strong.

* * *

I went about the business of my days now, discovering how very weak I was.

I wept constantly. While a part of me understood it was my pregnancy that made me sensitive, I knew my problem. Forlorn and lonely, I longed for company. But to be exact, I yearned for Max. His charm, his wit. His embrace. I was pregnant with my first child and alone in the world. And I ranted and railed against forces that kept me alone.

I could not eat. Nothing much appealed to me. Nora was a good cook and I assured her the problem was not with her. No. Only with me. I had no appetite, save for a meal eaten with someone whose company I craved. And I craved Max. His smile, his compliments. His regard. I was a young woman in love with a man whom many had spurned. And I cursed forces that had ruined our love and made me doubt him.

At night, I was worse. After a small repast, I walked the house in search of peace. I could not do my needlepoint. I could not read. I could not concentrate on anything except the memory of that bottle of laudanum as it had rolled across the floor of the conservatory. Yet . . . that bottle stuck in my brain. Why had Max had it?

Did he always carry it? If so, why had I not seen it before? Did he take the opiate himself? If so, I had never seen its affects. Why, then, did he carry it that day?

The lack of a reason drove me mad.

Lianne came to see me in late spring. Nora showed her out into the rose garden, where I sat in a white wicker chair, my girth limiting my agility these days.

She came and kissed my cheek and pulled up a

matching chair while I put my pruning sheers upon the nearby gardener's cart.

"How are you, Alicia?"

"I try to keep up my strength for my baby's sake."

"The wisest course. Max worries over you."

"He sent you?"

"No, not specifically. I came of my own accord. I am worried about you both. I saw Max last week. He was in town on business. If I had not seen him in the street and caught a word with him, I know he would not have come to visit. Still, I insisted he come to my house for dinner." She reached over and took my hands in hers. "He tells me little. Only that the girls cry for you constantly. But when he speaks, he cannot bring himself to utter your name. My unshakable conclusion is that the man is miserable without you."

I would not cry, I wouldn't! "He was not honest with me, Lianne."

"Certainly you understand why."

"I gather you don't believe in the gossip, either."

She sighed. "Let me simply say that for many, many years I saw reasons why Max would want his wives dead."

"Oh, Lianne!"

She put up a hand. "My dearest Alicia, I will tell you one thing. I do not know all the facts in these matters. I wonder if even Max does. But I do know one thing—I *know* Max. And I know he could not have committed such crimes."

She stayed for a few days, but no other words of hers destroyed me as completely as those.

Beginning the night she left and on into the hot summer evenings, I walked the floor of my bedroom, pondering her words.

I know Max, she had said. *And I know he could not have committed such crimes.*

Why did those words sear my heart? Why did they make me writhe in torment?

And then the first of my revelations hit me. If Max truly wanted a son—and I believe that that had been his primary motivation for marrying me—why would he try to poison me before I gave him one?

Without an heir, murdering me did not make sense. Or at least, not the same sense as the other murders did. No, because in both cases, the duchesses of Worminster had died *after* giving birth.

It was August before I admitted the second truth to myself, August before the significant evidence of the laudanum bottle paled beside other evidence, August before I admitted my complicity in my own downfall.

August, when I stood in my garden, thick with the redolent scent of roses, and confessed the truth I'd so long avoided. I had always known something horrible was behind the secrecy in the House of Wolff. I had known it for months. I had known many would hold Max responsible. For such a crime as murder of one's wife—or rather, of one's *wives*—I had known there would be questions to be asked, answers to be given, and shocks to be borne. I had known why Mrs. Timms was quick to take up for her master. I had known why Williams was too ready to save the souls of her two tiny charges. I had known why Gil drank and Adair destroyed and Caroline prevaricated. I had known, yes, yes, I had known in my heart of hearts for so long and I had ignored all these secrets.

268

I had known and I had not known. Purposely. For my own ends. My own benefits. Because I was attracted to my fiancé. So attracted, so enchanted, so in love with his looks and his manner and his devastating charm that I would abandon every precious rule I had ever learned, forsake every moral injunction I'd ever been taught. Just to have a few blissful moments, days, weeks to call my own. Oh, I'd had them all right. And if now some said I had lived with the devil, I admitted here to myself that I had loved every heavenly second of it.

I covered my face in my hands and cried bitterly.

Nora flew to my side and insisted on putting me to bed. Weary of the world, I let her lead me to my room. Sobbing, I fell into a deep sleep. Yet hours later some small noise awakened me. Frightened, I gathered my nightgown to me and struggled to prop myself on one elbow. Across the room, before the window, appeared one specter.

Big, long, lean. A giant male creature.

Max?

Yes. Surely.

He stepped from the shadows into the moonlight. "Darling, don't be afraid. It is I." He hovered near. His eyes, soft gray orbs of concern, flickered over me. "Haskins came at Nora's request." He bent and would have placed his hand on my brow, but thinking better of it, he withdrew. "They say you are not well. That you do not eat or sleep. I want you well, my love. Will you do that for me? Get well? Please."

Tears choked me and I could only nod. I sank back into my pillows, my eyes on the dearest sight I'd beheld in all the months of my solitary confinement. At his request, I would do anything. My eyes closed in peace.

Of course, when I opened my eyes the next morning, he had disappeared. Being baldly honest with myself, I admitted I did not really expect to see him. Still, my heart had captured the comfort he offered. And from the comfort came a seed of hope. Even though Max was not with me, the hope remained. Even untended, the seed germinated, took root, and grew.

Now into the last months of my pregnancy, I began for the first time to truly enjoy my condition and anticipate its conclusion. I now waited in welcome for my baby.

I thrilled to my baby's little kicks and punches. His rolling over and over like a gymnast in my womb made me giggle. His hearty appetite made me eat everything and anything Nora produced and bade me ask for seconds. His growing weight left me breathless with fatigue and bright wonder at this miracle Max and I had created together.

Snow fell early that winter. By the first of December, it was as deep as I remembered it at this time last year. Last year, when I'd first traveled to Wolffs' Lair. When I'd first seen Max and agreed to be his wife. When I'd first tasted love.

I put my hand across the great mound of my stomach and remembered those days, happy, thrilling, frightening, fulfilling days with my husband. Yuletide would be lonely without him and Mary and Elizabeth. New Year's would be worse. But hope, with the flower that sprang from the seed he'd planted months ago, blossomed within me—and I could not say why, except to anticipate my baby's birth.

Christmas came and went in a haze of preparations for the new arrival. Although my brothers had each invited me to spend the season with them, my condition prohibited even the shortest trip. Still, I sent Nora up to the Lair with a few small gifts for the staff and two handmade dolls for the girls. For Max, I could think of absolutely nothing that might denote all my feelings for him and so, at such a loss, I sent nothing.

Mrs. Timms came down in the ducal coach, laden with candies and sweets, a giant plum pudding, and a saddle of lamb for our dinner. I would have refused, but she stopped me short with the disclosure that the duke had specifically itemized the goods to be brought. In addition, he sent a few small presents, which he begged me to accept in the spirit of the season.

I could not deny him his wishes. We dispensed his gifts, ate his offerings, and then, seated near the spruce Haskins had brought in and decorated in my drawing room, alone on Christmas night, I tore open the gift Max had sent for me.

It was a square, flat box, which he had wrapped in colored paper and red velvet ribbon, a hand-carved mahogany box which I hesitated to open. Curiosity overcame any inhibition and the sight inside made me start.

It was a necklace and earrings of incredible value. New as those others he had once graced me with. Rare as his person. Incomparable as his love. The set displayed a thousand tiny diamonds twinkling up at me, each a perfect teardrop. Each the perfect sentiment to make similar teardrops fill my eyes.

"Oh, Max," I sobbed, "I am so sorry, my beloved.

I doubted you, and you apologize to me. There is no justice there.''

One week later, on New Year's Eve, I stood by the same bedroom window where I had last seen Max stand and across the miles of heartache I silently wished him a happy new year. Suddenly, my waters broke.

Quietly, I took to my bed. I, who had helped many a woman birth her baby, knew it would be hours before I needed assistance. So I let Nora sleep.

By dawn, my pains came regularly every half hour or so. When Nora came to check on me, she immediately saw my condition.

"Oh, mum, it's snowing hard again. I'll get Haskins to go for Doctor Quentin now. God knows how the roads will be later."

I let her do as she thought best. I, by now, had all I could do to concentrate on not screaming down the house when the pains came.

But in an hour, it was not Doctor Quentin but Hannah Mead who tramped into my bedroom, discarded her cloak, and peered at me with clear eyes.

"Hello, Your Grace. The doctor could not come. He's birthin' another baby in Wolffson. Haskins came for me."

I tried to smile at her and then thanked God when she came closer that I could tell she had not imbibed too much punch to welcome in the new year. No. Her gaze was steady and sure.

"Nora, 'ere, tells me you've been at your pains since last night."

"Yes, Mrs. Mead, but the pains weren't bad until dawn. Now," I panted slowly as another wave swept over me, "I am confused. They're getting stronger but not any closer, and since my waters are gone, I'm worried."

"Hmmm." She rolled up her sleeves and began to bathe her hands and arms in the large basin Nora had provided earlier. "And so ye should be. Let's take a look at ye."

I gripped the headboard spokes of my grandmother's big bed as Hannah bent to her investigation. When her face loomed into view again, she pursed her lips.

"Not good, lassie."

"What's wrong?"

"He's presenting feet first, Your Grace. We'll have to turn 'im. Can you bear it?"

"Yes. Is it possible to turn him? Is it?"

"Aye. I think so. But ye've got to be strong."

I snorted. "Mrs. Mead, I am stronger, wiser than I have ever been. Before God and all that's holy, I want this baby, Mrs. Mead. Do what you must and do it now."

Through gritted teeth, I breathed and quelled the moans I would have rendered. Hannah worked swiftly and, to her credit, skillfully. Oh, yes, I could feel her turning him, gently, deftly. I felt her withdraw just as quickly and then, then within moments, I could tell my baby was in position. He moved speedily now to join us. The move was breathtakingly fast, bone-wrenchingly glorious as he left me and came into the world.

"Ha-hah!" Hannah cried, as she received his slippery body into her hands. "I've got him, lassie. Yes, yes, don't fear, he is a boy! A grand and glorious boy!"

She held him aloft for me to see.

With his black hair and long, strong body, he most

273

certainly was Max's son. And when Hannah wrapped him in a pale blue blanket and tucked him into my arms, I looked into his newborn baby blue eyes and knew they would turn to his father's silver gray. This child was a Wolff in every aspect. I kissed his sweet brow and cuddled him close to offer him my breast. He suckled eagerly, lustily. Tears came to my eyes that his father did not share this moment with us.

"The duke will be wild with joy, Your Grace."

I glanced up at Hannah as she stood there with her hands on her hips, satisfaction in every line of her wrinkled face. "Yes, Hannah. Wild."

Her eyes met mine in frank examination.

"It is a word fitting for him."

"Tell me why, Hannah."

"It's not a story I've ever told to anyone, lassie."

I waited. My son lost the nipple and smacked his lips. I directed his mouth to his goal and he loudly resumed his sucking.

She walked away, rolling down her sleeves, picking up a kettle, a bowl, and an unused pair of forceps on her way to the window.

"I used to drink a lot of whiskey. I had lots of good reasons, I thought. Now and then, I can still be known to guzzle down too much. Like the night o' your reception last year. Did you know the duke didn't give one this year? Guess he didn't want to play the host without you. He sent Bigelow out to give everyone their annual sovereign, though. Good man, yer husband. Sad."

She turned and faced me now.

"I remember the night Cynthia finally went into labor. The duke sent Bigelow for me. A cold night in

274

September. It was the duchess Cynthia's first full-term pregnancy. The only time in all the ten years she and the duke had been married that she'd been able to bring a babe to term. She was a frail woman. Flighty. But you could see she loved him. Adored him. And while it killed her that she wasn't hale and fit, she tried repeatedly to give the man an heir. This time, she almost succeeded. She had stayed at home, coddling herself, and then for some unknown reason, she found herself in bed two weeks early.

"Not too early, said the duke and I to each other when she began to suffer with the birthing pains. Not so bad, we both agreed, when ten hours later, she brought into this world a lovely little boy. Not as big and strapping as your boy, there, Duchess. No, he was not. But he gave a good cry at the beginning, he did. I bathed him and swaddled him and gave him to his mother. Cynthia didn't want to nurse the child in front of her husband, and so I took the boy when the duke came in to coo and preen. He was so happy, he even cried a little, too, by God."

She bit her lip. "But there my recollections turn muddy, I'm sorry to say. The duke left, I think. The duchess and her baby slept, I think." She stared at me.

I raised my brow.

"I had brought a bottle with me. As reward for a good night's work, I downed the rest of it. I don't remember much clearly after that. Wish to God I did. All I know is that when I woke up, it was to the sound of scuffling. Fighting. I saw Cynthia strugglin' with someone, a woman was my thought. But as I made my way in to see about it, I slipped on a rug, or I think it

275

was a rug. The woman fled. I never saw her face, nor her hair because, she wore a mobcab.''

She smacked her lips and shook her head. "I'm not sure what happened after that. Maybe the duchess got out of bed to tend to me. Maybe the other woman came back in and they tussled again. I'll never know. Next thing I knew, I was awakened by the duke, standing with his wife in his arms, rocking her back and forth, crying and screaming, the bed a bloody mess. The whole room was wild lookin', if you ask me. There was struggle, all right. But who knew who the duchess had it with? Not me, I'm sad to say, sad to say . . . Then they found the baby—ahhh, that fine baby boy, he was dead in his cradle. Poor mite. He was dead. Gray, he was when I saw him.''

So it only appeared that Cynthia had died in Max's arms.

"And you never knew how she died or exactly when?''

"Died of a hemorrhage.''

"And the baby?''

"Obstructed air passage or smothered. Doctor Quentin said he could not really tell.''

"But Cynthia . . . ?''

"The duchess died of inattention. I live my life knowing she might've died trying to help me up from my stupor, lass. I've not forgotten it. Of course, people whispered that the duke and his wife had been having troubles. They say she had accused him of taking his attentions elsewhere. When it looked like she died in his arms, many said he had killed her by letting her bleed to death. Over the years, I wonder if that crime isn't all mine. I've wondered and I've hoped I might

276

repay him for the disservice I rendered him. But I've never found a way to recompense the duke for what I helped take from him—until now. I won't drink tonight, duchess. I promise you that."

"Thank you, Hannah. I have no fears."

"Don't you, lass? You don't listen to the stories, then. About your husband, I mean."

"Oh, I know the stories, Hannah. I believed them once briefly. But over the months, I have more reasons not to. Including your story tonight. Thank you. He would be pleased you had the courage to tell me now."

"I was ashamed for years. I hated to be near him, but he tolerated me, knowing what he knew. Then, when his second duchess came to term, she would not have me. She called for Doctor Quentin instead. Said she wouldn't have a drunken piece at her lying-in. I didn't much blame her. But I never liked her anyway."

"So you have no idea what happened when the second duchess gave birth to the twins."

"No, ma'am. Only what I heard about it." She came closer. "Do you want to hear it, lass? It's not a pretty story."

"Please, Hannah. I must know as much as I can."

She sighed and sank into a chair.

"He married Maribel a scant six months after he buried Cynthia. Many say the two of them had been close, if you take my meaning, for months before the Duchess Cynthia went to her grave. But that may be gossip at its worst. Who's to say? In any case, he married Maribel against all the rules of society.

"And according to the household staff, they were not happy. No, indeed. From the first, there were arguments as wild and free as the air you breathe. He said she gave her favors elsewhere; she accused him of the same. When it became clear she was with child, rumor said the baby was not his. By the time the birthing came, they barely spoke to each other.

"Her labor came quickly, and she delivered twins. Doctor Quentin was there and there were no problems, amazing as that was for such a petite lady as the Duchess Maribel. She delivered two healthy girls, and hours later, all secured, the doctor left.

"Who knows what really happened that night? The only evidence there was was found next morning by His Grace. Again, the man was found holding his wife, moaning for her to speak to him. But, of course, she didn't. She was dead. This time, no hemorrhage was the cause. No, there was no blood. No sign of struggle. This time, peace reigned in that bedroom. The only thing unusual in that room was an opened box of French bonbons upon Maribel's dresser. Bonbons like the duke always brought her. When Doctor Quentin tried to deduce what it was had killed her, he declared the bonbons laced with a strong dose of opium. Maribel was poisoned.

"Naturally, the rumors flew again. And again, the Duke of Worminster was rumored to blame for yet another wife's demise. But no one could prove it, even if they did believe it. Everyone said he had good motive. He had good chance. And he had the money to import French bonbons."

"But no real evidence was ever found that he put the poison in the bonbons, I presume."

"You're right, Your Grace. Never."

* * *

That night, I brought my baby's cradle within a hand's distance of my bed and posted Hans beside me on the floor. Hannah Mead slept in the anteroom, and Nora I sent to her own bed. Haskins I ordered to take up a position at the front door. I told him he had to keep his hunting rifle by his side. He did not ask questions; he knew what I intended.

I had given strict orders to them all. No one would get near me tonight. No one would touch my baby, either.

No one save the one man I longed for and knew would never come.

Chapter Fourteen

No one came. The snow was too deep, I told myself. But I knew—oh, yes, I knew!—eventually someone would come. Snow, rain, nothing would keep this person away from me.

Two days after my baby's birth, a sleigh rounded the front door. From my sitting room window, I couldn't tell whether or not it was Max, so I donned my robe and padded to the top of the stairs to see who it might be. Haskins quickly opened the door.

Doctor Quentin stood huddled there against the ravages of a bitter wind. "Hello!" he bellowed. "Let me in, man! I've no intention of murdering anyone!"

Haskins flung the door wide and tried to apologize.

Quentin stamped the snow from his shoes and shrugged out of his overcoat. "Arggh! It's all right, man. Don't fuss. Where is Her Grace?"

I descended the first few stairs, Hans by my side. "Here, Doctor. Do come up." I turned to lead him to my sitting room.

"I am glad to see you recovered so well. His Grace

sent me, as you might expect. The word has gone round Wolffson that you are delivered of a boy.''

I signaled to Nora to close the door and remain with us before I turned to him. Meanwhile, Hans flopped to the carpet.

''Yes, I am, and we are both well. It was Hannah Mead's good hand which saved us both. The baby was breach. She turned him. She's very good.''

''Yes, I always thought so, despite her affinity for a bit too much now and then. That accident she had when she tended the first duchess was regrettable, but certainly no reason for her to cease her ministrations. She didn't do anything herself to harm the lady. She did deliver her of a fine boy. Whatever she did afterward, well, she has paid for her neglect in great remorse.''

''Yes, but the mystery of what happened to the first duchess has had disastrous results on my husband.''

''Mmm. And on you, also. Otherwise, why are you here, Madam, and not at home?''

''I'll not avoid your logic, sir. When I first learned of the rumors, I was afraid they might hold some truth. But while I am not afraid of my husband any longer, I don't know if the culprit or culprits might return to do in my own baby. My husband must realize the same thing. He stays away lest he once again be near when terror strikes.''

''I am sad for you both that you endure this.''

''Thank you. Yet I feel that the time of reckoning comes soon, Doctor. I can wait.''

''I would like to say your husband can wait, too, but I can't.''

''He's ill?''

"Worried sick. He does not sleep but walks that labyrinth of a house at all hours of the night. He looks appalling. He fears for you both."

"He needn't."

"His Grace wonders if you might allow me to see for myself if that is so."

"You mean examine me? And my baby?"

"Yes, if you wish. His Grace stressed that I am to do it only if you so wish."

I nodded at Nora, and we three went into my bedroom, where Quentin deduced in rapid time that my son and I were hale and hearty. Then he left with a promise to return for periodic checks of our condition.

Two weeks later, Edward Perry drove up to the front door in a public carriage. He looked splendid in new finery and declared he had a new position with a shipping company in Manchester. He came laden with messages from my brothers and their families, plus fruits and candies and tiny toys from them for my son.

"Have you named him?" Edward asked, as I leaned over into the drawing room chair and placed my precious bundle into his arms.

"Yes, I have decided to call him David, after my father. I would have liked to have Max's thoughts on the subject, but . . . well, that cannot be for a while, anyway."

"If you are resolved that Max is really not to blame, why don't you go home to him, Alicia?"

"I can't, Edward."

"Is it your pride which holds you back?" He chucked my baby under his soft chin and cooed at him. "This lovely child is the best reason in the world not to stand on pride, my dear girl."

"No, Edward. Pride has nothing to do with it. Fear does. Somehow I know whoever was responsible for Cynthia and Maribel's murders must come again for me and mine. They stopped at nothing before. Why stop at a mere minister's daughter, especially when she has the son and heir?"

"Perhaps you're right," he sighed. "I hate to see Max so unhappy."

"You've seen him?"

"Yes. Good man, your husband. He came to find me in Manchester last spring, a few weeks after that horrible row when you left. He was bitter and wanted to apologize. Now, whenever he comes to Manchester, he visits me. I like the man, Alicia. Loving you as I do, I never thought I would like him, but I do. And I think you need to go home to him."

"In all good time, Edward. In all good time."

Going home to Max became a dream of my nights and my days. I would awaken to the feel of his arms about me or his lips claiming mine. I would stop my needlework and feel his warm hands to my own or pause at my bath and remember the touch of his fingertips. I would walk in my rose garden, the same garden that I'd once tended for my Grandma, and long for the sights and fragrances of spring and wonder if the joys of love could ever blossom in my life again.

I languished here alone. And I wanted—no, I *needed* good company. My husband's.

I had to end this torment, but how could I?

With my faithful Hans as guard, I sat in a garden chair, beneath a trellis entwined with the bare branches of Grandma's roses, while the winds of March stirred my longing for normality. While the question of when I might go home repeated in my head. Suddenly, it was late afternoon, the sun was setting, and Nora came to fetch me in for David's feeding.

I left my reverie and vowed to find a means to go home again. And soon.

The idea came to me soon after the post arrived later that afternoon. In it had come a letter from my brother Mark, the minister of a small church in Liverpool.

Mark had recently received my announcement letter of David's birth and he wrote to me now about the need to baptize the child.

"It is most fitting you do it soon, my dear, even though you are estranged from your husband. A child must never suffer for his parents' foibles, and this child, like any other, needs commendation to God's care. I urge you to baptize him soon."

I smiled and kissed the notepaper.

"Mark, my darling brother, how right you are!"

No sooner had I sent word of the impending event than I received another visitor, this time from the Lair.

A grinning Mrs. Timms presented herself in the ducal carriage filled to the brim with supplies for the day itself.

"His Grace wants you to have everything you need for the reception, madam," she said, as she stood in my mirrored hallway while footmen who had accompanied her filed past with boxes of foodstuffs and silver servers, urns, and God knew what else.

She herself carried one huge traveling case which she

carefully placed on the floor. "If I may have a word with you alone, Madam?"

I nodded to Nora, and we three went into my sitting room, where I chose a chair. Hans sank next to me and curled into a ball.

"Yes, what is it, Mrs. Timms?"

"I have something His Grace wished me to present into your hands alone."

She came forward with the case and unlatched it. Spreading its mouth wide, she took from its depths a plain white muslin undergarment meant for an infant. When she laid it in my lap, I could see its delicate embroidery of oak leaves about the neck and armholes. Next, she exhumed a silk and satin gown with the same embroidery on the gathered bodice and wide sleeves. Then, she brought forth wool knit slippers and a cap to match. Finally, she laid in my lap a creamy wool shawl of such delicacy and beauty I gasped.

"These, Madam, are the christening clothes for the heirs to the House of Wolff. They were commissioned by Charles the Second to baptize his son by Morgana Wolff. That boy Charles dubbed the first Duke of Worminster. Your husband wishes you to clothe your son in these for the event so that all might see and know that he acknowledges this child as his beloved son."

As I fingered the exquisite garments, tears began to fall from my eyes.

"Does he send me no letter, no message?"

"No, ma'am."

What harm could a piece of paper do? Yet I knew it was best that we not have any contact anyone could prove, even though my heart ached to see him, hear him, hold him.

Mrs. Timms curtsied. "I'll take my leave, ma'am, and wish you God's blessings."

Her choking voice made me raise my eyes to hers.

"How is he, Mrs. Timms?"

"As well as can be expected, Ma'am. He sleeps better, now that he knows you are delivered safely and that the boy is healthy."

So, many besides the good doctor knew that Max was tormented by the mysteries that surrounded us.

"The girls are healthy, too. His Grace hired a new governess last month. He had interviewed a virtual parade of women, I assure you. He finally chose a woman who came with solid references from the Earl of Surrey, whose girls had grown and married. She's a lovely woman, Ma'am. You would like her and approve."

"I am overjoyed and miss them terribly."

"They long to see you again, Ma'am."

"They will soon, I hope." I could not continue in this vein lest I crumble into uncontrollable sobs of loneliness. I skewed myself up and asked, "How are the others?"

She thought I meant Caroline's brood, and told me how each seemed to be healthy. "Lord Gilbert has been away for a while, but I will say, before he left, he and the duke seemed friendlier. Almost like the old days."

Though curious as to the cause of that, I could not bring myself to ask, if indeed the housekeeper would know. But of other things she would certainly have knowledge.

"And the staff? How are they? Bigelow and Dorcas and Cook?"

"Bigelow had problems this winter with a stiffness in his hands and feet. We nursed him with warming pans at night, and in the day, lots of molasses tea. It eased the aches, but he is glad for the springtime. Cook continues as she was, hale and hearty. But I have no knowledge of Dorcas.''

"But why?''

"You did not know?''

I shook my head.

"I presumed you would learn . . . eventually.'' Her robin's-egg eyes shot to Nora and back to me.

"Mrs. Timms, we three have seen few people here, and even if we did, Dorcas would hardly be a subject of discussion.''

"Quite right, Ma'am. Well, then, I will tell you that Dorcas is gone, Ma'am. Has been since the night you and the duke fought.''

"But where did she go?''

"We have no idea, Ma'am. Nor do we care. We know, you see, what she tried to do to you.''

I rose from my chair and the christening clothes scattered to the floor. Nora rushed to retrieve them. I stared at Mrs. Timms.

"How can you know?''

"Oh, Madam, how could we not?'' She saw my confusion and plunged onward. "The night before you left the Lair, the duke discovered her in your bedroom. She was dispensing laudanum into a pot of tea. He caught her and asked her what she was doing. He knew that you refused to take the potion and that you hid it away under your mattress. She could not explain herself; they argued and he turned her out, right there on the spot.''

Trembling, I sank back to my chair. So that's why he had the vial on his person that night! He had confiscated it from the hand of Dorcas, and I, frightened and confused as I was, had concluded the worst. I sat and wildly peered about the room.

Oh, Max, what have I done? Oh, my dearest love, how I have misjudged you, wronged you!

I ran a shaking hand through my hair. Did Max know then only that Dorcas had tried to administer laudanum that night, or did he also deduce that my maladies of the first few months had been brought on by Dorcas's evil ministrations as well?

Only he could answer that.

"Dorcas was always a cold fish, I'll tell you," Mrs. Timms continued. "Not trouble to me, but surly and indifferent. She could be sweet as taffy, though, when she wanted something. Lovely to the first duchess, and kind to the second, even though she really hated her."

I gazed at Mrs. Timms, my mind a whirl of questions and jumbled logic.

"And you have not heard from her? Not any of the staff or Lady Adair?"

"Not to my knowledge, Ma'am. Dorcas should know that once you cross the Duke of Worminster, you must stay well away."

She hung her head and looked fretful, embarrassed.

"Madam, I hope you don't think ill of me, telling you things that . . . well, that are not quite . . ."

"Proper?" I smiled reassuringly. "You have never crossed the line of propriety, Mrs. Timms. You have told me what you know to be the truth. And to tell *you* the truth, I did notice that most of what you tell me is about the house and its functioning. I will not reprimand you, Mrs. Timms. Your advice has been as helpful as your insight."

She quickly recalled herself and smiled. "I am very glad Dorcas is gone. The staff work better without a sour face among us, and we wonder if Dorcas's absence might mean you would return to us, madam."

"In all good time, Mrs. Timms. In all good time."

The Chapel of Mary and Joseph in Wolffson came into view as my carriage rounded the last bend in the winding road. I spoke to David of the wonderful event about to befall him and inhaled some measure of courage from the joy I would impart to my infant son.

I had chosen the chapel for any number of reasons. It was close. It was the church I had attended ever since I'd come to the Lair, and even though I had been a former member of the Methodist congregation, the vicar, who was, of course, of the established Church of England, was honored to have me.

"Miss Pennington," he had confided to me in his study three days after I'd first arrived at the Lair, "if it pleases you to attend my church, I have no quarrel with you. God accepts us all."

I had attended his church every Sunday morning, had sat in the pew assigned to the six dukes of Worminster, had become an active member of his parish. In the absence of my brother, Mark, I'd requested the vicar's attendance on Max and me. The little man had gladly consented to marry us. So, it was natural for me to go there for this occasion. It was also natural for everyone and anyone associated with the dukes of Worminster to go there today for this most dynastic event.

The chapel was a delight to the eye. Nestled in a valley just outside the village, the gray stone structure was squat and jolly-looking. Once the chapel to a Cistercian monastery, it alone remained of all its accompanying buildings. Surviving centuries of wars and deprivations and Henry the Eighth's reformation, the chapel beckoned to those near and far. Today, its miniature imitation of the gothic monoliths found in larger cities comforted me for the day's challenges before me.

Yet when the carriage pulled up to the main door, I bade the driver take me to the rectory's entrance. I did not wish to see anyone before the service. My baby boy would receive his sacrament without threat. Whoever came today to this event or to the reception afterward would meet me in my own good time and on my own territory.

Haskins swung open the door of the carriage. "Your Grace," he muttered, and handed me out.

I grasped his hand and stepped down to the stone path. I gathered David close against the winds of March and felt him cuddle nearer instinctively. I smiled and placed the family heirloom shawl Mrs. Timms had brought down to us up about his strong, round chin. He slept, thank God.

The vicar, who must have been watching for me from his study, bustled out the door.

"Your Grace, I am so delighted to see you this bright day." He came to my side and took my arm to help me over the stony path.

"Thank you, Vicar. I am delighted to be here. Hopefully, the clouds will clear and we'll draw a goodly congregation for my son's baptism."

"Oh, Madam!" he chuckled, and pushed his spectacles up his nose. "You have that now! The church is full to the vaults!"

We both laughed, he with more gusto certainly than I could summon. He was pleased he could officiate at such an important event. I was pleased so many had decided to attend. But I was terrified, too. For among the throng there must be not only Caroline and her two chicks, but the staff of the Lair, the villagers of Wolffson, my brothers and their wives and children, Lianne and Edward, and any other soul who took it into his head to see the son and heir to the Wolffs named in a church of God. Certainly among this throng must be the one particular person I sought to lure. Among the throng must be the one who would come forward and wish me ill . . . wish me dead . . .

Oh, God, I pleaded, do not let me be afraid *now*.

I shuddered.

"I know it is quite cold today," murmured the vicar, as he opened the rectory door for me. "I have a pot of tea, nice and hot, ready for you, Your Grace. That'll warm you before we begin."

He led me down the darkened hall to his study. When Haskins followed close behind, the vicar turned, and with raised brows, questioned the man's presence.

"This is my butler, Vicar Morrow. He serves also as my footman. So, as you might imagine, he is indispensable to me and accompanies me everywhere. What we say in private, he can be privy to."

"Very well," the vicar frowned.

The three of us entered the book-lined study. A warm room made so by the look and feel and smell of a thousand old works, the study seeped into my senses with a warm glow of sepia gaslight. I breathed more easily here.

But the vicar had become more agitated, wiggling

291

his glasses on his nose and looking about the room with darting blue eyes.

"Tea, Madam?" he queried, as he set me in a chair before his desk.

"Just a sip, thank you."

He began to pour and his hands shook. I eyed the liquid as it came from the cup.

Oh, what was I doing? Doubting a man of God?

"I see my wife forgot the sugar. Wait here a moment, will you, and I'll fetch—"

"No, Vicar, really, I suddenly don't think I care for any tea. I—"

He was headed toward the door. My eyes followed him.

But then my vision encountered another.

From an alcove emerged the man—the only man—who could make my heart stop. Tall, dark, sorrowfully handsome, he met my gaze. My heart paused and then sped on.

He looked wonderful. Terrible. Divine. Bedeviled.

I rose from my chair with my precious burden. The vicar disappeared through the door. Haskins moved closer to me.

Never taking my eyes from my husband's, I spoke to Haskins. "You may wait just outside the closed door, Haskins."

"But, Ma'am—"

"Do it, Haskins."

"Remain, Haskins." Max's eyes flicked to the servant and back. "I will take no chances with you, darling. I'll not trouble you for long. Indulge me, please, Alicia, for just a few moments. I do not want to debate what happened that night, or—'' He broke off with a glance at Haskins.

I had to help him.

"And I think such a discussion is best left for later."

Max shook his head violently. "Alicia, I came here hoping only that you might allow me a glimpse of my son."

"I'll do more than that, Max." And with that, I moved forward and offered the father his baby.

Max's expression went from bewildered to astonished and then to overjoyed. He extended his arms, and into them I settled his son, still sleeping angelically.

With his long, elegant fingers, Max removed the creamy shawl from the charming face and sturdy body of our baby. He took David's tiny hand and kissed the fingertips. "He's very beautiful. He's perfection." Tears welled in his eyes.

I moved closer and gazed down at our pudgy little boy. "He's very healthy. Strong and bright. When he awakens, you'll see how he coos and gurgles. How he loves company."

Max swallowed convulsively and his arms shook. Suddenly, he was returning David to my arms.

"Take him." His eyes shot to Haskins. "I count on you, man, to remember I held him for no more than a moment."

Then Max spun from us. Still in his greatcoat, he headed for the door.

"No, Max, wait!" I caught his sleeve. "You're not leaving?"

"Ahh, Alicia! Christ, what do you think I'm made of? I cannot remain—"

"Of course, you can!" I barred the door. "I want you here. He is your son, your heir."

"All the more reason for me to go. I want both of you to live a long and healthy life."

"We will. I promise you, Max."

"And I promise you I will stay far away so that no one may harm you."

"Why are you so stubborn? Don't you see, I *want* you here. What better way to catch a villain than to offer not only opportunity and reason, but also the intended accused?"

He scowled and grabbed both my arms with clenched fingers that dug through the layers of my wool cape with the sharp edge of an animal's claws. "I want no one near you, do you hear me? *No one!*"

"You cannot stop me. But even if you could, darling, you cannot stop them, whoever they are. Oh, Max, my love, don't you see? Life is long, and opportunities abound. If the culprit does not strike today, tomorrow remains, and all the tomorrows of our lives. Will you live your days wondering when and how and who it is that will strike?"

His fingers relaxed, his arms stole around me, and his expression fell from anger to despair.

"Alicia, I fear for you both. I fear so much I tremble at the thought. I came here today to see you and David just once. But I want you to know that I have provided what protection I can. I have given explicit instructions to my ten footmen, and they stand on guard today to any attempt to hurt you."

"Thank you. But you cannot keep them on guard for the rest of their lives. Help me find the villain, Max. Stay. Stay for me, because I want you. Please?"

He shook his head and tears started in his silver eyes, glistening them like diamonds. "What will the towns-people say?"

"Didn't you teach me long ago that they will say what they will? And that rumor is no match for the truth? Oh, Max, stay with me today! Come to the Dower House for the reception. I need you. You need to dispel rumor and find the truth, once and for all time."

"Your logic is superb, Madam." He was smiling even if his eyes were fighting back fat tears.

"I thought so, too." I grinned at him. "I think it's time we named your son, sir."

Max removed his coat, ran shaking fingers through his silver-streaked hair, and straightened his waistcoat and jacket. With a nod to Haskins, Max took my arm and we four left the study. Just outside the door stood the fretful vicar, who examined our demeanor, found nothing amiss, and then led us from the rectory through dim, winding corridors to the anteroom behind the chancel.

I cracked the door and peaked out to view the con-gregation. Merciful heaven, I had never seen so many people jammed into one place at one time. I was thrilled. Complimented. Terrified. Surely, one of those people . . .

Warm arms stole around me and warm words drew me back to long-needed comfort. "Darling, come away."

"The girls, Max." I turned into his arms and into some other subject. "Did you bring them?"

He grinned and thumbed a tear from my cheek. "I

could not keep them away. They are with their new governess in the front pew."

"I would like them to stand with us, Max. Haskins, will you fetch Elizabeth and Mary, please?"

Within a minute, two girls ran squealing to my arms while their father held their baby brother. Our kisses and hugs and endearments ended when their attention drifted to the boy whose birth they had once been taught to fear.

"He's very small," observed a bewildered Mary.

"He has our eyes," declared Elizabeth, as David awakened from his dreams to face reality.

Their father, who had knelt to show off the newest family member, smiled gloriously at them. "I hope he'll be as handsome as you both are lovely."

Mary harumphed. "And obedient, too."

They all three chuckled at some intimate joke. Without me, they had formed a solid bond of love and respect. Suddenly, I felt bereft. Forlorn.

"Darling," Max stood by me in a second, "what is it? Are you feeling ill?"

"Max," I whispered for his ears alone, "oh, Max, I want to come home."

Passion, fury, delight, and hopelessness mixed in a ripe blend upon his handsome face. "And God knows, my love, I want you there. Chin up. We'll have you there yet. Today, God willing. Come, now. Let's name this child of ours."

He took my elbow and nodded to the vicar, the girls, and Haskins. We emerged into the chapel, where sunlight streamed through stained-glass windows and dust motes floated in such profusion they obscured the brightness. I could not look at the congregation. I was too afraid.

But Max looked. Beside me, I felt him count heads and recognize faces and names, recording them in his brain for future reference. And when they saw him, when they knew that he accompanied me and David, when the ripple of recognition rose to a crescendo of gasps and ooos and ahhs, the very church seemed to vibrate in surprise. Gracious as he was, Max ignored them.

Instead, he led us to stand before the baptismal font, and it was there I realized David was still in my husband's arms. For all the world to see, this child was his. For God to bless, this child was ours.

And for whomever this child was anathema, here he was presented. Let him who wished him ill come forward, I prayed fervently. Please, let this agony be finished.

The ceremony went swiftly. Within minutes, David Maxim George Wolff was baptized before God and man. And within minutes, we five were inside the ducal coach, headed for the Dower House and the reception I'd planned.

I sighed and sank against my husband's side. He caught me close and kissed my temple. Thus entwined, we silently traveled to the place where we'd first met and where now all our troubles would be put to rights.

Chapter Fifteen

The throng that had packed the chapel came to my door in droves that afternoon. They came in carriage and on foot. They came bearing extravagant gifts and simple ones, some purchased in far-off lands, others handmade in nearby cottages, some packaged in bright ribbons and others plainly offered for the son of the lord of the manor. These Nora took and placed on a huge table in the hall that soon towered dangerously high with items of every shape and size.

While Hans took up his usual post at my feet, I stood in my wine-red drawing room with Max at my side, his arm conspicuously at my shoulder or on my waist, his eyes alert, his most engaging smile for me alone. We stood together against the uncertainties of our future and received those who would wish our boy well.

They sat in my morning room, ate in my dining room, debated politics and fashion in my drawing room, listened to a few bright young women render a little Mozart or Brahms on my grandmother's piano-forte. They came and spent the afternoon, inspecting my house and my servants, judging the worthiness of my cook, bowing to my husband and curtsying to me, offering their best wishes to the boy I held in my arms.

They came one by one to introduce themselves and peer at me and Max and David. They came to smile and congratulate and compliment. They came to inspect our demeanor so that they might retire to some discreet corner and mutter to each other of the obvious reconciliation of the duke and this, his latest duchess.

They were not malicious in this, merely human. I knew it and understood it. After all, they, too, had endured the horror of two unsolved murders, two unpunished murders. They were afraid as much as they were curious. And they, like Max and me, deserved to know the truth.

If I could, I would offer it up for public consumption this very day in this very house. But my eyes scanned the drawing room and I detected no one who had menaced me in any way.

David once more squirmed in my arms and began to whimper. He was hungry. I felt an answering tingling response in my bosom and knew I must retire to nurse him. I looked up at Max.

"Darling, I must attend to David. Remain and entertain our guests, will you?"

A fierce animal protectiveness suffused his silver eyes. "I will not leave your side."

I smiled. "It did not take you long to come full circle from this morning's need to be with me in a crowded room."

"We'll have Nora with us."

"Yes. Nora." I rose and David began to cry louder.

Trailing Nora, the three of us led the way down the long mirrored hall and mounted the alabaster circular

299

stairs in silence. We entered my chambers and I passed David to Max.

"Help me out of this gown, Nora, and hurry! David is starving, from the sound of it."

Poor Max was having a difficult time of quieting a hungry boy. I disappeared into my anteroom and Nora quickly let down my hair, stripped me of the layers of satin gown, two stiff petticoats, camisole, stays, and chemise. I donned one of my favorite lawncloth chemisettes which buttoned up the front, one simple petticoat, a jade velvet skirt, and atop it all, a full muslin canezou with long lace sleeves and tiny glass buttons going from waist to high-necked collar. This I left unbuttoned to feed my baby. This and two other cambric canezous were my usual attire since David's birth; not only were they comfortable for my more ample bosom, but they were easy to don and discard.

I told Nora she should remain in the anteroom while I nursed David. "His Grace will not let anything befall me, Nora, rest assured."

She nodded and threw me a weak smile. Even she did not quite believe the man was innocent. I sighed and entered the bedroom.

"Come with me, Max," I told him, as I led him into my sitting room to a rose-colored chaise lounge I used when feeding David. I arranged myself, unbuttoned my bodice, and looked up at Max.

He breathed heavily, his eyes on the swelling tops of my breasts.

"Give him to me, darling. He'll scream the rafters off if he doesn't eat soon."

Max handed David over and immediately the little

boy rooted for his dinner. I bared one plump hard breast and he latched on instantly.

"My God," Max marveled, as David crooned and sucked with ecstasy, "starving little mite, isn't he?" His eyes took in the sight of mother and son at peace.

"You have never seen this, have you, Max?"

He shook his head, not knowing whether to be embarrassed or just to give over to the utter fascination he really felt. "Cynthia was too embarrassed to let me stay to see her nurse our newborn, and Maribel refused to nurse the girls. She bound up her breasts minutes after their delivery and had me hire three wet nurses for the twins. Do you . . . does it hurt?" he asked in wonder.

"Not at all. It's delightful, actually. Almost as wonderful as having you . . ." and then I blushed and looked down at my baby suckling happily.

Max's hand went to my cheek. "Alicia," he whispered, "I love you, darling. You are so rare, so honest, so—"

I leaned against his palm, closed my eyes, and rubbed my cheek against his skin. "Max," I tried hard not to sob, "I want this over. I want to come home and live with you and love with you." Tears welled up and obliterated my vision. "I can't bear not knowing. They've got to come forward. I thought they would today." I was crying frantically now, and David lost his hold and whimpered. I led him to his source and he quieted. I did not.

Max encircled me in his arms and stroked my unbound hair. "Sweet love, don't. The day is not over. They will come." He held us securely as David finished his feeding.

301

Minutes later, a knock sounded on the main bedroom door and we both turned to gaze in that direction. We looked at each other.

"Nora will answer, Max."

We heard footsteps and muted voices.

I froze.

I heard footsteps come closer and pause.

Nora was saying, "I will ask Their Graces if they will receive you."

A woman's voice pleaded for the opportunity. Another one, deeper, repeated the hope. A man's echoed both sentiments.

Nora rounded the portal, her eyes rounded to the whites with fear.

"Milord, Madam, it is Lady Samuel, Lady Adair, and Lord Gilbert Wolff."

My eyes closed and I felt David pull away.

"Please have them wait for a few minutes, Nora. Take David, will you, please? And take him to the nursery. Take Haskins with you, and lock the door behind the three of you, do you hear me?"

Max stood and helped me from the chaise. "Darling, you will receive them with me."

My mind raced. I needed another. Another person who would stand guard, who would verify that Max could not, would not hurt me.

My mind raced. Who? Who?

I handed David into Nora's keeping and said, "Send Doctor Quentin to us, Nora. Before you show the Wolffs in, please."

She disappeared and closed the door firmly behind her.

I fell against Max's chest. If I could have burrowed

into him, ignored the world and all its problems, I would have gladly gone.

He understood, as he always had. He murmured little love words and tiny consolations. He stroked my hair, my back. His lips, buried in my hair, spoke of resolution of this mystery, ultimate freedom and joy. He turned me and rearranged my chemisette, kissed my breasts, and buttoned the canezou to the collar. He led me to a dressing table, sat me on the stool, took a brush, and tamed my hair. He found a ribbon and tied my hair back at the nape. Then, he leaned down into the mirror, captured my staring eyes, and whispered how he adored me and how he would never let me leave him again.

I fell back against him and his courage seeped into my soul. I stood and nodded. He lifted my lifeless hands and kissed each tenderly. He smiled tremulously and tipped my face up.

"We will face the world together, not just this day for this trial, but for all our days together."

"I would to God they were long days, many years."

He smiled more assuredly now. "And so they will be. An eternity together, nothing less."

Nora knocked and came in to announce Doctor Quentin. The tall, thin doctor entered right behind her.

"You sent for me, Madam. Are you ill?"

"No, no. My husband and I wished you to be present, that is all. As a witness, you see."

He frowned. "A witness to what, Madam?"

Max scowled at the doctor's impertinence. "We wish your presence, man, isn't that enough?"

Quentin was only partially cowed. "Yes, Your Grace.

Your wife was kind enough to invite me here, even though I did not attend her at the birth, and I—"

"Then do us a favor, Quentin, and sit quietly over there while my wife and I give this audience. *Please.*"

Quentin had trouble suppressing a smile. "Yes, sir." And with that he retired to a corner of the room and took a seat in a small boudoir chair.

Nora's eyes went from mine to Max's. He gave her a lift of his brows and she turned to fetch the three Wolffs.

In they came like soldiers to a front. Caroline, in dark mauve and cream. Adair, in a green which was too dark for her fair complexion. And Gilbert, still using his cane, but in better clear-eyed health than when I'd last seen him that horrible night in the library. He still had his cane, but he had another aura about him that I could not define.

Of course, I had seen them all briefly downstairs. I had greeted them first as was their due as the closest relatives. They had been civil—polite, even. I had returned the tone. They had moved on to mingle with the other guests and we had not spoken again. Why they should wish to see me privately now was not only frightening, but considering our past poor relationships, also unnecessary, unless . . . unless one of them meant to do me harm.

I stood, my husband at my side, and extended my hand. "Please, do have a seat."

Caroline smiled—truly smiled!—and chose an overstuffed chair to one side of a small settee.

"Thank you, Alicia. We do not intend to stay long. We know you must be tired. New mothers are so often fatigued."

She arranged herself in the chair like visiting royalty. Her two children, with less ostentatiousness, assumed perches side-by-side on the settee, but it was Gilbert who broke the silence and smiled at me.

"We wanted to have a few private words with you, Alicia, before we left." His eyes, so like his cousin's, ran to Max. "Perhaps Max has told you of a conversation we had with him recently."

"No, Gilbert. We have not had an opportunity to speak of much today."

Gilbert nodded and brushed at his trousers. "Very well. We three had a discussion with Max day before yesterday. We have petitioned Max to support us in a move." He glanced up to check his cousin's expression and mine. "I have found a position for myself, teaching English at a school in Chester. It is not much in pay or prestige, but I realized months ago that I really could not remain at Wolffs' Lair on Max's charity any longer."

I felt Max stiffen beside me, his hand going securely to my waist.

Adair glowered at the floor.

Caroline, more serene and gracious than I'd ever seen her, smiled at me sweetly. "I think it is a wonderful opportunity for Gil, don't you, Alicia?"

"Absolutely," I replied, and thought more wonderful the change in Caroline's usual acerbic disposition. What a pity her daughter did not experience a similar transformation.

"Yes, well," Gilbert cleared his throat, "I wanted, rather, *we* wanted you to know, Alicia, that we will be leaving the Lair within the month. Max has said he 'ill help us financially for as long as I wish. He's glad to see me take a stand for myself and for Mother and Adair. I rented a cottage near the school, and Mother and Adair will be in town, near genteel people. I wanted to come today to tell you that we were going so that you might consider that when deciding whether to return to the Lair." He flushed bright red in confusion.

"I never had any doubts about returning, Gil."

He blinked. "But—why, then, did you leave?"

"You know full well one of the reasons I wanted to leave."

He bit his lip. "Yes, I told Max about it."

I swung my gaze to Max.

"Gilbert came to me the morning you left, my dear. He told me much that I had suspected for years and had no proof of. He also told me much that explained your actions the night before you left the Lair."

"I'll add," Caroline jumped into the conversation, "that Gil has since changed his ways significantly."

"Mother, please, I will tell this. Alicia, I want to apologize for that horrible event in the library."

"Thank you, Gil. I accept your apology. I prayed one day you would come to your senses and give up the drink."

"It was what I did to you that night that humiliated me more than I ever thought possible. After I knew you fled the house, I blamed myself for acting so dastardly. What sin I kept hidden was what I revealed to you that night. You see, I . . . I was in love with Maribel."

"Oh, my God!" cried Adair, as she jumped from her seat and stared in horror at her brother.

Caroline closed her eyes as if the world had offered

306

up all its evils to her eyes. Her hand went to her throat and she convulsed but remained erect.

Adair wrung her hands. "How *could* you? How could you say that *here?* In front of *her?* Oh, my God, Gil!"

He eyed his sister coolly. "It's true, Adair. I will say it now, just once more for Alicia to understand, and then never again will I utter Maribel's name. I loved her, illicitly. She . . . she was a witch, you know. A witch. She would look at any man and smile as if he alone were the center of the universe. She would compliment you and pout and preen and offer up her innermost thoughts and all the while you thought it was for your private consumption."

Gil rose to pace to the window and back. "From the moment she arrived to act as companion to Cynthia, I saw her work her wiles on every man within shouting distance. I saw her smile at the gentlemen who came to dinner, or those who came for business discussions. She even tried to work on the good Doctor Quentin here!"

The man shifted self-consciously in his chair.

Gil raged on. "I saw her cull Max. My God, I even warned you, didn't I?"

Max swallowed hard. Admitting such indignity in front of so very many people was frightfully hard. "Yes. Yes, that's true. Gil came to me to warn me. We were good friends, Gil and I, before Maribel came to nurse her cousin, my wife. But Gil saw what Maribel was long before I ever did. I was the bigger fool because I did not see it myself. I was beguiled by her as so many poor fools were."

"And I was, too," Gil continued quietly. "She played on me until I was enchanted with her. No matter that I had been the one to warn others of her. But even I could not withstand the onslaught she could mount. Anyone could become besotted with her. She was evil. In her spell, I did things . . . well, let me say, I shall forever be ashamed of the things I did with her. But as God is my witness, those twin girls are not—could not be mine. I never went that far with Maribel. She wouldn't allow it. Perhaps she was afraid of committing the ultimate sin once she was married. Perhaps she could not lie with her husband's cousin for fear of arousing his wrath."

Caroline swooned.

The doctor jumped from his chair to catch her before she fell to the floor.

"Someone get me some water or smelling salts."

I ran to the other room and wet a handkerchief with cool water from an urn and took it in to him. He patted Caroline's forehead and hand and she recovered enough to loosen her own fichu.

"Really, Gil," she croaked, "must you go on?"

"Gil," Max said, "you really are doing in your mother and sister, here. I know you wish to confess to Alicia, but perhaps we could send your mother and sister out. They don't really need to hear this."

"Yes, they do, Max." He turned his eyes to each in turn. "They need to know so that they will cease their endless fantasies and know the truth—finally."

Adair advanced on him like a vicious cat. "You needn't tell me a thing, brother of mine. I *know*. I knew ever since the day Maribel came inside the Lair that she would lead us all to utter destruction. Mother knew, too. Never doubt. Ha! That you were so weak, so silly as to be caught in Maribel's trap, is a sin I'll never forgive you of. So take your righteousness elsewhere, sir. It cannot buy amnesty from me."

"No," he shook his head sorrowfully, "nothing buys amnesty from you. You are so hardened, so wizened to the truth of what you've become."

"Children!" Caroline admonished her brood like the woman I'd known her to be.

"No!" Gil shouted at her, and pointed a finger at Adair. "I've kept quiet long enough for you! You like to blame others for your failure to capture Max for yourself, but you must come to your Rubicon, my dearest sister. You must own up to certain facts yourself."

She clenched her fists. "I own to nothing."

"No?" He stepped forward and narrowed his eyes at her. "Why not tell us what you were doing in Maribel's room the night she died?"

She fell back, her mouth open and working.

"I saw you in the hall, opening her door. Tell us, sister."

She twitched one shoulder. "I went to visit."

"Did you? Why?"

As Gil advanced, Adair fell back step by step and Max gathered me to him, beyond her reach.

"I went to see how she was. She had had a difficult birth. Twins are difficult to be delivered of," she sneered.

"Aye, I grant you. But why go to her, taking tea and cakes?"

She frowned.

"I saw you with the tray, Adair. *Don't lie*. You got it from whom? Dorcas? Would your good friend the upstairs maid, our dear 'sister,' lie for you, hmm? Hah! You know it wouldn't be the first time.''

"Yes, I took Maribel tea and cake. What of it?''

"Why? You and Maribel were never friends. Why take her that? But better still, the question is, why was the tray not found in the room the next morning when Maribel was found dead?''

Adair went blank. ''I have no idea. Ask the staff.''

"I did.''

She shrugged.

"The footman in the upstairs wing recalled that no one called for him after two, when I saw you enter her room. Maribel did not pull the bell. Did you take the tray out with you? And if so, did you also wash the pot and cups by yourself?''

He looked over to Doctor Quentin. ''You were called to the scene the next morning, sir. Did you see a tea tray?''

"None.'' His eyes examined each person in the room. ''None. And everyone vowed they had not touched a thing, but had left it as it was when the duke found Maribel's body the next morning.''

I grimaced at his words and stepped forward. ''What was there in the room, then? Any indication of a struggle?''

"None. The duchess had died quickly, from violent convulsions, from the look on her face.''

"And you concluded she died of poisoning, Doctor. Why?''

He lifted his shoulders. ''It was simple. I saw a box of bonbons opened and two eaten from it. I examined them and found the bonbons dusted with opium.'' He glared at me. "The duchess died of a lethal dose of opium. She was poisoned."

"And you thought it was the Duke of Worminster who had killed his wife—?"

"Yes, because he admitted to having purchased the bonbons from a London confectioner a week before." He checked the look on Max's face and then returned to his chair, a tired man.

"You see?" bellowed Adair at the assembled company. "I did not kill her. Although, as God is my witness, I would gladly have strangled her for all she did to me."

She peered at Max now with tear-filled eyes. "Yes, I wanted to be your wife. From the moment I entered your house, I wanted to be your wife. You were so dashing, so charming, so intelligent. And Cynthia was no match for you. She was a simp, a twit. Sitting there in all her delicate finery, whining day in and day out about her malady of this and her affliction with that! Oooh, God, what a bore! How could you stand it, I wondered. But then, of course, I saw she changed for you. She would become the darling of your dreams when she entered a room. She would never show you what a dreary bit of baggage she really was."

She sidled closer to me and Max. "But you were such a gentleman, you ignored her foibles and chose not to see her for her true worth. Especially when she got with child and finally, for the first time in her life, she kept it to term!

"Ha! What a coup for Cynthia! What a disaster. No sooner was she pregnant than she was in bed—constantly. And she absolutely had to have amusing company. And I did not suit. I was too dull, too low-

311

born to read or play cards. Nothing would do but she'd have her cousin, the amusing, the glorious Maribel.

"Oh, God, Maribel came like a wind from hell. And she, just like her cousin, was one thing in front of the world and quite another in front of a man—any man, especially Max."

Adair sauntered forward now to rake her eyes over Max. "And you—you poor blind man—you fell for it. I watched you just as I watched Gil, and you both fell for her lowered lashes and her comely smiles. Her black lace and her black heart. What happened, Max? Did she tantalize you so you couldn't bear it any longer? Did my instinct deceive me, Max, or did you commit adultery with the viper?"

Max went white.

Caroline fell back against her chair and patted her forehead with the cloth I'd given her.

Gil stood silently while tears accumulated in his eyes.

Finally, Max spoke. "No, I did not commit adultery with Maribel, Adair. I will confess I wanted to, but no, God help me, I did not commit the act."

"She tempted you to, though, didn't she?"

Max pursed his mouth. "Adair, you stretch the bounds of propriety too far."

"She wanted to seduce you! She told me!"

His head came up and his face was the mask of a fiend.

"No!"

She avoided him. "Yes, she told me. She was *so* proud of herself. So hellishly proud! She said she had come to get you, and she would do it with any means. She laid a bet. I was aghast. I couldn't believe she'd play you so openly. But she did."

312

Reason surfaced in my mind and I had to ask more of this horrible revelation. "But even if she did plan such a thing, she couldn't predict that Cynthia would die. What good would it do Maribel to lure Max if it was only a liaison? She'd want marriage."

"So . . ." Adair turned on me, "don't you think she could remove the last impediment, too, if she wanted?"

"You mean Maribel killed Cynthia?"

"Wouldn't *you* kill for the Duke of Worminster, madam?"

I could not answer. What do you say to such a query?

Adair shook her head. "She thought she was better than Cynthia. Certainly healthier. More able to bear an heir for the cursed House of the Wolffs."

"But do you have any proof? Did she confess?"

"To me?" Adair laughed like the inmates of Bedlam. "Not to me, duchess!"

"But she confessed to me."

We all turned to Quentin, who sat slumped in his chair, his unseeing eyes upon the carpet.

We became a study in silence. A group of five with gaping mouths and bulging eyes.

"She was evil. I knew it the minute I saw her. Women like that are never worth a drop of emotion or an ounce of love. Yet they take everyone else's and crush it. She was such a woman. I hated her."

He raised his face and his eyes met mine.

"I loved her. But she was evil personified. She told me she loved me, and then, one day, she blithely decided she didn't. One day this, the next day that. She was quicksilver. Lust personified. She loved to be petted and adored. Yet she hated to be responsible for the feelings she evoked. She was evil. Diabolical. She told me one day when she came to my cottage how she had hated her cousin. How she loathed Cynthia's weaknesses.

"She told me how she deserved to be the Duchess of Worminster, and how she had planned it and Cynthia, in her weakness, had abetted Maribel's plan. She went to see Cynthia in her room the night Cynthia was delivered of a boy. Maribel meant to congratulate her, or so she told me. When she entered, she thought they were alone.

"Maribel wanted to see if Cynthia would survive. Cynthia had had a difficult birth, and Maribel was tiring of waiting for her cousin to sicken and die. Maribel had become a companion to Cynthia during her confinement only because she wanted to be near Max. Evidently, Maribel had long schemed to find herself a rich husband, and it pained her that her weak cousin had snared so rich and famous a one as the Duke of Worminster.

"When Maribel entered Cynthia's room, Cynthia was on to Maribel's games. She had been for some time, it seems. Then and there, she accused Maribel of betraying her trust in her own house with her husband. They argued.

"Cynthia revealed then that she had detected something awry in Maribel's attentions to Max. When Cynthia gloated that night that her position was now secured by the birth of the boy and that neither Maribel nor any other woman would take her place, Maribel became so mad that she slapped Cynthia. Cynthia

314

hit her cousin and called her a whore. They tussled there in the room on the bed.

"The midwife must have heard them, and rose to enter the main chamber. The two of them continued to wrestle until Cynthia began to hemorrhage and Maribel, caught in a blood lust, just kept pummeling her cousin. Then Maribel saw the midwife coming for them, but the woman slipped and passed out upon the floor. Maribel made to leave, but Cynthia taunted her, and Maribel returned saying she'd kill Cynthia and the boy. Cynthia made it to the cradle and got the baby out, intending to get help, but Maribel was faster and tried to tear the baby from her. Maribel fell, and somehow in the fracas smothered the baby. Cynthia had begun to bleed badly. But Maribel, seeing what she had done, became frightened and thought she could escape all responsibility if she left Cynthia to bleed to death. Maribel sought to cover her movements and put the baby back in the cradle and left.

"Unfortunately for the duke, he was the one to discover the bodies. The midwife couldn't disprove the conjectures, and so we had the beginning of the rumors. If those rumors served His Grace poorly, Maribel didn't care. The onus was off her. She took the reward and married the duke when he offered a scant few months later."

His haunted eyes met Max's. "My God, man, you even married her too soon. Not to observe the proper year of mourning only made the gossip worse."

Max raked his hair. "I know. But she was, as you say, evil. She was at me constantly. A veritable harpy. Seducing with eyes and lips and hands. Always there, always available. So damn relentless."

315

"Aye, Your Grace, in more ways than one, she was a killer."

Finally, I found some voice. "Doctor Quentin, you loved Maribel and you hated her. Did you also kill her?"

"No. But I wish to Christ I had." He began to weep. "I wish to Christ I had."

Chapter Sixteen

A scream pierced the stillness of the room. We spun in unison toward the door.

I ran for my bedroom and the others followed. I barely made it halfway across the room when my door burst open to admit one panting woman. It was one of the Lair's downstairs maids, dressed in her Sunday finery, wild-eyed and crying.

"Milord, Milady, oh come, come! Mrs. Timms sent me to fetch you."

Max strode toward her. "What's wrong, Carrie?"

"It's Hans, milord. Oh, milady, he's having a fit. Frothing at the mouth, and—"

I picked up my skirts and would have run, but Max had me by the arm. "If he's rabid, darling, you won't want to go near him."

"Come with me, then. Get a blanket, Nora. Two. Yes, thank you."

I wrapped my arm in one and handed the other to Max, who did the same. We flew down the circular stairs.

At the bottom, in front of the hall table where we

had stacked the presents, a crowd gathered to peer at the giant writhing dog. He lay on his side, his teeth bared, growling his agony while his legs wildly pawed the air. Beside him lay a few of the presents which had fallen to the floor, and just in front of him, a once pretty red velvet box, now savaged by canine teeth-marks. Opened. Almost empty. Yet inside remained one whole white chocolate bonbon. The others clearly had been consumed by none other than a hungry, curious Hans.

His legs slowed. His breathing labored. I wended my way through the throng, knelt by his side, and spoke to him. At my voice, his growing ceased and small whimpers met my ears.

"Sweet, faithful Hans. What has happened to you?" I began to cry and stroked his noble head.

His eyes opened once and rolled, and then he was gone from me.

Max drew me up into his arms.

"Bigelow," he called above the crowd, "Bigelow, man, where are you?"

From the back of the crowd, the butler came forward to face Max, who instructed him to take the dog away.

By now the crowd was over the initial shock and weeping or talking or making haste to leave.

Max drew me closer to his chest and raised his voice, "My wife and I thank you for coming. We regret the sad ending to a lovely day. Before any of you goes, we wonder if we might ask the person who brought these chocolates to step forward."

It was like asking the devil himself to identify and be exorcised. No one stepped forward. Everyone murmured and fretted and huddled together.

Doctor Quentin stepped forward and bent to pick up the mangled box and its contents. He smelled the box and the chocolate, then ran his finger over the bottom. It came away with a white residue which he eyed and felt between two fingertips. Then he peered up at Max.

"Sir, it is opium."

The crowd went mad. Some screamed or cried. Most hastened to leave. Thomas came forward, along with my other brothers, Luke, John, and Paul, and the four of them effectively barred the door.

"No one leaves," Max barked, "until we know who brought these."

Still no one took ownership.

"Very well, Bigelow, get me Nora. She's locked in the nursery with the baby. She placed the presents on this table, and she will remember who brought this."

I pressed myself against the solid security of my husband, but as I watched Bigelow climb the stairs, past Gilbert and Adair, I knew Nora would not come out for anyone but me.

"I will go with you, Bigelow." Max pulled me back, and when I turned and explained, he reluctantly let me go. "Max, do not fear, Bigelow is with me."

I mounted the stairs and followed the staid butler to the end of the hall. We were just about to turn when a strong hand grabbed me by the collar, pulling me backward so that my ribs felt the definite impression of the barrel of a gun.

I cried out, but Bigelow was not fast enough for my attacker. He turned and his bulging eyes nearly fell out of his head.

"Back off!" hissed Caroline to the butler. "If you want to see her live, back off!"

Muddled, frightened, the butler froze.

"Come this way," she said, as she jabbed the gun once more into my ribs. "Down the back stairs."

I walked forward as she commanded. My mind was whirling.

"What do you think you're doing, Caroline? You won't escape this."

"I can try. Run, Duchess. The faster you run, the longer you live."

We were moving rapidly down the stairs. Here, at the back of the house, no one would hear us, nor would they see us leave. Yet Bigelow would get Max. Max would come.

We emerged into the chilly spring air.

She nudged me forward along the path round the house toward the woods.

Within twenty yards, we made the edge of the trees, and the way she led me was along no cut path but over treacherous brush. The wind sliced through the trees and without a wrap, I shivered. She nudged the gun into my ribs to hurry me on.

My eyes scanned the territory before me. I had never walked these woods. I had no idea what treasures or disasters it offered. How was I to escape this situation, this madwoman?

But suddenly words Max had said to me long ago and for another purpose flooded my brain. Where logic offered no help, couldn't I rely on my instinct to lead me?

"Wherever you take me, Max will find us. He is not a man to be foiled."

She laughed like the demented. "You really love the creature! Max the Wolf. Max the Rake. Max the Rich, the Bold, the Honorable! How sick to death I am of hearing about the infernal Max!''

"Why?" I asked, as she prodded me over ragged stumps and stagnant puddles that made me pick my way at a snail's pace. "Why do you hate him so? He has been so good to you."

"By your definition, I suppose. By mine, he has been an idiot."

"And Maribel as well?"

"Maribel was my thorn. Maribel the whore. Who did she think she was, worming her way into his heart and his bed, when the honor belonged to Adair? Then, if that weren't bad enough, she had to work her wiles on innocent Gilbert. She deserved to die. She stood in our way. Just like you."

"So you had Dorcas try to poison me."

"Of course I did. She hated the Wolffs as much as I did. And you were so humble, so innocent. Bah! If it weren't for you, Adair would be married to Max now. I know it."

"I doubt it, Caroline. Your daughter is no match for him. Nor for any man. She is too bitter, too filled with gall to make any man a proper mate."

"And you, you simpering little minister's whelp, *you* should know what a good mate is, eh?"

"Yes, I do."

"Not by any measure I've taken."

"Oh, is a minister's whelp worse than a smithy's daughter?"

"You wretch!" Her fist struck me in the back of the neck.

The world reeled and I staggered, then fell to the earth on my hands and knees. I would not faint, I told myself as I blinked and focused on leaves and twigs and stones.

"Get up!" She was tugging at my arm. "Get up!"

I could hear voices, footsteps. Max? Max . . .

"Damn you, get up!"

I turned my face up to her. She looked this way and that about her as the voices grew louder, nearer. She raised the gun to my head.

I closed my eyes, prepared to meet my maker. "Dear God, forgive us our trespasses as we forgive those . . ."

A shot thundered in the air. The earth beside me shook. I felt nothing. No pain. No release. I merely marveled at how in the world death could seem so peaceful, so ordinary, when bliss was what I expected.

And bliss felt like Max's arms around me, Max's hands to my cheeks, Max's lips buried in my hair, whispering words of love and deep concern for my health and telling me how he loved me dearly and would never let anyone hurt me, now or in the beyond.

I searched his eyes and knew suddenly that this was life, not death.

My arms stole around his neck and I hugged him close.

But . . . Caroline? Where was Caroline?

I looked around and down. There she lay, sprawled upon her back, face up, her lovely Wedgwood blue eyes now serene, a bullet hole precisely through my chest.

Horrified, I turned my face into Max's chest and mutely wept for a woman who knew no redemption before she died.

* * *

An hour later, I sat in the chaise in my sitting room, wrapped in warm velvet and wool, hot chocolate on the end table and Max beside me.

He stroked my hair back from my cheeks and smiled. "You feel better now."

I took one of his hands and kissed the palm. "Always, when you are near, I am sublime."

His ministrations had brought me round. Taking charge of the hideous scene in the woods, he listened to Doctor Quentin pronounce Caroline dead, then ordered his men to remove the body and take it home to the Lair. Then, he lifted me high into his arms, bade adieu to our guests, and returned me to my chambers. There, he had directed Nora to get me a huge bath, clean clothes, and a pot of hot chocolate. Then he dismissed her, stripped me of the ruined garments I'd worn through the woods, bathed me, dried me, and attired me in clean cambric linen chemise and drawers, a green velvet robe, and two wool shawls. I had loved every caress, every tender ministration, and his gentleness had brought me from my silent horror to some semblance of normality.

He leaned forward and kissed my lips. "I would have died if I'd lost you now. I have been so forlorn without you this last year. I began to think I had dreamt the few months I'd spent with you."

"You are not alone in that. But I know now I owe you an apology—"

"You, apologize to me? No. Never."

"Yes, I misjudged you. I didn't trust you—"

"You had good reasons."

"All of them have since proved false."

323

"Yes, but you could not know that. The evidence was too overpowering."

"Caroline was very shrewd."

"Yes. Until the end, when her logic failed. She could not have hoped to get away with hurting you."

"She'd succeeded in so many other things. She hired Dorcas, you know, to administer laudanum. To addict me to the stuff, or one day to poison me outright, I know not which."

"I never thought Dorcas did the act without some instigation. But I had no proof of who might be behind it all. I merely saw her that night when I returned from my trip. I'd gone upstairs, even though I knew you were in the conservatory. I had a gift for you, you see, and I wanted to hide it in your jewelry box. Thank God I did. I found Dorcas holding the deadly bottle and stirring the potion into your tea. How in God's name she meant for you to drink tea instead of hot chocolate without noticing the heavy taste of laudanum, I have no idea. But she was never one to think everything through, either. I knew she couldn't be at the bottom of her own scullduggery. She left, and I was glad to be rid of her."

"You have never heard of her again?"

"No. I don't think she would be stupid enough to return within a thousand miles of me. She knows I'd take her before a magistrate."

I squeezed his hand and gazed into his troubled eyes. "Tell me about Cynthia and Maribel. All of it, please. I would hear the entire story from your lips, and then I promise I will never ask it of you again."

He sighed and examined my hands. "I should have told you long ago. But I was very afraid I'd lose you.

You see, when I made arrangements with your father, I was simply in need of an heir, not a woman to love. I'd had my fill of what I'd presumed was love. I suspected Gil of betraying me with Maribel, and the suspicion ate at me. I did not want him to inherit, and I—well, I simply wanted an heir. You had all the necessary attributes. You were young, healthy, and a female of the House of Wolff, with all the attendant qualities that implied. When I saw you, I was enchanted, yes. You were—you *are* so very beautiful. But more than that, you are so bright, so cheerful, so logical and intelligent. The combination intrigued me. I had never been intrigued by any woman's intellect or cheer. I had been far too intrigued by two women's feminine charms, and I had found that wanting in both of them.

"You, my love, were—are—so very different. Unique. And so, in the desiring, in the loving of you, I could not bear it when the mysteries began with you. The convulsions, the headaches, the stomach ailments. I was mad to find the perpetrator. Constantly on guard for you, I found myself the target of some menancing letter writer."

"The notes! I thought I detected a change in your behavior. Someone *was* threatening you, weren't they?"

"Yes. Someone with a very bad hand but a very genteel education. I knew the notes had to have been written by a servant, but composed by someone of better breeding. With the first note, I suspected Williams. She was being devilish toward the children and being caught at it by you. I knew that did not bode well. Then, when the second arrived, she had just departed.

When no more came my way after that, I concluded it was Williams who had penned them.''

"And do you think Caroline was the instigator of those as well?"

"I know Caroline made a point of being friendly with the governesses I hired. Except for this last one, whom I made sure she stayed far from at all times. I suppose we will never know for certain if Williams was put up to her evil by Caroline, but we can rest assured she will never bother us again. Over a month ago, I got word from a man of mine in Chester that a woman calling herself by the same name was found dead of starvation this January in a workhouse. Williams lived for retribution, but I think she found her own first.''

I shook my head. "I am sorry for her nonetheless. Poor misguided soul that she was.''

"You pity Caroline, too, I think.''

"Yes, she was not originally evil. Circumstances helped to make her so.''

"I know. I wish I could have corrected some of the unfortunate mistakes of my ancestors, but I tried and failed. I took the three of them in when they were in debt and had no one to turn to. I fed them, housed them, clothed them. My God, I even paid for Gil's last year at Cambridge. And then, of course, to see how Caroline despised me and Adair, in her odd way, pursued me. To see Gil fall for the machinations of Maribel . . .''

He raked his hair and would have risen to leave me. I captured his hand to hold him there. He would not meet my eyes.

"Darling Max, Gil was wrong to become involved with Maribel. He knows it, admits it. But he never

326

succumbed to the ultimate betrayal, it seems. He did know right from wrong, even if the very thought ate him alive. Certainly he has paid his debt today by helping to reveal all the mysteries of the last few years. Let him go, and let the bitterness go with him. I think one day he will return to us a better man."

"Ahhh, God!" Max caught me close. "You are so wise."

Through my own tears, I smiled up into his eyes. "So, now you think I am wise. How fortuitous for our life together, sir."

I ran one forefinger down his high cheek, along his jaw, and across his handsome mouth.

"I am overjoyed, sir, that at last you think me a suitable mate for the magnificent sixth Duke of Worminster."

"I *always* thought you the *perfect* mate, Madam!" He took my lips in a ravishing kiss and crushed me close. "You may be my third duchess, Madam, but you are my last. And for eternity, you will be my one, true love."

Epilogue

Dearest Lianne,

Max and I returned from London today a little the worse for the extended stay. We are not accustomed to the rigors of the city anymore, but David and his wife, Clarissa, insisted we attend the christening of their second son, John, and coupling that with the engagement announcement and party for our third son, Harry, we did have an eventful six weeks in town.

David and Clarissa are outrageously happy. Almost as happy, I daresay, as Max and I are—even after all these years. Our thirty-third wedding anniversary approaches, but we seem not to notice the age, only the depths to which our mutual love has grown. It is as it should be, as God intended.

Our other children seem to have acquired that outlook as well. Mary, with her Scottish laird and her brood of four girls, and Elizabeth, with her American financier and her twin boys, came also at Harry's request. Guy came, too. Still charming the deb-

utantes of the season with his dashing black looks and that splendid regimental uniform, he is not yet ready to pick one and settle down. Max chuckles and predicts when Guy finds the right girl, we'll have our heads spin with the haste he'll make for the altar.

In any case, for all our events this season, the pack of us displayed ourselves as quite a splendid family. So unlike the picture the old rumors made of the House of the Wolffs. So much more loving than those old vicious rumors of Max's sins.

Throughout the weeks, Max—wonderful Max—did nothing but beam. Nearing his seventy-third birthday, he cuts quite a swath through society, I'll tell you! He is still the master at polite conversation and deft observation. Still the beguiling man who captured my heart and mind years ago.

When I remember that horrible first year of our marriage, I still cringe. I remember it quite clearly, probably more so today, since I have just spent the last few weeks repeating the tale for the older grandchildren. Mary and Elizabeth had often told their chicks about the goings-on that year, but because they were only five when it happened, they always left out important parts. Their children, now at the impressionable ages of ten, twelve, thirteen, fourteen, and fifteen, hungered for the complete story. So I complied.

Settling all six before a blazing fire in the study in David's house on Grosvenor Square, I began with the day my father's solicitor told me I must wed the rich, the noble, the mysterious Duke of Worminster. The children were spellbound and, I must admit, I enjoyed the telling of it. We can forget sometimes how fortunate we are. The telling of the stories of our lives makes us not only remember, but also perceive the divine order there.

In the telling of this tale, I saw the order in my life quite clearly. I was the means by which the sixth Duke of Worminster was to bequeath his estate to a rightful heir. But my very presence brought forth more than that.

Max voiced it quite succinctly when I finished the story.

"Your grandmother," he affirmed, and took my hand to kiss it, "was the woman whose very presence would purge the evil from the family and make it pure once more."

They nodded their pretty heads and asked if we ever heard news of Dorcas again. When we told them no, they looked relieved and quite at peace with themselves and proud of their family.

Jocelyn, Mary's oldest, was the one who put the brightest cap on the story, though. She, who resembles her mother so completely in thought and careful manner, sat up on her knees and flashed joyous gray eyes at her grandfather and me.

"Grandpapa, everything changed from the moment our cousin Caroline died. Cousin Gilbert became free to become himself."

"That's true, my love," Max nodded. "He never would have been able to make such a success of himself as a writer if his mother had lived to judge his efforts at fiction."

"And Cousin Adair might still be a sourpuss and hate you both, instead of coming to family events like the christening and engagement and smiling and being ever so pleasant."

Max nodded. "True, true, Jocelyn."

"But you know," she mused, and then absolutely beamed with the joy of her next thought, "other things have changed as well. It's clear, whether you ever believed in it or not, that the family will never have any more problems."

I frowned. "What do you mean, my dear?"

"Look about you, Grandmama. We are four girls from our mother. A female Wolff who bore only females. And Aunt Elizabeth had only these two churlish lads." She playfully nudged the ten-year-old twins, Winston and Jim. "Then Uncle David has two boys. While you both have three sons—not just David, but Guy and Harry. Don't you see, my dears, with you have

ended the evils of the family? The true destruction of the curse on the Wolffs."

She's right, of course. I never thought of it that way. But then, over the past three decades, I have never had reason to look back and fear any such thing as a curse. My life has been a joy, nurtured in love and rich in many blessings.

I hope you consent to come for the holidays. We have not seen you in so long and miss your bright perspective.

All my love,

Alicia

**FOR OTHER WONDERFULLY
SUSPENSEFUL GOTHIC TALES FROM THE
TALENTED PEN OF AUTHOR JO-ANN
POWER, ASK YOUR BOOKSELLER ABOUT:**
Now Available!
THE MARK OF THE CHADWICKS
Praised by *Romantic Times* as:
"A FIRST-RATE TALE OF ROMANCE AND
SUSPENSE!"

Vanessa Chadwick had returned to England for one reason—the reading of her father-in-law's will. Stepping onto the chilly docks of Southampton, holding fast to the hand of her young son, the beautiful American widow tried to remain calm. But Graham Chadwick, her late husband's brother, quickly tested her resolve. Graham was a towering, muscular, exquisite specimen of a man, and their brief encounter years ago was one reason she'd fled . . .

Scandal was on everyone's lips then, and Vanessa expected some whisperings to follow her now; yet when the first threatening note arrived, and her son narrowly escaped an "accidental" injury, she knew someone desperately wanted her out of England. But Vanessa was through with running. She would go to the stone monolith of Castle Darnley, the house she had learned to fear, and find a way to stop her tormentors before they put a stop to her . . . forever.

**AND,
COMING TO BOOKSTORES IN
FEBRUARY 1994
WATCH FOR:**
THE HAUNTING SECRET OF
CASTLE TRAYMORE

HERE IS A SPECIAL SNEAK PREVIEW OF JO-ANN POWER'S NEXT EXCITING GOTHIC COMING IN FEBRUARY 1994
THE HAUNTING SECRET OF CASTLE TRAYMORE

August, 1891

Last night, they walked again.

They came from the dark, mere shadows, frail wraiths, wild forces. They came, the two of them. As they had so many times before. This time they said nothing. Nothing.

This time they glided from the shadows of the balcony and floated through the doors to my chambers. Just as before, I could see them before I really saw them. Feel them before I ever really felt the hair on my arms rise. Shiver before their chilling presences crossed the room, stood beside me, and peered into my soul.

This time, they came together; she first, strangely mute, and he, now a serene, tender gentleman, close behind.

She wore the white diaphanous stuff she had always worn when she appeared to me. Her long black hair flowed gently about her shoulders as her silver eyes greeted my stunned ones. Then she turned to tenderly survey the contents of the family cradle. She stretched out a hand to touch my baby son and paused to check her companion's eyes before she made so bold a gesture.

But he closed his stark white eyes and slowly shook his noble head. By that noble move, he said she must not touch the child. She must not taint him, predispose him. Her laying-on of hands might be a show of affection, but it was more for innocent earthly beings.

Not her.

Not him.

He came to stand beside her and gaze down at the sleeping infant. His visage, once demonic, now paternal, revealed the handsome brute who'd once walked the earth. He even smiled—or so I, in my vivid imagination, thought he did. It made sense that he would, of course, because he—of all people, of all the apparitions in this house—would rest more easily now. His tribulations, just like hers, had ended when mine had. It was quite natural, then, that they would come to inspect my boy. To admire him and confirm him as a Traymore.

I sat up, propped on one elbow to watch them. They seemed so at peace. So much in harmony with each other and the cosmos. It struck me suddenly how they walked together for the first time not as enemies, but as companions. And this I understood as a progression. This I took as a sign of some divine order in which I, the living, had affected the realm of the dead.

This morning, in the light of day, I gaze out over my garden to the sea and I am as much at peace as they. Enough time has passed since the terror that I can now be objective. Certainly, if those two have put the agonies of the years to rest, I can also. And I can do it more quickly, more expediently than they, because I have only a year between my terror and my redemption, not centuries.

Because I never pretended to be a philosopher or a wizard, I know no way to explain why this might be so except to tell the story and to tell it in its entirety. By recounting this tale, please know, dear reader, that I do not understand the progress nor seek to offer some patent rule by which others might assess similar phenomena and proceed to endure it or banish it. I seek only to tell the story of the two devils who walked into my life, nearly took it, and—in the haunting—almost destroyed my country, my household, and my love.

August, 1890

The door! Oh, please . . . I had to reach it before he caught me. If I didn't, I'd never, *never* feel safe anywhere in the world again!

I panted, racing, lifting my skirts higher and stretching my legs farther, faster to make my goal. I'd never let him catch me . . . never.

I reached the huge portal, grasped the knob, thrust it open, and slammed it behind me. With a frantic turn of the wrist, I swiveled the key in its lock. Threw the bolt home. Then collapsed against the barrier between me and my raging attacker. I clamped my hand over my mouth, stifling sobs of outrage. Tears coursed down my cheeks and I swiped at them with the backs of my hands.

He'd never have me. Never . . .

I heard him. His footsteps heavy on the Turkish runner. His breath as heavy as it had been against my bare breast. His hands—oh, Lord!—his moist hands under my skirts and groping for secret places, secret entrances.

He fell against the door and his gruff voice seeped through the jamb.

"Witch!" he seethed. "I'll have you. I'm your employer, you ninny." He jiggled the knob. "Let me in." His voice slurred with the Scotch whisky he'd been downing. "Let me in or I'll tell my wife you were impertinent. She'll throw you out."

I swallowed hard. I hated the street, but I hated being pawed by this beast more.

"You'll never find another position like this," he hissed, and rattled the knob again. "Let me in, I say!"

"Never," I whispered. "Tell her. Go on, tell her."

His breathing quickened. I could hear him through the jamb. I could almost see him, his round face growing redder, his wide nostrils flaring, his fleshy lips twitching in frustration.

"No one denies me. And you, little lady, won't do it, either. I'll tell her you're spreading your legs for the lot of the male staff."

"Do it," I coaxed. *"Do it."*

He cursed viciously and began to pound the wood.

I stepped back and hoped to God the door was as sturdy as it looked.

Presently he stopped and I heard him put his lips to the frame and whisper.

"If I tell her, she'll rue the day she brought you here. She won't think too kindly of her sweet little cousin. She won't even give you a reference, you know."

I knew. Oh, yes, I knew. I frowned as something else I knew began to surface in my frightened mind.

I crossed the room to my chiffonier and yanked open a drawer. I threw petticoats and chemises and corsets and pantalettes in a pile high atop my bed. I bent under the bed and slid out my straw reticule and larger packing case. I flicked them open and stuffed more clothing inside.

I went to my secretary and stuffed my writing pens and pencils into my stationery box. Then I grabbed at the manuscript I had hidden under my mattress. No one would ever acquire this by default.

I'd get out of here and I'd go today, before his wife, my good cousin, returned. I'd go and let him explain to her why I'd gone—as if she needed explanations.

I stopped in midmotion, my hands full of pages, my mind full of the horrible truth I now acknowledged.

Of course, my cousin Louise knew of her husband's tendencies! She had known all along what he did with the female staff. She knew and turned her eyes the other way.

No! That wasn't the whole truth, either . . .

I sank into a tiny wooden chair, my eyes wide and dry. Louise not only knew how her husband used the women on the staff, but she even supplied new victims for him! That's why the male staff—the head butler and the baron's valet—looked me over like prime meat from the butcher when I'd first arrived. That's why my cousin had oh-so-generously paid fifty pounds of my first years' wages in advance "for your father's debts," Louise had too graciously offered. No, it wasn't, as I suspected, a courtesy shown to me because I was the baroness's dear but impoverished country cousin from St. Ives. No! It was because I was the new offering to the Baron Hargate.

Merciful heaven, my cousin Louise *knew* her lecherous excuse for a husband would try to add me to his list. And she didn't care.

All that talk about how she couldn't bear to see me

337

penniless was just that—talk. Her wringing of hands over my father's accidental death was an act. Her solicitous nature over my sorrows, my accommodations, my proclivities. Oooo, how could she be so sinister?

My eyes flew to the door. Was he still there? Something crinkled and then slid beneath the door to me. Even from this distance I could see it was money. Money . . .

I laughed out loud. But I caught myself, afraid I'd lost my senses, and forced my mind to focus on the matter at hand. I rose and continued to pack. Louise was due to return soon from her afternoon calls. I'd see her. I'd tell her. Then I'd leave.

I turned and looked at the currency on the wooden parquet floor. I'd leave and I'd take not this money, but only a pittance of my hard-earned wages with me.

But the determined Baron Hargate wouldn't leave. He rattled the doorknob again. Emboldened still by the liquor he'd consumed this afternoon, he continued his quest.

"Let me in, honey girl. I'll be so good for you."

I heaved with fury.

"Get—away—from—my—door!" I yelled like a banshee. *"Get away!"*

I heard footsteps. Lots of them. Running. Coming toward my room down the nursery wing.

And I knew the baron had stepped away from my door.

"Milord," some manservant asked, "may I help you, sir?"

"What's all the screaming about?" asked a faint female voice.

338

"My lord"—that was Simmons, the butler—"may I accompany you to your quarters, sir?"

Baron Hargate inhaled so sharply I could almost see him pull his girth up with his dignity. "Why, yes, Simmons. Thank you. I was just asking Miss Sutton about her treatment of the boys, and she ran from me, you see. Terrible to have a governess beating the children. Shameful."

The swine. I'd see him roast in hell before he'd repeat that lie. If the baron's two sons suffered, it was because the man ignored them ninety percent of the time and intimidated them the rest. Where did love factor in such an equation?

But then, of course, it was quite clear to me that love was no factor in this house at all. If indeed it had ever factored.

All grew quiet in the hall. I finished packing and heard my two little charges, Reginald and Stanton, come in from their pony ride. In the nursery, I heard their boyish giggles and squeals between the connecting doors as they changed for their teatime with the help of an undermaid. Presently, she came to knock on my door.

"Miss Sutton, I know you're in there," she said, with a quavering voice that told me some member of the staff had revealed the goings-on of the past hour. "Masters Reggie and Stan would like to see you. May I bring them in?"

"No, Hettie. I am quite busy. I will see them, rest assured."

"Very well, if you promise."

"I promise, Hettie. Don't worry."

339

She pressed closer to the door and whispered hoarsely, "I do worry, Miss. This is not right."

"Quite so, Hettie, this is not right. But I will make it so."

"Oh, Miss, be careful. You'll upset the house."

"Hettie, don't be ridiculous. The house is already upset. Diseased, if you ask me. I will not let it continue."

"After you're gone, it'll be just the same."

"No, Hettie. It won't. Once the disease is diagnosed, the chances of it being remedied are greater."

"Oh, no, Miss. Not here. Don't tell the baroness."

I ran a hand through my hair. "No, Hettie. Now, please go away."

She muttered something and left.

Finally finished packing, I sat calmly with my cases around me. I waited in my chair, listening to the clocks in the house strike four, then half four.

Where was Louise?

Usually when she arrived from her afternoon calls, she could be heard all over the house. Wherever she went almost every afternoon, whatever she did, it had the effect of a tonic on her otherwise sedate personality. I'd often wondered if the moribund woman I saw in the morning had any relationship at all to the chattering, fluttering creature I saw sail out the door at three. She certainly went out to make calls more often than she received visitors. Odd, that she would love to make afternoon rounds but loathe having guests for supper. Odd, that she would deplore most public gatherings—christenings, receptions, balls—and adore to go out in the afternoon alone.

Or was it so odd? Where did she go? She never spoke

of many true friends. Was there another secret in this house? Another's actions to cover?

Oh, good heavens, where was my mind leading me? Was I merely applying fantasy to reality, as I'd always done, and had I devised another story, another fiction?

No. Some instinct told me no. I knew fantasy from reality, at base, at core, and the goings-on in this house had the ring of truth to them.

The only answer that remained for me was the quite logical one. I had not seen this reality for what it was, not merely because I knew my cousin Louise only slightly from childhood, but because I had been so forlorn after my father's death that I could not think. Could not see.

I walked in circles in my room. Yes, I had been quite beside myself with grief two months ago. Father's death had been a shock, especially the way he went. I had known for years of his predilection for alcohol. He had not been able to stay far from it ever since my mother had died five years before. But I never expected him to drink anywhere except at home by the fireside. I never expected he would someday drink himself blind at the local pub, begin his journey home, then slip and fall in the sand along the beach and drown. Then, when the awful event did occur, I never thought I would mourn his loss alone. All alone. Without his best friend. Without mine.

Tears started again, and I shook my head to ward them off. What had happened to Sean O'Ruark? Where had he gone? Where was he then, and where, oh where, was he now?

If I had had Sean then to lean on, to counsel with, I would probably not have taken this position with

Louise. I would have had his advice. His moral support.

Oh, who was I fooling? I didn't want Sean O'Ruark's advice or support as much as I wanted—had always wanted—Sean O'Ruark.

He was everything a man could be to a young girl. A young, impressionable girl, my mother had said.

"Don't be makin' eyes at the man, my pixie," she'd warned me. "He's handsome, dashing, all right, but he's much older than you, and he's got troubles by the bucketload."

I saw only the tall, red-haired giant who brought me presents of ribbons and silks from his ships. I saw the man who told me stories of a sheik's harem and a maharajah's ivory palace. I saw the ship's captain, the adventurer, the trader who arrived to have my father tally his shipping company's books. I saw a laughing man with crinkling, sparkling topaz eyes and rough, bass voice. I saw a gentle man, a generous man, the only man I'd ever dreamed would kiss me. Caress me. Tell me I was his.

But he was nowhere to be found. And I was left alone to come to this.

I choked on my tears and bit my trembling lips. So I would make the best of it. I'd tell Louise what I knew and begin the process again of making a good life for myself.

The clock chimed five times.

Now I knew if I waited any longer, I'd have a difficult time finding a room in town for the night. And I certainly would not remain here in this house of horrors tonight. Heaven knew what evils could occur here in the dark.

I had to brave the hall. I went and rang the bellpull behind the heavy draperies. I'd brave the hall, but when I did, I'd have my belongings by the front door, ready for my departure. I had to be prepared for any eventuality.

In minutes, Millbrook, the underbutler who had been assigned to my service and that of my two tiny charges, arrived and lifted my two cases. He followed behind me as I sailed down the circular stairs toward the head butler's pantry off the dining room. As I expected, the butler Simmons was there, counting the silver as was his usual wont before dinner.

I must have come round the corner on cat's feet, because he startled and dropped a few forks to the silver chest. He scowled at me over the rims of his glasses.

"When do you expect the baroness to return, Simmons?"

"She has returned, Miss Sutton."

"Well, then, I must speak to her. Where is she?"

"She is engaged, Miss Sutton, and cannot be disturbed."

I narrowed my eyes at him. He could be more impenetrable than a Norman castle wall.

"Is she in the drawing room?"

He rounded on me. "I said she is not to be disturbed."

I hoisted my skirts and pivoted. I was halfway down the hall before he found his voice—and a loud, irritated one, at that. But his command didn't stop me, and my persistence only had him scurrying after me so that he tried to bar the door.

"I cannot let you enter. I was given specific instructions not to—"

"Were you? Well, I have a few things to say to my cousin, and say them I will. Now, step aside, Simmons, or I will scream down the house until my cousin grants me an audience."

He quelled—or rather quaked—with the very idea that someone would threaten the morbid quiet of this atmosphere. He didn't like it, but he did step aside.

I entered, my head held high. At my height, with mostly everyone taller than I, I had learned long ago to walk as erect as my backbone would permit. The imperiousness made people listen to me, and as time went on, most came to respect me. Even my cousin Louise, whom I knew only from the two summers we had spent together as children, respected me enough and trusted me enough to care for her two sons. Yes, she had listened and respected me—at least when it came to the education and nurturing of her two young sons. I counted on a similar response now.

But at first glimpse of her, I knew such measured responses were not in her power today. No. Today she sat not suffused with chatter and gaiety, as was her usual mode after her afternoon calls, but wringing a handkerchief, overcome with anxiety. The cause of this extraordinary behavior was, I had to assume, none other than the man who sat before her and who rose as I entered the purple and plum depths of the drawing room.

"I had to see you, Louise," I blurted out, ignoring the apology I should have offered for my intrusion and failing to use the title she always wished me to use in front of her guests.

She rounded her eyes at me, gathering her dignity to her in spite of her agonies. "Really, Julia! Must you

344

break in? I would have called you presently." She waved a hand in the direction of the gentleman.

I frowned and looked him over. He was tall and dark, and handsomely attired in a navy suit that made him look like a man of order and constancy.

"This is Mister Mayo, a solicitor from Dublin."

I nodded politely and wondered why in the world Louise would bother to introduce me to her caller. He smiled engagingly at me, but I ignored his overfriendly manner and concentrated on my own needs.

"Louise, I must speak with you immediately."

It was her turn to frown. "Really, Julia. We will deal with whatever your problems are with the boys in a moment. For now, we must deal with Mister Mayo."

I started to object when she bade me sit.

"Yes, Julia, sit. Mister Mayo has really come to see you. And he tells me he will not discuss the full nature of his business with anyone *but* you." At that last, her nostrils worked as if she smelled something fetid. Her green eyes, so like mine, settled on me with the flamboyance of a challenge. "Mister Mayo has a very unusual message for you."

I looked at him now and truly saw him. He was young, no more than twenty-five. He was nervous, as his shaking fingers denoted. This, I was sure, was because he was intimidated by Louise, as so many were. But most of all, he was thrilled to speak to me about his mission.

He cleared his throat. "Yes, well, how do you do, Miss Sutton? I am honored to meet you."

Honored to meet me? It had been a horrid day, but his statement made me smile.

345

He took a sheaf of papers from the end table and held them aloft, displaying them for me.

"I have here instructions from my client in County Waterford, Ireland, that I am to convey to you, Miss Sutton."

Surely this was fantasy. Or some incredible mistake.

I smiled apologetically. "I am sorry, Mister Mayo. I know no one in Waterford, nor do I ever recall my father speaking of anyone he knew there."

"Oh, no, Miss Sutton. I assure you, it is you I seek." His soft brown eyes traveled to Louise and back to me. "If there was any question before, I know there is none now that I have spoken with Baroness Hargate." He crinkled his eyes at her in polite gratitude, but she was having none of it.

She clenched her jaw and stared at me. "It's true, Julia. Mister Mayo does have a missive for you." She worried at her lace handkerchief again, and I wondered at her distress.

"What is it, sir? I have no idea why you should be here."

He grinned now ear to ear, so pleased to speak of his mission. "I have the wonderful duty to reveal to you that your services have been sought after by a very kind gentleman."

I tried hard not to gape. I tried even harder not to clap my hands for joy. If this were true and someone wanted me, I could leave here quickly and with hope. Only reason intruded in such happiness, and I endeavored to find some logic to a very illogical proposition.

I couldn't help it: I returned his grin and then composed my features. "Sir, I have only lately become a governess for my cousin, the Baroness Hargate. Who

346

would seek me out from Waterford? My reputation as a governess cannot spread so wide so fast, since I have been with my cousin only a few weeks. Are they in dire straits, perhaps, to seek so far for someone so untried?''

Now he laughed. He threw back his head and laughed!

Louise seemed to exude a displeasure that even with his eyes closed he felt, for he recovered instantly and straightened his coat and his composure.

''Yes, well, ahem. I assure you that the terms of this agreement are very generous, far beyond anything I would describe as 'dire straits,' Miss Sutton.''

He sounded so sincere, the laughter died in my throat. Instead, an incredible pressure of burgeoning joy built in the region of my heart. ''Tell me,'' I whispered.

''I have here a letter for you from my client.'' He handed over the paper as I dug in my pocket for my spectacles.

''Thank you.'' I settled my glasses on my nose and began to read.

On translucent parchment, the handwriting rose up to greet me with brash strokes of thick black ink. Beginning with ''Dear Miss Sutton,'' the sender offered condolences upon the death of my father and how he— yes, *he*—and my father had been good friends. The sender apologized for his failure to attend the funeral or to send his sympathy before this, but he had been in America on extended business. When he returned to Ireland, learned of my father's death, and saw my advertisements offering my services as governess, he

347

immediately hired Mayo and Sons to draw up an agreement.

However, when Mayo and Sons journeyed to St. Ives with the offer, I was nowhere to be found. It took weeks before they were able to trace me to my cousin Louise in Somerset. He once more apologized for his failure to find me before I was engaged by the Baron and Baroness Hargate, but he hoped he might persuade me to consider the offer in any case.

He needed me, he said. He needed me very soon and very desperately.

What's more, he was willing to pay for that privilege. He then proceeded to substantiate the need by describing his two children, a girl, age seven, and a boy, age four, both of whom needed a constant influence on their young lives.

"And I," he wrote, "cannot give it them. Motherless as they are, they need a woman's guidance and nurturing. But I wish them to have not just anyone's love and care. I wish them to have the joy of knowing a tender soul, a brave heart, and an intelligent mind such as you possess."

My eyes watered. My heart pounded at the thought that there still existed such kind regard in the world. I adjusted my glasses and struggled to read the last paragraph.

He concluded with his offer to hire me with the stipulation that I sign an agreement which bound me for two years. At the end of that period, I could leave, if I wished, or sign another contract which would bind me to him in one-year terms. In return for this, he agreed not only to pay me the first year's salary in advance, but also to double it the second year.

Such terms would allow me to repay Louise's advance and then completely settle my father's embarrassing debts. Such terms would allow me to live in dignity in a comfortable position. Such terms would allow me to continue to write my little adventure stories and send them off to London publishers in the vain hope of fortune and fame. In fact, such terms would allow me to leave Hargate Manor. Tonight, if I chose.

And oh, how I chose!

I chose before I read the entire contract. I chose before I read all the terms.

The paper drifted from my hands and I raised my eyes to Mister Mayo.

"Sir, this is astounding."

"Yes," he sat back, "I thought so."

"The terms are more than generous."

I had all I could do not to dance around the room. I swallowed and tried to grasp sanity.

"The gentleman must be very wealthy."

"Aye, he is that. But from what I learned during his conversation with my father, he wanted to be quite sure the offer would be so attractive you could not refuse." He smiled again. "I see it worked."

"It did."

"He will be pleased. I must admit my father and my two brothers had quite a scare when we could not find you. We also had quite a greater one when we learned you were already employed. But I thought the terms might win you from any prior commitment. I was right, I see. And now that I have found you, the earl will be overjoyed."

"The earl?"

Mayo frowned again. "Yes, did you not read the letter? The man's signature?"

I lifted the papers once more to my eyes. Then, they fell from my hand to the floor.

"The Earl of Traymore?" I asked Mayo needlessly.

"None other."

A cacophony of emotions spread through me. Notes of fear. Pride. Terror. Joy.

"The Earl of Traymore" evoked images I'd nurtured since childhood. Images based on some truths, much gossip, and more conjecture. Images fueled by English-Irish politics and tensions. Images set ablaze by centuries of injustices and carelessness. Images that blended into one picture, one portrait of a man made noble by his actions and his beliefs. A man so vital to the Irish cause even Charles Parnell courted his approval. A man so virile women were said to court his favor. A man so bereft over his wife's death that he courted no one—and never would again. A man so legendary that even I knew he rivaled any hero I could create in my fiction.

The Earl of Traymore meant so many exciting things to me. Peer of the Realm. Irish lord. Member of Parliament. Adviser to Prince Bertie and Prime Minister Gladstone on matters of Irish trade. All facts gleaned from the London *Times*.

But gossip embellished the facts. The Earl of Traymore was unique in this day and age. He was a moneyed lord, and a moneyed *Irish* lord in a country devastated by famine and revolt. A rich Irish lord who nonetheless fought for land reform by sitting in the Englishmen's Parliament. A wealthy man who had not only inherited a sizable estate, but also earned more money from his commercial ventures, money gained from his family's involvement in manufacturing of two Irish products—glass and whisky. He was a shrewd businessman, one of Ireland's most respected. He was a wise politician. He was an asset at any woman's dinner party, witty, brash, and impossibly handsome. But in private, he was tormented by a loss he could not comprehend—the loss of his beloved wife. A stunning English beauty whom he'd wed on a whim and lost after five short years and the birth of a daughter and son.

He was a legend.

An enigma.

The most fascinating man to walk the British Isles in years.

And *he* was my employer.

"Mister Mayo, if you will wait here for me, I will sign this document and we will discuss exactly how soon I may leave for Ireland."

About the Author

JO-ANN POWER has dreamed of becoming a published writer since she was eight years old. Her dream became a lifetime career in communications: She was first a reporter and teacher, then vice president of a nationwide financial corporation and a public relations executive for national trade associations. She has worked on vital communications issues with media, Congressmen, Senators, and senior government officials.

Residing with her husband and three children in Maryland, she enjoys both a solo writing career and a collaborative partnership in writing with her friend and business partner Barbara Cummings. Look for *Risks* next month, a spectacular mainstream novel written by the Barbara Cummings and Jo-Ann Power team.

She is also the co-author, with Barbara Cummings, of a Victorian mystery series, titled *Clively Close* and released under the penname of "Ann Crowleigh." The first book in the *Clively Close* series, *Dead As Dead Can Be*, is now available from your bookseller. The second book in that series, *Wait for The Dark*, is due for release next month.

The Last Duchess of Wolff's Lair is Jo-Ann's second gothic novel. Her first was *The Mark of the Chadwicks*. She is currently working on her next gothic, *The Haunting Secret of Castle Traymore*, due for release by Zebra Books in February 1994.

Jo-Ann also writes her own column, "Reading Between The Lines," in the *Gothic Journal*.